Good Neighbors

"Connor's ability to richly develop each character and plot thread is fascinating even when the horror is reserved... the constricting pressure as the dread piles on makes this book hard to put down and even harder to go to sleep after reading. This is a great novel..."
-David J. Sharp, *Horror Underground*

Second Unit

"Intricately plotted and vividly layered with suspense, emotional intensity and strategic violence."
-Michael Price, *Fort Worth Business Press*

"Drips with eeriness...an enjoyable book by a promising author."
-Kyle White, *The Harrow Fantasy and Horror Journal*

Finding Misery

"Major-league action, car chases, subterfuge, plot twists, with a smear of rough sex on top. Sublime."
-Arianne "Tex" Thompson, author of *Medicine for the Dead* and *One Night in Sixes*

The Jackal Man

"Connor delivers a brisk, action-packed tale that explores the dark forests of the human--and inhuman--heart. Sure to thrill creature fans everywhere."
-Scott Nicholson, author of *They Hunger* and *The Red Church*

Also by Russell C. Connor

RUSSELL C. CONNOR

Visit us online at

DARKFILAMENT.COM

Contact the author at
facebook.com/russellcconnor
Or follow on Twitter @russellcconnor

Cover Art by SaberCore23 Artwork Studio
For commissions, visit sabercore23art.com

ISBN:
978-0-9864431-2-1

Third Edition: 2019

For the DFW Writers Workshop, for continuing to boost an already too high ego.

For Abs-tastic, for understanding.

For River Trails, for a childhood of inspiration.

For Spud, Kallik, Tally, and Graves, the reason I love animals. And write about them killing people.

Special Thanks To:

Joe "Bad Batch"-elder, for continued firearm knowledge and demonstration. He gives new answer to that immortal Hendrix question, "Hey Joe, where you goin with that gun in your hand?"

TABLE OF CONTENTS

DARK HOAUS

TALES OF THE JACKAL MAN

Do you know the one about the two boys? Yeah, I'm sure you do. Folks say they left the final football game of their senior year to while away Friday night by driving aimlessly. You probably did the same thing when you were their age.

The way I heard it, they had the windows rolled down, *Appetite for Destruction* blaring on the stereo, and the pressures of college and the real world were still months away.

The one driving we'll call Jimmy. This might be his real name, or it might not; in an urban legend like this, our characters are as two-dimensional as cardboard cutouts, so they can be passed easily from person to person and always remain someone's brother or son or friend or roommate. Jimmy is that suburban kid you see at the mall with the GAP clothes, the mess of hair jutting from under a sideways cap, and sneakers so white they glow.

His friend—let's say Dustin—is even more generic, if that's possible. His posture's a bit more slumped, his hair hanging limp in his face, but he could be that teenager you always see in the convenience store parking lot at all hours of the night.

They finished up a conversation about a girl from school, and then were quiet as Jimmy drove his car (which is another blank you can fill in when you retell this, but for now it's a gray Mustang) up the Westwood Strip.

"Hey, what the hell's wrong with you?" Jimmy finally asked, turning down the screech of "Welcome to the Jungle" so he could be heard. "You've been acting like someone jizzed in your ear all night."

"I don't know." Dustin was noncommittal as he looked up at the night. The sky was clear of clouds, with a bloated moon floating in the darkness. The lights of the Strip, a mile-long consumer paradise of shops, eateries, and the requisite Starbucks, drowned out the stars with industrial callousness.

"You're thinking about next year again, aren't you? Would you relax, college ain't a big deal, millions of people do it!"

"That's easy for you to say. The whole rest of your life is planned out. You'll play around for four years and then go work for your dad. Me...I have no idea what I'm doing. I don't have anything."

"You got me, man, and that's all that matters." Jimmy pulled to a stop at a red light. He glanced down at the clock, the first time the real world had intruded on them since leaving the game. "Shit! My father told me to be home by eleven-thirty!"

"You'll be lucky to make it by midnight now. You're dad's gonna be so pissed."

"Maybe. Not like he'll do anything."

"He said he'd ground you next time."

"So? He can't stop me from going out."

"He might take your car."

This sobered Jimmy. He sat, fingering his stick shift as thoughtfully as someone contemplating the cure for cancer instead of just trying to beat curfew.

Someone honked behind them.

"We'll just take the Dark Road," he said.

Something in Dustin's stomach plummeted as Jimmy revved the engine and started forward. "No, we fucking will not!"

Jimmy's mouth twitched angrily. "Why not? It shaves a good twenty minutes off our drive!"

He was no A student, but Jimmy knew the shortest distance between two points was a straight line. The freeway took them in a big circle, while the Dark Road was a direct link between the Westwood Strip and their homes on the other side of the Metroplex, with a quick run through the shitstain town of Asheville.

But to Dustin—who will be our voice of reason—there was a lot to be said for taking one's time.

"Look, do you trust me?" Jimmy asked.

"Yeah…"

"When every jock in school wants to kick your ass, who always stops them? I've never let anything happen to you, have I? *Have I?*"

"No. You haven't."

The Mustang cruised along. The freeway onramp was coming up on their left, but the Dark Road lay directly ahead. Dustin could see the point where the four-lane boulevard narrowed to two at the top of a gentle rise.

He had to say something to get Jimmy to stop.

"What about the Jackal Man?"

The words floated in the air.

Dustin watched Jimmy's face. He was sure he saw a glimmer of fear in his friend's eyes. "Don't be a chickenshit. There's no such thing. It's just something those creepy kids in Asheville made up."

This was what pretty much what everyone said, but the stories filtering out of the high school in the tiny speck of a town were told with complete reverence. If that were the extent of the myth's reach, it wouldn't be so bad—just another teen spook story, no different than the guy with the hook hand—but even the adults had spun yarns about it as far back as Dustin's father could remember.

Everyone from Asheville got a weird look in their eye when they talked about the Jackal Man.

'Mass hysteria' would be the term Dustin might use, if he knew what it meant.

The Jackal Man was Asheville's answer to the Yeti, the Metroplex's equivalent of Chupacabra, Texas's claim to Loch-Ness-size fame. He could often be found in that local rag, the *Weekly Digest*, right next to stories about Alligator Boy, and Satan's face materializing in clouds of disaster smoke.

The onramp crept ever closer. Dustin fully expected Jimmy to jerk the wheel at the last minute—*ha ha, just kidding!*—but then the Mustang was flying over the populated and well-lit highway. Dustin gave an involuntary squawk of fear and then reddened in embarrassment.

"What's the matter? You scared of the Jackal Man?"

"No. Just caught a reflection of your face and almost shit my pants." By his side, where Jimmy couldn't see, Dustin's hand gripped the armrest so hard his fingers left gouges in the leather.

"I told you, *the Jackal Man's ain't real.* Those morons didn't even name him right, for chrissake."

The last few houses on the end of Westwood Boulevard slid by the window in a blur, replaced by thick stands of birch and oak. Old Cyrus's shack was the last structure on the left, set back in the middle of a field before the greedy trees claimed all. Everybody in the county knew Old Cyrus. He lived farther into the woods of the Dark Road than anyone, and, in Dustin's book, that made him the goddamn bravest person alive. Once his decrepit hovel was left behind, they were all alone until they reached Asheville.

Leaves were just sprouting in the blackish woods during the cold April. The wind rustled the brittle branches and gave Dustin the impression of a crowd jostling for a position from which to grab at the vehicle. The streetlights along the side of the road cast glowing circles on the pavement for a short distance. Then they passed the last one, and the only illumination was the Mustang's headlights carving the road in front of them and the moon above.

"See? Nothing to be scared of down here," Jimmy said. This time he sounded like he might believe it.

A mile rolled by, and the woods sprawled out on both sides. The stars reappeared one by one as they escaped the light pollution of the Strip. When you got down to it, the Dark Road was really just an unnamed strip of tarmac running through a patch of land so underdeveloped it was like being on a different planet. The fact that such raw Texas wilderness lay in the middle of bustling civilization seemed amazing to Dustin, like it was left behind in the rush to urbanize.

The car passed over a rickety bridge spanning the Trinity River, long, steep beds sloping to a trickle of water, and then the road led into a canopy of deep woods. The branches hung over the road like skeletal hands. After another half mile, the trees on their left vanished. The woods ended in a line so abrupt and precise it must've been cut with God's own razor. An open field stretched out to the horizon, sparingly dotted with lone trees. The moon reflected eerily off a low ground mist.

"What is that?" Jimmy strained forward against his seatbelt.

A rectangular sign on two tall poles stood to the left of the road, where the grass met the concrete. Dustin was finally able to read it as the headlights swept across:

COMING SOON!
River Meadows Housing: Phase 1
A Lyles Corporation Project

Underneath the words was a picture of a smiling family that had stepped out of a time warp from the 50's, complete with a beehive hairdo for Mom, in front of a modest, two-story home.

"Who would want to live out here?" Dustin whispered.

"It's impossible. No way they can build houses."

"How come?"

"Ground's too hard. My dad told me. This land is made of some kinda weird clay. They can't put pipes in the ground. That's the reason there hasn't ever been anything built out here before."

Dustin felt no need to argue. The sign proved that *somebody* thought they could build houses on the field.

They could see the glow of Asheville now on the horizon, the flat radiance of electricity leeching the sky away from the stars once again. Civilization, or what passed for it around here, was only minutes away.

The car came around a tight curve in the road, Jimmy tugging smoothly on the steering wheel.

"See? I told you," he said.

Dustin started to nod, to tell him he was right, he was always right, he trusted Jimmy like a brother, and then something emerged from the woods along the right side of the road and stepped in front of their car.

They saw it at the same time in the cones of light preceding the Mustang. It stood on two legs, facing them. Dustin caught a quick glimpse of a slightly hunched back and arms drawn up at the elbows, as though it was uncomfortable standing upright. Dirty tan fur covered its body, mottled with small patches of black like a leopard.

After that...things happened fast.

Jimmy jerked the wheel, skewing them into the other lane, but it wouldn't be enough to keep them from smashing into the thing. Dustin cringed, but at the last second the creature leapt into the air. It landed on the still skidding car—one human shaped hand with two-inch long claws touched down on the windshield in front of Dustin—and then vaulted over in a blur.

Brakes squealed. Jimmy tried to straighten out, but one tire hit the ditch alongside the road at close to 45 miles per hour, bouncing the driver's side up into a corkscrew. They were airborne for a moment, both screaming in unison, and then the Mustang came down on its roof. The impact knocked their skulls against doors and dashboard. The front windshield shattered. Sparks flew as the vehicle slid another twenty feet across concrete.

Dustin hung from the seat, suspended above broken bits of Saf-T glass while the engine coughed and sputtered and died, cutting off Axl as he shrieked about being taken home to that place where grass was green and girls were pretty. He moved his head to look at Jimmy, who was unconscious but breathing as he dangled above the steering wheel.

Movement outside caught Dustin's eye. He spotted the figure as it loped through the haze of his vision and watched as it circled the car on all fours, stopping beside the open window of the driver's seat. A hand came snaking in through

Jimmy's window (*shit, that's no hand*, Dustin's sluggish mind insisted, *that's a straight razor with fingers*) and the claws on the end pierced the soft throat of his best friend and tore it out amid a gush of blood. Jimmy jerked several times, flopping against the leather seat, then went limp.

The figure came around the hood, heading toward Dustin. The car was filled with the sound of blood draining from Jimmy's body like the soft patter of rain. Dustin wanted to cry out, but couldn't produce even a squeak. Some part of him realized he was about to become part of the Jackal Man legend forever, and this time next year two other kids would be talking about them as they drove through these woods.

A head appeared in his window, features obscured by flickering shadows. He thought he could make out a feline face complete with small triangular ears laid back against a broad skull.

And its eyes. Luminescent green, like floating emeralds.

Its mouth opened. A harsh, mangled roar split the night. A full set of wicked fangs was set into that gaping hole, each as thick as Dustin's thumb.

That hand reached in through his window, those sickle claws sank through his neck, and there was no pain, only the sticky warmth and sweet smell of blood spilling up into his mouth and nose and eyes and darkness stealing his every thought...

But everyone knows that story, even if they can't tell you exactly how long ago it happened, or just who those kids were. Always just the same old tale with a new coat of paint. It and a hundred more about the Jackal Man have been around forever.

Why, I heard a new one just last week. The details have escaped me, but I'm sure I can get close enough.

Stop me if you've heard this one.

FRANK

THE BASTARD PAYS A VISIT

1

The Texas sun baked the earth with a ferocity even most lifelong residents never get used to, including a busy construction site in the middle of downtown Houston. Enclosed by a tall wooden fence, the yard stretched for nearly a quarter of a mile along Market Square.

A sign outside proclaimed it, 'THE FUTURE SITE OF THE HOUSTON SPRINGS MALL'. In the lower right corner were the less visible words, *A Lyles Corporation Project*. Some comedic soul had crossed out 'Lyles' with a marker and written 'Asshole', despite the grammatical problem this posed.

A foreman's trailer was parked on the dirt lot, pushed off into a corner. It had large windows, but the shades were drawn.

Frank Stanford sat inside this trailer in near darkness, trying to enjoy the dribble of cool from the air conditioner. A mess of papers lay scattered on the desk in front of him. The muscles in the back of his neck thrummed like an ill-tuned guitar—from sleeping on his couch, he had no doubt—and the pain coupled with the unbearable heat wasn't helping his disposition.

At last he moved, shifting through the pile on his desk until he found the report he wanted. Inside was a timetable showing where the mall construction project should be, and a small arrow representing where it was now.

These two were not close to one another. At all.

Frank Stanford detested being off schedule on a job.

He stood up, lumbered over to the window, and raised the blinds. The sunlight burned his tired retinas. When they adjusted, he watched the workers. He had six different crews out there, jostling for space and trying not to get on each other's nerves in the peaking summer heat.

They were some of the best crews he'd ever supervised, and the delay wasn't their fault. God Himself still needed a respectable seven days to create the universe. Still, it was time to give them a little motivation.

Remind them they were on the Bastard's dollar.

Frank opened the door to his trailer. Heat washed over him in a scorching wave. He paused on the threshold, reached into his shirt pocket for a crushed package of Marlboros and shook one out. He took several drags to get the refreshing spike of nicotine in his system, and studied the men at ground level as they mixed cement and drilled rivets, then looked at the crewmen on the upper floors, where the only thing between them and a long, painful fall were two-foot wide steel beams.

Didn't that used to be you up there, Frankie? a familiar condescending voice spoke up in his head. This voice, which had been tormenting him as long as he could remember, had a way of sounding a lot like his father when it wanted, the only man who ever called him 'Frankie.'

He dropped the cigarette to the dirt. Two fingers went in his mouth to give a shrill whistle. The work around him slowly ground to a halt as crewmen passed the word along. Frank stood ramrod straight with arms crossed over his chest as they clustered around him.

"Okay, fellas," he shouted. "As of today, we're nearly three weeks behind schedule. Anybody wanna tell me why?"

"Your manliness is a real distraction while we're trying to work!" someone yelled.

"I don't find that funny. Not one fuckin bit."

"C'mon Frank," Danny McGinty said from the front line. "We're doing the best we can here."

"Yeah Bossman," Ted Harwell agreed. "The Bastard's runnin us ragged. You know that timetable's all messed up."

"No, I don't know it," he argued, knowing it perfectly well. "I do know that if we don't follow it, all of us are gonna be in a world of hurt and unemployment. I don't want excuses, I want you guys out there doing the job. And to that end…we're cutting overtime and adding a full second shift."

This was met with instant outcry. Most of them needed the money they earned through overtime, but it would be cheaper for Frank's budget to cut it out entirely and just add a new shift of fresh faces that he could get more work out of. Of course, it would also mean longer hours for him unless he brought on an assistant foreman. Trish would not be happy. Or rather, less happy than she already was. But, if he was being honest, anything that kept him out of the house a little more would be a relief. As the rabble grew louder, Frank held up his hands to keep them quiet.

"I don't wanna hear it. You wanna bitch, do it to The Bastard and see what he tells you. Just make sure you're clocked out and gone by the end of your shift, because you're gonna be working for free if you stay longer. And if that doesn't motivate you, I'm taking away smoke breaks too."

They continued to groan as they trudged away. Someone muttered, "Like the world's in any big hurry to have another fuckin mall."

As the crewmen returned to work, Frank spotted one man in particular and called out, "Hold up, Garrett!"

Garrett Tanner crossed the lot back to Frank, a hangdog look on his face. "Listen Frank, if this is about me using the acetylene torch to cook that bag of popcorn, I didn't know it would explode like that…"

"What? No, look, I just wanna talk to you." Frank edged back toward his trailer, away from hearing range of the rest of the yard. "I just wanted to ask you…" He paused again to check for eavesdroppers, "About that military school you sent your son to."

"Andrew Academy?"

"Yeah. What'd you think of it?"

"Shit, that place was stricter than a maximum security prison. Did the trick though. Turned Davey's whole life around." Garrett frowned at Frank. "You still havin problems with Willie?"

"He's taking summer school for all the classes he skipped this past semester and he's gotten into two fights *there* in the past week. I think the kid's in need of a good, old-fashioned, boot-to-the-ass."

"I don't know, Frank. Every kid's different. The only reason we sent Davey is because he was gettin arrested every other week and wouldn't listen to a goddamned word we said. What finally swayed us was when the little shit pulled a knife on me because I wouldn't let him out of the house to go street racing at three in the morning." Garrett paused long enough to shake his head. "When he came back from Andrew he was a model citizen, and maybe it gave him a shot at a normal life, but… it's like he wasn't our son anymore. More like a stranger, after they sucked the life outta him. If you think you have any shot at reaching Willie yourself…I'd hold off."

"Now you sound like Trish. She defends that kid at every step."

"That's what mothers are for!"

The conversation was cut off by the sound of tires crunching across the lot behind them. Frank looked away from Garrett to find a long, dark limousine pulling in through a gap in the fence. At the sight of it, the noise level around them tripled as the crewmen built harder and faster. Frank's own heart rate jumped.

"The Bastard." Garrett breathed the word with the reverence usually reserved for Greek gods.

"You better get back to work."

Garrett scurried away to make himself inconspicuous, a luxury Frank envied at the moment.

Frank crossed in front of the polished chrome grill and around to the driver side. A man in chauffeur regalia got out and goose-stepped to the rear door. Frank watched the process from several feet back, hands clasped, trying not to fidget away his nervous energy.

What was the son of a bitch doing here?

Why now, of all times, when Frank hadn't even heard from him in three months? He didn't make surprise inspections and social visits sure as hell weren't his cup of tea. No, the only explanation was that he knew about the delays and intended to go bowling with Frank's head.

The driver yanked the door open.

And then Barry Lyles the Third—aka Third Reich, aka Larry Biles, aka The Bastard (that one not so funny since the recent death of his father)—swung around on the padded limo seat, placed his Italian loafers on the packed dirt, and exited the vehicle. He stood up to his full five-foot height and adjusted his tailor-made suit jacket. Lyles inspected him through sunglasses that probably cost more than Frank's entire outfit.

"Frank," he offered.

"Hello Mr. Lyles. I wasn't aware—" was all he could get out before the man strolled away in the direction of Frank's trailer. The limo driver gave Frank a sympathetic look before scurrying back to his seat.

2

Frank followed Lyles as he barged inside the trailer like he...well, like he owned the place. In fact, Lyles owned this and sixty-three other construction ventures across North America, but it was an empire inherited. Frank stood uncertainly in the doorway of his own office as the man went behind his desk and shifted through the mound of papers.

"It's wonderful to see you again, sir," Frank groveled, attempting to shift the magnate's attention away from the incriminating timetable in the stack. Lyles's hand brushed aside a blue budget report and, whaddaya know, there it was. Frank had even been kind enough to highlight the discrepancies.

"Been a long time," Lyles said.

"I was sorry to hear about your father. He was the reason I stayed with the company so long. He was...a good man."

"Yes, well, I wouldn't know. He spent more time with his employees than he ever did with me. This company was his goddamn reason for being."

For that comment alone, Frank wanted to reach across the desk and rattle the dwarf's teeth. Barry Lyles Jr. built the corporation from the ground up, and his son benefited from every drop of sweat. Frank had watched him grow from smarmy young man to coldhearted shark-in-a-suit.

Lyles's stubby fingers lit upon the pink sheet of paper. He lifted it by the corner, holding it to his face to study. Frank stood by, helpless and speechless.

"You look uncomfortable." Lyles looked up to meet his eyes for the first time. An amused smile tugged at the corners of his thin lips. He spread the pink sheet of paper across the desk. "I didn't come here to cry a river for my father. Why don't you stop drooling in the doorway like a retard and sit down?"

Frank entered the room and sank into the padded chair in front of his own desk. From this vantage point, even Lyles towered above him. The other man circled, staring down at his captive.

"If it's about the job, we are a *bit* behind schedule. But I think if we push we can be back on track by—"

"No, forget about that. Forget about this whole job, in fact."

Frank swallowed a frozen lump the size of a golf ball. So that was it. No reprimand; this would be used as an excuse to get rid of him. Twenty years with the company bought him no parole.

"I'm here to offer you a transfer to a *new* job."

"Um...say again?"

"And a significant pay raise." Lyles halted to Frank's left, gave that same predatory grin.

"I'm not sure I understand, sir." *Or I'm not seeing the catch.*

"Have you ever heard of a town called Asheville, Frank?"

The topic change with no segue was a tactic they must've taught Lyles in whatever school they trained assholes in nowadays. Frank rolled with it rather than try to swim upstream. "Can't say I have."

"It's a little pisspot up north, stuck outside DFW. Small town, tiny population, lots of woodland, just begging to be developed. My father purchased a rather large plot of land there, with the intention of turning it into a huge housing development."

"Oh, I did hear about that. River Trails, or something, right?"

"Meadows," Lyles corrected. "Phase one consists of forty houses slated to go on the market in mid-September. It's just a jumping off point to test the market; phase two will be close to 300. And I now find myself in the precarious position of being without a head foreman when we're less than halfway through."

"If you don't mind me asking, what happened?"

"I fired him. He wasn't getting it done Frank, and in this business, it's all about getting it *done*. We have contracts, we have deadlines. This is a huge project and, unlike my father, I don't have the time to waste on fuck-up's like Wesley Gammon."

Frank knew the name, but not well enough to decide if Lyles was talking out of his money-hungry ass.

"I'll be honest with you, Frank. My father sank a shitload of money into some projects out west that went sour. He pushed the Lyles Corporation to the edge of bankruptcy, then he croaks and goes out like a champ and dumps the whole thing in my lap. When it goes under, I'll be known as the bad son who ran it into the ground. I'm inclined to think the old goat planned it that way." Lyles chuckled sourly. He came up in front of Frank, bent so they were at eye level and placed his hands on Frank's shoulders. "This project could turn it all around for me though. So I'm going to be totally up front with you about this Meadows thing. This isn't a cakewalk job. There's one very big problem my father neglected to discover before he bought that godforsaken land."

Silence followed, and Frank was unsure if Lyles was waiting for him to inquire. He really just wanted the man's hands off his shoulders. It was like they were about to kiss.

"Know anything about geology?"

"Uh, nope."

"Me neither." Lyles stepped back at last. "But the *incredibly* expensive geologists I've hired tell me there's a layer of hard clay under the entire area that makes it all but impossible to build on. We're talking bedrock here, except three inches under the soil. The only way to lay a foundation is to blast through. It's proving to be a helluva roadblock. You think you're behind here—which you are, by the way—but it's nothing compared to the Meadows."

"'Blast through?' You mean with dynamite?"

"No Frank, with raindrops on roses and whiskers on kittens. Yes, with dynamite! Gammon hired some tech to do the work. Stay with me here or it's gonna be a long afternoon."

"Yes sir," Frank agreed through clenched teeth.

"Anyway, the point is, if you want the job, I need you out there by next week. We've got a house rented for you already. Feel free to take the family. I'm even willing to pay a bonus upon completion by deadline."

As much as he and Trisha could use the extra money, Frank wasn't witless enough to leap into this offer blind. She was pissed enough at him these days as it was. "That's very generous sir, but I'd have to give it some thought. You know, talk to my wife."

"More time is being lost as we speak. I need an answer today, right now. The only reason I came to you is because my father had so much faith in you. You were always one of his favorites." A peculiar, faraway look crossed his pinched features as the younger man said this. "Now, do you want to seize the opportunity, or do I find someone else with the balls to take this on?"

It *would* be nice to have the stress of the mall project taken off his plate. And there was no good reason for them not to go. Trisha was jobless, and Willie would be done with summer school soon enough. They could all use a vacation, even if it was just a change of scenery.

And if not, well...it might be nice to go alone, too.

"I'll do it," he blurted.

"Excellent." Lyles's grin was full of too many teeth. "You leave Friday."

Frank's mind whirled with all the questions he still needed answered. "Who am I working under?"

"I was thinking about calling in Damon Bradford. You know him?"

"I've worked with him before."

"Good, then it's settled. You go home, start the wheels rolling, and I'll contact you tonight."

Frank found himself ushered out of the trailer. The door slammed behind him, and he had the unshakeable feeling he'd just been conned by the carnival fortuneteller.

3

Frank parked his truck in front of his house in the eastern suburbs of Houston as afternoon dwindled toward twilight. He climbed out and clomped up onto his porch, but paused before going in. Dread resignation filled him, like a soldier preparing to enter hostile territory. Finally, he unlocked the door and stepped inside.

"*Daddy!*" The excited squeal filled the living room as Casey launched herself from the couch. He tossed his lunch pail aside and swept his five-year-old daughter off the floor before she could crash into him. His tired back screamed in protest, but it would have time to rest when she was too old for this.

And that time would come all too soon. His son had brought that truth crashing down on him.

"Why are you home so early?" she demanded.

"They released me on my own recognizance." His daughter was a female mirror of him, black hair and a cute, round face that matched his at every chubby angle. One more reason to curse his name when she came of age. "What have you been up to?"

"Mommy took me to the park today! I got pushed on the swings!"

"Sounds like a perfect day." He planted a kiss on her forehead. "Where's your brother?"

"He's in his room."

Of course. The boy only came out when his body required food or a restroom to continue functioning. It was more like they had a boarder living under their roof, one who was quiet, unobtrusive, and kept to himself unless confronted.

"Probably playing video games. Let's go stop him from being antisocial, whaddaya say?" A few seconds later they stood in front of the closed door of his son's room. Frank pushed it open without knocking.

William Stanford, or Willie, as they'd called him since the day he was born, slouched down on his bed, staring vacantly at his small TV. He wore a black t-shirt with a slogan extolling the virtues of something called a 'Seether,' and rumpled black jeans at least three sized too big that hung off him in folds like the loose skin of an elephant. His fingers moved expertly across the PlayStation controller in his hands.

"I'm home," Frank announced.

"Daddy's home," Casey echoed.

"Hey." The boy's eyes left the screen for only a second, flicking up and back down.

If Casey looked like Frank, then fifteen-year-old Willie was all his mother. Harder to notice the resemblance though, after he spiked his sandy brown hair up into orange tips and darkened his eyes with what Frank feared was mascara.

"How was your day?" Frank asked. Willie shrugged. "Oh really? That's good. Mine was fine also." No way to know if the boy was upset or just in his normal funk. He moped twenty-four hours a day; a smile at this point might shatter facial muscle. Frank waited a minute in the doorway with Casey becoming heavier each second.

Might as well go for broke. "Something bothering you?"

"No," he said too quickly. His hands stuttered on the controller and the depressing music indicating a loss of life came from the television speakers.

"He can't go to school no more!" Casey tattled eagerly.

"Shut up! That's not true!"

"What's going on? What's she talking about ,Willie?"

"Nothing! Leave me alone! I'm sure *Mom* will tell you all about it!" he shouted, making the word 'Mom' sound like something between toe jam and the Hanta virus on the desirability scale. Willie threw down the controller and pushed past his father, giving his sister a hateful glare, and went into a door down the hall. "Guess I'll go in the bathroom to get some privacy since you all come to stare at me like some fucking zoo exhibit!" He slammed the door.

Frank sighed. He said to Casey, "That went pretty well, didn't it?" She smiled until her eyes squinted and nodded.

He found Trisha in the kitchen and sent Casey back into the living room. Frank stood in the doorway, watching his wife as she peeled potatoes while listening to the soft sounds of Shania Twain from the radio by the sink. She was thin and delicately curved, brown hair cascading down her back, skin at least two shades darker than his, every move graceful as she flowed around the room in a sleeveless summer dress. The material was light and breezy and almost see-through. He was surprised to find himself becoming aroused.

When was the last time they'd had sex? Two months, maybe three? The tension between them had been thick enough to cut with a chainsaw since Willie's problems began. And when he told her he'd taken another job for the summer without consulting her, he might need Viagra before he got another shot.

"So why are you home so early?"

"Eh." He shrugged. "Good day?"

"You could say that," she said without turning around. "*You* could say that, but I wouldn't."

He took a chance, ambling across the kitchen to slide his arms around her stomach. She stiffened reflexively—only for a moment, but enough to skewer his confidence. "Why is my daughter the only person that can show me any affection when I get home?"

He was shoved away as she went back to working on the potatoes.

"While you're at work Frank, I'm the one who's been going to parent-teacher conferences at the school. Willie was expelled from the summer courses after that last fight, and now the administration says they don't want him coming back in the fall."

"What? That's ridiculous!"

"Tell them that, like I've been trying to all day. They feel he's—how did they put it?—a 'danger in a public school setting.'"

"They have gangs roaming the halls and *he's* the danger?"

"So now," she continued, "we either enroll him somewhere outside of the Houston school district or send him to a private school, neither of which sounds too affordable to me."

"There's no way out of this? We can't pay them or...?"

"No Frank, they're not mobsters, you can't bribe them. Their decision is final."

He gripped the counter, disappointed and frustrated. A year ago, his kid was a straight A student, never in trouble a day in his life. Now Frank was terrified he was going to wake up some night with the boy standing over him, knife in hand. "I *told* you. I told you letting him dress like that and listen to that music would lead to this. But no, he's got to 'explore' and 'figure out his path.'"

Trisha turned on him with fire in her bright eyes. "That's perfect. Blame me. You know this is exactly what I wanted to happen, Frank."

He sighed. "I didn't mean that. It came out wrong. So what do we do?"

"You tell me."

Frank shrugged, ready to throw up his hands and give the whole mess to whoever wanted to clean it up...and then a smile found its way onto his face. She expected a miracle, but in lieu, he would give her practicality.

"What if I can solve all of our problems?"

"Kool-Aid with rat poison?"

"I'm serious, Trish."

"Then what are you talking about?"

"Let's go in our room." No use giving her access to cutlery and pans when he delivered the news. Frank led her down the hall and into their bedroom and shut the door. She collapsed on the bed. "Barry Lyles paid me a visit today."

"From the grave?"

"His son."

"I'm sorry. How did you survive that encounter?"

"Never mind about that. Long and short of it is, he offered me a job with an increase in pay, and I took it."

Her face brightened at that announcement. "That's great! God knows we need it. I'm really happy for you."

He took a deep breath. "Don't be. Not yet."

"Oh Jesus. Why do I get the feeling you sold yourself into slavery?"

"Nooo, nothing that bad." He chuckled and then said in

a rush, "The job is in another city up north, and we're all going! But it's just for the summer!"

"Woah, woah, how far up north?"

"Asheville, Texas. He's already rented us a house and we're supposed to move up there by next week so I can take over foreman duties."

She was very still, and then struck like a cobra. "How could you accept something like that without even calling me?"

"It was a spur of the moment thing, honey!"

"But I can't just pack up and leave! I need to be looking for another job! We can't survive much longer without me working!"

"You're exaggerating! The jobs will be here when we get back. Besides...my bonus for this will keep us afloat."

"Bonus?"

"Yep, for completion on time."

She groaned. "Frank, I don't know..."

"Then think of it as...a vacation. Together, as a family."

She thought about that, then shook her head. "No, Frank. I don't think now would be the best time for you to go traipsing off either, but if you have to do this, then you can go by yourself."

He got down on one knee. "We really need this time together, Trish. This will get us away from all the distractions, and we can spend some real quality time with Willie. It... It'll give us some..." he flailed for an appropriate word, "perspective!"

"You don't honestly think it will be that easy, do you? That we'll spend a few months in a different house and Willie will be himself again?"

"It couldn't hurt to try! He turned into that holy terror in less time!"

She put one palm against his cheek and smiled, so much weariness in her face that it hurt him to look at it. "Frank, I'm sorry, but I'm not going anywhere. If you want to follow Lyles into the sunset, fine, but the kids and I are staying right here."

"So that's how it's gonna be? There's nothing I can do to change your mind?"

She leaned close. He could see the finality in her eyes. "It would take something extreme."

The door to their bedroom burst open, causing them both to jump. Willie stomped into their room, a tornado of black with an orange top.

"Might as well just confess before you find out anyway. I pierced my tongue today. Me and Miles did it ourselves." He opened his mouth and shoved out his tongue. A small metal pin with a glinting silver ball on top impaled the meaty part of the muscle, which looked red and badly swollen. He reeled his tongue back in and stood defiantly, waiting for them to pass judgment.

Frank looked at Trisha.

"When do we leave?" she asked.

4

"For the whole rest of the summer?" Miles whined in disbelief.

Willie nodded, sitting on the porch in front of his house, his legs—clad in another pair of oversized black jeans that engulfed the lower half of his body—dangling off the edge beside the stairs. It was Tuesday, but the summer had already reached the lazy pace where the days no longer had their distinct feel. Miles paced in the yard in front of him with his arms hugging his chest over a black shirt with white lettering that read, 'Eat Shit, Dickhead.' If Miles ever told anyone out loud to 'Eat Shit,' Willie would start watching for the apocalypse.

He reached down and pulled a handful of grass from the lawn and threw one blade at a time into the summer breeze. "Yup. That's what they said."

"Aw, man...dude...*man!*" Those words had enough emotion to convey everything his best friend thought about the situation. "Your dad's got a real shitty job!"

"I heard that, Miles." Willie's father drugged a trunk full of clothes past them to load into his truck. He stopped long enough to take in the boy's shirt with one arched eyebrow, then said to his son, "Why don't you make yourselves useful? You can help me hook up your mom's car to the tow hitch."

"Um, no thanks. That's cool." Miles gave a weak laugh and scurried to sit down next to Willie. He was shorter and chubbier than Willie, with glasses that rested against his bulbous nose, and five piercings. The glittering studs and hoops protruding from his skin outnumbered the facial hairs he was currently capable of growing. "Do you think they'd let you stay at my house?" he asked in a low voice, after Frank Stanford stomped away.

"Could I?"

"I don't know if my folks would be cool with it, but if you snuck in and out..."

"Naw, that's all right." As much as Willie dreaded this trip, the idea of spending the summer as a fugitive was less appealing. "I think my dad'd make me go with them anyways."

Willie's mom came out of the house carrying a suitcase that had been in their attic for three years. He couldn't even remember their last vacation, a drive to SeaWorld in San Antonio when he was eight. Not that he was fooled by the exaggerations they were using to get him and Casey excited about going. If this was a 'vacation' then next time he went to take a shit, he would just call it 'scenting the bathroom'.

"Willie, you better go inside and start packing!" she yelled. "You haven't done anything to get ready and we're leaving in an hour!"

He mumbled an assent into his chest that was incoherent to even Miles. This was how he communicated with them now, and it was as automatic as swallowing after chewing.

Certainly made hiding the tongue ring easier. It'd hurt like a bastard when Miles did it, and Willie was afraid it might have gotten infected, but the swelling finally went down. He was just thankful his parents let him keep it; the damage was already done, after all.

His mother gave him a look that was part frustration and part concern, then took the suitcase out to his father.

"This sucks donkey balls, man! What am I supposed to do all summer without you here? It's no fun sneaking out without you, and I won't even have anybody to go to the big concerts with! Linkin Park is comin, dude, *Linkin Park!*" Miles groaned and leaned back against the porch railing.

Willie didn't bother to remind him that he had bigger monkeys on his back than which bands his poor, dejected friend would have to see all alone while he was stuck in a house in an unfamiliar town with his nagging parents and bratty sister like some kind of reality show conceived by Satan himself. He wanted to tell Miles to stop his bitching.

But he didn't, because Miles was his only friend these days.

"I better get going. Guess I won't see you again until the first day of school?"

Willie grimaced. He hadn't mentioned his permanent expulsion and now wasn't the time. "Sure, man. I'll call you when I get back."

Miles held out a hand and Willie gripped it so that their thumbs interlocked. "*Da-svidan'ya,*" he began.

"Don't spit on ya," Willie finished the old schoolyard rhyme. Neither of them had any idea what it meant anymore, but it'd become their standard send-off.

Miles hopped on his bike and rode away, careful to go around the far side of the truck so Frank Stanford wouldn't see him. Willie sat for a few long minutes, marveling at how cataclysmically unfair life could be, then slowly got to his feet.

His father passed him at breakneck speed, wheezing and sweating. He shouted over his shoulder, "*Go pack, Willie!*"

"*I'm GOING!*" he yelled back, as anger swept through him. There was a ready supply of it lately, bubbling below

the surface, as though he'd developed a new gland that se-
creted pure, uncut, chemical fury instead of hormones. A
'shit-uitary' gland, maybe. He stomped into the house and
back to his room, slamming the door.

An open suitcase waited on his bed. He jerked drawers all
the way out of his dresser, letting them clatter on the floor, then
grabbed underwear and socks and threw them at the suitcase in
wads. He gritted his teeth as he unplugged wires from his game
system and tossed it in as well. Then he stalked to the closet to
retrieve the bulk of his clothing.

The inside was one long hanging rod. The left half held
all of his black shirts, ridiculously big jeans, spiked belts,
and other accessories: the wardrobe he'd acquired in the last
year. The right half held the straight leg blue jeans, slacks,
and crisp dress shirts that had been the staple of the old Willie Stanford. Neither had done much to raise his social level
above that of algae in the pond of high school.

He froze in the doorway and clicked his tongue ring
against the inside of his teeth, torn about which clothes to
take. Finally, his hand went to the darker section.

"The other stuff wouldn't go with orange hair," he muttered, as if in apology.

Besides, this would *really* bug his parents.

Willie grabbed clothes off the rack in handfuls, and
shoved them in his suitcase. After it was jammed full, he was
panting and red in the face from the effort, wondering how
things had gotten so screwed up, how the one person whose
approval used to be so important could take one look at his
orange hair and dark clothes (and the mascara he'd been
swiping from his mother) and think he'd gone insane, like all

of it made him a different person.

So what? He wasn't ashamed, and Frank Stanford could just deal with it.

Of course, all that pride would be small consolation at whatever 'behavioral readjustment center' he ended up at next year. He'd heard his parents talking about Andrew Academy. Fine, let them send him. His prison sentence was only another four years, at most.

It's not too late to turn it all around.

He contemplated that while he stared at the leftover clothes in the closet.

Da'svidan'ya, don't spit on ya, he thought, but without much remorse. He zipped up his suitcase, and dragged it toward the door.

"Everybody ready to go?" his mother asked in the car. "Nobody needs a pee break?"

"Ready, Mommy!" Casey shouted. Willie sneered and stuck out his studded tongue at her. She wrinkled her nose in disgust. "Why does Willie have that thing in his mouth?"

"He thought it would be fun to have a hole in his tongue to match the one in his head," his father said, glancing at him in the rearview mirror.

"Oh, ha ha, you're such a comedian. Can I just ride in mom's car?"

"Only if I can strap you to the luggage rack."

Casey giggled and his mother smiled at him crookedly, obviously holding in laughter. Willie grunted. "Still be better than this."

As his father put the truck in gear and pulled away from the curb, Willie glanced back at their house. It looked somber and quiet as he watched it dwindle.

And then an odd thought popped into his head.

Suddenly, for some reason...he knew he would never see their home again.

5

Traffic thinned as Interstate 45 carried them away from the clogged streets of Houston, through rolling Texas landscape, and then into the heart of Dallas, where the streets were more like a maze than a planned network. They stopped only twice for Casey's bathroom breaks and still arrived in the city in a little over four hours. From there, it was a relatively quick jaunt into Arlington, and when they reached the far side of the city limits just before entering Asheville—a town represented on the GPS by a tiny black dot no bigger than a pen nib—Frank succumbed to the pleas to stop for a bite to eat.

"We're almost there!" he protested, although he really didn't know if it was true; the GPS seemed to be having trouble plotting their route in the final leg of the trip. "Don't you want to see what the house looks like first?"

"Frank, unless the refrigerator is stocked, we're going to starve."

"We're gonna *starve?*" Casey howled.

Frank sighed. "See what you started?"

"Let's just stop now for something so we don't have to get out again." Trisha's jaw was set forward like a cocked catapult.

"All right, fine. I need to let the GPS recalibrate anyway."

They were on Westwood Boulevard, the street Lyles had given him in his hastily rattled off directions. A sign ahead proclaimed they would be crossing over Highway 30 soon, but the GPS seemed to think there was no way into Asheville from the south. When he tried the directions app on his phone, it told him the same thing. And going all the way around on the freeway and coming in from the north would add an extra hour to their drive. He pulled off the road into the lot of an old gas station.

"Willie, take your sister inside and pick out some sandwiches and candy bars. Don't let her out of your sight."

"God, I'm not a babysitter, you know."

"Just do it, son."

"I don't want to."

"Dammit, do you have to argue with everything we say?" Frank snapped.

Willie looked at him blackly, so full of hate Frank felt a moment of irrational fear. He got out, took his sister's hand, and led her into the gas station. Frank watched them disappear through the front doors and became aware of his wife's scrutinizing eyes upon him.

"What?"

"Did you have to be that rough?"

"Jesus Christ, Trish, you heard him! He's cruising for it!"

"Do you not remember what it was like to be his age? They lash out and then withdraw, lash out and then withdraw."

"What is he, a hormone-riddled jack-in-the-box? I'll tell you something Trish, the parents of those nutball Columbine kids probably said the same thing, and look where it got them. You have to start taking charge of them at some point. Do you know what my father would've done if I whined like that?"

"No, but I'm *sure* you'll tell me."

"Don't start, all right? Just don't start. It's too hot."

Frank reached past her to the glove box for the old paper state map he kept inside, hoping it would give him a different answer. He opened his door, got out, stretched, and spread the map on the hood. Trisha came to join him.

"Where are we?"

"Right here," Frank said, pointing at the prominently titled Westwood Boulevard. "This street runs across the freeway and then there's just this...road. Even on the GPS, it's not labeled, and I can't tell if it heads into Asheville. On this, it just looks like it peters out."

"Then go ask someone in the station."

"I don't need directions."

"But you obviously do! God, why do you have to be so difficult?"

He blinked at her stupidly, as shocked by her outburst as Willie had been by his. It was a cycle; the Stanford family Circle of Irritation. They passed anger around like a winter cold.

He gathered up the map in a fist and stormed into the building. When he pushed open the door, a wave of stale heat washed over him. The counter was to the left, and a grimy clerk was hunched on a stool with a fan blowing on him. He was reading a magazine and drinking from a juice box, but he looked up at Frank and held the hand with the beverage up in greeting. Frank nodded and went to find his children on the second of the station's three rows of goods, picking out candy bars.

"They don't have sandwiches," Casey told him.

"Well, this will have to tide us over then." He grabbed Butterfingers for himself and Trisha and herded the kids to the counter. As their purchases were rung up, Frank opened the map on his phone and held it out to the clerk.

"Can you tell me if this road takes us into Asheville?"

The attendant wore stained overalls with a patch that said 'Earl Dean.' He had greasy hair that fell past his shoulders, and sweat poured from him, despite the fan spinning on the counter. "Shore! The Dark Road'll take ya right in thair! Cain't miss it!" His Adam's apple bobbed as he mangled each word with backwoods Texas twang.

"Dark Road? It doesn't say that on the map."

"That's just what folks 'round hair call it. Really dudn't have a name. Whatchoo wanna go to Asheville for anyway?"

"Business," he said, handing over cash.

"Okay," Earl Dean agreed. "But they don't have nuthin thair. Just dirt and more dirt."

"What a coincidence! That's *exactly* what we're looking for!" Frank said. Willie snickered and Frank shot him a grin, a pale echo of the days when they used to laugh about everything together.

The three of them gathered the food and started for the door. As Frank's hand touched the glass, the clerk called, "Well, you folks be caireful on the Dark Road. Don't let the Jackal Man getcha!"

They froze at the strange warning, even Casey.

That other voice spoke in Frank's head again, and this time it didn't just sound like his father, it *was* his father, speaking straight from the depths of memory.

They're out there, it whispered. *They're lightning fast and got claws like steel razors. Now take this gun Frankie, and GO GET 'EM!*

A shiver built in him, despite the stifling air in the station. He hadn't thought about that in a long time.

He turned and saw the clerk's eyes twinkling with anticipation. Earl Dean was practically jumping from foot to grungy foot in his eagerness to elaborate.

Frank would've been content to walk out of that roadside station without ever hearing what homespun fairy tales the man intended to tell. The very thought of playing this man's fool filled him with a potent mixture of revulsion, anger, and, queerly, fear.

However, he wasn't the one that finally took the bait after fifteen seconds of confused silence.

"Jackal Man?" Willie repeated. "What's a Jackal Man?"

Earl Dean grinned wider, a few teeth poking between his lips like chunks of meat in murky soup. "Guess you folks is from farther off than I figgered. The Jackal Man lives in the woods out on the Dark Road!"

"What does he do?" his son asked, approaching the counter.

"*What does he do?* Why, he *kills* folks, son, whatchoo think he does? He kills them that's stupid enough to trespass in his woods!"

"Like the Jersey Devil?" Willie asked. "Oh, or the Mothman! That's cool!"

The greasy attendant bent over the counter toward Willie, his face losing its impish grin and becoming stone serious. "No, it ain't cool," he said softly. "This is a real nasty fella we're talkin about. Worse'n any of them. A big, mean cat monster. Fangs and claws and shit. All polka-dotty, like a leopard."

"Daddy?" Casey asked uncertainly.

"He got a couple of kids a few months back too! Jumped on their car and climbed in through the window to eat 'em!" Casey whimpered and jumped at Frank's hand.

"That's enough buddy," Frank cut in. "Peddle your urban legends to someone else. You're scaring my kids here."

"I'm not scared," Willie said quickly.

"Geez, mister, I didn't mean nuthin. Just a friendly warnin." The attendant stood straight and wiped his hands on his coveralls. He seemed to come back to himself, then looked down at his feet sheepishly.

"Buncha baloney," Frank muttered, turning to go. "C'mon kids."

Casey followed, holding his hand, but he saw Willie hesitate, taking several looks back at the man behind the counter.

"Ask anybody in Asheville," Earl Dean told him. "They'll tell ya."

Willie nodded before exiting the store.

Casey was almost in tears by the time they got to the car. "Is that true, Daddy, is that true? Don't make me go in the woods!"

"No, that man was an idiot, sweetie. He doesn't even know a jackal is a dog. Surprised he didn't tell us to say Bloody Mary in the mirror five times too."

"Or take out our livers and leave us unconscious in a bathtub full of ice!" Willie added.

Frank glared at him. "It's just a story. They're ALL just stories."

He got them back into the rear seat of the truck and climbed behind the wheel. Trisha asked, "Did you find out if that's the road?"

"Yep." *The Dark Road*, he almost added. He suddenly craved a cigarette.

"What's wrong with Casey?"

"You don't wanna know, trust me."

~ ~ ~

Five minutes later, they were in the thick of the woods, and Frank began to understand the title. At night, without any lights, this place would be pitch black. The trees were gruesome somehow, scraggily branches jutting from packed rows of thin trunks, all fighting for light, food and growing space as prickly bushes weaved between their feet and shallow bogs filled the only breaks in the continuous line of trees. No wonder the place was being razed to make room for the next wave of white-collar housing.

They drove through the wilds and across a bridge over a torpid stream before the left side of the road cleared of trees, and they saw a sun-beaten meadow dotted with a few oaks.

"There's a sign, Frank!" Trisha cried, startling him enough to cause his hair to bristle.

A large square board by the side of the road announced that the River Meadows Housing Development was just ahead.

"Good, let's check this place out."

They flew past the sign, and only Willie noticed the markings in the corner. By the time he figured out what they were, they were speeding away, and he didn't have time to double check.

They looked like claw marks.

Large, ragged claw marks.

6

The site began three yards from the edge of the road. The steep ditch hugging the pavement was worn down and evened out by heavy machinery into a dirt path that would one day be a street leading through the middle of the lot.

The place was deserted. Houses, nothing more than frames at various stages of development, stood in two rows on both sides of the dirt track, facing one another. A white, portable trailer was at the back of the lot, straddling the middle. A lone bulldozer sat to the left of the first house. Frank got out of the truck, leaving his family in the air-conditioning, and went to the center of the yard. He counted nineteen partially finished structures. He was expected to have forty identical, cookie-cutter tract houses built by the end of the summer for Lyles's Phase 1 marketing experiment.

He could easily envision what old Barry Jr. had seen when he looked at this land: an expansive neighborhood with green faux lawns and luxury cars and American flags and basketball goals over every garage. Another natural reserve falling victim to urban sprawl. Until then, it was just trees, a strip of thick marsh grass to the south, and the unnamed road running by it all.

He ambled toward the trailer, looking into the shadow-steeped house frames along the way. A green storage shed about the size of a walk-in closet stood beside the trailer. The door was ajar, and he pulled it the rest of the way open to look inside.

Stacked in neat rows were about thirty black metal boxes labeled 'DYNAMITE!' with numbers and barcodes beneath.

"Jesus help us," he whispered. "They don't even keep this shit locked up."

Besides that, the temperature in the shed was somewhere close to the surface of the sun. As far as he knew, heat was a bad thing where dynamite was concerned.

He tried the trailer next. Also unlocked. Inside was a small scuffed desk, a leather chair cracking open in several places, a file cabinet, and a stool. A tiny A/C unit was wedged in one of the windows, enough to cool a few fleas if they didn't overexert themselves.

"Real classy, Lyles. Don't spend too much money." Frank thought of what the man said about the company teetering on bankruptcy. If it were true, he could expect more cutbacks in the days ahead. He closed the door and used a key from the ring Lyles had given him to lock it this time.

Asheville itself was a further five minutes up the road. The first houses appeared like random bits of wreckage from a plane crash, and then they were in a maze of short residential streets.

"The map says there's some kind of main street towards the center of town," Trisha said. Frank had seen it, too. It was the only discernible landmark; everything else was clustered around it like suckling puppies.

"We can look for that later. For now let's just see what kind of dump Lyles has us in." He sensed rather than saw the sharp look she gave him.

But after following the directions and pulling to a stop in front of the address written on the pad, they sat in the truck, stunned and speechless for a full minute.

"It's...huge," Trisha stammered.

"Two stories," Willie added.

"We have a *forest* in our backyard," Frank said in amazement, taking in the trees that covered the area behind the house. He had expected the place, deep down, to look like something from the *Munsters*; instead they had gotten *Leave it to Beaver*, complete with gleaming white sideboards and freshly painted green shutters on each window. A wrap-around porch ran half the length of the front and disappeared around the side.

"Let's see the inside!" Trisha urged.

They hurried to the door, carrying only the bare essentials. Casey squealed in eagerness to get inside. Frank found the right key and let them into the spacious living room. The furnishings weren't extravagant, but most of it was better than what they had at home. The living room alone was home to a matching light blue sofa and loveseat with a television that was twice as big as their own.

"Wow!" Willie yelled. "Dibs on one of the rooms upstairs!" He took off for the staircase at a full run and, for a moment, he really was that excited thirteen-year-old boy again, if you could ignore the orange hair spikes. Casey followed on her big brother's heels. A few seconds later, he called down, "We have big TV's up here, too!"

Trisha smiled at Frank and he slipped an arm around her waist. He kissed her on the top of the head and she ran a hand across his chest as she leaned into him.

They spread out through the house, starting the air conditioner and allowing the mustier rooms to air out. It seemed Wesley Gammon had used only a small portion of the house. Trisha headed for the master bedroom downstairs while Frank checked out the kitchen in the back.

Now, *this* place was a sty. Trash rotted in the wastebasket by the screen door leading to the backyard. Dishes had been left in the sink to crust and mold. The refrigerator was stocked with expired food growing new life forms. He would need a biohazard suit to get some of this out. The axe had come for Gammon without warning, apparently.

"Frank!" Trisha interrupted from elsewhere in the house. "Frank, come here!"

He found her in their sunken master bedroom, also devoid of any decorum but complete with a king-size bed. She was in front of the room's huge walk-in closet, holding the door with one arm and leaning on the frame with the other. He came and looked over her shoulder.

"Was the last guy fired or executed?" she asked.

The closet was full of clothes, all crammed together at the front of the rack where they would be easy to reach. Mostly jeans and t-shirts for a man built narrower than Frank, a few pairs of khaki slacks and dress shirts hanging crookedly toward the back. Curiously enough, every shirt in the closet, whether dress or casual, had the name 'Wesley' stitched onto the right breast.

"Guy really wanted people to know his name," Frank said, rifling through the clothing. The man had skedaddled in a supreme hurry, leaving the place like a vacant ghost ship.

"Well, throw it all out," Trisha said with a shrug.

He put them in a garbage bag he found in a kitchen cabinet, along with the expired food and unsalvageable dishes. He carried it out the back door, where the wraparound porch held battered lawn furniture and a table.

Frank stopped with his foot halfway across the threshold.

A fat dead squirrel lay on the back porch, stretched out right across the base of the door, bushy tail straight out, tiny limbs curled up on its belly. Its head would've reached to the other side of the door jamb, if it had one.

The neck of the little creature ended in a shredded stump; otherwise, there wasn't a mark on it. Looked as though some animal had gnawed it off, then left the body here for the blood to drain. A dried maroon puddle beneath was baked into the wood by the summer sun. The body was old, a week or two at least, the skin already taken on the crispy, hardened look that dead rodents got.

"Great. Have to watch the wildlife. Probably had rabies."

As he looked at it, an unexpected chill slipped up his spine. What was wrong with him all of a sudden?

Little Frankie, did that mean old store clerk stir up some bad memories?

He picked up the squirrel by its tail. The upper part of its body was glued to the porch by the dried blood. It made a noise like fabric tearing when he yanked. He stuffed the tiny corpse into one of the garbage bags and carried them around to the back of the house.

"Yoohoo!" a high voice called, as he dropped the bags into garbage cans.

An elderly woman in gardening clothes came stumbling

out of the large copse of trees behind their rent house. She wore a large floppy hat designed to either keep her wrinkled face out of the sun or send signals to airplanes in flight, and she waved a gardening trowel in his direction with one hand and carried a wicker basket of pecans with the others. Frank waved back and walked out to meet her.

"I'm Iris Bush. I live in the house just behind the trees here." She might not be Queen Elizabeth, but she had a lot more breeding than the redneck from the gas station.

"Frank Stanford." He offered a hand before realizing hers were too full to reciprocate.

"I never got to meet the man that lived here before you, but I wanted to catch you while I had the chance and make it perfectly well understood that *this*," she pointed to the trees, circling them in the air with her garden trowel, "is *my* property. I own this entire pecan orchard."

"O...kay," Frank said with a questioning frown.

"I didn't want you to partake of my nuts. As long as I tell you now, there won't be any misunderstandings further down the line."

"Yes, I'm glad you said something." Frank gave an exaggerated nod while trying not to giggle at the phrase 'partake of my nuts.' "My family just loves pecans. *Loves* 'em. In fact, I was just telling my wife how I could go for a big bucket. We would've had your trees here stripped bare within the hour."

Iris squinted at him. Frank kept the serious face. At last she said, "What brought you to Asheville, Mr. Stanford?"

"Well, we're renting actually. My company moved me here."

"And what company would that be?" She had a grandmotherly air about her, but not the friendly, cookie-baking kind. This was the sort that boxed your ears if you didn't eat all the cauliflower on your plate.

"The Lyles Corporation." She stared at him. "They're the ones building the houses out on the…" he couldn't bring himself to say *Dark Road*, "road to Arlington. I'm the new foreman."

At the mention of the houses, a look of disgust passed over the old woman's face. She backed away as though he might reach out and strike her. "You're part of *that* group?" she asked shrilly.

"Is there a problem?"

Iris was already heading back into the safety of her precious orchard. Her last words were shouted over her shoulder. "There certainly is! If you knew what was good for you, you'd pack up and go back to wherever you came from! Asheville doesn't need any more houses, especially not…out there!" And then she was gone, back to hoarding her 'nuts'.

"Crazy old biddy," Frank grumbled. "I hate pecans."

7

"I thought it might be fun if we went out after all, explored town to see if they have a swimming pool. The kids would love it and we could sit around all afternoon in the sun, relaxing..." Trisha hopped up on the counter in the kitchen to await his reply.

Frank shook his head, though nothing in the world sounded better. "Can't. I have to get a crew together so we can start work tomorrow."

"Today? We just got here, Frank! I thought you said this was going to be a vacation!"

"It is, but it's a working vacation for me. You knew that, it's the whole reason we're here. If it rains this week, I'll be losing time as it is. You guys have fun, and I'll catch up if I get done."

Her jaw worked as she looked away. "You said you would be able to spend more time with us, with Willie. You *said* that Frank. Or was it just a lie to get me here?"

"That's not fair. Don't simplify things down to black and white. I have a responsibility here, one that puts food on the table. I seem to be the only one able to do that lately."

He might've slapped her and received the same shocked, hurt look. "Low blow. Remember, *you're* the one that told me not to worry about it." She slid back off the counter and stalked out of the kitchen.

Lyles had given him the number for a Rafael Barrio, with instructions to contact him to get a crew together. Frank put his phone to his ear but had to lift it away when the line was connected. Spanish music blasted out of the earpiece.

"*Bueno?*" a voice asked.

"Uh, is Rafael there?" Frank shouted over the music.

"Speaking, *muchacho!* What can I do for you?"

"Hi, this is Frank Stanford! I'm the new foreman at the River Meadows site!"

The music cut off. "Oh yeah, man! It's good to finally hear from you! I thought they were going to shut that place down for good!"

"No, no, the job's still on. Listen, Lyles told me you would be able to put me in contact with a crew."

"I think so *amigo*, if they're still available. Most of the guys Gammon had working out there have drifted on to other jobs. It was hard enough to find people willing to work out there the first time but now...I don't know, man."

A burst of static across the phone made Frank think he'd missed something in the man's statement. "Wait, I don't understand. Why would it be hard to get people to work?"

The voice on the other end hesitated. "Well...you know how things are in Asheville, man."

"No, I don't. I just need to know whether you can get me the guys or not, because work needs to start up again first thing in the morning."

"Hey, why don't we meet to discuss this? You busy?"

Frank sighed. "Not at the moment."

"I can be in Asheville in twenty minutes. There's a bar called The Howler on Mission Street. Know where that is?"

"I just got into town an hour ago."

"It's the main road, you can't miss it. Anyway, I'll meet you out front in half an hour."

"Sounds good."

Frank hung up and went into the kitchen. They'd eaten only an hour before—leftovers from Gammon's reign in the house—but he was starving again. In one of the empty cupboards he found a box of stale Ritz crackers that he used to keep his stomach from growling. He heard doors opening on the other side of the house and Trisha calling the kids down.

Frank lit a cigarette and took a long, soothing drag around a mouthful of cracker.

Willie hadn't packed a swimsuit, but he wouldn't so much as put one leg in the pool even if he did. He was pale white in contrast to the tanned bodies that usually hung out at such places, and his ribs stood out on his narrow chest. Besides, water would only make his colored spikes of hair fall down.

"C'mon let's go!" his mom called from downstairs.

He considered refusing, but he was anxious to see what the town of Asheville had to offer. The thought had occurred to him that this was a new place with a whole new set of people, and maybe they would be friendlier to someone like him. Maybe he would even *impress* them. This fantasy continued to unfold until the entire town's populace of teenagers worshipped him like a pagan god.

Willie bounded downstairs, giving Casey a good knock on the top of the head along the way. She tattled on him.

"Willie, don't do that," his mom scolded, a bit harsher than necessary.

He mumbled an apology and ran for the door.

"You can't swim like that." She pointed at his black t-shirt, torn jeans, and boots.

"Not gonna swim. Can we go now, or do you have a thousand other questions to ask me?"

"I'm going to ask you something all right, if you don't watch that smart mouth."

Willie went outside before his shit-uitary gland could flare up and make him say something that would really get him in trouble. He got into the Honda and stretched out in the back seat. The sun was warm and pleasant shining through the windows on him, and he closed his eyes and dozed like a contented cat while his mother wound through the back streets of Asheville.

"Found one," she announced. "Doesn't look half bad either."

He sat up. The pool was small and fenced in, behind an activities building. Next door was a library and across the street was some sort of rec hall. Most of the kids swimming appeared to be around Casey's age, all accompanied by mommies. No one he would want to hang out with.

Where were all the high schoolers on this stupid summer day?

"Do I have to stay here with you guys?" he asked casually.

His mother looked over the seat at him and cocked an eyebrow. "You're still supposed to be grounded, you know."

He grimaced. "Aw c'mon. If we're gonna be stuck here all summer, at least let me see the town."

"You won't get lost?"

"Do I look five? No offense, Casey."

"Can I trust you not to cause any trouble?"

He scowled and shook his head. Just like everyone else, all his teachers in school, she believed him to be the root of the problem. No one ever stopped to think that maybe it was the other guys that started the fights.

"I'm going to take that as an agreement. Just...be careful."

"I will. Geez." He opened the door as she and Casey went into the pool area. He needed to put as much distance as possible between himself and them before someone his own age saw him. The rec hall across the street looked like a good place to start.

Willie crossed over the lanes of non-existent traffic roaring down this town's dusty main street and went up to the entrance like Doc Holliday entering the OK Corral. The front double doors were tinted glass, so he couldn't see inside. He held his breath and pushed the door open.

The interior was a pool hall and arcade, ancient classics like Pac-Man and Galaxia along the back wall and billiards and ping-pong in the middle. The place was packed with teenagers, the noise level tremendous.

He walked inside. When the door closed behind him, the majority of light in the place went with it. Overhead fluorescents glowed weakly. He waited in the doorway, trying to come up with a plan.

Some of them were staring, but he couldn't pinpoint which ones without being obvious. They looked as strait -laced as he'd imagined, as groomed as he used to, with carefully cropped hair, jeans and t-shirts—and a few collared shirts on the roper types—but instead of feeling cool, he just felt out of place. His tongue ring clinked nervously against the back of his teeth. What had he expected, someone holding a sign with his name on it, like a limo driver at the airport?

His confidence evaporated when he spotted a group of huge athletic guys playing pool several tables away, the same kind that used his head to close locker doors at school, that dubbed him 'Wet Willie' and spit water on his crotch so he looked like he pissed his pants. He tried to seem uninterested but noticed when one of them tapped the others and pointed slyly in his direction.

Willie dug in his pocket for a quarter, found the courage to cross the room, and started a game of Donkey Kong.

His interest was minimal, so when their reflection appeared in the glass screen over his shoulder, he saw them instantly. He didn't turn though, until one of them tapped him on the shoulder.

There were three, all towering over him. They wore jeans and cross-hatched shirts, a little more country than the bullies back home, but infected with the same asshole disease. The one in front smiled at him, but Willie recognized that smile.

"You new around here, kid?"

Willie nodded.

"That's great." The two galoots behind him snickered. "What's your name?"

"Uh...I'm Willie." This brought another laugh from the goons. Some of the other kids turned to listen, taking in his clothes, his hair.

"Willie, huh?" The guy leaned forward until their eyes were level. "Who said you could come in here looking like that, Willie?"

"No one. I just thought—"

"I don't care what you thought, freak. This is our town. Did you see a sign on the way in that said, 'Fucking Douchebag Tools Welcome?'"

"Do all the kids where you're from dress as ugly as you?" one of the others asked.

"And are you wearing *makeup?*" the other added.

The back of Willie's throat burned.

"You're just another little punk we don't want here. Like those other two idiots. Well, right now, I'm giving you a choice, and you better feel lucky I'm in a forgiving mood. You can either leave right now and never come back here, or," he grinned even wider, "we can use that orange head of yours for the five ball."

Willie swallowed the burning lump. He was scared, but the anger was blooming in him again, the same anger that always got him in trouble back home. It seemed like a different voice that said, "I don't know. Tough choice. Can I finish my game if I let you beat on me for awhile?"

Fire bloomed in the boy's face, tempered with surprise. "What did you say?"

"I just figured we should probably establish an exchange rate. You know, something like one punch is equivalent to another five minutes?"

The guy raised one fist scarred across the knuckles.

"I'll go," Willie ceded, before that fist could descend. God, if he got in another fight, he would never hear the end of it. They moved out of his way. He could feel the eyes of the entire room upon him as he trudged to the door.

"Fuckin freak!" one of the assholes yelled after him.

The sunlight nearly blinded him. Tears streamed down his face. He used his bare arm to swipe them away. You'd think when you were kicked as much as he was, used for a punching bag by everyone you came across, you'd eventually give up. But not Willie Stanford; he just kept right on trying to make friends, like a little lost puppy-dog. And when being himself didn't work, he'd tried to become someone else.

Then just end it.

He wasn't sure where that one came from. The word 'suicide' rolled around in his head like a sticky marble.

He crossed the street and smashed against the chain link fence around the pool next to where his mother lay stretched out in the sun.

"Can we leave?" he shouted. He knew he was crying and looked ridiculous, but he couldn't stop. To make it worse, the ladies at the pool were staring.

"Willie, what's wrong?" his mom asked as she sat up.

"Nothing's wrong! Can we just go?"

"We just got here! Calm down and tell me what's wrong, sweetie."

"I'm not your sweetie! Never mind, I'll just walk home!" He started down the sidewalk until he realized he didn't even know where 'home' was. He growled and clenched his fists. "I'll be in the car!"

The interior was sweltering in the one-hundred-plus-degree temperature. He lay in the back seat again and pressed his red face into the searing fabric with what he hoped was enough force to smother himself.

8

As Frank drove slowly through the streets of Asheville, looking for Mission Street, one face became evident: this town was laid out weird.

He wasn't a city planner, but he knew zoning laws, and beyond that, he knew what was typical—what was just plain *normal*—for a suburban area in Texas like this.

For starters, the streets were far too close together. You could throw a stone from the front yard of one house and hit another three streets away. Ditto with the spacing of the houses, all crammed next to one another like cavemen huddled around a campfire. River Meadows looked like there was enough room to play regulation football on each lot compared to these. And the streets were all angled funny, giving easy access to the middle of town.

And then a broad, four-lane road ran perpendicular ahead of him. It looked to be a commercial district, businesses squashed together just like the houses. He took a guess and turned left.

Frank passed another gas station, a few eateries, a mechanic shop, and an elementary school while keeping an eye out for the bar. There was a single engine fire department, a tiny building no bigger than the video store next to it.

It was tempting to say that the whole setup was quaint, a throwback to simpler times, but it just wasn't true. Besides the fear elements inherent in their architecture, there was an uncomfortable, almost angry vibe in Asheville. He remembered what Lyles has said about the clay in the ground off the Dark Road. Maybe it was radioactive or something.

He spotted a large structure up ahead and slowed out of curiosity. Sedans with red and blue bulbs on top were parked outside and a there was a sign above the entrance.

The Asheville Police Department.

It was no skyscraper, but it did seem abnormally big. Frank had seen smaller law enforcement departments in major areas of Houston. What in hell did a dustbowl town like this need with such an extensive police station?

He saw the Howler finally, a rectangular building whose short side faced the street. The only parking was the short row in front and along the alleys on both sides. At this time of day, only three cars sat in front, so Frank had room to squeeze in.

The interior of the bar was gloomy and silent. The tables in the middle and booths against the right hand wall were empty. Two customers squatted at the bar, nursing beers, and neither of them looked like a Rafael.

"Help you?" the bartender asked.

Frank jumped. The man was hidden at the cash register by the entrance door. "I'm looking for a guy named Rafael Barrio."

"Don't know the name."

"I don't think he's here yet."

"No, I mean I don't know the name at all. I know everybody in this town, and that one's not ringin any bells." He squinted at Frank. "And while we're on the subject, I don't recognize you either. You just passin through?"

He remembered Iris Bush's reaction to him. "More or less."

"Feel free to have a seat and wait for your friend. I'll pour you a drink."

The thought of sitting in here alone for even a few minutes, with these dour faces scrutinizing him, made him nervous. "No, that's okay. If he's not here, I better wait outside." He backpedaled and was soon out on the sidewalk.

"Hey, you the foreman?"

Frank looked around. A wiry, dark-skinned Mexican stood at the corner of the building. He wore a thin, sleeveless white shirt and jeans, with a ball cap on his skinny head. He looked like someone pedaling drugs, lurking in the mouth of the alley. "Yeah. You Rafael?"

"That's me, *amigo.*"

"Why weren't you inside?"

"I said I'd meet you *out*side. I try not to go in too many public places in this town. They don't take real well to strangers."

"I'm glad it's not just my imagination." The heat was unbearable, even with the sun on its way out of the sky. Frank plucked at his shirt beneath the armpits. "All right, you brought me out here, so now tell me, can you get me the guys or what?"

"I can get you the guys, no problem. I made some calls and I figure I can have you a crew of at least forty out at your site tomorrow morning. They're all gonna be Hispanic though, most of them fresh over the border and not exactly ripe, if you know what I mean." Frank arched an eyebrow and Rafael smiled. "No green cards."

"Aw, c'mon!"

"That's kinda why I wanted to talk to you in person and not on the phone. Never know who's listening. Anyway, you're lucky I was able to get you that. A few of them were on Gammon's crew, but it's only the desperate ones that were willing to come back."

"Why? What's so hard about doing a job out here?"

"Not out here, man. Out *there*. On the Dark Road."

"Because of the clay?"

Rafael gave him a blank look and then chuckled. "Yeah, right. The clay." When Frank didn't join him, he trailed off and asked, "You really don't know about Asheville, do you?"

"I'm beginning to think I don't."

"Well, don't get me wrong; the clay is bad enough. Gammon might've had the whole miserable thing finished if not for that clay. But beyond that..." He frowned at the sun, pulled on the bill of his cap. "You ever hear of the Jackal Man?"

Frank snorted. "Don't tell me that same bullshit story again."

"Hey man, I'm like you, I think it's *loco*. But the folks around here...they *believe* it. They think there's really some kinda monster out there, and you guys building the houses are making him mad. They don't want you out there, or in their town. When that land was bought, they sent around a petition to stop it. It was all over the news."

"Lyles didn't tell me that!" Frank was surprised the man's father would go through with such a purchase if he was receiving flack from the locals, but even so, his son was who Frank was really mad at.

"It's true, man. Everybody around here's been pissed about it ever since. Most of the guys on your crew are gonna be nervous as hell working out there. But that's all I can do for you. Take it or leave it."

"Jesus Christ, an urban legend." Frank shook his head in disgust. "Forty guys, huh? And they'll be there at seven in the morning?"

"Most of them need work so bad they can't afford not to be. Like I said, in from *Me-hi-co* and not even a peso to their name."

"Perfect."

"Hey, don't worry so much! You look like you're halfway to a heart attack already!" He slapped Frank in the gut with the back of his hand. "How you wanna go about paying these guys? We're gonna need to set something up under the table."

"Shit. Let me talk to the project manager. He should be in town soon."

"Just have him call me then." Rafael walked away, heading towards a purple Cadillac parked in the alley beside the building. He stopped and turned back to ask, "So, where'd Gammon end up, man?"

"I don't know. I never met the guy. You know what happened?"

Rafael shrugged. "Some of my guys told me he just didn't show up one day, and Lyles told them he was fired and a new guy would be here soon." He frowned. "Good dude though. I had a few *cervezas* with him. Anyway, good luck, Stanford. Hope the crew works out for you. They're a little rough around the edges, but they know their jobs. They can build you a house, no problem."

"Let's hope so," he said.

Frank found a grocery store on the way home and bought some essentials. He knew he was probably being paranoid after what Rafael told him, but it felt like every eye was turned on him. In the canned food section, he looked up and saw a clerk jump and then become engrossed in checking the prices on the gum at the register.

On his way home, he noticed the streetlights.

There was one every half block, and all of them came on at the first hint of darkness. And they didn't just shine a weak circle of light down on the sidewalk either. Their combined illumination created a glow that drowned out the stars, a false daylight. Perhaps he'd found the cause of the angry vibe in this town: they hadn't gotten a good night's sleep in who-knew-how-long. The electrical usage must be phenomenal.

It all pointed to one inescapable conclusion.

This town was scared of the dark.

He thought about Rafael's story again.

"Jackal Man, my ass. What a crock."

Trisha and the kids still weren't back. He stocked the pantry and refrigerator, smoked a quick cigarette on the back porch, and sat down in front of the big TV with a beer to flip through channels.

Finally, as night was really coming on, he heard the Honda pull into the short driveway. A few seconds later, Willie tore through the living room without even looking at him. He took the stairs two at a time, and Frank heard his bedroom door slam.

He lifted the beer to his lips and took a long swallow.

Trisha came in next, with a sleeping Casey on one arm.

"Do I even need to ask?"

"I would prefer if you didn't," she answered. "Would you take her upstairs?"

Frank carried the girl to her new room. She snuggled under the blankets, looking precious and incapable of growing up. Had Willie ever been that cute?

In the hall, he considered knocking on his son's door, but didn't. The boy had to be the one to stop all this foolishness, all this moodiness, all this radical appearance-changing.

Trisha was in the shower in their room. He waited outside for her.

"You didn't come," she said as she toweled off and changed into pajamas.

"I didn't feel much like swimming," he said. "Besides, I didn't think you wanted me there."

"Don't be a martyr. We all wanted you there."

"Even Willie?"

"Well...maybe not Willie."

"What happened?"

"I don't know, he wouldn't tell me. He wondered off and when he came back, he was in that mood again. Bitter and angry at the world."

Frank nodded but said no more on the subject. "You still mad at me?"

"I'm too exhausted to be mad at anyone right now." She pulled sheets out of one of the boxes they'd brought with them and made the bed. He helped her tuck them in and then watched as she slipped beneath.

Frank knelt by her side of the bed. He stroked her arm and cheek with one finger. "It's kind of early to be sleeping. Do you want to...?"

"Not tonight." She yawned and closed her eyes.

Frank went to the living room, turned off the TV and the lights. He checked to make sure the front door was locked and then, on second thought, opened it and went out into the yard. A light glowed in the house across the street and in the other homes sandwiched along the avenue. He could hear a thousand insect voices singing even over the audible hum of the streetlights.

And that vibe was still there. Telling him to get out, telling him he wasn't wanted here.

"What have you got in store for me Asheville?" he asked.

9

Asheville became a ghost town each night, its population drying up, all businesses shutting down at seven so the owners could scurry home. The Howler alone braved every night until two a.m. so the adventurous could drown their boredom in alcohol. The yellow neon beacon was even brighter than the army of streetlights, and it was the only place still populated as the clock hands wound round to midnight on the night that the Stanford family blew into town.

Except the police station, of course.

The large building Frank saw was home to about three times as many officers as the norm for a town the size of Asheville. People living there had always felt the need for protection, and a little extra on their taxes was a small price to pay.

Through the arched double doors in front was a small reception area and front desk. After dark, only one dispatcher relayed calls to officers on patrol. Tonight it was Curtis Walz, a twenty-six-year-old rookie, with the force for barely a year.

He hated when his turn at this shift came up on rotation. There were never any real calls at this time of night; if anything important happened after the town's self-imposed curfew, it was domestic violence or drunken citizens.

Which wasn't to say the phone on the desk in front of him didn't ring often.

Even as he settled in and attempted to read a paperback true crime story, the buzzer sounded. He reached for the receiver.

"Asheville PD, Officer Walz speaking. What is your—?"

"Oh God, you gotta help me!" A young male voice, stricken with fear.

"What is your emergency?" Curtis tried to keep his cool. He knew where this was going.

"The Jackal Man is after me! I saw him on the Dark Road...and n-now he's chasing me!"

"Stay calm, sir. Where are you now?" Curtis glanced at the police tracing equipment built into the phone. The call was coming from a payphone close to the south part of town.

Near the Dark Road.

"I'm almost home! I managed to lose him long enough to make this call! He—shit, he's right HERE! Oh no, NOOOO!" A series of disgusting squishy noises like someone smacking a mouthful of jelly, and more whimperings. When he was sure he would get nothing else rational from the caller, Curtis set the phone back on the cradle.

Asheville P.D. logged such calls all night, every night, ranging from the spooky—like this one—to the obvious pranks ('a jackal is a *dog*, you hillbilly!' was frequent). The record in one night was two hundred and eight calls, originating either from in town or the surrounding cities.

As a non-native of Asheville, Curtis Walz didn't like those numbers. Not one little bit.

The procedure was, if a call seemed real, the dispatcher reported it to the officers on patrol. However, the few dispatched calls rarely turned up anything solid.

But not all the time.

That was true. They were all before his time, but in a few cases, bodies had turned up.

And what if...just what *if*...this was one of them, right in his lap...and he fucked it up?

Curtis reached for a dispatch radio, but changed his mind. He didn't want to be teased about getting spooked. He needed a second opinion, someone to be in on his decision, right or wrong.

He grabbed for the phone on the desk instead and dialed an extension within the station. Distantly he heard a phone buzz inside the squad room.

"Shruff here," a weary voice answered.

Curtis sighed, relieved the man was still here. But of *course* he was still here. He was *always* here. None of the officers could pin down when he slept. "Sir, it's Curtis up at the front desk. I just got a call about the...you know."

Detective Shruff came to attention. "Yes? What's going on?"

Curtis explained the call. "Do you think I should get somebody out there?"

"Where, exactly, did it come from?"

He checked the trace equipment again. "About five blocks from where the Dark Road starts."

"Then, no. Disregard it."

"Thanks." Curtis rubbed his eyes and felt some of the tension drain away. He tried to laugh. "I guess the Jackal Man doesn't come into the city, huh?"

"Maybe. But no one would've been able to survive for five blocks on foot if he wanted them."

Curtis swallowed.

"Have a nice night, Officer."

"You too, Detective." Curtis replaced the phone, no longer so thankful that Shruff was working late again. There was an example of everything wrong in Asheville. Even in a land of lunatics, the detective was still crazy enough to stand out, which was why the other officers gave him a wide berth.

But that...neck thing...probably didn't help much in that department.

The incoming call line buzzed. Curtis picked it up and gave his chant.

"Officer Walz, this is Betty Blackburn at 219 Theodore Terrace. The Jackal Man is eating out of my garbage cans again!"

WILLIE

THE PUNCHING BAG TAKES A HIT

10

Frank rose at five and left the house before the sun was up. Even devoid of people and with the quiet of dawn upon it, Asheville still felt ready to split down the middle and swallow him up.

At least the ugliness of the woods was less severe in the somber light of morning. The site was as he left it, except now an orchestra of crickets held concert in the field to the south. Their tempo was frenzied, as though trying to squeeze in as much screeching as possible in the last strained minutes of night. Sounded like several of the bands Willie listened to. He parked his truck beside the trailer and went inside.

In the filing cabinet were complete records for the project, proving Gammon had been at least as meticulous as Frank himself. That didn't bode well. If Gammon was legitimately trying to finish the neighborhood, then what made Frank think he could do it?

"Cause I'll work these poor bastards to the bone if that's what it takes."

There was a dynamite inventory with the records, a bar-code present for each box the Lyles Corporation ordered from the supplier. He had to admit, if there was one thing that turned his stomach about this project, it was that dynamite. The price tag beside each barcode was a larger numerical amount than he paid for his first car. Frank decided to do his own sight inventory.

The darkness of the meadow was fading as he stepped out with a clipboard and headed to the green shed, texture creeping back into the world with the sunlight. A low ground mist covered the grass and sprawled across the construction yard. Frank's legs were lost in the soupy murk below the ankle. The cricket symphony was still in full swing, crescendoing every few minutes with a sustained *ree-ree-reeeeeee*, that vibrated his teeth.

He unlocked the door and did a quick count of the boxes against what the records showed.

Five short.

Frank couldn't have been caught more off guard if one of them had grown legs and kicked him in the balls.

He counted twice more, heart pumping out a little more ice than blood each time, and found the same inconsistency.

It was possible the boxes had been used and Gammon failed to record them. Possible, but Frank couldn't count on it.

He took the heavy boxes down from their stacks one at a time—a fifteen-minute job in itself—and checked each barcode on the list off.

Five of them gone, any way you sliced it.

Five very expensive, very dangerous boxes of dynamite unaccounted for. Ready to blow off some kid's face or arm or leg.

Frank scratched his thick chin and stared at the clipboard while his mind raced. He was so engrossed that he didn't notice when the crickets of the meadow fell silent in unison, as though a conductor had brought them all to a close with his baton.

The silence proved to be more oppressive than the chirping. He finally glanced up. The ground mist lay thick across the meadow, providing more than enough darkness to fool the crickets into thinking it was night.

But now there wasn't a sound, not a whisper. Frank had never heard—or *not* heard—anything like it.

There was an irregularity in the mist far out in the meadow, a break in the smooth, even surface. He stepped past the trailer, squinting into the rising sun. Maybe his eyes were playing tricks on him, but it seemed to be moving closer, like something down in the grass was splitting the mist as it slouched toward him.

They're out there, Frankie, his father whispered. He froze in place, hating that voice and the power it still held over him. He could remember that night with crystal clarity, an incident so silly when you boiled it down, but so important and vital to his young mind...

A noise came from his left, by the trailer, something stealthy and slithery. He jumped and honed in on the noise, but could see nothing in the white mist. Suddenly he was aware of how alone he was. No, there was no such thing as a Jackal Man, and it might be resurfacing memories making his mouth go dry, but fear was still fear no matter what caused it.

Frank took a step back, toward the illusion of safety offered by the construction yard. He had backed up past the trailer and onto the dirt when something fell on his shoulder.

He spun and knocked the fleshy thing away but choked off a scream. Frank raised a fist until he realized he was looking into the face of a burly Hispanic man.

"I here...for job?" the man asked, confused and scared, and jerked his hand away. "Jo-ob?"

Frank calmed both his thudding heart and his ragged breathing. "Yeah," he said. "Job."

By seven-fifteen, Frank had forty-two men lined up in neat ranks in the middle of the yard, like a company of soldiers. True to Rafael's claim, every one of them was Hispanic and downtrodden. Frank had done his share of roofing and building in his youth, and, if he tried it today, he would be dead in an hour. Yet a good portion of these men looked older than him.

"All right fellas, listen up-o." He pantomimed this with a cupped hand behind his ears. "How many of you speak English?" Approximately twenty hands went up. "Please translate for those that don't *comprende*.

"My name is Frank Stanford, and I'm the new foreman of this site. Our goal here at River Meadows is to build forty homes by our deadline at the end of August. I don't wanna see anyone lagging and I don't wanna have to ride you. First time I don't see you spilling sweat, you're gone." He paced as he gave the speech, eyeing as many of them as he could, but now he stopped and looked over the whole group. "Now, who has experience with this type of construction?" After the translations had time to worm through the crowd, nearly every hand went up. "Good, then get organized. We're gonna start at the front and work our way back. I should have a rough schedule for the plumbing contractors in a couple of days, so do what you can until then. Go to it." The group dispersed, and after a quick thought, Frank called out, "Hold on!"

He came back to stand in front of them and asked, "Were any of you with Gammon when he was here?"

A man in the front raised his hand, and Frank came closer to ask, "What's your name?"

The man was about Frank's size, eyes flinty and sharp, an almost angry set to his mouth. "Gerrardo," was all he offered.

"Did you know anything about the dynamite he was using? Did he keep close track of it?"

"He kept it locked up, if that's what you mean," someone said from further back in the crowd.

"Do you know who else had access to it?" Frank looked at Gerrardo again, who had his head tilted back so he could stare at Frank down his nose.

"Why you askin?"

"I need to know. We have five boxes missing and I intend to find out where it went."

"You think we took it or somethin?"

"Did I say you took it?"

"You...call...police?" another man asked, in broken, heavily-accented English. He was thin and wiry, with a tiny beard and a swath of dirt stuck across the left side of his face by sweat.

"I haven't yet. I'm still trying to figure out if a crime has been committed, Mr...?"

"I am Jaime Garcia," the man answered mechanically, a statement probably memorized for usage in America.

Gerrardo was still watching him; Frank could feel his angry gaze and wondered what the guy's problem was. "Look folks, let's just put it like this: if it doesn't happen again, then we got no problem."

Frank started to walk away and heard someone mutter, "Maybe it was the Jackal Man." He let the comment slide with an inward groan.

~ ~ ~

By noon, the heat was an actual presence in the field. It cut through the men with heartless persistence, seeped through cracks in the trailer while Frank tried to reorganize the contents of the filing cabinets.

A shadow flitted by the trailer's window. A knock came at the door. Frank lifted the dirty blinds across the window in the trailer door and gasped at the sight on the other side.

A face glared in at him, completely bald except for a few long strands of gray hair that sprouted behind the ears. It had only one good eye with a rolling, brown orb in it; the other side was a puckered, fleshy hole. Frank fell away from the door in disgust and the face on the other side of the glass cackled, tilting its head back to expose a jiggling Adam's apple.

He recovered and jerked open the door. "Can I help you?"

"Name's Cracker." The cryptkeeper smiled gleefully, displaying the only two teeth in his head. "You must be the new fella. I'm the dynamite guy. Gammon had me scheduled to do some blastin today."

"Okay. Jesus, you...you gave me quite a scare."

Cracker held out a hand for Frank to shake. It was missing the pinky and half the thumb. Frank stared blankly, unable to help himself. His unease only caused Cracker to bray laughter again.

"Don't worry, young fella. Sometimes I scare *me* when I look in the mirror."

"No, it's not that. Listen, we just got back up and running today. You think you can come back tomorrow to do... whatever it is you do?"

"Sonny, for as much as the Lyles Corporation is payin

me, I'll cut my dick off and have it for supper tonight if you tell me." This joke instigated a fresh round of shrieky laughter. "But we best git on it tomorrow, 'fore that gully-washer hits later this week. Can't do it when the ground's wet!"

"Will we have to stop work?"

"Weeeeelllll, it's all directed charges, but for safety's sake you'll prob'ly wanna clear me a little runnin room. We'll be blastin down at the end here, by your trailer."

"Then try and come around twelve and we'll do it at lunch when there are less men around. Is it...just you?"

"Yessirree."

"Hey, tell me something. Is it all right for that stuff to be sitting out in the sun like that?"

"Why? You 'fraid it's gonna blow ya back to the Stone Age?" he giggled. "No foreman, you're safe. That's hi-tech, synthetic explosive out there. Only extreme heat—like fire, let's say—would set it off, or a blast cap set by a trained professional like yours truly. See ya tomorrow then." Cracker started to hobble back across the lot, and Frank saw he also had a fake leg.

He couldn't resist curiosity. "Wait, Cracker? I hope you don't mind me asking, was it...was it explosives that did all that to you?"

Cracker looked at him somberly. "Rabid wolves." He wiped a sudden tear from his good eye. "Killed my grandma, then got me when I went to see about her. I 'as saved by a local lumberjack."

"Oh. Oh, I'm...sorry."

The gimp snorted again. "That's Little Red Riding Hood, you big dope. Yep, I done blowed myself up." He limped away, and Frank closed the door just in case the weirdos were being drawn to him like moths to a flame.

11

By the afternoon of Willie's second day in Asheville, the boredom got so thick it dulled his senses and sapped his strength.

Daytime TV sucked, he had no friends to call, and even videogames sounded like too much trouble, leaving him in the funk of depression while he tried not to think about yesterday. He roamed the house, listening to the screech of bands like Chevelle and 30 Seconds to Mars on his iPod while inspecting the place more closely. He explored the attic, hoping that previous owners had left behind possessions for him to rifle through, but the place looked like it had never been used. In the back of one of the upstairs closets was a few old porno mags, but even this entertained for all of ten minutes. He actually played Barbies with Casey for a short time, a fact he would fight to the death to keep from Miles.

That was why he jumped at the opportunity when his mother asked if he wanted to accompany her and Casey to the park up the street.

His mother looked shocked before a sly smile turned her mouth. "Summer boredom, eh?"

He shrugged.

"C'mon, we'll find somewhere to get a milkshake when we're done."

Willie rolled his eyes, too cool to enjoy anything so droll as a milkshake.

They walked four blocks up the street. The park was small and deserted, which was good, because Willie would've gone home if there was the slightest trace of the Asheville hellspawn. Playground equipment took up the front, close to the street, and a cement pathway led into a thicket of trees at the back for a 'Scenic Nature Trail.' A sign stressed the trail was closed after dark, and he thought of those ragged scratches on the sign in the woods for his father's construction project. As his mother pushed Casey on the swings, Willie wandered up the path.

It was shadowed under the canopy of trees and relatively cool, a respite from the relentless sun. The trees grew more dense the further in he went, becoming a tangled mess of undergrowth and exposed roots. The path meandered through the trees at a lazy pace. He strolled along, enjoying the quiet and solitude.

Willie had never been in the woods before, never gone camping or hunting. The one time he made such a request to his father, the man barked a huffy denial and left the room.

But it was kind of nice. He had the urge to sit under one of the trees and take a nap, like a new age Tom Sawyer. He had to smile at the idea of himself in a big, floppy straw hat and overalls.

The smile was still in place when he smelled the smoke a few seconds later. He recognized the sharp reek of cigarettes just as a teenager stepped out from behind the tree ahead of him.

He was a few years older than Willie, maybe even out of high school, but shorter and broader, with black hair that hung down his neck and a face scarred by acne. He dressed head to toe in black, and wore a black leather jacket even in the sweltering heat. From underneath the collar, the protruding edge of a tattoo was visible on his neck, but Willie couldn't see what image the wispy lines formed. The guy raised the cigarette Willie had smelled to his lips and took a casual drag.

Willie wheeled around, intending to walk right back down the path. Another boy stood behind him, barring the way, this one tall, thin, and gawky, almost the proportions of one of the gray, big-headed aliens people always claimed kidnapped them. The left side of his head was shaved, the right full of blond, slicked-back hair, and a nose ring glittered against his skin. He had a lopsided smile on his big lips.

"What the fuck is this, Zerk?" the one with the cigarette asked, flicking it into the bushes and running the hand through his dark hair. Willie glanced at him but kept his eye on the tall one and the path to freedom beyond. He kept his hands from shaking, but his tongue ring clicked against his teeth like machine gun fire.

"Don't know, Nails. Looks like someone out for a midday stroll." The tall one leered. He had fake contact lenses that changed his eyes from human irises to circles of green flame.

Willie suddenly remembered the arcade, and what the honky-tonk bullies said. That Willie was a freak…

Just like those other two.

He was looking at Asheville's entire punk population.

"Hey kid," the one called 'Nails' growled. When he moved, a wallet chain rattled against torn jeans. "I'm talking to you. Least you can do is look at me."

This is it, I'm done for, da'svidan'ya, don't spit on ya. Always a punching bag. Line up Asheville, everyone gets a turn.

Willie moved to face him.

"I ain't seen you around here before. You new, or just lost?"

"Little of both, I guess."

The one at his back gave a single snort of laughter. Nails continued to stare. His tattoo, Willie now saw, was a skeletal arm that reached from under the neck of his shirt and wrapped around the side of his neck, so it appeared the bony hand was choking him. "You a narc or somethin? Gonna tell ol' Shruffy we were smokin?"

Willie blinked at him. "Um, what's a 'Shruffy?'"

"Let me put it this way: who the fuck is dumb enough to go into the woods anywhere in Asheville?"

He could've bit his tongue, but God, it was hard. As far as self-esteem went, bruises were always better than humiliation. "Well I guess I'm looking at him, aren't I?"

The other boy glared at Willie for several seconds and then...burst into laughter. "That's pretty good, dude. He's a real tough one, huh?"

"Guess so," the other boy agreed.

"I'm Nails. That's Zerk. So who're you?"

"I, uh, I'm Willie."

"You don't sound too sure. Bitchin hair though. And a kick-ass shirt." He pointed to Willie's Ozzfest shirt. "And you got a tongue piercing too? Been wantin to try it, but it sounds like more pain than even I can handle."

"Naw, it wasn't too bad. Did it myself. Cool tattoo."

"Yeah, I had to hitch a ride to Dallas to find someone willin to do it, me bein underage and all." Nails strolled to the side of the path to lean against a tree. "So Willie, you just move here or what?"

"Not really. I'm here for the summer."

"This ain't exactly a tourist town," Zerk pointed out. He moved around Willie to stand beside Nails. The two of them looked like a punk version of Laurel and Hardy.

"Tell me about it. In a tourist town they're friendly to you."

Zerk cracked a smile. With his wide lips, it seemed to split his head in two. Nails laughed again. A thick scar appeared by his mouth, running from the middle of his chin in a jagged curve around his lips and up to his pockmarked nose. "I guess you met some of those shitheads from town."

Willie nodded eagerly. "They're complete assholes! They're like...Children of the Corn, or something."

"Don't worry about them." Zerk waved a gaunt hand. "Their cowboy hats are the only thing keeping most of their heads from caving in. This town has a serious redneck infestation."

"So what brings you here, Willie, if not the fine dining and friendly locals?"

"Oh, my dad's job. We're from Houston."

"Houston, huh? I lived in Houston with my dad for about three days. Not bad."

"It's all right. You guys aren't from here either?"

"I moved here two years ago, and my dad's been too drunk to outrun the creditors since." He jerked a thumb at Zerk. "This poor bastard's had to live here his whole life."

"But not much longer," Zerk said. "When we graduate this year—"

"*If. If* you graduate."

"Yeah, *if* I graduate, I am so outta this inbred town. I'm goin to Hollywood, get me some kinda acting job, maybe in porno flicks, and then I'm gonna bang chicks all day and get paid for it."

"He's real optimistic for a guy with the body of one of those starvin African kids, ain't he?"

"Yeah," Willie said, "Glass-is-half-full kinda guy."

"My grandfather's always sayin that!" Zerk exclaimed, his green-flamed eyes widening in delight. "He's always like, 'I see my glass as half empty and you see yours as half full,' and I'm like, 'What are you talkin about, old man? I didn't have anything to drink!'"

This time it was Willie's turn to laugh.

Nails lit another cigarette. "Like I was sayin, man, it's not wise to be out here. See, there's this thing around—"

"The Jackal Man, yeah, yeah, I know all about him."

Now they looked at him with drawn brows. "And you still came out here alone?" Zerk asked.

"What's the big deal? It's just a story."

"The Jackal Man ain't just a story! He attacks people all the time! See, I heard it from this guy that gets me beer, who heard it from his next door neighbor, that he got these two kids in a Ferrari just a couple of months ago."

"No dude, it was a convertible. He got inside and ripped them right outta the seats," Nails corrected.

"Was that it? Anyways, when they found 'em, one had his eyes gouged out and the other one..." Zerk paused, bit his lower lip like the world's hammiest soap star. "The other one got his fuckin *arms* torn off. It's true."

"Every word," Nails confirmed.

"Do you guys actually know anybody that's seen him?" Willie asked. "Firsthand, I mean."

The two boys exchanged a look. "Well...no," Nails said. "But that's not the point. We just take it as our responsibility to warn newcomers, is all. If you wanna go walkin into the woods and get your ass sliced, that's fine by me."

"Thanks. I'll also be on the lookout for the Abominable Snowman while I'm at it."

A voice called out his name from down the trail.

"Oh shit, that's my mom." The last thing he wanted was for her to see these guys. "I gotta go. It was...weird meeting you guys."

Nails looked at Zerk, who shrugged, and then said to Willie, "We're goin to the mall up on the Strip tomorrow. You wanna hang?"

Willie answered before the question was even finished. "Sure!"

"All right, meet us here at the park around ten. See you later, Willie."

He sauntered back down the trail until he was out of sight, and then flew all the way back to the park.

12

Dinner was more enjoyable than Frank could ever remember. They belonged on a postcard: Trisha serving up the meal while humming, Casey eating without complaint, and Willie— wonder of wonders—animated and jabbering and answering questions. Frank could've sworn he even saw the kid smile.

And then it was over, the comfortable moment bursting like a soap bubble. Frank was doing the dishes when the doorbell rang. He heard Trisha talking to someone, then the kitchen door squeaked open behind him. She came in, followed by a handsome black man dressed in a charcoal suit.

"Damon!" Frank beamed as he set down the dishtowel. He hadn't seen the man in nearly two years, since they worked together on a hotel in Houston.

Damon Bradford's hand shot out and Frank pumped it heartily. He was tall and thin, a pair of gold-framed glasses with circular lenses perched on the end of a squat nose. "Look at this domesticated SOB here! Got him whipped pretty good, don't you Trish?"

She rolled her eyes. "Don't let this display fool you. I can't even get him to put down the toilet seat without a session of Congress."

"How was the trip down?" Frank asked.

"Lousy. Flight was long and uncomfortable and airport security did everything but shove a bomb-sniffing dog up my ass. I thought I was never getting back to this shitty state."

"Took you long enough! You trying to let me finish the whole damn thing?"

Here Damon hesitated, smiled awkwardly, and said, "I was in Tulsa with Lyles and the entire Board of Directors for the past week."

"The Board? Why did the Board wanna meet with you?"

Damon glanced at Trisha and shrugged.

"All right, I know when I'm not wanted." She slid between them to get to the sink. "You two go talk shop and I'll take care of this."

"Thanks, babe. You want a beer, Damon?"

"Whatever you got."

Frank went to the refrigerator and pulled two cans out. He handed a Coors to Damon and led the way out the back door of the kitchen. A weak porch light outside shown down on a few pieces of battered lawn furniture. In the dark, the bloodstain from the squirrel blended into the wood. The orchard was shadowy and silent, Miss Iris Bush presumably in her home, sitting on her pecan pile like Scrooge McDuck in his vault. The night was humid and warm, the lingering heat of the day still enough to cause a veil of sweat to break out on Frank's forehead. He sat down in one of the chairs, and Damon followed after wiping out a few specks of dirt from the seat bottom to make way for his expensive suit.

Frank popped the tab on his beer and took a long swallow. He put the can next to him on the ground and lit a cigarette before he said a word. In the stagnant air, the smoke curled up from his hand and created soft wisps when he exhaled. "So you met with the Board?"

"Weren't you quitting those the last time I saw you?"

"I cut down. I only smoke now when the urge is really bad, and if my wife can't stop me, you sure as hell can't. Now c'mon Damon, what gives?"

Damon reached up, loosened his tie and undid his collar. "Shit Frank, I like to think we're friends, so let's just lay the cards out. This is some bad business we've gotten ourselves in to."

"What're you talking about?"

"I drove by the site on my way here. Surely you must realize even after one day that it's going to be near impossible for you to wrap this thing up by the end of August."

"Well, I...I wouldn't say that. I've got a pretty large crew and if we push it, there's a good chance we can do it."

"I wish I had your optimism. Or the drugs you must be on." Damon took three long swallows, Adam's apple bobbing. "I feel sorriest for you, Frank. Lyles told me I had to take this, but you had a choice. You should've opted out. Believe me, if I could've warned you, I would've."

"Damon, if you wanna 'lay the cards out' then lay them out. What's going on? What did the Board say?"

"The Board...is getting ready to oust Lyles and take over the Corporation. They just need a reason, and they've been looking for one a long time. This disaster we call River Meadows is it."

"Shit! You're joking! They're gonna can Lyles?"

"If you had the power, wouldn't you?"

"Good point. But what do we have to do with anything?"

"Lyles has one legal way to save himself, one chance to get the courts on his side and maybe recoup some of his losses if the Board goes hostile. If he can prove that the project failed as a result of employee negligence rather than bad investment..." Damon held his hands out, palms up, as though shoving the dangling sentence away.

Frank nodded along until the full impact got through.

"That's right," Damon said, seeing the horrified look that spread across Frank's face. "We're scapegoats, my friend. You, me, even that poor bastard Gammon. We're the ones that are gonna lose our jobs, so Lyles can keep his. It was all I could do to sit in that boardroom and not climb over the table to beat the blue out of his blood."

Frank's teeth ground together with nearly enough force to chop his cigarette in half. He tossed it away and ran palms through the bristles of his scalp. "Oh God. Oh shit! What am I gonna do? What am I gonna tell Trish?"

"Listen Frank, don't panic yet. Right now let's just keep our eye on the prize. If you think you can finish this project, then do it and we all go home rich. If you can't, I suggest you start looking for another job. I wouldn't have told any other foreman about this, but you and I go way back."

"This doesn't make any sense! Why would he fire Gammon if he meant to blame the whole thing on him anyway?"

"There's a rumor—and if you tell anyone, I'll deny it—that Lyles asked him to torch the place so he could collect the insurance and opt out."

"Bullshit. I wanna talk to this guy."

"Good luck. I can't find him. Nobody knows where he went."

"Well, wherever he is, he must be naked." Frank told him about the clothes in the closet.

Damon drank his beer to the last drop and put the can on the table. "I don't know about that. I can only say it doesn't look too good for us either."

Frank doubled over in the wicker patio chair. His stomach was churning like a washing machine. "Old man Lyles really left us with a shit storm to clean up, didn't he? So much for a legacy."

"What? You...you think Lyles Jr. bought that land?"

"That's what the Bastard told me. His father nearly bankrupted the company."

"This purchase was made eight months ago, Frank. Lyles died nearly a *year* ago, leaving the company, I might add, as solvent as ever."

"Oh, that lying weasel!"

"They told him the place was a bad investment. Told him about the clay and how hard it would be to develop. He didn't listen. He looked at that field and saw a goldmine. Hell, even if we do our part and those houses get built, they're still going to have a hard time turning a profit. You've probably noticed how much the dynamite costs."

"That's something I wanted to talk to you about. There are five boxes of it unaccounted for."

"*What?*"

"They were gone when I got here. I don't know what happened, but I'd feel a lot better if we had some security measures set up for that stuff."

"Did you call the cops?"

"And tell them what? I don't even know when—or if—they were taken."

Damon nodded. "First thing tomorrow I'll call a security company and have them put up a chain link fence. And we'll get a big guard dog. Fair?"

"I guess. That's all I need, to spook the workers even more. They think I'm accusing them of stealing the dynamite."

"You think they did?"

"I don't know. In any case, I can't afford to stop and find new ones. According to the guy that got me the crew, it was hard enough to find people willing to work out there."

A curious smile came over Damon's face. "Why?"

"Well...because of...see, they think..."

"It wouldn't have anything to do with the Jackal Man, would it?"

Frank nearly choked on the last of his beer. "How do you know about that?"

"Some gas station attendant told me about it on the way into town."

"My good friend Earl Dean."

Damon chuckled so hard his shoulders rose up and down, glasses throwing off chinks of reflected light. "What's up with this thing?"

"It's just some stupid local myth. Dumb urban legend cat monster thing. Sounds like something from a Stephen King novel."

"No it doesn't. It sounds like a movie Elvira would host. Somebody needs to teach these hillbillies some biology. A jackal is a dog."

"That's what I said!"

Damon finished off his laughter with a sigh. "All right, I'm gonna get out of here. Let you get back to family time."

"You staying in town?"

"Hell, no! I'm a five-star hotel kind of man, you know that. Downtown Fort Worth. I'll take care of as many of your problems as I can tomorrow, then I'm flying out to San Antonio for a meeting and I'll be back here Friday. We'll have dinner or something. Paint this town red."

"We're gonna need a lot of paint," Frank muttered.

They walked around the side of the porch to Damon's rented BMW rather than go back inside. They stopped beside the driveway, the darkness pervaded only by the light from a rather fat moon above them. Frank couldn't see Damon's face in the shadows, but he stared at the rim of his glasses.

"Goodnight, Frank," he said. "Don't let the Jackal Man bite."

"Get outta here before I do to you what I should've done to Lyles."

Damon chuckled and got into his car. He pulled down the driveway and drove away. Frank waited until he was around the corner before going inside.

He decided he would tell Trisha nothing until he had no other choice.

13

Thursday morning held none of the upbeat tone of its predecessor. They would never be finished; Frank saw what Damon meant now, what optimism had blinded him to. And no matter how much he yelled or screamed, the whole world seemed to move in slow motion.

His new perception of the project was only the first of his distractions. Damon, true to his word, had a security company called Arcus show up at ten o'clock. They scrambled around the perimeter of the site, rolling out a chain link fence with a gate facing out onto the Dark Road. Frank also got several crewmen to move his trailer further back into the field using his truck, to give Cracker more room for whatever he did with that dynamite.

At some point during the chaos, his cell phone rang. He fished it out of his pocket and flipped it open.

"Frank Stanford here."

"And just where would 'here' be?"

He recognized Lyles's voice. He swallowed rage-laden bile and said, "On the site, sir."

"Then take a look at those houses you're building for me and tell me what you see."

"Not much, considering it's my second day on the job."

Lyles didn't speak for several long seconds. "You keep in mind, *Frank*: those houses go on the market September first, and I don't have time to fuck around. You understand?"

God, Frank prayed he hadn't sounded like such a dick when he'd said nearly the same thing to the crew the day before. "Perfectly, sir."

"Get it finished, or you'll go the way of the wild Gammon. Say hello to Damon for me."

The connection was broken before Frank could bother to answer.

Cracker arrived at ten minutes until eleven.

"You're early."

"Ain't no never mind. I don't charge extra for earliness." The man cut loose with his awful laughter.

They went around to the dynamite shed and Frank unlocked the door. Cracker dug around the interior as Frank gave a friendly wave to two of the guys from Arcus Protection. They ignored him while they unrolled the fence past the trailer and out into the open field.

"Looks like you're missin some crates since the last time I 'as here," Cracker said over his shoulder.

"Don't worry about that. If you need more, the company will buy it."

"Okay, sonny, don't get your panties all bunched up. Just wantin to make sure you wasn't tryin to steal my job." He tittered and fixed Frank with his one, rolling eye. "Or maybe the missus told you she wanted more fireworks in the bedroom."

"Listen Cracker, I wish I had time to stand around and jaw with you all day...on second thought, no, I don't. Could you just light the fuse or…push the button or…just give us the damn hole in the ground, okay?"

"Yes, your Majesty." Cracker hefted two of the black boxes from the inside of the shed. Frank followed him out to where the next foundation was marked off on the left side of the lane with stakes in the ground.

Cracker hobbled to the middle of the rough square, then squatted with the boxes in front of him. He opened the latches and pulled the lid off. Frank leaned over his shoulder, curious as to what multi-thousands of dollars worth of high-grade dynamite looked like. Sweat ran off his nose, dripping onto the strange contents.

A clear cellophane package contained caps and wires on the right side of each box. On the left were circular mounds, like the side of a tennis ball cut off and painted white. He had, he realized, been expecting long red cylinders with fuses sticking out of the end, like a Bugs Bunny cartoon.

"How powerful is that stuff?"

"Well, these here," Cracker pointed to the white mounds with a finger that ended at the top knuckle, "are directed charges. If you use 'em proper-like, the blast is directed in one direction and you got a controlled explosion. What I do here is almost more of a seismic vibration that breaks up that clay under the ground enough to be shoveled out."

"Okay," Frank said, marveling at the transformation from Hee-Haw to Bill Nye. "What about if they're used improper…like?"

"You mean if you threw gasoline on 'em and lit 'em on fire?"

"For example."

Cracker's usually smiling face turned into a deadpan stare. "Then you got some problems, foreman. 'Less you can outrun the devil hisself." Frank continued to watch until Cracker said, "Do you mind? Yer in my light. This is gonna take awhile anyway. Go play with your crew. They didn't look too happy when I 'as comin up here."

That was an understatement. Frank had felt uneasy stares all day, but couldn't determine the cause. He walked around the site, checking work here and encouraging more there. He caught Gerrardo glaring at him from one house only to turn and find Jaime Garcia sneaking furtive glances at him from another.

Cracker found him a half hour later. "Set to go, foreman. Clear these guys away."

Frank whistled. The workers gathered in the middle of the lot. The technician held a fistful of wires in one hand and a small, disc-shaped device with a single button in the other.

"Are you sure this is safe?"

Cracker flapped a disfigured hand. "I been doin this my whole life!"

Frank lifted an eyebrow. "Yeah, that's what I'm afraid of."

"All the force of the blast goes into destroyin the ground and leavin you a nice, shallow hole. There might be some clay thrown up, but it ain't gonna be a nuclear blast." Cracker rolled his eye around the gathered men. "Now comes the fun part. Ever'body ready?"

"Wait a minute." Frank took one more look around the lot. All of the workers were right here with them. On the far side of the blast area, out in the field, the two security guys hauled the fence around the last side of the lot. "Are they gonna be okay?"

"They'll be fine." Cracker, with a pyromaniac's delight, plugged the ends of the wires into the disc. After a dramatic pause, he pushed the button.

A dense cloud of brown and gray matter shot into the air from the blast site with a sound like a cannon firing under a giant pillow. It began to settle at once, and the ground beneath their feet trembled as the shockwave passed through. Frank waited patiently for it to stop.

Funny thing though; it didn't.

His teeth chattered from the increasing vibrations. He tried to calm his fluttering heart; perhaps this was all just part of the show. A steady rumbling came from the tortured ground where Cracker set the charges, radiating out like ripples in a pond. Some of the men actually swayed on their feet.

"What's going on?" Frank shouted, surprised and terrified to find he could barely hear himself. An awful grating drifted up from the earth, like the creak and groan of old floorboards.

Cracker stood up, but his bad leg slipped out from under him. Frank and several of the crewmen leapt to catch him before he fell on his face. "I...I don't know! Somethin ain't right! It's never done this afore!"

Frank looked toward the blast site, waiting for Godzilla to rise from the ground. He could see the security men on the far side attempting to keep their own balance as they clung to the fence spool. Then, as he watched, the ground crumbled under them. The earth gobbled them up along with the fence spool, then belched up another cloud of dirt.

"*Jesus Christ!*" Frank yelled. The heaving and rumbling subsided; they no longer moved like men in drunken stupors. He sprinted toward the area where the Arcus guys had fallen, wheezing after two steps from a combination of his own excessive weight and the blistering sun. From somewhere, he could hear that bastard Gerrardo laughing maliciously. "*What did you do, Cracker?*"

"*It weren't me, it weren't me!*" The man bawled somewhere behind him.

Frank passed the blast site, ran by without stopping, but did notice a shallow, almost perfectly square hole, filled with hunks of gray rubble. Several of the faster workers passed him by in their haste to reach the security men.

He skidded to a halt at the edge of a newly formed pit. It was also a rough square, stretching about ten yards across on all sides. At the bottom, six yards down, lay the two men in a jumble of twisted chain link fence and half buried in chunks of dirt and clay. The fence ran up out of the hole in a crushed mess and back to where they'd sunk the last post further down the line.

Frank stepped closer to the edge. Dirt crumbled away beneath him, almost spilling him into the pit on top of them. He scrambled back, clutching at offered hands for support. When he was as close as he dared, he yelled, "You guys okay?"

One of the men moved, pulling his leg from under the chain link. "I...I think so!" The other one sat up. "I'm okay," he said after spitting out a wad of dirt.

Cracker hobbled up behind Frank. "I didn't do nuthin! You can't sue me!"

"You sure as hell did *something!* And would you shut up with that sue crap?"

Cracker knelt at the edge of the hole and eased forward. "The explosives did exactly what they were supposeta! This musta been some kinda natural cavity in the ground! See them walls?" He pointed and Frank saw that the sides of the pit were made of clay rather than dirt, with a slightly curved appearance. "The ground coverin this thing was so thin, you're lucky no one fell through by walkin on it! That explosion vibrated the ground at just the right frequency to bring the whole mess down!"

Frank's anger died. He could see what Cracker meant. The dirt and clay that had covered the pit left a ring around the top edge no more than a few inches thick. As the blasts extended further into the field, it was only a matter of time before they got close enough to open it up.

And how many more of these things were out there? The next one might be deeper, a drop sufficient to shatter bones.

"Get something to haul these guys out!" To the men standing at the bottom of the hole, Frank asked, "You sure you're okay? Don't need an ambulance or anything?" The perfect culmination of his problems would be a lawsuit against the Lyles Corporation for unsafe practices.

They coughed and gave him a thumbs up. He heard a small sigh escape Cracker as he whispered, "It weren't my fault. How in blazes was I supposeta know?"

"I know. It's fine, nobody's blaming you. Go on home and calm down. I'll give you a call when we need you again."

"Fuck that. I'm gettin drunk. Scared me outta two weeksa sleep." He limped away from the pit.

Frank looked back at the hole they uncovered as a ladder was lowered into it and the men climbed out. He had actually heard of this before, at a convention some years back. Builders all over the southwest ran into these sinkholes, pockets of air trapped when the molten materials of the earth's crust were cooling. They had ruined projects.

But the question remained: was this an isolated incident, or were there more of the little beauties waiting to be discovered? In a perfect world, Frank wouldn't know and wouldn't care—it was surveyor negligence, after all—but he had a crew to protect. If he let them knowingly keep working and someone got hurt, that was his ass on the lawsuit paperwork, right alongside the company.

Then again, what the hell was he going to do, report it to Lyles? He already knew the response to that. He would just have to see what Damon wanted him to do.

For now, he had houses to build, if only to spite the man making him do it.

When the head of the team from Arcus approached him later that day, Frank expected to be informed that the two men were hurt after all. Instead, the muscular man said, "We finished with the fence."

"Great. You guys did some fast work."

"Standard security job. We ran the fence out a good distance from the property to give you some breathing room. Of course, on the south side we had to extend it a little further because of the...hole. It's on the inside of the property. And we can always come back to take it out further when you need it."

"The gate?"

The man pointed toward the road. The fence was four yards high, the gate wide enough to admit a single car. A large birch tree sat beside it, limbs hanging over the top from the outside of the fence. "Here's the key."

Frank clipped it to his ring. "All right. Looks good."

"Not so fast. There's also the matter of the dog."

Frank stared at the man. "Dog?"

"Yeah, the guard dog."

"Damon actually got a dog? I thought he was joking."

"Don't worry about it. He's harmless. *If* you know the right commands."

The man walked toward the front of the compound, to a large white pickup truck parked outside the fence by the Dark Road. An animal carrier sat in the back. A Doberman stared up at him with two glazed chocolate eyes.

"He doesn't look very mean."

"He was tranquilized for the trip over. Trust me though, once he wakes up, he'll be patrolling like a little soldier. Won't you boy?" The man made kissy-faces into the cage door and, before Frank could ask if they wanted to be alone, he opened the carrier and lifted the droopy-eyed animal out. The dog didn't have the strength to lift its head. He passed it to Frank, who accepted it like a sack of furry potatoes. "His name is Caesar. Keep him inside your trailer during the day and don't tell anyone his relent command or they can get in here whenever they want."

"What's the command?"

"Glad you asked." The man pulled a huge bag of dog food out of the back of the truck and put it on the ground. "Every morning when you get here, you'll have to say 'Hail Caesar.' At least until he gets to know you."

"Heel Caesar? That's it?"

"No *hail*. As in 'all hail.' And you better say it right, cause he can tell the difference."

"Real cute."

The man climbed into the security truck. "Take care of him!" His truck bounced over the uneven terrain and onto the Dark Road.

Frank looked down at Caesar, who managed to lift his head and whine. He drug a rough, slobbery tongue across Frank's cheek.

"This just keeps getting better." He sighed and carried the dog back to his trailer.

14

Willie couldn't escape from the house without admitting to his mother where he was going, but he certainly didn't confess who he was going with. She seemed happy he wanted to get out, but insisted on driving him to the mall.

It was awful when parents cared.

Casey provided the answer to this problem. She woke up with a sore throat and fever, and his mother spent the morning searching for a doctor that would take new patients on short notice. She agreed to let him go alone after he promised to 'take the bus' (the fact notwithstanding that he didn't even know if Asheville *had* a bus) only after he agreed to a three o'clock pickup. Willie dressed in his most torn-up pair of jeans and an Avenged Sevenfold t-shirt and took off down the street.

Nails and Zerk weren't at the park when he arrived a little before ten. Nowhere on the nature trail either. Not that he ventured far up it; the Jackal Man was probably no more real than gremlins, but why test fate?

Emotions raged as he collapsed on the swings. They were joking with him. He could imagine them somewhere now, in a basement filled with cigarette smoke, laughing at him.

A tap came on his left shoulder. Willie jerked his head around to find the space behind him empty, then heard a laugh from his right. He turned to find the duo standing in his blind spot, giggling like loons after playing the oldest prank in the universe.

"Gotcha!" Zerk's contacts looked like bolts of blue lightning today.

"Glad you showed up." Nails wore a plain white t-shirt and jeans, but still with that beaten leather jacket over the ensemble. "I had my doubts, but Zerk here never lost faith."

"Solidarity brother." The gaunt boy held up a fist.

"I haven't really been out at all," Willie said. "Unless you count the arcade."

Nails grimaced. "Ugh. Haven for the terminally redneck. I wouldn't be caught dead within a mile of that place."

"There's so much useless testosterone from all the cowboys packed in that place, you could launch a rocket to Uranus. Or Their-anus, as the case may be." Zerk grinned, and Willie realized he was liking these two more and more. They weren't whiny like Miles. They'd shed those last few human emotions and become exactly what Willie was striving for: detached and sarcastic.

"So, um, how're we getting to the mall? You guys have a car?"

"Shit, we don't even have a license."

"Bus?"

Nails snorted. "Yeah, right, a town with no McDonald's has a bus. We got bikes, man."

"Oh." Willie looked down at his feet. "I don't have a bike."

"No problemo," Zerk told him. "You can hop on the back of mine. Long as you don't pop a boner or something, you fag."

Though he was overjoyed at the offer, the smile they exchanged did not inspire confidence.

~ ~ ~

"*Isn't this fun?*" Zerk screamed over his shoulder.

"I don't know." Willie clung to his back. "I'll let you know when I can breathe again."

Zerk had only a beat-up Huffy with a seat just big enough for Willie to squeeze on the back, but Nails perched atop an oversize, tricked-out BMX, hand-painted with black crows and snakes, chrome-plated spikes along the handlebars and pedals, and fake chain spokes. His baby, paid for by delivering newspapers in his 'other life,' as he called the time before his mother died and his father began his daily dives to the bottom of a beer bottle.

At the breakneck speeds they pedaled, the trip lasted only an hour. They took main roads out of Asheville, traveling in the breakdown lane of the freeway at one point. When they emerged onto a busy street and were almost struck by a passing truck, Willie finally felt like he'd reentered civilization. The mall, a two-story, sprawling structure with multiple parking garages, only reinforced the feeling of being home.

Nails and Zerk chained their bikes to a rack near the front door. Willie noticed two girls a little older than him on the other side of the entry, sitting on concrete posts as they waited for rides. Hair glowing in the sun, curvy bodies in shirts that displayed smooth midriffs, and legs stretching for miles beneath tight skirts. He subtly stared at them while trying to maintain an air of cool detachment.

"Hey ladies, you waitin for me?" Willie flinched as Zerk shouted out next to him. The two girls halted in their conversation and looked up at the three of them. At first Willie thought Zerk knew the two, until he yelled, "And I got plenty of friends to go around!"

126 RUSSELL C. CONNOR

The girls rolled their eyes, stood up, and walked around the corner of the building away from them.

"*Daaaamn*, did you see those two, Willie? I'da given my left nut to have a go at them. After I'm done, of course."

Willie's cheeks burned, but he frowned and said, "Don't get me wrong, I'm no expert or anything, but I don't think screaming at them is the way to go."

"But I wasn't gonna get 'em anyway."

Willie continued to frown in confusion.

"Jesus Willie, get with it! If I can't have those girls, then who cares what I say, right?" He cleared his throat and recited, "'How luscious lies the pea within the pod that duty locks!' That's Emily Dickinson. Means if you live with inhibitions, you live in a prison."

"Don't pay attention to his crap." Nails lit a cigarette. "Shithead thinks he's a philosopher just because he goes and reads poetry at one of those gay-ass coffee bars where they all dress in black and wear berets and have goatees. Including the women."

"Hey!"

"But he is right about one thing." Nails squinted at Willie. "You got the look, but your attitude definitely needs some work. We're gonna have to teach you some manners."

They wove their way through the mall, and for the next few hours, Willie was witness to a host of juvenile pranks and hi-jinks. Spitting off balconies onto people, pulling the mobile kiosks out of place when the owners weren't looking, and unplugging the games at the arcade were but a few of the items on the duo's troublemaking resume.

And Willie didn't participate in a single one. He couldn't even look his two companions in the face as the day wore on.

When three o'clock approached, he found himself in the mall's only comic book store, leafing through back issues while the elderly clerk eyed them as if their faces were on a wanted poster behind his desk.

Nails wandered up next to him and picked up a comic. He thumbed the pages one at a time. "You read a lotta these?"

"Yeah, I guess."

He closed the book and looked at the price on the cover with exaggerated disdain. "These things get more expensive every day. Only one way to solve that problem." To Willie's horror, he curled the book into a tube and put it inside his jacket, shoving it into an interior pocket.

Zerk snickered. "It's easy, Willster. Check it out." He knelt, checked the circular shoplifting mirror mounted in the corner, then ripped open an action figure package and stuck the toy in his sock. "For our burning amusement later."

"You gotta live *sometime*, Willie. We do it all the time. Never been caught."

"Go ahead," Zerk urged.

Their eyes bore into him from both sides. It felt like a last chance kind of situation, his final opportunity to show they hadn't been wrong in taking him under their wing. He suddenly understood what Zerk meant earlier. Inhibition and fear were strong prisons.

Riding the impulse, Willie spotted an appealing title, took it down, and secured it under the waistband of his jeans. The tingling sensation all over his body prevented him from backing up the visual input with his other four senses.

He was numb.

And it felt good.

A grin spread across his features, one that was mean and nasty and fit all too well.

Nails smiled back at him. "Thatta boy. Take whatever you want. The old coot that runs this place is blind."

They spread out through the store on their shoplifting spree. Willie's euphoric high kept up until he felt like he was floating down the aisles.

Finally, Nails sidled up next to him. "That's enough, man. Don't get too greedy. Let's get outta here."

Willie moved as fast as he dared with all the contraband shoved into his pockets. He felt smug, superior. Zerk fell into line behind them, a smirk on his wide mouth.

They passed the register, where the gray-haired old man still eyed them as he checked out another customer. Nails seemed to pass as close as possible, to shove their thievery under the proprietor's nose. Willie didn't look away as he walked by, but instead held his head up as though he were the center attraction at a parade. The sheer gall in the act made it even sweeter.

And then his heart jumped out of his chest as a hand yanked up the bottom of his shirt from behind.

"Look, this kid's stealing!" he heard Zerk shout.

Willie's muscles became steel rods, locking him in place. He felt his face go red as the owner's jaw dropped open behind the counter.

Nails shouted, "Run!" He took off, but Willie remained where he was—he was busted after all, fair and square, and good morals said he had to wait here for the handcuffs—but then Zerk shoved him from behind until his feet were forced to move. They charged back into the mall proper, where other consumers stopped to watch the commotion.

Willie followed Nails through the throng, Zerk at his heels. The old man chased them only as far as the door, bawling for security, then went back inside. Nails charged out through the nearest emergency exit, letting in a stream of a harsh sunlight, and waited in the alcove beyond for Willie and Zerk.

"Why'd you do that?" Willie demanded between gasps.

Nails laughed and coughed all at the same time. Zerk fell to the ground holding his side, rolling in delight as stolen merchandise fell out of their hiding places on his body. "Oh man, Willie, I'm sorry, but you shoulda seen your face!"

Zerk squealed, "Don't worry, the police sketch artists won't be able to recreate that beautiful mug of yours!"

Willie smiled uncertainly. "I...guess it was pretty funny."

"Damn right it was!" Zerk's laughter trailed off as a thought occurred to him. "Shit, Nails. You don't think this'll get back to Shruffy, do you?"

"What does it matter? He doesn't have jurisdiction here, he's an Asheville cop."

"Who is this Shruffy guy you keep talking about?" Willie asked.

"Detective Marcus Shruff. Local cop that always gives us shit."

"But if he finds out it was us, he'll hand us over to the Arlington PD, man." Zerk's eyes became owlish circles in the middle of his head. "You know he will."

"He won't! Jesus Zerk, it looks like Willie has a bigger pair than you!"

"I don't know whether to take that as a compliment or not," Willie mumbled.

Nails laughed and reached in his jacket for a plastic baggie. "Only one thing to do to steady your nerves after something like that."

Willie was horrified all over again as he saw what was inside. "Jesus Christ, *marijuana?*" he asked in a shrieky voice.

"C'mon Willie, it can't shock you *that* much." Nails rolled a joint on his lap with expert flair and produced a lighter from the interior of his jacket. "For guys like us, it's almost a social responsibility. If we didn't smoke a little once in a while, the world would collapse from all the poor uptight fucks walking around on it. We're maintaining a balance here."

"Yeah, why don't you try telling that to my parents." Willie looked around, sure a SWAT team would be descending on them.

"Two roads diverged in a wood, and Willie Stanford chose the one with less tokin'," Zerk said, winking at him.

Nails touched flame to the end of his little bundle of joy. "So what's the deal, Willie? You up for this?" He watched the tube of twisted paper as it was passed to Zerk.

His mind reeled under a decision that he honestly believed was only encountered in after school specials about peer pressure.

In the end, the choice was taken away from him, as a familiar shadow fell across his shoulder.

15

At close to two-thirty, Frank's cell phone buzzed again. He excused himself from several workers. The pit in the corner of the yard was roped off now, and Frank stood facing it as he answered.

It was Trisha this time. "Frank, listen, I need a big favor."

"What's up?"

"I'm at the doctor's office with Casey still. It took forever to get in and he's prescribing medicine that we need to have filled and—"

Frank jumped as an electric drill started up close to him. He walked away from the construction, past the trailer where Caesar the Guard Dog now slept, toward the pit. "And?"

"And I told Willie I would pick him up at that mall outside town at three o'clock, and there's no way I can get there."

"The mall? How the hell did he get to the mall?"

"He took the bus."

"The bus? I thought he was grounded!"

"He wanted to get out, and I don't blame him. Look, you're closer than I am, could you just run there to get him and drop him off at home?"

Frank stood very still, internal and external heat boiling him from both directions, and became fixated on the pit across from him. Suddenly he could think of nothing but that hole in the ground. He said into the phone, "I'm really busy here."

"Of course you are. You always are. Look, I'm not going to beg you. Willie can just sit there thinking we forgot to pick him up. I'm sure that will improve his attitude."

The pit. It was hypnotizing him, like a great big eye in the ground. For some reason, his father's voice floated through his head again. This town seemed to be bringing it out in him.

"I'll get him," he said, barely recognizing the sound of his own voice. "I'll leave now."

Trisha sounded stunned. "Okay, well...thank you."

Frank put the phone back in his pocket without letting his eyes leave the pit.

The mall was just like any other Frank had helped build. The universal law seemed to be that wherever there was empty space, teenagers would be there to loiter in it.

He cruised past the main entrance at a crawl, scanning the groups for Willie. Surely Trisha would've told the boy to meet her here. He felt the first twinge of fear.

Frank left the front entrance, circled the building, and started back toward the front when he saw a flash of orange tucked away in a small indentation in the building.

He pulled to the curb and got out, walking around the building and into a small alcove with an emergency exit. His son was here, along with two other punks he didn't know, one of them moronic enough to wear a leather jacket in hundred degree weather. He started to call out, but his tongue died in his mouth as he took in the scene. He could only stare as the one in the leather jacket held out a suspiciously pungent cigarette to Willie.

The one in the coat noticed the adult among them first. "Whattaya want, old man? Take a hit?" Frank wanted to throttle the little punk.

Willie turned, guilt already spreading across his face. Frank grabbed him by the t-shirt collar before he could speak and hauled him out of the short alley, away from his friends, drugs, and a pile of what could only be contraband merchandise.

His son twisted in his grip, trying to get his feet under him. Frank opened the passenger door, shoved him inside, and marched around the vehicle. He pulled away from the mall with a squeal of heated rubber.

"So this is it, huh? This is what it's come to? You're doing drugs?"

"No, I didn't do them!"

"You sure could've fooled me."

"But that's the thing, I really didn't! He offered and I didn't even have a chance to say no!"

"Right, that's the way it works." Frank took a corner too fast. "And what about all that stuff on the ground? I suppose you were wearing a wire for a sting operation on the local shoplifting ring?"

Willie's jaw worked, but no words escaped.

"Son, do you know what would've happened if you had gotten caught?" He paused, but the boy still didn't speak. "Answer me! Do you?"

"No."

"You would've ended up in juvenile hall! That's prison for kids!"

"I know what it is. I'm not an idiot."

"I don't think now would be the best time to make that claim."

Tears welled up in Willie's eyes. "What do you care anyway? Wouldn't it make you and mom happy to have me sent away?"

"Oh don't even try playing for sympathy!"

"You were gonna send me to Andrew Academy."

Frank twitched, glancing over at the boy. "That's different."

"No, it isn't! You just hate me so much because I don't fit into your perfect family! You want me gone!"

"Willie, you're kicked outta school! What should we do with you?"

"I don't know. Whatever." Willie swiped at those tears and looked away.

"That's no answer. 'Whatever' never solved anything. What are we going to do about this?"

Silence stretched out while his son stared out the window. "Dad," he said quietly, "I know things have been bad lately, but you used to trust me, right?"

Frank swallowed. The solemnity of the question got his attention, turned down the heat on his anger. He nodded.

"Then please, please, just...trust me this time. Whether you think I did it or not, just believe me when I say I'll never put myself in that situation again. Please just let it go, and don't tell mom."

It had been so long since the boy asked him for anything. He was reminded of that hint of the old Willie present at the dinner table the night before. He wanted that kid back, wanted to have them swap identities like some sort of multiple personality disorder.

"Keep it between us, huh?"

"Please."

"And you won't pull something like that ever again?"

"Never!"

"Okay, but you're still grounded. You don't go anywhere unless it's with your mom, got me?"

"Yes, yes." Willie nodded quickly.

"Don't let my trust be for nothing." Frank turned onto the road that led to their house. "Is it too late for me to ask you to wash the orange out of your hair as part of this deal?"

Willie smiled a little and shrugged. "Probably."

They drove home in comfortable silence.

16

Outside town, the River Meadows construction site was abandoned for the day, stacks of lumber and a single bulldozer waiting among the house frames. The workers had left when it got too dark to see, happy they would be earning extra time but exhausted from being under the thumb of their new taskmaster, who some were already calling 'the Hammer.' Gerrardo and several others grouped together on their way out, talking rapidly in Spanish and shooting the evil eye at the place over their shoulder. The gate was locked behind the very last man by the Hammer himself. The shadows first lengthened as the sun went down and then fattened to take over the land entirely.

Now the structures within the compound were silent monuments. Crickets and frogs sounded from all over the field and the tall grasses of the dry marsh a short distance away.

Caesar was fully awake, the tranquilizers worn off hours ago. He had been released and left with a supply of food and water in two hardhats at the door of the trailer. The master of this place gave the relent command repeatedly as he went about these activities, though Caesar made no motion to attack.

He was a lean animal, coarse black fur on a body that tapered to a point at either end, and ears clipped to make him more intimidating. He knew his job: to walk the perimeter of wherever the humans left him and watch for intruders. To keep such intruders out, at any cost, till the life was gone from him. Caesar had done this many places, in a multitude of temperatures, weather, and terrain.

And yet this place…this place was different from them all.

His canine senses were on fire, prodding him to be more alert than training could ever make him.

This was about *instinct*.

He patrolled the south side, walking through the area that would eventually be backyards, and gave the huge hole in the ground a wide berth. This section of the compound tweaked his senses especially hard.

He continued walking the length of the fence, which faced the tall marsh grass less than fifty feet away. His padded feet had carried him into the next circuit when the wind brought a peculiar scent. He stopped and lifted his nose.

The noise level in the field abruptly dropped off. The night creatures fell silent in such coordination they might have scheduled their cessation ahead of time.

The dog's brown eyes probed the long blades of grass moving in the night breeze. As he watched, they parted slightly in one place, the motion too forceful to be wind. In the darkness, two small, green circles shimmered.

A growl built deep in Caesar's throat.

Something low and sleek slipped out of the grass and circled the enclosure at a distance, working around to the front. There was an overwhelming grace to its movement, and it kept to the shadows with the uncanny knack of the most experienced predators.

The Doberman growled again and followed the scurrying shape to the gate. It was on the other side of the tree next to the fence; he could see its tail twitching. Caesar issued a warning bark and displayed jagged canines to scare the aggressor away.

But the thing on the other side of the fence wasn't intimidated. The creature climbed the tree with quick, strong appendages. Caesar craned his head back and watched it leap from limb to limb without a sound. The green orbs stayed fixed on him.

He backed away as it swung to one of the limbs that hung over the inside of the fence. Then he got a good whiff of the thing's odor. The musky scent filled up his nose and head, an ancient, primal smell.

His survival instincts overrode his training, telling him to run, because here, in this fight, *he* was the weaker specimen.

Warm piss puddled on the dirt beneath him.

The creature leapt from the branch and landed on two legs in front of him, the supple body curving until its forelimbs rested on the ground.

Caesar whined in terror and tried to run, but the thing was on him before he could, wrapping thin arms around his neck to pin him. A grinding pain flashed up his side as he twisted his head to snap half-heartedly at the hand that held him. There was a hiss. Claws sank into his throat and ripped it out. Blood sprayed in one arterial gush from the ragged tear.

He died with a gurgling whimper in the thing's embrace.

The creature holding the dog carried him by the neck to the edge of the pit uncovered earlier that day in the dynamite blast. It stood perfectly still, gazing down into the hole, and then turned away with Caesar's body.

SHRUFF

THE DETECTIVE FINDS A TRAIL

17

Now that there was a gate to unlock, Frank upped his arrival time at the site to 6:30. It was Friday, his third day on the job with two houses completed, seventeen more at various stages, one safety accident under his belt, and a big pit that would have to be filled at some point.

He just couldn't worry about secondary shit anymore. If he wanted to save his ass, he needed to focus on the bigger picture, and that was getting the houses built. No more explosives, no more fences or non-essential personnel traipsing through the site, no more *distractions*; just sweat and blood from here on in. He would grab a hammer today and get some work done himself.

His truck sat with the engine idling and headlights casting dusty circles on the fence while he unlocked the gate. The crickets were back in full swing. Frank twisted the key in the lock and pushed the gate open as they continued their song. He stood in the entrance for several seconds, scanning the site for a shadow among shadows.

"Where the hell is that mutt?" His voice was small in the yard. "*Caesar!*" he called. No answer, and he didn't know what kind of aspersions it cast on his sanity that he expected one. Some goddamn watchdog.

He started back toward the truck, saying over his shoulder, "Just in case you're listening, 'Hail Caesar.' When I call that security company, it's gonna be '*Hasta la vista* Caesar.'"

Frank parked his truck at the back of the site and got out with a thermos of hot coffee. "No distractions," he reiterated as he came around the corner of the trailer.

He stopped in mid-stride.

The large window to the left of the door was broken. Triangular shards clung to the frame. Before his anger could properly flare about the vandalism, he noticed a more curious anomaly.

On both sides of the door were dark streaks, like paint slopped on the cheap aluminum siding in a quick slash with a large brush. It was hard to make out the color in the weak rays of the still-rising sun. Frank came closer and ran his finger down one of the marks. Most of the substance was crusty, but in the thicker patches, the air hadn't dried it yet. Frank's index finger came away with a stain. He tilted his hand to catch as much of the light as possible.

The stain was red. A rich maroon.

Could be ketchup. Sure, it was perfectly reasonable to assume some vandal had wiped ketchup on the sides of his door, like a trailer trash version of the Passover...but then why did he have some serious goosebumps going on?

There was a loud thump at his feet and Frank jumped, his skeleton attempting to tear free of his skin, before he realized the thermos had slipped from his other hand.

He sniffed the tip of his finger and thought he caught a whiff of copper. It was definitely blood. He wiped it on a clean part of the trailer, wanting the smear off him, and then rubbed the flesh on the fabric of his jeans. He turned away from the trailer in disgust.

His jaw dropped open as he faced the unfinished houses he'd driven past without a glance. The sun peeked over the horizon now, and he could see from the steps of the trailer that all of the frames had splashes of red on the wood beams and sheetrock walls. The early sun made them look more vivid, jumping out at him like a 3D movie.

Frank thought again of the story of the Passover, and felt an actual gag coming on at the aptness of the comparison. A more horrifying thought surfaced: what had been used to decorate his site?

Where in hell had the blood *come from?*

He grasped the doorknob of the trailer with his eyes shut and unlocked it with a shaking hand. He just wanted inside, to call the police and try to get himself under control. He jumped into the trailer...and gasped.

Caesar lay on his side on the fake wood surface of Frank's desk, staring ahead with glassy eyes. The Doberman's underbelly had been torn open from groin to muzzle; thick ropes of entrails hanging from his stomach off the front of the desk, above a coagulated pool of blood in the floor.

Frank stumbled back outside as he dug in his pocket for his cell phone.

A platoon of Asheville PD's finest swarmed over the site within an hour, poking at bloodstains and taking samples. As the workers arrived for their shift, they were asked to wait outside the fence perimeter to keep from damaging potential evidence. The Hispanic men gathered around the front and sides in tight clusters, peering through the chain link, some of them lamenting at the sight of the gruesome mess.

No distractions, Frank thought again, with a grim smile.

He wandered around helplessly, attempting to elicit an update from the officers, who were close-lipped about when they would be packing up the circus. None of them seemed anxious to get the job done, and looked at him with veiled malice. Was it imagination, or more of the prejudice he'd experienced at the hands of this warped little town?

After half an hour of fingerprints or DNA or whatever the hell they were doing, the body of Caesar was carried out of his trailer in a clear plastic bag. Outside the fence, the Spanish Hail Marys started up all over again. Part of Frank couldn't imagine ever setting foot inside the trailer again; another insisted this was ridiculous.

And yet a third part was thinking about his father, campfires, and stories about birds with razor talons and beaks like alligator jaws.

He felt a tap on his back. A squat man with a long, bald runway over his skull stood behind him.

"Are you in charge of the building here?"

Finally, someone who would speak to him. "I'm the foreman."

The little man sprang into action, going from serene to frantic as he flashed an ID in Frank's face. "James Buchanon of the *Weekly Digest*. Let me be the first to ask, who do you believe is responsible for this *ritualistic slaying?*" The final two words were pronounced with just the right amount of flair.

"What?"

"Anyone with a grudge against the company? Out to get your boss, what's-his-name, Lyles? Or could this be the work of a psychopath?" Buchanon produced a miniature tape recorder and shoved it toward Frank's mouth. His eyes reminded him of the gas station attendant's—good ol' Earl

Dean—too eager to push the right buttons and get the right responses.

"Psychopath? What are you talking about?" Frank backed away. Buchanon followed him with the recorder held out like a weapon.

"Look around, buddy. This wasn't done by kids on drugs. And if it was, they got a serious dealer problem." The man flashed teeth in a crooked smile. "Is there any possible connection with...the Jackal Man?"

"The only psycho here is *you*, buddy!" Frank shouted. He snatched at the tape recorder, and Buchanon danced out of his range. Frank marched forward now, herding the reporter back toward the exit.

"C'mon man, cut me some slack! Just give me one quote I can use!"

"I'll give you the front page story: Pissed-off Foreman Beats the Shit Out of Trespassing Reporter!"

Buchanon was nearly at the gate now, walking backwards so he could keep an eye on Frank. "*Just a few more questions about the slaughter!*" he yelled, much louder than necessary, glancing at the Hispanic men outside the fence.

"It's not a slaughter!"

"Jesus James, go on. Get outta here," a new voice said from Frank's left. Someone had appeared beside him, a younger man with brown hair that flopped into his eyes, in a blue oxford shirt and...

Holy shit, Frank almost yelped aloud. *What happened to his neck?*

"C'mon Shruff, this is news! You can't keep the news from the people, how many times I gotta tell you cops that?"

"Once more ought to do it," the man at Frank's side said with a tired smile. "Now go on. You'll get your official statement from the police. It'll be filled with these amazing things you might want to try working with some time. They're called 'facts.'"

Frank snorted laughter. Buchanon retreated outside the fence, where he began speaking with the workers. Several of them, Gerrardo in particular, looked all too eager to talk.

18

"Tabloid trash," his rescuer said. "I wouldn't use the *Digest* to wipe my ass." He regarded Frank with murky green eyes. "You Frank Stanford?"

Frank had more trouble tearing his gaze away from this man's deformity than Cracker's missing body parts. His neck was a snarl of scars, flesh standing out in livid, mottled ripples all across his throat, starting just above the Adam's apple and extending to the collar of his shirt in a roughly circular pattern. "Last I checked."

"I'm Detective Marcus Shruff. I'm in charge of the investigation."

"Great, nice to meet you," he recovered. "Listen, is there any way we can get him away from the site? He's bothering my workers."

"Bothering?" He waved a hand at Gerrardo, still speaking rapidly to the reporter. "That guy looks cozy enough to propose marriage."

"Okay, he's bothering *me*. How the hell did he find out about this so fast anyway?"

"As shameful as it is to admit, he probably got a tip from someone on the force. Don't worry about Buchanon though. For the most part, he's harmless. Just be glad you don't have a hundred reporters from more reputable media out here."

"Why? Cause some sicko butchered a dog? I could understand local news, but I don't think it warrants the eyes of the nation or anything."

Shruff smiled, a boyish grin that could probably break hearts, if not for that scar. "People around here take a real interest in what goes on in these woods. The media knows it, and they give the people what they really want nowadays: truth with a twist of fiction."

"Info-tainment, huh?"

Shruff touched the tip of his nose. "No reality in front of a camera. Not anymore."

"Okay, so then tell me: what's so special about these woods?"

"C'mon now, Mr. Stanford. Don't tell me you've been in town more than five minutes and you don't know about the Jackal Man."

"I do." Frank sighed. It sounded stranger coming from an honest-to-God police officer. He used his sleeve to mop at his brow. "I was just kinda hoping you'd tell me it was an endangered coyote habitat or something. Is it too much to ask for one sane person in this whole town?"

The detective laughed easily, and, despite the blood-strewn battlefield they stood in, Frank found the sound relaxing. "I used to ask myself the same question. Gave up on that search, though."

"Okay, never mind about local folklore. Just level with me, and tell me what's going on. Who did this?"

"Well...what if one answered the other?" Frank cocked his head, and Shruff continued. "You're an intelligent guy, so I won't try to bullshit you this was some kind of animal attack."

"I don't know how an 'animal' big enough to do...*that*,"

an image of Caesar, slit open like a roasted pig, flashed behind his eyes, "would've gotten in here in the first place, but I do know animals don't finger paint when they get done killing something. And they don't deposit the remains on your desk like a present either."

"Depends on the animal. I had a dog that brought me dead birds all the time."

"This wasn't a dog. It wasn't an animal at all."

Shruff smiled wide, but it didn't reach farther than his mouth this time. "You're right. We're agreed on that then. It wasn't an *animal*. Let's take a walk." The detective shuffled away across the dirt lot. Frank followed him to one of the blood smears on a nearby house frame that was still two days from being completed, if they ever got the chance. "First of all, I can tell you without a doubt that all the blood we're seeing here couldn't come from that dog. In fact, I'd be willing to bet that all of this out here is from a different species altogether; rats maybe, or squirrels, we'll have to do some analysis."

"Squirrels?" Frank repeated, too sharply. *Squirrels with no heads Frankie, squirrels left in a dried pool of their own blood, squirrels left as little presents for* you.

"That's right," Shruff said with a cocked eyebrow. "You know something I don't?"

"No, I just…that is…I mean, how can you be so sure?"

"Call it a hunch."

"Never believed in those."

Shruff just shrugged and walked deeper into the house's structure without extending invitation. Frank followed, stepping into the dry shade of the interior. His eyes took a minute to adjust going from blinding sun to deep shadow. When he could see again, he marveled at the thoroughness of the perpetrator. Maroon decorated every surface in the same haphazard manner. He sucked in his gut to keep from touching any of them, telling himself it was for evidence purposes instead of admitting that the place really, really gave him the screaming jeebies.

They passed an officer who seemed to give a wide berth around Shruff without looking at him. The detective beckoned to Frank, and together they entered the skeletal frame of the kitchen, which was, thankfully, shaded by the partially finished floor of the upper story.

"This is what I really wanted to show you," Shruff told him. In the shadows, his scar was like the pitted surface of the moon. He pointed beyond the entryway. Frank moved past him and was walloped by a rank odor hanging in the air, like a YMCA locker room magnified a thousand times. He breathed through his mouth and found what Shruff brought him to see.

On the sheet rock, where the outlets for the stove and dishwasher would eventually go, was a fully formed handprint. About waist height, dipped in blood and pressed to the white wall between two-by-fours as neat as a police fingerprinting.

Something about it wasn't quite right.

"I guess that rules out the animal theory," Frank mumbled. He stared at the print, trying to figure out why it looked wrong. Yet again the story of Passover occurred to him, and he finally realized the connection: it was as if someone was marking territory, claiming the house as their own. "Who would do this? Who in a town this size would be that severely disturbed?"

Shruff leaned against a vertical board. "Just for propriety's sake, let's cover all the bases, Mr. Stanford. Do any of the employees—or anyone else, for that matter—have a grudge against you or your boss or the company?"

"Ha! Might be easier to ask who doesn't."

"Bad enough to do something like this?"

Frank thought of Gerrardo, of the rumors he'd heard around town, about the missing dynamite and the missing Gammon. It felt like too many pieces from completely different puzzles being jammed together. "Not that I know of. There's been some stuff stolen, but nothing like this."

"How long ago was that?"

"Before I got here. Maybe a week or so ago."

"What was stolen?"

"Just…just small stuff. Stuff we had lying around." *Like a bunch of idiots.*

"That leaves the random—gang killings or cult sacrifice, both of which are unlikely around here…or something else entirely."

"Like what?"

"Did you really take a look at that print, Mr. Stanford?"

Frank looked again. And this time it popped right out at him.

The handprint could better be described as a *paw* print, just like a little puppy or kitty would make: a palm sectioned into pebbly pads, except these pads stretched up into long, dexterous fingers.

About an inch or so above the end of each of the strange digits was a small circle of blood, barely the size of a pin nib.

Claw tips. Curving from each fingertip to make its own impression.

"Gotta be a fake."

Shruff was silent.

Frank leaned closer, looking for the little MADE IN CHI-NA that had been molded into the fake rubber on the Halloween glove. But if it was forgery, his eyes weren't trained enough to spot it.

Below the print was a dark stain on the bottom of the sheet rock where it met the concrete foundation. A yellowish puddle, dried to a sticky film, and he realized the pungent smell (*animal den*, his mind hissed) was wafting from the stuff.

"What's that?" he asked.

"Don't know. We have samples."

"Looks like piss. Then again, if you're willing to murder a dog, you're enough of an animal to whiz in the corner."

"I thought we agreed it wasn't an animal."

"Goddamn it, you know what I mean."

"Let's head back out." Shruff said, and Frank understood—on an instinctive level only, for the detective gave no outward sign—that he was just as nervous being in here.

The kitchen was dark and oppressive now, though one entire wall was open to the elements. Frank suddenly pitied whoever would eventually live in this house and cook in this kitchen.

"So quit trying to keep me in suspense and just tell me what this means," Frank demanded as they ducked under a low beam in the living room and emerged into the brutally welcoming sunlight.

"As your friendly neighborhood detective, I can't say for certain. There's a lot of lab work and forensics that go into these things." Shruff was in front of Frank, facing the trailer and the back of the site. He suddenly glanced over Frank's shoulder.

"Well then, when are you going to be through?"

"We're finished here. I'm going to ask you to keep your guys out of this house until we finish the investigation."

"You can't do that!" Frank exclaimed. "We have to work in there! We're on a schedule!"

"You want us to solve this case, don't you?" Before Frank could answer, the detective asked, "What is that?"

Frank realized what he was talking about a half second before he turned. The pit. Late yesterday they put up tape on stakes to mark the hole to prevent further accidents. He'd left Damon a message about it, but had gotten no call back yet. Shruff slid around him and made his way across the lot.

"That's nothing, just an accident! It's dangerous to go much closer!"

They stopped within several feet of the pit. "That's quite a deep accident. You guys mining for gold or something?"

Frank wiped at his eternally sweating brow and shook his head. "Let me level with you here, Detective. I've been in town less than a week. I've been on the job three days, only to find out the site was burglarized, we had a very lawsuit-worthy dynamite mishap yesterday, and today I get here to find that someone played tic-tac-toe with our guard dog's guts. My boss is gonna fire me if I don't finish this project. I don't have time for this."

"Okay. Now let me level with you." Shruff looked into the pit as he talked, the scar tissue on his neck stretched taut. "I told you that, as a detective, I had no idea what's going on. As a human being, just a friendly face on the street, I'll tell you this: run. Leave town. If your boss is gonna fire you, let him fire you. Just get yourself out of this mess. You seem like a nice guy, and I don't want you to get hurt by all this."

"Hurt by *what*, for Christ's sake?"

Shruff stared into the ground for a long moment. "Have a good day, Mr. Stanford. I'll let you know as soon as I have something."

He walked away, back toward the gate. Frank stood dumbfounded, staring after him.

~ ~ ~

The eyes of the workers were on him as he walked back. Frank bellowed, "C'mon fellas! You waitin for Christmas? Let's get some work done!"

They remained statues, faces unreadable.

"Shit," Frank wheezed. He sauntered over to the gate where the majority were gathered. "What's the matter, *eses*? Are we building today or not?"

Several conferred in Spanish. A man Frank thought was named Enrico told him solemnly, "We can't work in there. It's marked."

"Marked? What are you talking about?"

You know exactly what they're talking about, Frankie. The ghost of his father still used the nickname, but it was no longer teasing.

"This is an omen," Gerrardo spat, eyes flashing as they had during their first confrontation two days before. "A *blood* omen."

"A blood omen? Jesus, you sound like a buncha witch doctors! You're here for labor, not reading tea leaves! What do you think is gonna happen if you come in here?"

"This is a warning. Left by the Jackal Man."

"I'm so sick of that name I could puke. What do you know about the Jackal Man? Not something you heard from someone else. What do *you* know?"

Gerrardo's nostrils flared like unfurled cobras.

"Have you ever seen him? *Have any of you?*" Frank looked around, but got no response. "Then why are you so scared of him? Just, somebody…give me a straight answer!"

Gerrardo breathed deeply, the chest of his white t-shirt expanding. "You don't have to see something for it to hurt you. This is about caution, you understand?"

"You know, I thought you Mexicans were all about being men. But I don't see any men here. I see children willin to go back to their families jobless because of the Boogieman!"

"Can't find another job if you're dead."

Frank ran a hand down his face in frustration, stretching out his skin and creating hollows under his eyes. He saw Gerrardo flinch back from the ghoulish sight.

"Okay, here's how it's gonna work." Frank drew a line in the dirt with his foot from gatepost to gatepost. "Those that want their pay can cross this line and get to work. Those that don't, can fuck off."

For one strangled moment, Frank was afraid they would all really leave, abandoning a job because of a trumped-up nursery rhyme. Enrico stepped silently forward with his head down, a scab crossing the picket lines. Others followed, including the nervous Jaime Garcia, and Frank's breath came easier with each addition. When it was all finished, only Gerrardo and a group of twelve others remained on the opposite side. They turned in unison and walked away, several of them casting regretful glances behind them, like Adam and Eve leaving Eden.

"Thank you," Frank told the others. "Summer's wasting. *Andale*."

They scattered to work and Frank walked quickly back to the trailer. He was going to track Damon down and give him a full report, and then insist he get down here. He wasn't prepared for this, public relations and police investigations weren't his job goddammit, and if Damon wanted to save his ass, he would handle it.

Frank stepped inside and found the day's next surprise waiting for him.

19

Just breathe, Marcus Shruff thought, as his unmarked police car raced up the Dark Road toward Asheville. *C'mon, in and out, one at a time...*

But he couldn't. His lungs were filled with glue, and his chest shuddered with the effort. He'd kept his cool in front of the new foreman, looked like an actual professional for a change, but that was the best he could do.

Black spots spun across his vision as the panic attack sank its claws in; pardoning the expression, of course. He'd gone to a doctor for them several years back, hoping for asthma medication, and was told they had nothing to do with any condition of his body.

The doc gave him the name of a good psychiatrist instead.

One of his hands came off the steering wheel and rubbed at the deeply scarred flesh of his throat.

It was the trees. Out in the meadow, in the open, the anxiety was manageable, dampened enough so he could at least function. But now, with those god-awful trees pressing in on both sides of the road, it was like...like...

A coffin, he finished, and instantly wished he hadn't.

And then his car passed the Spot, and the sound of Axl Rose's voice floated through his head like a distant echo, the smell of spring filled his nose, and he knew he was going to faint.

The hand at his throat stopped its subconscious massage and moved protectively over the evidence case on the seat next to him. Its presence was like a security blanket dragging him back from the brink.

I got you this time, fucker, he thought. *You poked your head out a little too far, and I'm more than happy to chop it off for you.*

"Can you get someone to run this to the lab in Fort Worth, along with the canine body they brought in?"

The cop manning the closet that constituted the Asheville police station evidence locker was young, another out-of-town rookie. Policing was the only profession where outsiders were not only accepted, but came close to outnumbering the natives. Of course, when you hired as many officers as Asheville did, you exhausted your local candidate pool pretty fast.

It also meant an abundance of fellow cops who never got used to the twisted mess of scar tissue stretched across his neck. The rookie's eyes planted roots in it as Shruff slung the evidence case onto the desk in front of him.

"Um...well, I...um..."

He was rescued from terminal stuttering by his superior, Sergeant Cormack, who stepped between Shruff and the desk. Even the case being out of his sight for these few seconds caused Shruff's stomach to knot.

"What do we got here, Shruff?"

"Just some samples from that call down at River Meadows. I want to get it to the lab in Arlington this morning."

"Uh huh, uh huh." Cormack tapped the metal side of the

case. "Evidence drops are Mondays, you know that. We can keep this in storage till next week."

Shruff pulled his lips tight. "I know when the drops are, Sergeant. I want a rush on this. Please."

Cormack leaned in, covered his mouth with one hand, and asked, "Did uh...did the Chief okay that, Shruff?"

"Since when does the Chief have to okay a rush on evidence analysis by a fucking senior detective?"

"Fine." Cormack pulled back, snatched the case up, and thrust it at the rookie. "Officer, get all this logged and make sure it gets to the lab within the hour." He threw a sneer at Shruff. "The detective here thinks he's found a trail."

"Yes sir." The young cop took off with the case, casting one fearful look back at one or both of them.

Shruff eyed Cormack but said nothing.

He turned and made his way through the station. Every eye that met his—rookie or veteran, domestic or foreign—slid off and rolled away, heads bowing deeper into desks, conversations terminating, the aisle in front of him clearing.

This treatment stopped registering with him long ago.

Detective Shruff made it to his cubicle in the far back corner of the squad room and stared at the clock.

He was still staring fifteen minutes later, trying not to count the seconds since the evidence case left his possession, when Chief Windham poked his head around the corner of the cubicle.

"Marcus, a word with you?" He heaved his bulk onto the edge of the desk without invitation, trying to look casual when Shruff knew this was anything but. "I understand that situation out at the construction site was awful. Just a real mess. But do you feel it was necessary to rush those samples out for analysis?"

"Well, it's part of an ongoing investigation—"

"Goddamn it, there is no *ongoing investigation*," Windham snapped. "And you know that."

Shruff met the man's angry gaze head on. "I think those samples will show otherwise."

The police chief put a hand over his eyes and squeezed. "Marcus, you were an outsider when you came here asking for a job, same as me. With your...*history*...I was hesitant to hire you on, but I gave you a shot because you said you wanted to make a difference."

"And I am."

"Yes, you certainly are. For the worse." Windham shook his head sadly. "I've been here 28 years, and I can tell you, no one in this town wants this dredged up. They don't want to face whatever truth is out there in those woods. They're comfortable with whispers and stories."

"Okay." He pushed back from the Chief. "Then what do I tell the Lyles Corporation and the foreman out there when they want to know what killed their dog? What smeared blood all over the houses out there?"

Windham winced at the word 'blood.'

"This isn't town business anymore. This isn't hunters swearing they saw Bigfoot. This isn't teenagers wandering into the woods and coming out in body bags. The real world is coming to Asheville whether you like it or not, and they're gonna want answers, not a bunch of ghost stories."

"Oh really? And just what would you tell them, Marcus, if I indulged this obsession of yours? We both know what those samples will say when they come back. The same thing all the other reports in your little collection say." He tapped the bottom drawer of the desk with his heel. "Oh yes, I know all about it. Every one has the same thing, in big red letters." He held up an open hand and punctuated each word as though framing it. "FAMILY FELIDAE, SPECIES UNKNOWN. So what do you think you'll accomplish by pushing this?"

"I don't know!" Shruff jumped up, squeezed around the man in the narrow space, and started into the main room. Eyes turned to him, and this time they didn't turn away. Probably all figured it was the murderous snap they'd been expecting. "Maybe I just want you people to stop being scared to go outside at night! To get up off your asses and DO something about it!"

"Where are you going?" Windham shouted after him.

"To the lab!"

"You're on the clock! The lab will send the results when they have them!"

"Then call it a vacation day! Trust me, I have plenty of those saved up!" Shruff stomped out of the station amid a slew of stares.

20

A man sat at Frank's desk.

In his chair, to be more precise, reclining, legs resting on the bloodstain where Caesar had been displayed like a butcher's daily offering. He inspected his fingernails with the flair of royalty, cleaning them with a bowie knife that looked long enough to gut an elephant. Frank stared at him, utterly at a loss. No one had come in the trailer since the cops left; he felt sure he would've seen someone of this hulk's size even during the labor standoff.

"You're here! Sweet Jesus, thought I'd be waitin all day!" The man at the desk looked like the illegitimate love child of Arnold Schwartzenegger and the late Steve Irwin. Tall and muscular, thickly built, and wearing leather boots that had seen a fair share of rugged terrain. Above these were a pair of stained khaki shorts, exposing a length of hairy, toned legs. He wore a loose blue work shirt, and the ensemble was topped off by a ridiculously dented hunting hat with a wide brim turned up on one side, the kind they wore in movies set in Australia. A ponytail curled from the back of the hat and disappeared down his back. "Well, come on in! Doorway's no place to linger!"

"Who the fuck are you? How'd you get in here?"

"Now, now, no need for that." He slipped the bowie knife into a sheath in his boot and swung his feet off the desk to stand. He towered over Frank by an extra half foot, hat almost brushing the ceiling. "Didn't mean to dance in your pansies, just wanted a word with you. If you're the foreman, that is." He moved aside in the cramped quarters so Frank could get behind his desk.

"I asked you two questions. You haven't answered even one."

The man smiled, a shark's toothy grin. He had the coldest blue eyes, drops of frozen Arctic sea water that make Frank want to shiver. "I can see you're gonna be stuck on this. Name's Deegan. I nosed around in here, but I couldn't catch yours."

Red washed over Frank's vision. He was so tired of meeting colorful new people. "The only name you're gonna catch is Mr. Stanford."

"Fair enough boyo, fair enough. Nice to meet you."

"Can't say the same. How'd you get in here?"

"I walked in, same as you. Doesn't matter though. What does is the fact that I have a proposition that may be useful to you."

Frank groaned. "What are you, a salesman? Listen pal, if you haven't noticed, you picked the wrong day to ask me if I wanted to buy a vacuum cleaner."

Deegan glanced down at the desk, at the tacky, dried bloodstain like an image from a Rorschach test. His nostrils quivered above his grin. "I did notice. Looks like you had some trouble."

"Yeah, some psycho broke in and butchered our dog. Say, you wouldn't know anything about that, would you?"

"More than you might think."

Frank had thrown out the question without thinking, but the seriousness of the reply threw him off track. His mind forged an image of this man burying the knife in his boot into the Doberman's stomach. He suppressed a shiver.

It must've shown on his face though, because Deegan tilted his head back and laughed as he crossed the room. The only other seat in the trailer was a stool in the corner beside the broken window, and he moved it into the middle of the floor and perched on it like a vulture. "No, I didn't do it, Mr. Stanford, but I know who did. I took the liberty of examinin the leavings."

"Are you another cop? A reporter?"

"Wrong again. I'm a hunter."

This time the shiver came and he lurched into motion to hide it, moving around behind his desk. *We're goin huntin, Frankie*, his father whispered, and Frank's dislike of this man was sealed by the mental association. He sat where Deegan had been only minutes before. "What do you want?"

"Well, I'm a bit of a…let's say, 'specialty' hunter. In other words, I'm not some queer that gets his jollies shootin Bambi's mamma. I prefer my prey a bit more dangerous. And rare."

Frank recalled that short story, read years ago in high school, the one about the man that hunted people. Unease was rapidly turning into fear. His father, damn his father and that thirty-year-old bullshit. Every time the word 'hunt' was mentioned he felt like someone socked him in the spine. "Listen Mr…Deegan?…I don't care if you hunt rhinos with your bare hands. It doesn't mean jack to me."

"Actually, it does. As I said, I have a proposition for you."

"Then get to it."

"All right." Deegan's eyes locked onto Frank's like guided missiles. "You have a problem. In fact, this whole town has a problem, from what I hear. I want to solve it, at no cost to you."

Frank narrowed his eyes.

"The Jackal Man, Mr. Stanford. The thing that did this to your dog. I've come a long way to hunt him."

Frank coughed. Put his hand on his desk and then jerked it away. Anything to keep from meeting that gaze. "Ah... let's just skip the fact that your request is a little nutty, and approach it from this angle: why in hell are you asking me?"

"This area is all owned by the Lyles Corporation, correct? And you're a representative of that company? Just wanted to introduce myself, seeing as our paths might cross on occasion."

Frank leaned across the desk. A new thought occurred to him, that this bruiser had been trotted out by Asheville to run him out of town. "Uh, maybe you didn't get the memo, but the Jackal Man ain't real. I don't know what woodwork you freaks are crawling out of, but I had a cop here before you, he didn't come out and say it, but he hinted at the same thing. It's insanity. Mass hysteria."

"If you don't think he's real, then you have nothin to lose by staying out of my way and lettin me get on with the hunt. I'm not asking for a paycheck for services rendered, if you're worried about that. I assure you, I'm a professional."

"A professional lunatic. The last thing I need is a crazy man running around my site with a gun."

Deegan remained frozen so long Frank thought he'd gone to sleep with his eyes open. Then, without warning, he leapt off his stool and recrossed the distance between it and the desk in a heartbeat.

Frank flailed as he tried to protect himself, but the man fell to his knees in front of the desk. Frank was trying to figure out if he was going to beg or perhaps offer a blow job when he collapsed across the top, laying his right ear against the cheap fake wood, right in the middle of the bloodstain, and rested his hands to either side of his head. The fold in his hat kept it from being knocked off.

"He stood right here, on all fours," Deegan whispered, holding out the last word. The hand in front of his face swept the scarred top of the desk. "You can see the indentations where his claws rested. These suckers are so long and heavy he can't even retract 'em to keep from leavin a trail." Deegan's fingertips grazed the wood in a semicircular pattern, sweeping back and forth over some perceived imperfections.

But he thought of the handprint Shruff had shown him on the wall of the incomplete house and found it too easy to picture what this man was describing.

Deegan turned his head so his chin rested on the table, his hat hiding him from Frank's view. There was a sharp intake of breath, like a nose candy sniff. "You can still smell the pheromones he left when he brought the dog in. There's a lot of anger, a lot of fear. It's all so fresh I could probably taste him if I wanted." At last he raised his head to Frank, who had scooted his chair back away as far as the wall would allow.

"I am not a rash man, Mr. Stanford. Hunting gives you patience, if nothin else. I've been to far too many places where the stories were fake, where Goatman and Batboy were just the fevered imaginations of the local populace. I'd planned to scope things out before I committed to talkin with you, make sure I wouldn't be wastin both your time and mine, but this is all the evidence I need. The Jackal Man is the real deal, boyo, and sooner or later...*someone* is gonna bring him down. I want it to be sooner, and I want that someone to be me."

The last vestige of hope that this was a joke or scare tactic died in Frank.

With Deegan still kneeling in front of the desk, he whispered, "Get out."

For the first time, Deegan was the one put off stride. He frowned.

"Get out now," Frank repeated, "or I will call the police."

There was a flash of what could only be fury in those cold blue circles, there and gone, and then the smarmy smile returned to melt it. He stood up. "I guess that's what I get for tryin to help someone out. With the way you're actin... you'd think I was dangerous." He winked. "But I couldn't be *dangerous*, could I?"

"All right you son of a bitch, you had your chance." Frank reached for his pocket. "I don't take threats from complete—"

The sentence evaporated. Deegan was gone, the door to Frank's trailer standing open to the heat.

Frank got up, crossed the room at a run, and looked out the door. The lot was swarming with workers, but he couldn't spot the hunter.

"Boo!" Deegan swung around the outside of the door where he'd been standing and shouted the word in his face, causing a jolt through Frank's system. He was still clutching his chest as Deegan chuckled, waved a hand, and said, "Be seein you." He strolled away across the lot.

Crazy townspeople, superstitious construction workers, cryptic cops, zealous hunters. It was like the fucking Village People of the straitjacket set. If they started singing "YMCA" he was leaving, and Lyles could shove it.

The phone went off in Frank's hand, almost causing him to drop it. He'd never been so jumpy in his life (well, maybe not his *entire* life) as he'd been since crossing the Asheville city limits. He answered and found Damon waiting on the other end of a static-filled line.

"I just got back into town. How are things progressing?"

Frank told him exactly how things were progressing. He didn't even get to the innuendo-laden conversation with the detective or the intense Deegan maniac. He kind of wanted the hunter to recede to the dim corners of his memory.

"Jesus Christ! Someone killed the fucking dog?"

"That's what I said. Listen Damon, you have to get back here and help me clean this up. We're down to maybe thirty guys and I have no idea what to do about this investigation."

"First of all, don't worry about the crew. I'll get you more guys if I have to ship them over from Mexico City. I'm just worried things might be worse than we thought."

"Why? What do you mean?"

Damon's voice wavered in and out on the phone, but Frank could still detect the hesitation in it. "Let's get together tonight. Go out for drinks. That town's got to have a bar somewhere in it."

Frank thought of the dimly lit interior of The Howler and the dopey, yet slightly angry, faces of its inhabitants. "Yeah, it does, but Jesus Damon, what the hell's going on now? I remember when this job used to be about building houses. Now I feel like I'm in the middle of the X-Files."

"If so, it's a conspiracy episode. Look, I'll meet you at the site tonight around seven. Keep all this mum."

"That won't be a problem," Frank said. Who was he going to tell?

Damon hung up, and Frank slumped against the door of the trailer.

21

Shruff killed most of the day working on other cases that Asheville assisted surrounding municipalities with due to their abundance of manpower. Then, after the samples became a corkscrew twisting through the base of his brain, he headed into Arlington, hoping he'd given the lab boys at least a few minutes with the samples.

He arrived at the central downtown police station and entered behind a handcuffed youth struggling against his patrolmen captors. Inside, several officers shouted a greeting; several others yelled a taunt. Since both were more than he got back home, he took them in stride. It was almost like he was a real person here, outside the bubble of hostility and weirdness over Asheville.

The female receptionist was a young blond that always flirted with him but whose eyes had a habit of straying to his throat every few seconds. Around him, everyone had the bedroom eyes of a vampire. Just as well. He could never focus long enough to be serious about a relationship.

Shruff rode the elevator up to the fifth floor, turned two corners, and pushed through the door marked FORENSICS.

"Well, look who's back," the older woman behind this reception desk said. "Does this look like a gym to you, Shruff?"

"Uh, no?"

"Then quit using our equipment and find your own lab."

He gave a rare grin. "Phil around?"

"In his office. Sure he'll be thrilled to see you."

"Who wouldn't?"

He wove his way through drug labs, DNA sequencers and ballistic testers, greeting a few white-coated lab techs without being intrusive, until he reached the office of Director Phil Howard. Shruff entered without knocking.

Phil looked up from a microscope on his desk, blinking a few times before his eyes came into focus. "Jesus, Shruff, your shit just got here this morning!"

"But you've got something for me, right?"

"It takes hours just to even prep a sample like that! I won't be able to run an STR or send it through CODIS till next week!"

"I'll save you the time. You're not gonna find any DNA matches in the database."

"Don't I know it. But we do have crimes of our own to solve here." Phil shook his head and rubbed the bridge of his nose. His bald head gleamed in the harsh fluorescents. "Fuck you and your goddamn Jackal Man shit! Anything to get you to leave me alone! I know pit bulls that let go of a bone faster than you!" He reached for a folder of papers on his desk. "I ran the sequencing and did a quick species comparison, all right? You gave us the blood, the body of the dog, the unidentified sample—believed to be urine—and..."

"The photographs. Of the handprint."

Phil slipped on a pair of reading glasses. "I'm going to make this quick. The blood wasn't all dog. Looks like different species of rodent, but I won't know what until final analysis."

"That's what I thought."

"You find any bodies out there?"

"Nothing besides the dog."

"Takes a lot of itty bitty mice and chipmunks to get that much blood, you know. You didn't find a single one?"

He shrugged.

"Anyway, regarding the dog," Phil read again, "the wound was examined, trace DNA, yada yada, blah blah, came from something of—"

"Family *Felidae*, species unknown," Shruff finished.

"You got it. Or as we like to call it around here, the Asheville special. We think the species should be called *Shrufficus*, if it's ever found. What do you think?"

"I think I'm glad you haven't found it, Phil."

"Anyway, that's all I can tell you without some serious work-ups."

"What about the urine?"

"The only thing I can tell you about the urine is that it's not urine. Got the same DNA in it, but no waste matter. All chemical, all pheromone."

"Huh?"

Phil removed the reading glasses, and laid the report down. "Listen Shruff, this isn't our deal. When we need help with an animal case, we bring in a professional. Why you haven't done so in the past five years is beyond me."

"Because this is free. Asheville PD isn't gonna pay to bring in an expert to talk about something they don't want to hear. Besides, what do I have to give them except a bunch of stories?"

Phil slapped the folder on his desk with the back of his hand. "This stuff, and the pictures of the handprint, there's not much we can do with those."

Shruff's face fell. This was what happened, every time. He got a lead, something concrete, and then it all came to a brick wall at sixty miles per hour. "What do I do now?"

"I'm referring you. To somebody more in line with what you need, someone else to feed this obsession. You're sick Shruff, you know that?"

"Just give me the name."

"Bob Oakland. He works at the Fort Worth Zoo as their expert on big cats. Now, God knows I don't believe in all that Jackal Man crap, but I sent copies of everything over to him already. He's expecting you, and he'll talk to you for free. Godspeed, and get outta here."

The zoo was further out of the way, but he didn't mind. Shruff hadn't been to a zoo since he was ten. He'd developed an intense fear of them right around the time he turned eighteen.

At the ticket booth, he flashed his badge to get in without charge, although they seemed like they still wanted a donation. The zoo had fallen on hard times. Much easier to watch Animal Planet these days.

He was pointed in the direction of the big cats area and started off on broad, plant-lined avenues. The tourist crowd was no more than a trickle. Most of the animals were being fed, keepers utilizing low traffic volume to take the displays out of the window. Already he felt light-headed, pulse audible in his throbbing ears. He walked under a faux wooden archway with the words 'Cat Country' and passed tigers, bobcats, and mountain lions with no more than a glance, but paused when he reached the cheetah.

Shruff studied the face for a moment. Black pattern of

spots, ears pointing off the head in two triangles, sleek fur. Its eyes, murky and shaded, stared coolly back at him.

His breath caught, and he moved on before panic could settle in.

When he reached the lions, he found something to distract him. A man in khaki shorts stood inside the enclosure close to a door in the fake mountain backdrop. He was old, in his sixties, thinning hair as white as fresh snow. He also looked too thin and bony to be doing what he was doing.

In his hands was a fireman's hose going full throttle, the pressure enough that he could barely stay on his feet. The spray blasted directly into the face of a lion that sat ten yards away. The king of beasts looked like a wet sock now, mane hanging around his face in limp strands. He tried to roar, but water filled his mouth. He raised a paw the size of a dinner plate to slap at the stream.

"Bath time?" Shruff shouted over the gush of the hose.

The man gave a pleasant grin. "Whether he likes it or not!"

"Can you tell me where I can find Bob Oakland?"

The hose shut off. The lion shook like a wet dog, grumbling deep in his throat. "That would be me. Which must make you Detective Shruff. Come around the back so we can talk." Oakland retreated into the concrete mountain, dragging the hose behind him. The lion gave him one last baleful look.

Shruff entered through an employee only entrance, praying he wasn't walking into a cage of rabid baboons. He found his way back to a small utility room where the older man was winding up the hose amid shelves of tools and feed. They shook hands. Oakland's face was as weathered and wrinkled as the rest of him, but full of life.

"Phil faxed me all your findings, with some notes of his own." Oakland turned his head to the side, examining Shruff at an angle. He waited for the vet's eyes to play over the twisted scar on his neck, but he kept his gaze carefully above nose level. The man would ask eventually though, everyone did, and then Shruff would have to decide which lie to tell. "You don't look like a detective. Too young."

"And you look a bit old to be lion feed."

"Touché."

Shruff had practically been jittering with excitement on the way over, but now he didn't know how to start the conversation.

Oakland relieved the pressure. "I know all about Asheville's answer to Lizard Boy, Detective. I believe his name is the Jackal Man, although I am curious how that particular moniker came about. Every description I've ever heard was of a cat, which is also why, I assume, you came to me. You are aware that the jackal is a member of the dog family?"

"I like to think it's one of those legendary misnamings, right up there with Columbus calling the Native Americans 'Indians'. From my research, I think the root actually comes from the fact that the sound he makes is more like a bark than a meow."

"Or maybe it just sounded scarier than Leopard Man." Oakland smiled at him sidelong. He was clearly having fun, but Shruff couldn't tell if it was at his expense. "Sounds like it might have overtones of the Egyptian deities, Anubis and so forth."

"I think you give the people of Asheville far too much credit." In an effort to turn the conversation away, if only long enough for him to plan his approach, he asked, "If you don't mind me asking, what kind of experience do you have with this sort of thing?"

"Well, if you mean modern day mythological creatures, then none. But if you're talking about cats in general, I assure you, I'm the best you're liable to find in the great state of Texas. I contributed to over two hundred reports over the last thirty years and participated in numerous field studies dealing with every aspect of exotic feline species. I only stopped that because the younger crop was coming up behind me and my body just couldn't take the grueling wilderness for months on end. I took a position here because I'm always needed, and I can still do the work I love. It sure beats those retirees that become door greeters at Wal-mart." His words sped up near the end, leaving him out of breath. "And in spite of all that, a better question would be, why come to me, Detective? Why not find yourself a good cryptozoologist? That's the study of—"

"I know what it is. I wrote my thesis on it."

Now Oakland looked like he was really struggling to hold back laughter. "Then you know the difference between the concrete and verifiable animals that I deal in, and the possibly non-existent ones that they do."

"This one exists."

"You have a long road to convince the rest of the world, Detective."

"I know that. That's why I need a professional, not some quack hunting the Jersey Devil or Bigfoot."

"Ah, how badly you want your town's legend believed, and yet you quickly pass off others who request the same."

Shruff had nothing to say to that, mostly because it was true. He hated urban legends; they all sounded like the boy who cried wolf these days.

"So, what exactly do you want to know then?"

"For starters, tell me about the yellow liquid we found.

They told me it wasn't urine."

"It's not. Some of the big cats have a gland above the anus that squirts out a special scent fluid used to mark territory. I recognized the composition as soon as I saw the fax."

"That would explain the smell."

"Pungent, was it? Yes, I imagine so. But then there's the photograph."

"Yes?"

"I can honestly say I've never seen anything like it. Sure, it *resembles* a paw print, but the fingers are splayed with each digit separate, and it has an opposable thumb, for God's sake. It's got to be the most laughable hoax ever perpetrated."

"But just suppose," Shruff pushed, "just pretend, that it came from an actual, honest-to-God cat. What would be the significance?"

"Besides an evolutionary track unlike anything the planet has ever seen? Which, by the way, is utter horseshit. But if you stay with the cat theory, there are plenty of felines that claw to show ownership. That's why cute, fluffy Mittens will tear your drapes to shreds. Somebody is trying very hard to make it look like a cat is starting a territory dispute."

"So you really believe it's a fake?"

Oakland nodded. Much too quickly for Shruff's liking.

"What about the scent fluid? How easy would that be to fake?"

"Admittedly, not very. With this sort of composition, you would need access to the real thing, and of course, the DNA workups tell me this is from—however little I want to admit it—a heretofore unknown species of cat. But if you're trying to goad me into siding with you that the Jackal Man is real, you're wasting your time. The furthest I'll go is to say you might have an undiscovered species of wild cat in your woods, Detective. One that's fueled Asheville's hysteria for a long time."

"If that were true, how come no one has ever caught one or killed one? How could an animal stay hidden for so many years in such a populated area?"

"Species stay hidden in the public view all the time. Just last year they discovered a new strain of butterfly in downtown New York City."

Shruff clenched his teeth. "I'm not talking about butterflies, Mr. Oakland."

The other man shrugged. "You want something more from me, I'll be happy to go out to the place and have a look. I've got nothing to lose and, who knows, maybe it's not too late for me to get another credit to my name if we discover you've got *Felidae Shrufficus* running around out there."

Shruff scowled. "Did Phil tell you to say that?"

"He didn't tell me *not* to say that."

"Whatever. Listen, I'll have to talk to the foreman out there, find out when we get on the site. He seems kind of jumpy about the whole thing."

"Can't say I blame him." Oakland ripped a scrap of paper from a clipboard on one of the shelves and scribbled down a number. "That's my home number. I don't have a cell. Let me know when you find something and I'll be at your disposal. Keep in mind, they're forecasting rain for tomorrow. If the evidence isn't protected, it'll be gone."

"Thank you," Shruff said, resisting the urge to say much, much more.

22

Damon arrived at the site shortly before six-thirty, as the last of the workers were leaving. Frank showed him around the carnage-filled yard. He guessed the way he'd described it over the phone hadn't done it justice, because Damon lapsed into a rare silence. They didn't speak a word, except in mutual agreement to leave when the ground gobbled up the sun and the shadows got too deep. They took separate cars to the The Howler.

It was Friday night and the place was jumping, or as jumping as Frank assumed it ever got. They kept their silence as they mounted the steps where Frank had talked with Raphael Barrio mere days before. As they entered, the fifteen occupants grouped at the various tables swiveled to look at the newcomers. Most turned away, but several lingered too long. The bartender was different than the man Frank had seen earlier in the week. Other than that, the place was still the same dismal, dark dive. Somewhere, the musical stylings of Tim McGraw played low.

They drifted to a table, plopping into the first empty chairs. Frank watched his friend carefully. The disturbed look on his face was like a mental patient doped up on too much Thorazine.

Yet it was Damon that answered first when the waitress came to take their order. "Beer," he rasped. "Anything. Just get me drunk quick and keep 'em coming."

"The same," Frank said. After she left, he let his attention wander. A man at the bar caught his gaze with an angry frown and knitted eyebrows.

A bad idea, coming here. They knew who he was now. He and Damon wouldn't be able to talk freely.

McGraw switched to a plucky Big and Rich tune, and still they said nothing. Frank laced his hands together.

Damon spoke while staring at the tabletop. "Why the hell would someone do that Frank?"

"There aren't too many reasons. Either it was just some random thing...or somebody was targeting us. Targeting the site. We're not exactly popular in this town." Several men at the bar snuck not-so-covert glances in their direction. A group at the back whispered and pointed behind Damon's back. Frank squirmed in his chair.

"Why?"

"For the same reason those Mexicans are afraid to work at the site."

The conversation at last grabbed Damon enough for him to look up from the table. "Are you...are you telling me this is about that fucking *thing*? The Whatever Man?"

"Jackal. And yes, somebody is trying to scare us off, that's all." Deegan slipped through his thoughts, there and gone with a hearty, 'Boyo.'

"That's *all*? You say, 'that's motherfucking *all*?'" Damon's usually deep voice grew more shrill on each word. "Shit, Frank, this is not your ordinary, run-of-the-mill vandalism! I don't even want to think about how crazy a person has to be to do something like that! Not to mention the fact that whoever did it got close enough to a trained guard dog to kill it by hand!"

The waitress arrived with a drink and a dirty look for each of them. Frank took large swallows from his stein, the edge of his tension draining away after the liquid got to his stomach.

"I mean, I thought this was supposed to be a cozy little town," Damon continued, his voice becoming incrementally louder. "But you got psychos carving up dogs in the middle of the night in the woods and using their blood for graffiti!"

"Damon, keep your voice down!"

But it was too late.

"Hey!" one of the locals shouted from the far end of the bar. He slid off his stool and sauntered over to them.

"Now you've done it," Frank growled. Damon turned in his chair to see what was coming.

The man was blue collar all the way, a dark mechanic jumpsuit halfway zipped and filthy work boots. A crowd of locals followed him. He reached their table and asked, "You're some of them dudes buildin out on the Dark Road, ain't ya? Some of them *River Meadows* fellas." He made the venture sound like a racial identity.

"Maybe. Who wants to know?"

"Gotta tell you boys, we think that's a bad idea. A *real* bad idea."

"Excuse me," Damon said softly, "we were having a private conversation. This doesn't concern you."

"Oh, but it does. It concerns everyone in this town." He sat down in one of the two empty chairs at their table and the crowd backed off, sitting in chairs and on nearby tables like kindergarteners at story time. There was something familiar to Frank about the entire set up. "You know, we tried to do things the legal way, but we can get rougher if we gotta. That is, if the Jackal Man doesn't run you out first. Heard he's still pickin the last fella outta his teeth."

"You tell 'em, John Boyd!" someone in the bar testified.

Damon cleared his throat. "You believe in the tooth fairy too?"

John Boyd smiled. "Ain't never seen the tooth fairy. Can't say the same for the Jackal Man."

"That's bullshit," Frank snapped.

"You callin me a liar?"

"If you're pedaling a story like that, yeah, I am."

The two of them stared across the table for a long moment, and then John Boyd relented. "Yeah, I useta be like that. All my life, growin up here, I didn't really listen. And then one night, I'm comin home after a job down south, and I took the Dark Road. Passed right by that field you're buildin in."

His eyes glazed over as he lost himself in the story. There was such a degree of intense deep thought in his expression that Frank became convinced that one of two things was happening: the man was telling the truth, or he *believed* he was. The rest of the bar dwellers listened raptly, though they'd surely heard the story before, and again Frank was struck by an uncanny déjà vu.

"I look over to my left, and right out in that field I seen somethin. Just kind of…caught my eye, you know? And, like a dumbass, I slowed to check it out. And there's…there's somethin standin there. Watchin me." Now the entire bar was frozen. The bartender had stopped work as he listened. The waitress killed the last twangy strands of Garth Brooks to allow silence.

And Frank finally understood his familiarity with this tableau.

That night when he was twelve, it just kept coming back to that, sitting around a campfire with his father and four other men, listening to that goddamn story, being sent into the woods, darkness all around, the feel of a hunting rifle in his sweaty little hands...

John Boyd was still talking, unaware one member of his intended audience had retreated into memory. "It stood on two legs, but that was really all I could see of it. It was just too dark. But it had these glowin eyes. Green. Wasn't no further from me than I am from the door right now." Everyone turned their heads to measure this distance and nodded approvingly. "I had come to a complete stop now, tryin to figger out what someone would be doin out there at that time of night. And this thing raises a hand up, like it was reachin for the sky...and I seen claws on it. Big ones, must've been... I don't know, a half foot or so. Then...it lets out this awful roar...and starts chargin me. It covered half the distance before I could get my foot on the gas. I floored it...and... well...I never took that way home again!" He raised his beer and several of his buddies clinked their glasses to it.

Frank wiped at his brow. "That is...the dumbest...most ignorant thing...I have ever heard anyone say. *Ever.*"

Damon snickered.

John Boyd pounded his beer on the table, an arc of brown splashing across the front of Damon's suit, and leapt out of his chair. "You goddamn outsiders think you know everything, don't ya?"

Frank stood, eager for a fight, anything to get his blood moving and not let them see how shaky he was. "I sure as hell know when I'm being fed a shit sandwich."

"Cause it matches the shit in your brain!"

Boyd grabbed the collar of Frank's shirt and pulled back with the other hand.

Damon jumped to his feet to intercede and was dragged back by the crowd. Frank's hands flew, one hoping to deflect a blow and the other rearing back.

"Hold it right there, all of you," an authoritative voice called from the door.

Frank looked up to find the detective from that morning coming into the bar, in all his hideously scarred glory.

"I ought to throw you in the drunk tank for inciting a riot, Boyd."

"They started it." The man released Frank and stepped away. Damon was set free and came around the table to stand beside Frank.

"Hello, Mr. Stanford." The detective turned to the bartender. "Under the circumstances, I'm sure you won't mind waving the tab on these two. I'm taking them with me."

With a final sneer at their attacker, Frank turned to go.

"You'll be lucky if you don't hear from my attorney," Damon sniffed. John Boyd pretended to quake with fear as they left the bar.

23

Outside, Damon threw up his hands and shouted, "Jesus Christ! Was this just the Friday night, rough-up-the-new-guys routine or were they really ready to fight us over that story?"

Shruff spoke before Frank could answer. "People around here take the Jackal Man very seriously, as I tried to explain to Mr. Stanford. And fighting for a belief can bring out the worst in people."

"Who is this guy, Socrates?" Damon stood at the top of the steps as he spoke, trying—unsuccessfully—to wipe beer off his suit jacket. Frank saw him sneak a look at the scar marring the newcomer's throat.

"This is the investigator working on the case at the site. Detective Shruff, right? This my boss, Damon Bradford."

"Oh. Thanks for stepping in. They might've moved on to lynching if we'd been in there any longer."

The detective gave a tired smile and came to a stop on the stairs down to the sidewalk. "I know it won't mean much, but they're not bad guys. They just care about their town, and they're really scared about what you guys are doing out there."

"Enough to butcher a dog?" Frank asked.

"They're not responsible for what happened. I know everyone in this town. I may not like them, but I *know* them, and not one person here is capable of the kind of violence that occurred at the construction site."

"Then who is?" Damon demanded. "The dog didn't commit suicide! Surely you must have some leads or theories or something! And don't tell me it was the fucking Jackal Man!"

"I think it's very important you understand something about this town." Shruff's face was as serious as any preacher that ever proselytized about damnation. "The Jackal Man isn't just some story that a bunch of drunken hicks made up to amuse themselves. The history goes back, you understand? The Indian folklore from the tribes that used to live in this area mention something, some...*being*...whose land must be kept 'sacred and separate.' Their word for him translated to 'Green Eyes Glowing.' And then the Spaniards swung through here, plundering everything they could get their hands on. De Soto came right through Asheville with one expedition. From them you get several accounts of what they called, 'the Night Stalker,' something they claim came into the camps at night and slaughtered the men. Asheville was founded and settled, but every time the town expanded and ate up a little more of the land to the south, something bad would happen. Town fires, unsolved murders...animal mutilations."

Frank thought of the town's construction. All those homes huddled together. If the detective was right, the town was literally *built* on fear. "Is all that common knowledge, or have you just done some homework?" *And maybe filled in the gaps with your own imagination?*

"Most of it's lost to history, just vague references in town bulletins or newspapers from other cities. But, more recently, there is a documented case file surrounding those woods. A lot of very real people, with real names and real families, have either disappeared or been found dead out there over the past few decades, including your foreman Gammon."

Damon twitched. "What do you know about that?"

"I know Gammon's brother was the last person to ever hear from him. That he called and said he'd been fired and planned on leaving town, and then...nothing. We investigated, cooperated with Missing Persons, but came up empty. Your boss Lyles asked us to keep it quiet." Damon shot Frank a narrow-eyed look. "So maybe now you understand why they take this 'story' so seriously."

"Okay, so it goes back." Damon had that quiet, intense tone again. "But you didn't answer the question. If none of the townsfolk killed our dog and vandalized our site, *who did?*"

The detective looked from one to the other, lips on the verge of parting. Something about him reminded Frank of Willie when he wanted to tell the truth but couldn't seem to turn off the lies. "I...I don't know. I need more time, and I need back in the site."

"No." Frank shook his head. "You've done everything you can, and now this is over. We don't need anyone else slowing us down."

"I can't force you. I was on my way to your house when I noticed your truck parked in front of the bar. To be honest, I could never get a search warrant. No judge will give me permission to pursue this. Folks in this town may talk about the Jackal Man a lot, but they're not big on taking any sort of action."

"Jesus, you really believe in him, don't you?" Damon stared at him as though he expected antennae to sprout from his forehead. "But not like those idiots in there do. You... you know something."

Shruff just stared at his feet.

"Frank," Damon said, still studying the detective, "do you have an extra key to the site?"

"The one I was gonna give you."

"Give it to the detective."

Frank started to lean close and whisper before he realized it wouldn't make any difference. "Do you really think that's a good idea?"

"Give it to him, Frank. I trust him more than anyone else in this town. Besides, I want to know who killed that dog, and where Wesley Gammon disappeared to."

Frank pulled the key from his ring and handed it to the detective.

"Thank you." Shruff looked anxious to leave now that he had what he'd come for. "It was nice meeting you both. As soon as I have anything definite, I'll contact you." He left them standing on the steps of the Howler, all but running to his car.

"What was with his neck?" Damon plucked at the loose skin beneath his own chin. "You don't suppose...?"

"Don't even fucking say it, Damon."

"How did he even survive whatever did that?"

"I don't know, and I really don't know if giving him free reign of the site was the best idea. We should just let this whole thing die. You didn't really buy into that crap, did you?"

"Of course not." But the way he said it didn't entirely convince Frank. "But since he won't find anything, what does it hurt to let him look? Besides...there *is* another possibility, the one I didn't want to mention over the phone. Have you considered the fact that maybe Lyles is responsible for this?"

"Lyles?" Frank tried to imagine the short man tearing the dog apart, blood splattering on one of his Armani suits, and then skipping around the site with a paint pail.

"Well, maybe not Lyles himself, but he could've hired someone. Just a little roadblock to make sure you don't finish the work. Maybe even hoping to scare you away. The Board certainly couldn't blame him if no one was willing to do the job."

"You really think he would resort to something like that?"

Damon raised a sardonic eyebrow.

"What about Gammon?" Frank asked. "You think Lyles had anything to do with his disappearance? I mean, Jesus, did he have him *killed*? To keep him from talking?"

"The only way to find out is to let the police in on it. That detective seems eager enough to find out."

"Yeah, but I kinda want to make sure I don't disappear the same way."

"He wouldn't let you bring Trish and the kids if he was planning that."

"It kind of makes you wonder, if the people who live here don't want us to build these houses, and our own boss doesn't want us to build these houses, what the fuck are we building them for?"

Damon chuckled, but the sound was strained. "I don't want Lyles to win on this one. I want to see the look on his face when we finish."

Frank nodded, not bothering to bring up the fact that either way, Lyles would win. If they didn't finish, he fired them, weathered the lawsuit from the Board, and washed his hands of River Meadows forever. If they did, he sold the houses and made his profit.

They said their goodbyes and departed.

24

Even though the matter seemed to have blown over, shame and guilt lingered for Willie the rest of the day, and he tried to stay out of the same room as his mother. When she announced his father had a meeting after work and would be home late, he didn't know whether to be relieved or not. He slumped upstairs to his room without dinner, closed the door, and flopped down on his bed to read comics until sleep overtook him.

He was two panels into his first issue when there was a small noise at his window, a sound as tiny as the *tic* of a second hand on a clock.

Willie peeked over the foot of his bed. With the lights on, he could see only the reflection of his room in the glass, laid over a backdrop of dark night beyond. He stared into the strange negative and thought he saw something move in that muddled black.

But his bedroom was on the second floor, with only a narrow ledge outside.

Tap. Tap, tap.

This time he heard it clearly, saw the glass tremble, causing the reflection to quiver like a mirage.

Willie stood, but instead of going to the window, he went

to the light switch beside the door. Muscles tense, he flipped the switch.

And gasped at the horrible face with fiery red eyes leering in at him.

Then the face transformed, features spreading out until Willie at last recognized Zerk. The boy pulled away from where he'd been smooshed against the glass and laughed hysterically. The bald side of his head was so pale it actually glowed in the moonlight. His contacts tonight were solid red ovals.

Willie sighed in relief and crossed the room to slide up the window. "What the hell are you doing here?"

"Classic man, classic. You shoulda seen your face!" Zerk hung halfway off the roof. The rest of him clung to a rain gutter on the side of the house. Nails was in the yard below, waving up at him.

"Thanks a lot for yesterday, you assholes! I thought my dad was gonna kill me!"

"Well, you ain't dead, so it couldn'ta been that bad."

"How did you know where I live?"

Nails whisper-yelled from below, "There ain't too many people that move in or out of Asheville, Willie!"

"Fine, you found me. What do you want?"

"We're gonna hang out, Will-ster," Zerk said. "Wanna go with?"

He'd thought he would only be too happy to never see this pair again. And now that they were here, offering companionship, he found his anger fading. He wanted *friends*, damn it, he wanted somebody on this planet besides Miles to think he was cool, and, for some unknown reason, these guys liked him.

"They really will kill me if I sneak out, especially after yesterday."

"So let 'em." Zerk shrugged. "You think too much."

"Some would say that's a good thing."

"Yeah, but sometimes you gotta live for the moment. Party tonight; face the music tomorrow. Grab some rose petals while you can, or whatever. I've been living by that philosophy since I was eleven, and just look at me now." He raised his hands to strike a pose and almost fell off the roof.

It was eerie how close Zerk came to reading his mind.

"Get out of the way." Willie stepped out onto the roof.

Less than ten minutes later, they were riding bikes down deserted streets, Willie once again perched on the back of Zerk's seat. Nails and Zerk whooped and hollered as they rode, weaving as close to one another as possible without colliding. A night breeze sprang up, ruffling his hair as they rode, and Willie wanted to laugh at the feeling of freedom coursing through him.

Nails slowed his pace until they were even. "So did your old man beat you yesterday or what?"

Willie was shocked at the idea. "Naw, I'm just kinda grounded, but it's a secret between him and me. He made me promise not to do it again. And of course, it was kind of implied I couldn't hang out with you guys anymore."

"Wow. That's a cool dad," Zerk said over his shoulder.

"Yeah, my old man woulda kicked my ass all the way to the town line."

"Only if your dad got sober enough to know who you are."

"Shut up, Zerk."

Willie had to stop and think about that claim. His dad? Cool?

And here he was, betraying the man again. Suddenly, this ride didn't feel so exhilarating anymore.

They rode on, turned a corner and traveled down a long road with no houses on either side, and no streetlights above. He ducked under Zerk's arm to see in front of them. Ahead, the road disappeared into an ocean of black where the outline of trees floated. It looked like an open mouth with fangs made of tree bark, and they were riding toward it without slowing.

"Wait a minute, where are we going?"

"The woods," Nails replied. "Duh."

"The *woods*? What about all that stuff you told me, about the Jackal Man?"

Nails grinned. "He doesn't kill *everybody* that comes out here. Did we tell you about the two kids in the convertible, like, ten years ago? One of 'em lived, and spent the rest of his life in an insane asylum!"

"You said they both died, and you said it just happened!"

"Did I?" Nails turned his head, audibly cracking his neck. "Well, I heard it both ways."

Willie held on to Zerk tighter. The night seemed cold now, and pressing. The darkness around them would've been absolute if not for the moon, visible in the small strip of sky that the trees on both sides of the road didn't crowd out. He stared into the gloomy woods. A thousand shadows moved and swayed in there, like people rocking hypnotically to slow music. Even if the Jackal Man was a story—which Willie was *almost* convinced of—there could be other things in there just as dangerous.

"Relax dude. We come out here all the time," Zerk said. "Testing fate, you know?"

They rode in silence. The trees to their right ended abruptly, and a field overtook the side of the road. Willie recognized the place from when he'd driven through here with his family on the way into town.

Somewhere just down the road was that sign with the claw marks.

Nails stopped pedaling to scan the meadow. "We haven't been out here since they started building those houses though. Everybody in town's so pissed off about it, we thought we should come out and show our support."

"My dad's the foreman. That's the reason we're here."

"No shit? Your dad works out there?" Zerk raised his arm from the handlebars and pointed into the field. The squat silhouette of houses under construction interrupted the horizon, like tombstones at the top of a hill in a horror movie. The only difference was, those movies usually had a full moon, if only for lighting purposes. The three of them didn't even have the benefit of a single flashlight.

Suddenly the dark felt so tight it was claustrophobic. Willie longed to turn around and go back to the safety of the streetlights.

Their pace down the road had slowed, and he hoped one of his companions would say they were bored and suggest going back. But instead, Nails stood up on the pedals of his fancy BMX to pump them harder and shouted, "Let's go check it out!" He crossed in front of Zerk's bike and rode through the rough grass.

"I don't think we should do that," Willie said. Too easy to imagine one of these guys vandalizing something expensive that his father would spend the next ten years taking out of his allowance. "It's all locked up and...and they have a big guard dog!"

"Cool! Let's tease it!" Zerk pedaled after Nails with Willie nearly teetering the bike over.

They abandoned the rides in a steep ditch beside the road and went to stand at the gate.

"Here poochy! C'mon boy!" Zerk taunted.

They stared through the fence links, wrapped their fingers through the mesh. On the other side, the houses held their secrets, each one a cave that could lead to the depths of the earth.

"I don't see any guard dog."

"I thought I heard my dad say they got one."

"Well, let's get a closer look, shall we?" Nails hooked his fingers into the fence and hoisted himself up. He dug the toes of his boots into the mesh and climbed. Zerk followed. Willie stood at the bottom until one of them called him a pussy and then started up, not because he was having anything that could be remotely mistaken as fun, but because he didn't want to be left alone on this side of the enclosure.

He was coming down the other side when Zerk, the first one to touch down, bounded into the seat of a big, yellow bulldozer parked next to the fence. "Look at me! I'm a construction worker!"

"Naw, too smart for you," Nails told him.

"Bitch! I'll kick your ass!" Zerk jumped down and chased Nails, who ducked between two of the house frames. Willie was left alone, trying to follow the sounds of their chase with uneasy steps. They came back out far ahead of him, crossing the dirt lane and then disappearing amid the structures on the opposite side. Quiet fell across the yard.

"Guys? Where'd you go?" He came forward, peering in their last direction, but his eyes weren't strong enough to penetrate the dark crevices.

A furtive noise behind him. Willie turned to the opposite row of houses. It came again, a softly shuffled footstep, but he couldn't pin down the source. He knew only one thing: there was no way Nails and Zerk could get across the wide dirt lane separating the houses without Willie seeing them.

He felt watched. The sensation was entirely new, but instantly identifiable. Alien eyes played over his skin, eyes with intelligence driving them, and perhaps malevolence.

Don't be stupid, he thought, waiting for his alter ego to back him up.

But the other Willie, so good at getting him into trouble, remained silent.

Willie backed away without much thought besides escape—anything to get out of the view of this presence—and slipped into the dark cover of one of the houses. He hid behind a wide piece of particleboard and watched the other houses for movement in the shadows. Blood, quickened by fear, pounded in his ears like waves on a rocky shore.

He was tackled from behind without warning, his unreleased scream turning into a gasp. Zerk spun him around and slammed him against the wall with Nails looking over his shoulder. He cackled. "Got you again, Willie!"

"Shhhh!" Willie whispered savagely. "There's somebody in here with us!"

"Huh?"

Zerk looked above Willie's head, squinting in the darkness. "Yo man, wait up. What is *that?*"

Willie twisted his head up to see a streak of something dark staining the speckled wood, only visible because of a shaft of moonlight streaming through the half-finished roof.

"Looks like paint," Nails said.

Willie looked around. "It's everywhere!"

The random slashes surrounded them, deeper darkness in the shadows and night. They spun in slow circles, taking it all in. Through a missing wall, Willie could see similar markings on the other houses. He hadn't noticed them on the way in.

"This is way creepy," Zerk murmured. "Like, satanic-ritual-creepy."

"I'm telling you, there's something in here with us!"

"Some*thing?* Dude, you just said it was some*one!*"

"Quiet, both of you!" Nails cut in. "Listen."

The sound they heard was faint.

Footsteps.

Someone was walking right down the middle of the aisle between the houses, crunching in the dirt. A shadow, cast by the sliver moon, flitted across the broken surfaces of the construction as the figure passed by.

Willie glanced at Nails. The boy's face was as ashen as Zerk's. It made the gruesome tattoo on his neck even darker, the fingers no longer in his skin but resting *on* it, a real hand reaching to throttle him. His eyes bulged from their sockets. Seeing the older, tougher guy in the grip of fear made Willie feel like he'd swallowed acid.

And that was why he pushed through it to do what they couldn't.

On legs that no longer had any feeling, Willie crept to the end of one of the sheet rock walls and watched the movements of the figure outside.

25

Shruff flew away from the bar, breaking numerous traffic laws.

The key to River Meadows burned through the material of his jeans like a live coal. He hadn't been on the Dark Road after sunset in six years, you couldn't have dragged him out there last night, and now he couldn't stop his hands from steering the vehicle that direction.

He drove with one hand so he could call Oakland with the other. The zookeeper picked up on the third ring, sounding even older on the phone.

"It's Shruff."

"Detective? I was expecting a call tomorrow."

"I have a key to the site and permission to check the place out unsupervised. How fast can you get here?"

"You want to look around *now*? In the dark?"

"About as much as I want to stick my finger in a socket, but I want you to have a crack at this stuff while it's fresh. Like you said, if it rains tomorrow…"

Oakland took a long minute to reply, and when he did his voice was huskier, softer, pressed into the phone. "I'm kind of in the middle of something with a lady friend, Detective. The kind of activity that you, being a young man of consenting age, should also probably be engaged in at this time of night instead of bothering me."

Shruff didn't know if this was comical or sickening, but, either way, the man was seeing more action than he had in the last three years. "Fine, have fun. But guess who won't be getting any credit when we discover a brand new species out here. This is your last shot at greatness setting sail."

He was sure the elderly man would hang up at the sophomoric taunt, but Oakland sighed and said, "You sure know how to hurt a man, Detective. I can be there in an hour, if the aforementioned lady friend doesn't detain me further by removing choice body parts."

"You know where?"

"I'm sure I'll find it."

Shruff got back in his car and drove.

He reached the maw of the Dark Road, where the trees yawned in the darkness from the end of the town streets. Panic hit him like a flu bug sped up to epidemic proportions.

Sweat broke out over his entire body, pores working in unison to grease him up like a piston. A tremor rattled his muscles, and he knew if he hadn't been holding the steering wheel so tightly, his hands would be shaking. His head thrummed, vision kept trying to blur. His stomach churned more and more violently as the car idled at the edge of the woods.

God, why did he keep doing this to himself? When would it be enough? When the woods were burned to the ground and the damn thing was on an autopsy table for the whole world to see?

Would that finally balance the books?

"Not even close," Shruff muttered. His foot slammed the gas.

The dark crept in to fill the spaces between the trees, conjuring shapes in the shadows. He passed the spot again, once covered with wooden crosses and memorial flowers but now no more than another patch of woods and grass on the side of the road. Shruff turned his head away.

The site was ahead, and he slowed his car and pulled carefully off the road. He was indeed shaking badly, and the sickness in his stomach and head was growing in throbbing lurches. His lungs worked like a bellows, but he couldn't get a satisfying gulp of oxygen.

And yet, he knew the hour would drag by if he sat and waited for Oakland. Most might think it rash—not to mention immensely stupid—to leave the vehicle, but glass and plastic and metal were no protection from the Jackal Man. Another fact gleaned from personal experience.

Shruff opened his door and stepped into the night. The air was fresh and filled with the repeating screech of crickets, but he wasn't fooled. The world was just as tense as him, every shadow ready to spring.

He felt under his arm for his nine-millimeter security blanket. The Jackal Man might be long-lived, able to surf the tides of time with the longevity of an immortal, but Shruff wondered if a bullet might change his disposition. He pulled the gun from its home next to his ribs, checked the ammunition and safety, and forced himself to return it.

His flashlight was under his seat. He used the beam to navigate his way through the dirt to the gate. Using the key Frank Stanford gave him a half hour ago, he opened the passage just wide enough to slip through and then closed it again.

The lane down the middle of the two rows of houses had transformed with the coming of night. It was a funhouse hallway, twisted with dread, the houses monuments to un-earthly gods.

Nevertheless, he breathed easier as he looked around the site, moving the flashlight beam in a sweeping pattern. Everywhere the blood smears leapt out at him. He wanted to see the pit at the far end of the lot again, but from where he stood, it appeared to be Outer Mongolia.

Shruff took one step forward and heard garbled voices bouncing between the houses. The sweating and shortness of breath returned until he assured himself that ululating spirits were the least of his worries.

An aluminum ladder leaned against the wall of one of the last houses on the right. Shruff picked this up and carried it with him. At the edge of the pit, he swept his flashlight around the inside. Only large chunks of dirt at the bottom, like the dregs of a giant soup bowl.

Anti-climactic. But had he really expected a neon sign saying, 'Jackal Man: This Way?'

He lowered the ladder and shoved it into the rubble until he was sure it had a solid base. He climbed down with the flashlight tucked under his armpit. His shoes crunched into the grit at the bottom. He moved the flashlight beam over the walls. The side the ladder leaned against was clay, the same hard clay that had been legendary in Asheville for as long as the Jackal Man. He studied the walls, looking for symbols, scratch marks, *something*, some sign that he was on the right track.

Shruff swung the flashlight around again, moving the beam up and down, then halted. The wall to the left of the ladder was *almost* all clay. At the bottom, the gray mineral deposit ended in a downward curve near his shins and a thin layer of dirt waited beneath that. It looked like a cross section of a temporal geologic strata survey, where the stages of evolution are frozen in layers of soil and rock.

He knelt gingerly on the knees of his slacks. Moved away a few large pieces of clay and debris. With one hand he held the light steady, and with the other he reached forward and dug at the layer of dirt along the bottom of the clay pit wall. It was moist and loose.

He continued until his fingers hit empty air.

His hand came up as fast as if he'd grabbed a flaming log in a fireplace. A crack nearly two inches thick and a half a foot wide began at the point where the wall became the floor. A miniature abyss framed by soil, one so deep and dark that his powerful flashlight couldn't penetrate it. He held his palm against it and could feel a weak draft dribbling out, air discernibly cooler than the muggy Texas night around him. He wanted to put his cheek to it, but was too afraid a hand would come shooting out to grab his throat, one that had been reaching for his neck for over a decade now.

Of course, it could be just another natural hollow in the ground connected to this one. It could be...but he didn't think so.

Shruff had gone to Carlsbad Caverns in New Mexico when he was six. There were tiny cracks in the rock like this in several places that, they were told by the guide, led away to entirely different cave systems. He'd crammed his face into those holes and breathed in the flat air and felt, deep in his marrow, the vast spaces that stretched beyond. He got the same sense of largeness when he looked into the hole he'd just created.

A system of caves and tunnels, carved into walls of solid clay.

Where something could live undisturbed for centuries.

He heard voices again, clearer this time.

Someone was in River Meadows with him.

His next breath wouldn't come. A wave of dizziness rocked him, and he had to lean against the side of the pit for a moment to keep from passing out.

Shruff slunk up the ladder and peered over the edge of the pit like a trenched soldier. He played the flashlight beam across the house closest to him, and illuminated three ghostly pale faces watching him from between support struts.

He screamed, wordless sounds of abject terror...but stopped when the three faces screamed back at him.

"Okay, you three, I'm a cop!" he shouted, the tremble in his voice not as bad as he feared. "Come out right now with your hands up!"

And out they filed, one little, two little, three little teenage punks, and lined up outside the house in the beam of his flashlight. "Shruffy? Zat you?"

Shruff smirked. "Zachary Murphy and Nelson Kredell. In case the fence didn't tip you two maggots off, this is private property. Which makes you trespassers."

"Shit, you know that's the least of our rap sheet," Nelson, a.k.a. 'Nails,' sneered back at him. Indeed he did; he'd arrested this seventeen-year-old four times for petty larceny, minor alcohol and drug possession. "Besides," Nails continued, "that didn't stop *you*."

"Ah, but I have a key and permission to be here, which is more than either of you even have at your own houses."

He climbed the rest of the way out of the hole and brushed his pants off before hauling the ladder back out. The other boy with them was smaller and younger, dressed the same but without the bravado that usually went with the black clothes and punked-out hair. He looked pale with fear.

His eyes flicked back and forth between Shruff's face and the scar on his neck, as though trying to decide between being polite and getting a good eyeful. "Who are you?" Shruff asked, in as rough a voice as he used with the other two. When the boy seemed unable to get his tongue moving, he softened and said, "What's your name?"

"Willie Stanford," the boy mumbled.

"Wait a minute, not...Stanford, as in Frank Stanford?" The resemblance to the foreman was nil, particularly with the orange spikes of hair standing up off his head.

The mention of the name got the boy to look up. "He's my father."

"Small world. I was with him in town not even an hour ago. I'm guessing he doesn't know you're here?"

Willie shook his head.

"What's going on here, Shruffy?" Zerk cut in. "Who put all this shit on the houses?"

"That's on a need-to-know basis, and you don't need to know. This is a police investigation."

"Aw c'mon, cut the crap! Is it...blood?"

"*Blood?* That's pretty inventive. You working for the *Digest* now or what?"

"Well it sure looks like blood," Nails insisted.

"What's down in the pit then?" Zerk asked.

"Dirt. Bugs. Slimy things. You know, all your ancestors." Zerk grinned sarcastically at him while Nails gave him the finger. God, they reminded him of a Marcus Shruff that could've been. In an effort to distract them, he asked, "All right boys, what are we packing tonight?"

Nails spread open his leather jacket—worn even during the heat wave last summer—to show the interior lining, and held up his hands. "Clean as a whistle, Shruffy. Feel free to search though. I know how much you like to feel on dudes."

"So let me ask, what in hell are you idiots doing out here?"

"Just came to scope the place."

"In the middle of the night? How long have you two lived in this town? I assume your friend here," he pointed at Stanford's kid, "knows about...?"

Willie perked up the tiniest bit. "I know about the Jackal Man, if that's what you mean."

"Well, I can't leave you out here. Let's go, out, all of you."

"Oh c'mon, man, you're not gonna take us home, are you?"

"You bet your dumb ass I am."

"You gonna tell our folks?" Zerk demanded. "You know they don't care!"

Shruff couldn't argue with that sentiment, as cheerful as it was. Nails lived with his father, who spent days at a loading dock and nights at various strip clubs. Zerk's parents lived on the north edge of Asheville, practically in Fort Worth, where the houses had actual space between them. They were never home, usually traveling the world and leaving their son's raising to hapless caretakers who could no more control the boy than they could.

Willie was obviously a different story. Kids that showed some humility were usually more scared of their parents than they could ever be of a cell. This quality was etched into every worry wrinkle on his face, written on the hunched way he stood, as though trying to shrink into himself. He may not even know it, but he cared what his parents thought of him.

"Besides, we got our bikes!" Nails argued. "You can't haul both our rides in your pig-mobile, and I sure as hell ain't leaving it here to get stolen!"

Shruff looked at his watch. If he were punctual—and Shruff couldn't imagine the zookeeper being anything but—Bob Oakland would be here in twenty to thirty minutes. He had no time to run them all over town to their houses. Not all of them, anyway.

"All right, you two get a head start out of here, but I want you to stay on the road and go straight back into town. I'll escort you to the town line. And if I catch you out here again, I *will* book both of you. Your parents may not do anything to you, but in another year, I'll be able to make life very unpleasant for both of you."

He scared Zerk with this threat, but Nails's eyes hardened. He bristled with anger. "What about Willie?"

"Him, I'm taking home. You got a problem with that?"

"Nope, see ya!" Zerk ran for the gate. Nails stared at him a moment longer and then did the same without a glance at Willie, who looked ready to burst into tears as he watched them go.

"Don't worry. You're not in trouble," Shruff told him.

"That's what you think."

They trudged back through the empty site to his patrol car. Not another word was spoken as Shruff started the vehicle, pulled carefully onto the road, and started back into town. He drove slowly, allowing the other two time to get back into town safely.

They passed Nails and Zerk after a few minutes, pumping their bikes at top speed. He went around them on the passenger side. Their heads followed the car, peering in at Willie, but this time it was the thin, pale boy that ignored them.

"So where'd you meet those two?" Shruff nodded his chin at the duo as the car edged by. They'd reached the first of the houses, so he figured they should be safe now.

Willie shrugged and found the door handle to be the most fascinating thing in the universe.

"I know they may seem like fun, but if you hang around them, you're setting yourself up for trouble. That's not a speech or anything, just plain truth."

"They've been cool so far," Willie said. "They're the only ones that have."

"This town can be a little...standoffish." Shruff thought of John Boyd almost tearing into the boy's father. "But you're better off alone than with those two. I mean, look where they took you tonight..." He trailed off, not knowing how much was too much.

The boy snorted and mumbled, "It's stupid. All those Jackal Man urban legends. He's not even listed on Snopes. I checked."

He sounded so much like his father and probably didn't even realize it. "I know it seems like that, but I promise you, there were these two boys—"

"Yeah, I *know* about the two boys!" Willie growled. "Were they driving a Lamborghini in your version? Or a hovercar? Did the Jackal Man fly in on a jet pack and rip out their still-beating hearts? Or did one of them live and go crazy and have to be locked up in a mental institute?"

Shruff had to grin at the irony. "No, no fancy cars, no blood and guts," he said. "And the one kid definitely didn't get thrown in the nuthouse. He just went away for a while and people forgot who he was."

The boy shot him a look, glanced at the scar, then returned to looking out the window.

Shruff had found the address for the Stanford home earlier in the evening by simple process of elimination; there were, after all, only three houses for rent or sale in the entire town. They pulled to the curb in front of the one he narrowed it down to and figured he guessed correctly when Willie climbed out without a word and waited to be escorted to the door.

"Hey," Shruff called him back. "Think you can sneak back in the same way you got out?"

Willie's eyes widened. He nodded.

"Then go do it. And stay out of the woods. I'm serious."

He took off around the side of the house. Shruff watched him disappear before driving away.

26

By the time Shruff arrived back at the site, Bob Oakland waited in his car at the gate. The man wore faded jeans and a short sleeve golf shirt that showed off the taut muscles of the young man he used to be, covered by the leathery, liver-spotted flesh of the old man he'd become. He stepped from his small Lancer and walked to meet Shruff.

"You know, I've been in the wilds of Africa in the dead of night with a pack of lions. And I've been in Amazon jungles so deep you couldn't see the sun at noon. But *this* place...this place is spooky." Oakland shoved his hands in his pockets and shivered. "That, or your damn stories have gotten to me, and that upsets me greatly."

"Why is that?"

"Because if I start treating this 'Jackal Man' as a monster instead of just another species of exotic cat find, all is lost. I become one of the yarn-spinning denizens of yon town." Oakland's cheerful face melted into a glower. "Don't ever keep me waiting again, Detective. Not after you roust me from bed to help you."

"Sorry. Unavoidable."

Oakland had brought his own flashlight, and together they went into the site. Shruff led the way back to the house he'd shown Stanford earlier in the day. The zookeeper studied the swatches of blood along the way like Sherlock Holmes, sans magnifying glass and pipe.

"You say these are all over the site?"

"Yes, at random, from what I could tell. Some of them are pretty high up."

Oakland nodded thoughtfully. He spoke with his nose mere inches away from a smear that resembled a crooked 'Y'. "I noticed. If this is a new species of cat, it's a diligent one. This is already more effort put into a simple territory marking than anything I've ever seen. Makes me lean more toward nurture than nature, if you get me."

"I do not."

"It's a fake," Oakland clarified, and Shruff's heart sank.

They climbed into the kitchen, where the dank aroma still hung in the air. Oakland breathed it deep. "Smells like an animal den, that's for sure. That's what the scent gland is designed for. Any animal within five miles is going to steer clear of this."

"If there *are* any animals within five miles. Keep in mind how many were probably slaughtered for the artwork out there."

"And yet, you didn't find a single body." Oakland went to the handprint and knelt, bringing his flashlight to bear on the image. "There's a lot of detail here your photograph didn't catch."

"Do you still think it's a fake?"

"I've never seen a cat with...well, fingers like this, so if does turn out to be an animal, it's the find of the century. But the shaping of the pads and the texture resemble some panther prints."

Shruff didn't know what to make of that, so he asked, "Out there, when we were coming in, you said you had to treat this as cat rather than monster. So what would make it a monster? Those," he tripped on the word, "fingers?"

Oakland's eyes sparkled in the flashlight as he hunkered in the dirt of the unfinished kitchen. "That just makes it mutation, Detective. That's all evolution is, after all, mutation that sticks, a successful experiment from Mother Nature. Intelligence though—if it were found to reason, like a man..." His eyes drifted away. "Now *that* would be something to terrify. Where did you get your scar, Detective?"

The question was so quiet and monotone Shruff almost didn't recognize it as one. He whispered, "Animal attack."

"I already know that; I recognized it as soon as I met you. *Which* animal?"

Shruff sighed. "Let me show you something."

They went back out the same way. "If there was a new species out here, where would you suspect it lived?"

"Most of the jungle cats usually live in trees, with the exception of lions. Wild cats make dens in the ground or in caves all the time. In desperation, animals can make a home just about anywhere."

The pit was in front of them, and Shruff shone the flashlight on the sheer wall. "Even in that?"

"Well, I don't know about that. Dirt is one thing, but any cats out here couldn't burrow through solid clay like that."

"Not even after centuries? Not even with sticks or rocks?"

"Tools? You've gone from animal to monster, Detective. I can't endorse that until I've seen proof."

"Then we can start with this." With a dramatic sweep, Shruff moved the circle of light back to the hole he'd dug.

Gone.

A small slope of dirt and clay was piled against the base

of the pit wall in place of the entrance he'd opened into deeper darkness.

Oakland put a hand on his hip. "Eh...what's up, doc?"

Shruff couldn't answer. He stepped away from the pit and looked at the rows of solemn houses. They stared back with black, uncaring eyes. He began to pant again, like an asthma patient.

"What? What is it?"

A flash of green in one of the houses on the left, darting and small.

"I think we should go now." Fear tightened his belly and groin. He took Oakland by the elbow and pulled him away from the pit.

"Detective, I'm not as spry as I used to be, but I'm not decrepit," the man said, shaking free of his grip.

"Shhhh!" It was as if he'd given the command to the night itself. The normal sounds of the meadow were gone. Even the crickets were holding still.

And then, from behind them, came a roar that echoed across the entire field, attempting to refill the night with noise.

"The only cat in this hemisphere that roars is the jaguar, and they haven't been seen in Texas in two centuries." Oakland paused as he waited for the sound to repeat.

"Go," Shruff wheezed. Panic stole every breath. "Go right *now*."

Oakland went without having to be asked again, which was good, because Shruff had no idea what he would do if the man didn't. He was unprepared for this encounter, even after all the planning, the dreaming, the pleas for a chance at vengeance. He looked back every three steps as they ran, slowing his pace to match the other man's.

"Oakland, can you move your elderly ass?"

"We can't be twenty-eight forever, Detective."

"This from...the man...that was about to engage in a sex marathon." Shruff was gasping now.

"Perhaps I ought to be carrying *you*."

"I'll be okay, it's just...a panic attack."

They slipped through the gate and Shruff took the time to throw the lock on and click it shut, wanting to laugh at the illusion of it all. If the beast wanted them, no fence would slow him down. Oakland headed for his car, parked several yards further from the gate.

"Not that way! Get in my car!"

Oakland faltered. He turned around, facing Shruff's vehicle and the looming construction site, and Shruff heard him say, "Good Lord."

He looked up from the process of disengaging the car locks. A shadow raced through the field near the marsh grass, nothing more than a blurred, bulleted mass, coming at them with incredible speed.

"Oakland!" Shruff reached for his piece, but the old man finally got moving and hopped into the passenger seat.

Shruff jumped in, slammed his door, gunned the engine and spun out, looking in the rearview mirror only once. The low, sleek shape was gone.

Breath, the first full one in minutes, filled his chest.

Something crashed onto the roof. Oakland squawked next to him.

The car bounced onto the black road, increasing speed from zero to forty in what felt like years. A screeching noise assaulted them from above, like a rake against sheet metal.

"Get it off!" Oakland screamed, and Shruff wondered if, on any of those nights on the veldt or those afternoons in the rainforest, he'd ever been attacked this savagely.

Shruff pulled the wheel to the left and then swerved back

right just as abruptly. A limb—furry and lean and toned—fluttered across his front windshield, seeking a place to hold on. He pumped the brakes once out of reflex and then slammed the pedal all the way to the floor.

The car screeched to a halt, throwing them both against the dash. Shruff tasted blood after his lips caromed off the steering wheel. The thing on top of the car crashed onto the hood in a tangle of splayed limbs and then slid off the front, out of sight.

"Jesus, its structure!" Oakland exclaimed breathlessly. "With a spine like that it could be bipedal or—"

The dark shape rocketed up and landed back on the hood, hunching low to the metal, face inches from the glass...and after an entire decade Shruff was staring into those glowing eyes again. That night came back to him, so like this, the moon riding low, spring itching under the skin, hanging upside down in the car...

Let Oakland try to say it wasn't a monster now, that there was no intelligence in those darting orbs of furious, almost radioactive green.

The moment stretched out longer than the bounds of reality could possibly have sustained it, and then the creature broke the standoff by raking its claws violently across the glass and pounding at the rooftop in a frenzy.

"GAAAAAAAHHHH!" he heard Oakland scream, before realizing it was himself. He tromped the gas again. This time he wouldn't stop until they were back in Asheville. He would parade through the streets with the Jackal Man on top of his car like a hood ornament, drive all the way to the White House, if that's what it took.

They came to the last bend before the end of the Dark Road, and Shruff saw he was going too fast. He released the gas and hit the brake again, but the back wheels slid out into the grass bordering the concrete. The car bounced, and went up on a precarious two wheels.

"Christ, NOT AGAIN!"

He couldn't lose control of the car, not this time, or there would be no escape for either of them. It would finish what it started with his throat.

From the corner of his eye, he saw the dark shape bound off the roof and disappear into the woods.

He continued twisting the wheel, but instead of braking he went *with* the speed. After several long seconds, the driver's side hit the pavement once more. The car fishtailed for another few yards, and then they were cruising along steadily.

"Take *that*, you BASTARD!" Shruff screamed triumphantly. "Well Oakland, what do you think n—?"

The words died in his throat. The old man's chin rested against his chest.

"Bob?"

The vet's head came up wearily and slowly. One eye was half closed. He garbled, "My...heart..." and clutched weakly at his breast.

"Oh God, hold on, just hold on," Shruff crossed the city line of Asheville and headed toward the small hospital on the far side.

27

Cyrus Griffin—or Ol' Cyrus, as most people in Asheville referred to him—was a stick figure as he moved through the rooms of his decrepit shack. He was considered a resident, but only by a whisker; his hovel was just inside the invisible city line running a shallow length through the woods.

He rarely ventured into town, and had attained a legendary status as some kind of friend to the Jackal Man.

But Cyrus was just an old man whose daughter insisted more vehemently each year that he move to Dallas to 'be closer to her' (which *really* meant a one-way ticket to the nearest nursing home), an old man trying to hold his rotting house together so he could continue to do the one thing that gave him any joy in life: tending to his beloved horses.

He hated people. Perhaps that was part of the appeal of living on the Dark Road, where others feared to come. The rest of Asheville had tried everything to scare him off when he built the place with his own two hands thirty years ago, but he didn't budge. He now had seven horses, and the stables were in better condition than his home.

At eleven o'clock, Cyrus was reading in his threadbare lounger. After dog-earing a yellowed page, he set the book aside and climbed, with some effort, out of the chair and hob-

224 RUSSELL C. CONNOR

bled to the bedroom on his bad hip. His head had just hit his rock-hard pillow when one of the horses screamed outside.

He sat back up. He'd never heard his animals make such a noise. All seven were corralled in the open-ended stable, with spacious stalls for each.

The others took up the appalling racket. Underneath the squall, he could hear the thuds as they tried to batter their way out of the wooden enclosures.

Cyrus swung his legs out of bed. His skinny chest hitched, stretched so tight his ribs showed through. His only weapon, an ancient Winchester rifle, was in the closet. He retrieved it, saying silent prayers for the horses. After firing his lantern, he gripped it in one hand and the rifle with the other.

On the porch, he hesitated. Only a few of the horses were making noise now, but that was even more terrible, like singular voices crying out from a dead battlefield. The broad side of the stable was visible from the front of his house, and the boards bulged outward as one of the horses kicked.

His bare feet were silent in the grass. Cyrus put the dim lantern beside the entrance so he could steady the rifle with both hands. He realized he hadn't even loaded it. Only one animal could be heard now, making a pitiful mewling noise. "Whoever's in there, I'm comin in armed!" His voice cracked.

Cyrus swung around the corner with the rifle held ready to bluff.

Someone darted out the other side of the stable. He caught only a flash of movement.

Cyrus ran past the far wall of the stable and found the yard deserted. He looked around his field and up toward the Dark Road in time to see the figure fly into the woods on the far side of the street.

He started to give chase, but knew it was pointless. And really, he didn't care who was in his stable (although he had a pretty damn good idea already), only what they had done. He swapped his gun for the lantern and entered the long stable corridor.

Light hoisted high, the feeble rays were stretched to their limit. All the horses were gone. That is to say, their heads, usually visible above the stall doors, weren't looking back at him. A dark liquid spread across the floor from Meredith's stall.

"No," Cyrus moaned. "Aw, no. Please God in heaven, no."

He went to Radish's stall, the first on the left. Peered over the door. An anguished cry escaped him at the sight of the gore from the horse's ripped throat. He went to the next and Sam, named posthumously for his wife, raised her head to look at him with wild eyes. A large, ragged hole in her belly leaked blood and viscera. She whinnied miserably.

Cyrus, tears in his eyes, went back to the house to get ammunition, and loaded his rifle. He put a bullet through her head with a crash that echoed in the empty woods.

The other horses were in worse shape, all dead. Cyrus began to cry until anger overshadowed his grief.

He knew the culprit.

No, he wasn't any friend to the Jackal Man, but he had no doubt the creature was real. Cyrus showed respect by staying out of his way, and always believed the same courtesy was paid to him. The beast wanted to be left alone, and Cyrus was the last person to fault him for that. But, after thirty years of peaceful neighboring, something had driven the creature to such malicious lengths.

Those bastards up the road, building those cheap houses. They were hammering and drilling and bulldozing and *blast-*

ing with fucking dynamite, like a bunch of reckless cavemen, too dumb to realize that if God wanted them to build there, He wouldn't have made it so difficult.

The Jackal Man was losing what little land he had, and making his case heard in the only way he knew how.

Striking out like a scared, wounded animal.

Again, Cyrus couldn't blame him. He wanted to, *God* he wanted to, but that was like blaming a tornado for the damage it caused. As he thought about his own war with his daughter to protect his way of life, Cyrus actually felt a sudden kinship with the creature.

Well, the Jackal Man would have an advocate now. Petitions hadn't done any good, so it was time to take a step up. Cyrus didn't like Asheville, but the people there would listen to him, even at this late hour. His voice would sway others also, folks from outside town, old friends like James Buchanon of the *Weekly Digest*. If they made a big enough fuss, the legitimate press would come.

Either way, tomorrow they would put an end to this Lyles Corporation once and for all.

ASHEVILLE

THE TOWN TAKES A STAND

28

He held the rifle close, against his narrow chest.

There was only darkness around him and a sense of motion, like many fingers brushing against his skin. It took several seconds for him to realize they were tree branches.

He took hesitant steps through the encroaching darkness, blind to all. He was looking for something...and it was looking for him, too. From far away, he could hear distorted echoes of his father's shouted encouragement, and laughter from a chorus of drunken men, but they couldn't help him.

From close by, a branch snapped. He could sense a presence now, something malevolent and tense, coiled and ready to strike, and when it came, no gun on earth would be able to save him.

He stepped backward, trying to escape now, flight over fight, and with a roar, the thing in the woods leapt at him...

Frank jerked awake from the nightmare that was mostly memory and opened bleary eyes. Someone had tied his spine in a knot as he slept on the couch. He'd stumbled home after leaving the bar, couldn't sleep, stayed up watching television, and passed out with it still playing. He sat up and rubbed a hand across his rough cheek.

It was close to 7:30, Saturday morning. He was late. Frank retrieved a change of clothes from the bedroom while Trish slept and dressed in the living room without the luxury of a shower. He let the T.V. continue running, the weatherman warning of the violent summer storm to sweep through tonight.

Then the screen switched from weather maps to the anchors at the local news desk, who gave their spiel introducing a new segment, and then to a female reporter standing in front of someplace very familiar.

River Meadows, filmed from the edge of the road. A crowd of people stood behind the reporter in the gray morning, some of them holding signs he couldn't read. In the near distance, Frank could see the fence and the unfinished houses in the site beyond.

"Thanks Lance," the reporter said. Frank punched buttons on the remote until the volume went up. "I'm here just outside the town of Asheville, where a sizeable group of protestors have gathered in the early hours to picket the construction of this housing project." The camera switched away to a sign for the project. "The Lyles Corporation began building River Meadows in late May in what previously had been a wilderness area. But what's unique about this protest is that the people aren't upset about the destruction of the land; they're fighting the work to keep from disturbing a creature they call 'the Jackal Man.'" Her eyes widened on the last few words, eyebrows raising like Vincent Price.

A protest. There was an actual fucking *protest* going on at the site?

Frank gave a short bark of maniacal laughter. "What next God, huh? Rain of frogs?"

The reporter turned to the people waiting behind her. Frank was glued to the set, sinking into the floor on his knees to watch. One of the men said into the reporter's microphone, "People who don't live here aren't gonna understand. But this is somethin Asheville takes very seriously. Stop buildin, or the Jackal Man will have his revenge!"

"What sort of...'revenge?'" she asked dramatically, giving a glance to the camera.

"Why don't you ask Cyrus Griffin what happened to his horses last night?" The man looked deep into the camera, and the reporter's condescending smile faded. The man stepped past her, crowding her out of the shot entirely. "We invite anybody that wants to help to just come out. If you don't believe in the Jackal Man, then come because you don't like to see wildlife bein destroyed or because you don't like corporations runnin all over the little guy." A cheer went through the crowd around him. He stepped even closer to the camera, and Frank had the very surreal feeling the guy was looking right at him. "And we advise the people who work here not to even bother showin up."

It was hokey, but at this point, Frank had stopped listening. He was glued to the throng of people behind the speaker where, for just a second, he could swear he glimpsed a tall figure in a dented hunting hat...

Frank pulled out his phone as the reporter asked various people in the crowd what the Jackal Man looked like. "C'mon, why are you reporting this, isn't there any real news going on?" He tried calling Damon's cell, but it went straight to voicemail. Then he dialed the hotel number the man had given him, but the operator couldn't locate him.

Frank hung up. The room spun around him. What was he supposed to do about this fiasco? This wasn't his problem, he was supposed to have superiors to kick this sort of thing up to, but he sure as hell wasn't going to call Lyles.

The workers would be arriving now—those that dared to do so—and he couldn't afford any more delays. Frank would have to get the gates open before they got there.

He turned the television off, denying the urge to put his fist through the happy reporter's face, and left.

The sun broke the horizon as he reached the site. The crowd had grown since the interview earlier in the morning. Cars were left along the sides of the street for miles down the Dark Road. He could see the main body of protesters with reporters milling around them, but other, smaller groups had pitched makeshift tents or set up lawn chairs to enjoy the parade.

Groups of college girls danced with their faces painted to look like cats. A fat man in robes proselytized to rapt listeners. People surrounded a long haired hippie-type with a guitar.

It was a fucking circus that had drawn every kook for miles. He scanned them all, searching for the berserk hunter.

He wondered if Lyles had already been contacted about this by one of the media outlets—it only made sense, after all—and could imagine the man laughing his ass off.

When they saw Frank's truck, they organized themselves into a marching line in front of the gate and chanted a slogan like something from the back of a cereal box.

"Leave the Jackal Man! Don't destroy his land!"

"Yeah…that's gonna be stuck in my head," Frank grumbled.

He found a gap in the cars big enough to allow his truck to pass and drove through the mob, right up to the gate. As he opened the door and stepped out, he expected them to rush him, but they only continued to march and chant.

Frank strode toward the gate and was surrounded by reporters like seagulls around thrown bread crumbs. Microphones were thrust in his face, the bright lights from cameras making him squint. He spotted the face of the pretty reporter jostling for a position among her male colleagues and even that rotten scumbag Buchanon, with pad and pencil ready. Questions were thrown at him with more speed than he could hope to answer.

"Get back!" Frank yelled, feeling like a monster fighting to escape the villagers. More of them everywhere he turned, blocking every step. The protestors only stood back and watched, the chant dying as the media did the work for them. Most of them laughed.

He fought his way free and pushed through the crowd. He unlocked and pushed open the gate, then went back to his truck through the throng of reporters.

"Do you believe in the Jackal Man yet, Mr. Stanford?" Buchanon called out.

Frank bellowed, "No, I do *NOT!*" The reporters fell silent to capture his words. It was quiet enough to hear the words of the street preacher across the field, as he proclaimed the Jackal Man was the living embodiment of Jesus Christ after the resurrection. "He doesn't exist! These people are all trying to get some attention, attention *you're* giving them!" His finger swept the gathered crowd.

One of them answered him, stepping forward. He recognized that deserter, Gerrardo. "I tried to warn you! You're crazy if you think you can get away with this!"

Frank climbed back into his truck and drove into the lot, blaring his horn. The reporters descended upon Gerrardo with a fresh barrage of questions and Frank shouted, "I'm gonna call the police on all of you!"

Once inside his trailer, with the door locked, he did.

29

In the few hours it took for someone to respond, the crowd harassed Frank's workers as they arrived. Most looked so terrified, they probably thought it was the immigration office waiting to cart them off. Jaime Garcia scuttled through like a crab. More protestors appeared, some serious, others seeking to take part in what was quickly becoming the next Woodstock.

Frank waited outside with his crew, or the half that showed up for work. Hammers rose and fell haltingly, without the steady rhythm he liked to hear.

And then someone else was squeezing through the fence, and Frank saw it was Shruff.

He walked out to meet the man. "I called hours ago! Why hasn't anyone come before now?"

"We're having a busy morning."

"Can you do anything about these goddamn freaks?"

"Not unless you can repeal the First Amendment."

Frank watched the detective, whose eyes flicked left and right constantly. He sweated a little more than the early heat of the day could account for, and his face was even paler than Frank remembered. His scars stood out in sickly pink lines against his pasty skin. "You all right, Shruff?"

"Didn't sleep real well."

Frank nodded. "You and me both. C'mon, let's go inside."

Shruff seemed all too happy to do so, taking one lingering glance at the pit as he mounted the steps. Once inside, Frank almost sat on the edge of his desk before remembering the bloodstain and instead elected to pull his chair from behind it and sit down. "Have you found out anything?"

"You could say that. Listen, Mr. Stanford—"

A digital bleating cut him off. "Hold that thought," Frank said, and pulled out his cell phone.

"What the fuck is going on out there?" Lyles squealed.

Frank stammered, "I can explain, sir!"

"You damn sure better! What kind of circus are you running, Frank?"

"Sir, to be fair, none of this is my fault!"

Shruff respectfully turned away from the conversation, looking out at the protestors.

"You're responsible for *everything* Frank, that's what being a goddamned foreman means! Why didn't you even notify me?"

"Well, I only got here a few hours ago—!"

"That's bullshit, this happened two days ago and you know it! Now, it was probably that dynamite tech's fault, but you're in charge of rectifying these situations!"

Frank gave a dumbfounded, "Huh?"

"So you're playing ignorant when I've got two lawyers in my office this morning representing some company called Arcus, who say two of their men were hurt in an explosion? They're fucking suing us, Frank!"

Frank sucked in air through his teeth in relief. "I'm sorry sir, that was a company that Damon hired to do some security work—!"

"I'll talk to Damon soon enough. And straighten this all out when I get there."

"You're coming here?"

"As soon as I can get a flight out."

"I don't think—"

"We'll talk then, Frank." The phone went dead.

So this was it. Lyles wasn't even giving him a full week to finish, let alone three months. The trailer felt smaller, and he put the cell phone on the desk as he leaned back to stare at the ceiling.

"Are *you* all right?" Shruff asked.

"Aside from the fact that I'm about to be fired, the site's gonna be shut down, and I can't find my boss, yeah, I'm just great. Oh and don't forget the hundreds of protestors screaming for my blood, that's a bonus."

"Lyles...he's going to shut down the site?"

"That was the plan all along. He's losing money on this whole thing and looking for an excuse to get out." Frank raised his head to look at the other man. "So don't worry, we'll be cleared out of here soon enough, and your town can go back to making up stories for the tourists."

"I truly am sorry. Asheville hasn't been very good to you, and I'm ashamed of it, trust me."

"Whatever." Frank regretted coming in the trailer. With the broken window, the meager air-conditioning did no good. The interior was a stifling oven with the nauseating under-smell of blood. He stood and went back to the window to try and catch any sort of draft and stared out at the protestors. "Can't you do *anything* about them? I mean, this is private property!"

"The second they see police cars coming all they have to do is step onto the road. I could get them for not having a permit, but the judge won't uphold it."

"Goddamn it! What the hell got them so stirred up they picked now to do this?"

"You didn't hear?"

Frank shook his head.

"A guy named Cyrus Griffin lives on the other end of the Dark Road. He's got a little horse ranch. I went out there this morning, even though he didn't want the police involved."

"Yeah, the horses. They mentioned it on the news. What's that about?"

"Somebody killed them late last night. Slaughtered all seven. He's the one that put this demonstration together."

"Jesus," Frank whispered.

"Mr. Stanford, I need to know something. Are you going to continue working? Are you going to...to stay out here?"

"Until Lyles forces me out. If only to spite him and those lunatics out there."

"Okay. I won't try to argue you out of it, but do me this favor. Get a gun. Go today, and buy a rifle so you don't have to go through the waiting period." His eyes were wary as he spoke, his face haggard and drawn.

The dream flickered through Frank's mind, the alien feel of the gun in his hands. His jaw worked until he choked out, "What, for the protestors?"

"No...yes...I don't know. I don't think anyone from town would try to actually hurt you, but we're getting a lot of other weirdos from the outside world. Look at it this way: even if you don't believe in the Jackal Man, *someone* killed your dog. *Someone* killed those horses."

"But a rifle?"

"There's something out there Mr. Stanford, something dangerous. You might need some protection. I don't know how to put it any simpler than that."

Frank continued to stare at the detective and felt another cold chill at the haunted look in the man's face. "What's going on? There's something you haven't told me."

Shruff shook his head. "It might not matter, not if your boss shuts the site down. Besides, you wouldn't believe me anyway. Just get that gun and...be careful. Don't stay out here alone." He opened the trailer door and stepped out. "I'll see what I can do with the crowd on my way out."

"Thanks," Frank replied, without any heart. He didn't like the way the man said that last, that *he* wouldn't believe him, as though the fact that Frank didn't put stock in stories about a centuries old cat monster put *him* in the minority.

I'll be damned if I let them start making me feel like I'm the crazy one.

Nevertheless, Frank grabbed his cell phone and walked out of the trailer to find the nearest gun store.

Shruff approached the gates, an intimidating experience worse than public speaking. And it was no use picturing them in their underwear, because some of them were. Most of these were the faces of people he saw at the laundromat, the diner, and the drug store, and all of them expected him to be on the opposite side of the fence. If this was war, he was consorting with the enemy.

The assemblage hushed as he approached, all except the preacher on the other side of the mob. It seemed unreal that he'd stood in about the same spot only hours before while running for his life, but he had a dent in his hood to reaffirm it any time he needed. That, and Bob Oakland lying in a hospital bed at Fort Worth Memorial. He knew he looked like shit, but at least the panic attack hadn't kicked in yet.

Mindful of the cameras trained on him, he held up his hands and shouted, "Listen folks! I appreciate the fact that you want your concerns addressed, but there are better ways to go about it!"

The speech was met with boos and hisses. One of his neighbors stepped forward from the crowd, a man that lived down the street from him for four years and mowed Shruff's lawn when he was too busy to do it. He barked, "What are you doing, Marcus? I know what happened to you all those years ago. Why don't you want this stopped?"

Shruff blanched. Had he really been stupid enough to think his secret was safe, that these people hadn't dug into his past the second he moved to town? "Nobody wants them out of here more than I do. But you can't force people around to your way of thinking, not like this. You think you're changing anything by coming out here? You're just giving everybody another opportunity to laugh at us. Come to Asheville, see all the crazies who believe in the Jackal Man!" He scowled around at as many of them as he could, forgetting the cameras and reporters and preachers and college kids and speaking strictly to those he knew. "Go home, folks. Do this the legal way and if it doesn't work...let *them* worry about the consequences." He jerked a finger over his shoulder at the construction workers and then pushed through the crowd toward his waiting car amid a barrage of questions.

By the time the segment aired on the nine o'clock news—near the end, where they always put humorous news oddities like lottery winners or stupid criminals—they would've dredged his story up, and then it wouldn't be two nameless, faceless boys in that old story anymore.

He escaped the mob's prying eyes and headed toward the hospital.

30

Frank could list many reasons for not getting a gun, the least of which was that he suspected he might pass out the second he held one. Perhaps more pressing was the fact that he would likely be out of a job by Monday, and, of course, Trisha would be more than happy to twist his scrotum into new shapes if she found out about it.

After he fought his way through the chanting crowd outside River Meadows, now devoid of reporters, he checked his phone to find there were two gun shops in Asheville, which wasn't the most cheerful sign for a town that didn't have a Wal-mart. One was a pawnshop specializing in guns and ammo, and he headed that way.

There were two customers inside—two black boys with basketball jerseys looking at video game systems—and a bored counter girl. The aisles were lined with musical equipment, computers, and appliances, but no guns. Frank asked the girl where he could find the weaponry. She pointed past him to a corner of the store and said, "Talk to the guys next door."

Frank found a doorway with a red curtain like the type video stores put across their X-rated sections. He felt even more embarrassed when he had to suck in his gut to get through the narrow entry.

On the other side was an interior decorator's wet dream, if that decorator was a card-carrying member of the NRA. The walls were covered in camouflage and netting hung from the ceiling, full of what appeared to be plastic plants and fake vines. American flags hung at random, as well as enough armaments to stock a decent-sized militia.

Frank turned to the left, to another glass counter manned by a fellow in a stained yellow t-shirt polishing a disassembled firearm. A larger man worked further down the counter with his back to Frank, his girth obscuring his activities from view.

The polisher's eyes rolled to him. "Help you?"

"I hope. I need a gun."

"Not planning on killing anyone with said gun?" the man asked, as he fit two of the pieces back together to form a handle.

"Not yet."

"Well, it's not much use to buy a gun unless you're gonna shoot something with it."

Frank approached the counter, glanced at the fatter man. He was sorting ammunition. Frank turned his attention back to the polisher and said, "What difference does it make what I'm gonna do with it? Do you sell guns here, or is this the militia training center for the southwest?"

The fat man turned from his work to look at Frank, blinking owlishly through thick spectacles.

The polisher kept at it, never bothering to glance again at Frank. "You looking for a pistol? Do you have a license to carry?"

"No. I need a rifle."

The clerk put down his work and pushed away from the counter, his stool rolling to a glass case of upright rifles along the far wall. "Anything in particular, or do you want me to blindfold you to pick one out?"

"What do you recommend?"

"Well, to tell you that, I'd have to know what you're using it for, now wouldn't I? Can't sell you a BB gun if you're hunting an elephant."

Frank shuddered at the word 'hunting.' "I don't know, forest game."

"You don't look like a hunter."

"Let's just say I'm picking it up."

"You look familiar," the fat man squeaked in a girlishly high-pitched voice from the opposite end of the counter. "Do I know you?"

"I don't think so."

The polisher looked closer at him for a minute and then said, "I can show you some nice .22's. Perfect for that amateur hunter looking to take down some mighty big butterflies."

"Just show me something powerful. And cheap, preferably."

He lifted a walnut-colored rifle down out of the case. "Simple .250 Winchester, bolt action, single bullet chamber. Easy to use, not too much kick, and the precision is decent. Unless you're going on safari, I highly recommend it."

The man held the gun out, but when Frank didn't move to take it, he set it gently on the counter. Frank stared at the burnished metal and brown stock. He couldn't remember what kind of guns his father owned, or what he'd stuck in young Frankie's hands that night before pushing him into the woods, but memory insisted not only did it look like this one, but it *was* this one. He felt ill looking at it.

"Hold it if you want. See what you think."

But he didn't want to hold it. He didn't even want to touch it. He wanted to bolt from this store and not look back. But instead, he raised his hands, forcing them to grip the weapon in the right places, and raised the stock to his shoulder as though he did it every day. He could feel its power, like a live electrical line in his hands.

"How's the weight?" the man asked.

"Feels good," he heard himself answer through a swimming pool of Jell-O. The room was stuffy and invasive, swallowing his senses until he was on the verge of fainting.

"You could easily put a man down with that. This one's in pretty good shape, but it's stripped down, no frills or sights or anything. I can let you have it for...oh, about a hundred. One-fifty and I'll throw in a sling and a box of ammo."

Frank was twelve again. Alone in the woods. The dream from this morning came hurtling back to him...the art gallery at the site...the bizarre hunter...one big blur of blood and violence. He was ready to put the gun back down and crawl away when the fat man spoke again.

"Hey, wait a minute! We're not sellin that to him!"

Frank turned his head, some of the dizziness wearing off when he focused on something besides the gun. The fat man slid off his stool and stood in the aisle behind the counter with his plump hands on his hips. The polisher asked, "What's wrong with you?"

"I know where I've seen him before! He's one of those damn River Meadows guys! I saw him on TV this morning!" The fat man gave him a fierce look. "Get outta here! We don't want your business!"

Rage flushed away the last of Frank's nausea like used toilet water. Why had he ventured into town to buy this? This was further proof of why, exactly, he needed this gun.

So the first time one of these loons decided to go one step past segregation and have a lynching, he would be ready.

The polisher glanced at Frank, no longer chipper and superior but rather frightened, and then back at his compatriot, who bawled, "Who knows what he wants that rifle for? These guys are nothing but trouble! I said it when they moved in and I say it now! Get outta my store!"

Frank stepped forward, slamming his hands down on the counter on either side of the gun hard enough to rattle the glass. He leaned across and divided the time while he spoke alternating between glaring at the polisher and the fat man. "Listen, you fanatical sons of bitches," he barked, "the only reason I'm buying this gun is to protect me from all the crazies in this town like you two. So you either sell me this gun," he picked up the weapon and didn't experience a single jolt of discomfort, "or I will call every building and health inspector I know to run over this place with a fine tooth comb. You'll have so many violations, it'll take you a lifetime just to get this place up to code. Then I'll start on whatever lean-to shanties you call home. Your Jackal Man nightmares will look like a wet dream when I get through with you."

The fat man's face fell during his spiel. He glanced at the polisher, who swallowed and nodded.

Frank whipped out his wallet. "Visa all right?"

31

Willie spent Saturday in his room, the guilt from betraying his promise to his father—and worse, not getting caught for it—making him avoid all close encounters of the family kind.

He heard a commotion from his mother and sister downstairs around noon, something about the television. He turned on the set in his room and found his father on one of the local station newsbreaks, in front of the same place Nails and Zerk had brought him to last night. Frank Stanford looked kind of crazed, waving away cameras. Willie's sister begged their mother to tape it so she could show her friends back home and was told gently—but with the barest hint of laughter, he thought—that it was nothing to be proud of.

Willie heard the sound of an engine late that afternoon, and watched from the window as his father took a long, sheet-wrapped bundle from his truck and ran into the garage with it. Still no one came to check on him. Why couldn't they do this when he *wanted* to be ignored? When dinner was ready, he refused to go down, now more out of stubbornness, even though he was starving. The sky outside darkened prematurely with thick clouds, and he heard the first distant peals of thunder. The ol' shit-uitary fired up in response to the fact that he'd been forgotten.

That was why, when a familiar tapping came at his window, he slid the drapes open instead of ignoring it.

Nails and Zerk both crouched outside his window this time, hanging off the roof. Zerk pressed a fast food burger in waxy wrapping to the glass, and Willie felt a wrenching spike of gratitude. He slid the window up and snatched the food away. His visitors slithered inside, closing the window behind them.

"Geez, what are they doin to ya in here, Willster?" Tonight Zerk's eyes were fluorescent green, the pupil's almond-shaped, like a cat's.

"Oh, shut up! Do you know how much trouble I could've gotten in thanks to you guys?"

"Us? What'd we do?" The look of innocence on Nails's face was well-practiced. A fresh bruise darkened his cheekbone, and he appeared to be wearing the same clothes from the day before.

"You brought me out there and then you just took off and left me with that detective!" Willie wolfed the burger in two angry bites.

"Okay. Next time we'll pull a GTA and waste the cop that's got you in custody. I didn't have anything planned for the next 50-to-life." Nails plopped down and stretched out on his bed, boots and all. "Besides, it's not like Shruffy took ya to jail. We've been there, and trust us, you got off easy."

"Yeah, and we brought you food as, like, a peace offering," Zerk added. "What did he tell your folks?"

"Well...nothing. He let me go."

Nails grimaced. "That fuck. He busts us every chance, but he lets *you* go? What are you complainin for?"

"You're right, I'm sorry. Listen, thanks for the food, but you gotta get outta here before my dad sees you."

Willie reached for the window. Zerk put out a hand to stop him. "Hold on, hold on! We want you to come with us again."

"Where now, to blow up a preschool? Kill a few nuns?"

"Dude, you got a real attitude problem tonight. It's not good for your chi."

Nails sat up on the edge of the bed. "We're goin back to the construction site."

"Hell no, I'd *rather* blow up a preschool! Why would you wanna go back there anyway?"

"That hole. The one Shruffy was in. Aren't you even the least bit curious what was down there?"

"No, because it was probably dirt."

"Maybe. But we know Shruffy, and when he climbed outta that hole, he looked *guilty*."

"After he looked like he was gonna shit his pants, that is," Zerk added.

"Think about it, Willie. He goes down there in the middle of the night and plays around in a big hole in the ground. Why else would someone do that if they weren't hiding something?"

Willie didn't know the detective as well as they did, but the man did seem in a hurry to get them away from that hole. And Shruff had let him go instead of tattling to his father, which would've forced him to admit where he'd been as well. "What do you think it could be?"

"Me and Zerk've been talking about it, and we think... there's treasure buried down there."

"*Treasure?* That's too dumb for even my kid sister to come up with. Why would treasure be buried out there?"

"Could be a lotta reasons."

"Like Indians, or pirates!" Zerk said gleefully.

"Okay, a little history lesson here, guys: Indians didn't have treasure, and pirates buried theirs on the beach, not three hundred miles inland."

Nails pounded a fist into the palm of his other hand. "I don't know, maybe Shruffy put something in there himself! Shit, don't be so negative!"

"I just don't see any reason to go digging in the dark for lost Mayan riches in some place where the cops've already run us out!"

"You want a reason?" Nails leaned forward, thrusting the bruise across the right side of his face more fully into the light from Willie's bedside lamp. "My old man decided to beat the shit outta me last night. Thought I took his cigarettes, which, trust me, with the shit he smokes, I did *not*. I'm done with it. Whatever's down in that hole could be our ticket away from this town."

"We're goin to California!" Zerk threw his arms around Willie and did a little jig on his gangly legs.

"That's right, man, we're leavin tomorrow, one way or another. Gonna find a place on the beach and have more girls than you could imagine, and party every night. And we're willin to take you with us because we like you, but if you're gonna keep bringin me down with this bullshit, then stay here and be miserable." Nails pushed past them, shoved the window up, and began to climb down the gutter.

Zerk released Willie, calm again, and rubbed the bald half of his head. "We're not totally brain dead, Willster. We know it's stupid. But we got a dream, and we wanna share it with you."

Willie sat on the windowsill. He didn't believe for a second that there was gold buried at his father's construction site, but the idea of leaving this crappy life behind for good?

That was all he'd thought about. He wanted that numb feeling back, and they seemed to be the only ones that could give it to him. Maybe this was even what the premonition had been about when they left Houston.

All it required was one last trip to that place.

He could do this. They obviously wouldn't miss him around here. He could be free of all the teachers, the assholes at school, and his father.

"But I'm telling you, there was something else out there last night, and it wasn't that cop. I could feel it watching us."

"You've seen too many movies, man." Zerk let out a nervous chuckle. "We'll be careful this time. Keep an eye out for Shruffy. Then you can come stay at my place and we'll leave in the morning!"

Determination was slipping, and Willie was almost out of excuses. "But it's about to rain."

"So? You melt if you get wet?" Zerk climbed out the window, got a footing on the gutter, and turned around. "C'mon, once more for old time's sake."

"We don't have any old times, Zerk."

"And we never will if you don't hang with us."

Willie took one last look around the room. Nothing here he wanted to take, nothing here he would really miss. He could just shed his life once and for all.

He swung his leg over the sill.

Rain pattered against the tarmac as they arrived on two bikes fifteen minutes later, droplets of water that sizzled from the day's stored heat. The protestors were gone now, but they'd left behind a trail of trash, clothing, and even a few lawn chairs. They hid the two bicycles in a ditch, and Willie joined the older boys at the fence, scanning the night for sounds and movements. The raindrops sprinkling his face increased in size, frequency, and strength until they covered him in a layer of greasy water.

No chase through the houses this time, no attempt at banter over the steady drumbeat of rain, no lingering over the dark streaks on the wood, faded by two days of blistering sunlight. Willie waited to feel that presence from last night, but they seemed to truly be alone.

The dirt lane leading up to the hole had turned into one big mud slick. Nails's feet flew out from under him at the edge of the pit. He slid ass first over the side, landing with a splash at the bottom. The curses from below were audible even the steady growl of thunder from the west. "Goddamn it, get a ladder and get down here!"

Willie could see only the vaguest outline of the other boy on the floor of the pit. The cloud cover clamped down on the world, leaving them no moonlight.

"And take this!" Nails's leather jacket came flapping out of the darkness. Willie caught it before it could smack him in the face.

He hung the jacket on a nail jutting from a support beam of the closest house, where it was protected from the rain. Lightning forked across the sky—a single crooked bolt, cruel and brilliant—while he and Zerk retrieved a ladder from the interior. As they dragged it to the hole, Willie wiped sopping orange spikes out of his face and said, "I don't think we should do this!"

Zerk glanced at him, face illuminated by another jagged whip of lightning, his half-head of hair plastered over his gaunt skull. He didn't answer. Together, they lowered the ladder down into the pit.

"Go on down," Zerk invited.

"This is your idea!"

"Ladies first."

"I hope lightning strikes while you're on it." Willie leapt for the ladder, going down as quick as he dared. His sneakers squelched into a thick layer of goo at the base. Nails was behind him, easier to see now with close proximity. His white t-shirt was drenched, and the tattoo along his neck and chest was visible like a network of veins pumping black blood. He grabbed Willie's arm and did the same to Zerk when he reached the bottom.

"*You gotta see this!*" he shouted over the growing cacophony of the storm.

He led them to a dark corner of the pit and crouched. Willie and Zerk hunkered beside him.

"*What're we—?*"

"*Wait for the lightning!*"

It took nearly half a minute. But when it came, Willie found himself staring into a dark crack nearly a foot high in the corner. The flash was just enough time for him to see the water sluicing down the side of the pit was actually eroding away more of the dirt and washing it down into the crack, like a raging river cutting away a valley floor. Beyond that was...

Nothing.

Darkness. A void, yawning into eternity.

Nails squinted. "*We shoulda brought a flashlight!*"

"*Wait! I have this!*" Zerk dug in the wide pocket of his huge jeans and drew out a key ring with a plastic circle the size of a quarter attached to it. He squeezed a button and a dribble of light oozed out.

"Oh yeah, Indiana Jones has got nuthin on you guys," Willie muttered, but the rain fell too hard now for them to hear him.

With the new light, they could see the crack had grown to nearly two feet high and twice as wide. They leaned in, Zerk directing the flashlight, and saw a slope beyond it, a slide downward into the bowels of the earth. The water in the bottom of the pit reached the lip of the crack and spilled down the ramp in shallow runnels.

"*It's a tunnel!*" Willie shouted.

"*Ha! We told you!*" Zerk whooped. "*Hello buried treasure, goodbye Asheville!*"

"*This is what Shruffy was looking for!*" Nails leaned forward to stick his head into the crevice. "*It's dug right into the clay! I'm going down there!*"

"*That's crazy! There could be a drop! You could fall! Break bones!*"

Zerk shook his head madly, water drops flying off. "*He's right, man, we can't do this!*" He grabbed Nail's wrist, pulling him back, and cried out, "*What if he's down there?*"

"*Who, the Jackal Man?*" Nails smacked his friend's cheek. "*That's just a story!*"

Before they could react, he sat down and pushed off, sliding down the slope like a water park ride. The darkness swallowed him.

His voice drifted back out a second later. "*Come on down! It's safe! Bring that flashlight too! I can't see shit!*"

Zerk swung his legs into the crack.

"*Zerk, man, don't!*"

"*He's my best friend!*" Zerk detached the tiny flashlight from his keys and gave it to Willie. "*Throw that down when I get to the bottom!*" He shoved off into the abyss.

Willie stayed poised at the top and decided that he was not going down there. Fuck Zerk, fuck Nails, fuck friendship or popularity or whatever he thought he was getting out of his newfound relationship. Nothing was worth this, no easy way out of his miserable life, even if the Jackal Man was just regurgitated crap.

They could have their flashlight. He was going home.

When he heard the cry of, "*Ready!*" he leaned forward to toss it down, and the embankment crumbled beneath his hands.

32

Willie tumbled headfirst down the slope, yelling uselessly as the last bit of light swept away.

He landed with a bone-jarring grunt against someone's feet, face down in two inches of muddy water. Willie rose up on his arms, spitting out grit and water that tasted like old socks, and then was helped back to his feet. The staccato feel of the rain was gone, but the sound of it was still above his head, muffled by yards of earth. He was wet and slimy from the insides of his sneaker to the depths of his ear canals.

"Where's the flashlight?" Zerk's voice echoed so much, it was hard to tell which side of Willie it originated from...but not enough to distort the stark panic. Willie finally picked him out by his glow-in-the-dark contacts, which were even brighter down here.

"I...I don't know! I must have dropped it on the way down!" He heard splashing as the older boys spread out to look. Willie stared upward at the crack, which might as well be a pinprick of light from a distant star. Water gurgled at the opening and washed down the slope toward them.

"It's gone now," Nails said. The echo repeated 'now' until it became a meaningless syllable.

"Jesus Nails, what if it floods in here?" Zerk asked.

The water was up to Willie's ankles, the swiftness of the current tugging at the cuffs of his jeans. "Or caves in."

"It won't, quit being such pussies! We're down here, so let's see where this thing goes."

Willie didn't bother to point out that if the tunnel didn't go up at some point, they were going to have to fill out new place of residence cards at the post office, address reading, 'Gaping Hole in the Ground.' He thought of every story he'd ever heard about people getting trapped in flash floods and how stupid he always suspected they must be.

Nails barked directions. "Zerk, stay on that side and feel along the wall. I'll stay on this side, and Willie, you get in the middle. Hold hands so we keep together."

They formed a line three abreast and moved down the corridor. Zerk's hand shook in Willie's. The feeble light from the crack disappeared entirely, leaving them in a world of darkness.

The tunnel widened and narrowed at varied intervals, never enough to be claustrophobic or for them to not be able to reach both sides by stretching. It never turned, never branched. The ceiling seemed to remain a fixed distance above their heads, and if the floor sloped any further, Willie didn't notice.

He expected the air to be dank and moldy, but it smelled musky. This was probably the first time this place had ever seen water like this.

"How much further do you wanna go?" Willie asked, and the loudness of his own voice made him flinch, like speaking in a quiet museum. They must've descended after all, because the rain was no more than a whisper somewhere above.

"I don't know. A little further. Until we find something."
Nails's answers came with the rapidity of machine gun fire.

"Nails...what can you possibly think we're gonna find?"

"Did you hear that?" Zerk asked abruptly.

They came to a stop, the three of them still holding hands
like the Goth version of Hansel and Gretel. The only sound
was the quiet rush of water, which now came up to their
shins.

"What?" Willie asked.

"Keep going," Nails pushed.

"What did you hear, Zerk?"

"Just *move!*"

"I don't think there's any treasure down here," Willie
said.

"Goddamn it, I don't care about any treasure!" Nails
roared. "But there's *something* down here, and Shruffy
damn well knew it, too! If we can't be rich, we're gonna find
whatever it is, and then we'll have that son of a bitch by the
balls!"

Willie frowned even though he knew neither of them
could see it. "That's what this is about? You getting even
with that cop? What do you think, he's got drugs down here?
Dead bodies? We're in a fucking tunnel halfway to China!
He sure as hell didn't dig it himself!"

There was a whisper of movement in the dark and then
Nails was on him, shoving him to the wall and bearing down
on his chest. "You listen to me," he spat, breath blowing
across Willie's nose. "I like you and everything, but if you
say another fuckin word that's not to the tune of 'yes sir,'
I swear to *God*, I will kill you and leave your body down
here."

"Okay. Fine."

The pressure disappeared from his chest and Nails growled, "Get back in line. Zerk, you're on the left."

They fell into formation, the current threatening to pull their feet out from under them with each step. Zerk's hand shook in Willie's, but he didn't bother to give reassurance, because he had none left to dole out.

Zerk's other hand trailed along the tunnel, the fingertips dragging across an uneven surface of rough clay. He was so deeply lost in thought that when the wall suddenly disappeared from his light touch, it almost didn't register.

At first he thought the tunnel widened beyond his reach. But when he stretched out, straining away from Willie, he caught a draft of cool air. His eyes strained for some sort of visual stimuli, but he might as well have them closed. He halted, dragging the line down as Nails marched on. "Hey guys, there's another—!"

A questing hand—pebbly and rough—came snaking out of the dark to grab his outstretched arm. Something that felt like razor blades dug into his skinny forearm. He screamed as it yanked him away from his friends.

Willie was thrown to his knees in the water by the sudden motion. Nails landed almost on top of him with a splash. Zerk's screech faded away as it bounced between the walls and then all was silent, except for the soft rush of water. The two of them crouched, Willie shivering and straining his ears for further sound.

When their companion yelled again, a wordless cry of pain, it came from far, far away.

Nails shouted, "Zerk, this is not fucking funny, man! Get back here!"

"I think he went that way!" Willie reached out and found Nails's head in the darkness, and turned it by the ears to face the direction Zerk had been pulled in. He wasn't even sure it was the right way himself anymore. The dark had turned him around, and severe claustrophobia was setting in.

"What's he doing?" Nails demanded. Willie moved forward with grasping fingers until he touched the wall. He found the edges of a branch in the tunnel three or four feet in width. Fetid air blew past him. The diversion of the shallow current at the split created random eddies and whirlpools that he could feel through his jeans.

Zerk's scream again drifted to them from far down the tunnel.

Da-svidan'ya, don't spit on ya, Willie's mind whispered.

"Zerk's not playing."

"I know," Nails said coldly. "We gotta get outta here."

"We can't just leave him!"

"And we can't help him either! We'll have to send someone back! If we stay down here we'll both..." He trailed off, and Willie's balls shriveled into raisins. "Wait a minute, *there* he is!"

Nails was at his shoulder, and Willie wondered how the older boy could see anything. "Where?"

"Down there!"

Willie could see nothing but the same inky darkness...at first. His eyes were so disused they didn't realize they were back in action. Far down the tunnel were two tiny pinpricks of green shining flatly against the dark.

"That's him, he's got in those stupid contacts!" Nails said. "Hey Zerk! Quit messin around!"

The eyes didn't blink.

"That's not Zerk."

An unearthly roar filled the tunnel. Bestial and primal, choked with rage. The green specks came at them like fired missiles. Willie heard the sounds of something splashing through the water.

"Run!" Nails commanded. Willie felt him flail away from the offshoot. They collided, and Willie fell again into the cold flood, deep enough to reach his chest when sitting, the current attempting to drag him away. Nails's watery flight sounded panicked.

Unfortunately, it was in the wrong direction, further underground.

Willie yelled, "Stop, you're going the wrong way!"

Water splashed into his face as whatever was in the passages with them entered the main corridor. He saw the floating green irises hone in on him before turning after Nails. Willie got to his feet, leaning heavily against the nearest wall.

"*Watch out Nails! It's COMING!*"

He heard the older boy cry out. The roar came again, pure fury expressed in echoed surround sound. It froze him, hardened his muscles, which was, he knew, exactly what it was supposed to do. He broke the paralysis and ran the other way. The water was up to his hips now, and gaining strength. Willie had to push against the current, each step weighing a ton as he lifted and replanted his feet in the muck along the bottom.

After an eternity, he realized he could see again. The texture of the walls crept out around him. He hit the steep slope and sprawled against it. The opening into the pit was visible above him. There was now a waterfall to rival Niagra flowing into it, splashing down on him with thunderous force.

He dove into the spewing water and tried to climb up the mud, but slid right back down.

"*Noooo!*" he moaned, the crash of water drowning him out. He could see the night sky up there, clotted with rain. He dug his fingers into the ramp to find purchase. Every handhold washed away between his fingers.

He was trapped.

Stuck with whatever else was down here.

Don't beat around the bush, Willster, Zerk said in his head. *You know what it is, it's the Ja—*

"*It's not real, there is no Jackal Man!*"

He felt his mind slipping, wanting to argue with itself until it whittled away to a lump of subconscious functions doing nothing more than keeping his body alive, when an odd clang came from above, ringing above the waterfall. Something rectangular appeared at the lip of the crack just feet above him, hesitated, and then plummeted down the ramp. Willie jumped out of the way as the aluminum ladder he and Zerk had lowered into the pit landed next to him. He realized the storm must've washed it down. Its base settled into the mud and leaned against the incline, stretching all the way back to the surface like a stairway to heaven.

Willie scrambled up on hands and knees until he was able to crawl into the pit. Rain pounded him again.

He reached back into the hole, expecting something to pull him in, and snagged the top rung of the ladder. Grunting, he hauled it out and replaced it against the wall of the pit. He was back on soggy ground and running for the gate in seconds.

Willie reached the fence, scaled its slick links, and looked back only after he swung a leg over the top.

During a quick bolt of lightning, he saw something else come crawling out of the pit.

Willie's feet and one of his hands slipped in his distraction. His other arm was nearly wrenched out of the socket as it caught his weight for a moment before his grip vanished. The ground rushed up and knocked the air from his lungs.

He stood, eyes bulging, unable to breath, and clutched his chest as the thing streaked across the lot toward him. It was too fast to be Nails or Zerk, a shadow marked only by those glowing green eyes.

His breath caught like a sputtering motor. Willie ran for the ditch where they'd left the bikes. It was flooded now, but he waded in, snatching at a handlebar and coming up with Zerk's bicycle. He wheeled it to the road, watching his pursuer as it scampered over the fence in two quick bounds.

Willie straddled the bike, legs barely reaching the pedals set for Zerk's tall, lanky frame. He stood and put all his weight down on first one side and then the other. His speed rose, tires kicking up thin flumes of rainwater. When he looked to his left, he saw that it—*not human, oh God, nothing like a human*—was running after him on two feet, cutting across the yard to head him off. He swept past it, neck craned over his shoulder. When lightning flashed again, he looked into its face.

And screamed.

Willie pushed harder and acquired a precious few feet of ground. He looked back for the last time and saw the creature perform an odd, graceful dive—like someone tripping but turning it into an acrobatic flip—and then it was running on four legs. It could've been a cheetah behind him now.

And it was gaining.

He had been pedaling for what felt like an eternity. Ahead were the first houses of Asheville. The stingingly bright street lights beckoned. Sudden anger invigorated him, causing him to grit his teeth and push harder until his legs quivered with the strain. Civilization flew by on both sides, but he didn't stop. He finally chanced another look back, expecting a tornado of claws and teeth, but the road was empty.

The Jackal Man—just a story, a myth, a legend—was gone.

Willie rode home, dove off the bike onto the front porch of his temporary home, and collapsed on the threshold.

33

Frank and Trisha listened to every word of the terrified boy's story until he seemed to run out of words, then sagged in his mother's arms on the couch. Trisha held him, swept fingers through his wet hair, and looked up at Frank. "What are you waiting for? Go call the police."

He stared down at them and crossed his arms. "No, absolutely not."

"*What?*"

"I don't need any more publicity down at that site! Today we have a hundred protestors and reporters! Can you imagine what it'll be like tomorrow if they hear this crap?"

"Frank," she said, as Willie shook against her like a hypothermia victim, "those kids could be *dead*. You're telling me you're not going to call the police?"

He realized he sounded ridiculous, but he had enough people trying to shut him down without having a hand in it himself. "Trish, even if we call them, what are we supposed to say? Those two are probably playing some kinda joke on him! He didn't see what this thing was!"

"It was *him!*" Willie cried suddenly, his face buried in his mother's chest. He lifted his head and shouted at Frank, "It was the Jackal Man!"

"Oh God," Frank groaned, and then immediately thought of the rifle sitting in the garage, wrapped up in rags beneath a workbench.

Willie jumped to his feet, coming so close to his father that Frank's slight gut grazed him. Frank didn't recoil, didn't flinch, although he suspected his son was on the verge of hitting him.

"It was him," Willie repeated. Tears threatened to spill from both eyes, but he spoke slower. "I know it was him. I saw him."

"You sure you weren't high? You can see a lot of things when you're hopped up on dope or speed or whatever the hell you went out there to do!"

Willie's eyes blazed, the tears evaporated by that fire.

"What's that supposed to mean, Frank?" Trisha demanded. "Willie's never done drugs!"

He kept his gaze rooted on the boy. "You wanna tell her, or should I?"

"You promised you wouldn't. You *promised*."

"And you promised to knock off all this bullshit!"

"All right, fine, those guys were into drugs and you caught me with them one time!" Willie held his hands up in surrender. "But that has nothing to do with this!"

"How can I trust anything you say?"

"All right, enough!" Trisha stepped between them. "Frank, goddamn it, if you don't call the cops, *I* will."

"All right, Jesus, I'll call!" He retreated to the phone. "You know, this should be Damon's fucking problem, but I can't find the asshole!"

"So grow up and deal with it yourself. And then you and I are going to have a talk about honest parenting."

"That's one to look forward to," he muttered. Frank

stabbed buttons on the phone, doing exactly as his wife had asked.

Shruff had finally passed out on the couch after watching a news story where every detail of his accident at the age of 18 was drudged up for the viewing public. They called it a "bizarre mishap," a title so pretty you could put a pink bow on it. Truth be told, it really wasn't even all that interesting, but mix in urban legend monsters, today's protest, and a generous helping of unstated implication, and it became a juicy find, elevating the whole shebang to lead item in a few local venues.

Chief Windham called soon after and told him to stay away from the station for a few days. He didn't sound happy with everyone's favorite obsessive detective.

When Shruff answered the phone next time it rang, he was prepared to tell another reporter which orifice microphones fit best in, but by the time Stanford finished explaining, he was pulling on fresh clothes.

"Christ, those two have fucked up now!"

"You know these kids?"

"They're from town, just some teenage troublemakers. I...uh, I found your son out there with them last night, and ran them out."

"Oh really? He conveniently forgot to mention that."

"Don't get too down on him. He seems like a good kid."

"You let me worry about disciplining my son. I called you because I want as little attention as possible. You saw what those people were like today."

"Yes, don't call anybody else, don't do anything until I've had a chance to go out there." The words were out before his stomach put in its vote about this idea.

But if he didn't help those two idiots, who would?

"You say your son claimed there was an underground tunnel?"

"Something like that, but it's hard to get the complete story out of him. He's pretty shaken up, I'll say that much. Do you wanna talk to him?"

"Not now. I need to get out to your construction site." He paused. "Those boys are in a lot of trouble, Mr. Stanford. If they're even still alive, they need help right now."

Silence came from the other end of the line, and he suddenly heard the way he must sound. Stanford finally said, "I'll go out there with you. Swing by my house on your way and I'll wait for you in the front yard."

Shruff felt such unexpected relief he wanted to burst into tears. The only thing he wanted less than going back out to those woods at night was to do so alone. "Okay. Fifteen minutes."

The rain stopped by the time they reached the site half an hour later, but large puddles waited everywhere. The merciless sun would dry everything out by midday tomorrow, but for now, the air was muggy. The moon peeked from behind the broken cloud layer, throwing just enough light on the world to make the shadows leap off the ground.

"You do have a gun, don't you?" Frank asked. It was the first words to pass between them since Shruff had picked him up.

The detective patted his side under his left arm. "You buy that rifle yet?"

"Yeah. A .308. Should I have brought it?"

Shruff looked across the field through the front windshield

and asked, "What about your boss? You get a hold of him yet?"

Frank shook his head.

Shruff squirmed around to lean into the back seat of his car. The man was so pale now he appeared to glow in the dark. His hands shook every time he took them off the steering wheel. He emerged with a large flashlight and Frank saw him glance at the marsh that ran parallel to the property before saying, "Let's go check it out."

Frank unlocked the gate for them to slide through. Steam rose off the houses and the construction equipment, giving everything a hazy screen. Beyond the fence, a ground mist clung to the meadow like gravy. The rain had washed away the crickets for the night, and a wet silence hung over the woods.

The pit edge had been eroded away by the rain into a sloping curve. The ladder still leaned against the wall as Willie said, but the last foot of it was buried in a layer of brown soup.

Shruff glanced at him and aimed the flashlight into the hole, hand jittering. Both men sucked in a breath as he switched it on.

The bottom of the pit was a smooth wall all the way around, no cracks, no gaping holes leading to tunnels, no nothing. Just clay and slick mud.

"He lied." Frank's jaw clenched hard enough to hurt. "I knew it. Probably getting high with those bastards and hallucinated the whole thing."

"No, he didn't. I saw the tunnel when it was just a tiny crack in the wall. It was right there." He waved the flashlight beam against one wall of the pit.

"You? When did you see it?"

"Last night, when I caught your son here."

"So I gave you the key, and you came running out here in the middle of the night? Jesus, you're as bad as he is."

Shruff squatted at the edge of the pit, peering closer into the hole. "There's no way that mud could've filled it in, not if it was as big as your son says."

"So what does that mean? Someone covered it up deliberately in the last hour?"

Shruff didn't speak. To Frank, he appeared to be having trouble breathing, his chest rising and falling in long, deliberate strokes. "I took Willie home and when I came back, it was gone, just like now. All I can figure is that the rain opened it up again, and then, after Willie escaped...someone closed it up."

"Or maybe this town infected my kid with your hysteria."

The detective looked up at Frank and then past his shoulder. He swept the flashlight beam up so fast Frank jumped, raising his fist to swing at whatever was sneaking up behind him.

"For someone that thinks we're all crazy, you sure are jumpy." The detective motioned with the flashlight. "Take a look at that."

Frank turned to see the circle of light trained on the house at the westernmost corner of the lot, closest to the pit. Something soggy and limp hung from one of the boards, under the cover of the rudimentary eave. Shruff lifted it off the nail it was caught on, spreading out the sleeves of a rain-moistened leather jacket. "This belongs to Nelson Kredell. He was one of the boys your son said was down here."

"I know, I saw the idiot earlier this week. He was wearing that thing in hundred degree weather."

"He never goes anywhere without it." Shruff stared at the bed of marsh grass outside the site again.

"So maybe he forgot it this time. It was raining and he just wanted to leave after scaring my son."

"Okay, let's assume he did. But they wouldn't have forgotten the bike, especially since your son took the other one."

They slogged back through the site, legs covered in mud up to their ankles. At the front, Frank locked the gate again and they strolled along the Dark Road, shining the flashlight into flooded ditches. It didn't take long before they saw metal glinting under the misty surface of a deep puddle. Shruff thrust an arm into the water and pulled a bike out by the pedals with the flair of a David Copperfield trick.

"Nails loved this bike. Hand-painted it himself. No way he would leave it here."

"Goddamn it, what do you wanna do then? I'm a little too old to be playing Sherlock Holmes, so stop beating around the bush and tell me what's going on."

"I've tried to, Mr. Stanford." Shruff let go of the bike, allowing it to crash down on its side, and whirled around. "Everybody in this town has tried to, but you don't want to hear it."

"Look, I heard all about you on the news, all right? I know what happened to you when you were a kid—"

"You *don't* know," Shruff barked. "You don't know what it's like to grow up with a roadmap of hell printed on your throat. To live in a town where they still tell stories about you and all you can think about is getting your hands on the thing responsible. To hang upside down while you bleed out and your only friend dies next to you. You don't know about any of those things, so don't tell me you do."

Silence stretched out, so deep Frank almost wished for the cacophony of the crickets. They stood uncomfortably, the effect of the story much better than the one John Boyd told in the bar.

"So...you think the Jackal Man killed this kid that was in the car with you all those years ago?"

"The cause of such wounds from the accident would've been impossible. Look it up yourself. And I know what I saw, so if you tell me otherwise, we're gonna have a problem."

Frank said nothing. Obviously the man was upset, he could understand that, but...

Why don't you tell him your story, Frankie, his father rasped. *After all, he told you his. Maybe it'll help him understand why you think this is all a big practical joke. Everyone's in on it: this detective, Willie, Damon, Trish, the rest of this town. Even Lyles. They're all waiting in the bushes and the minute you show any sign of believing this crap, out they'll come to laugh in your face.*

He didn't believe that, but he *couldn't* believe the other; there was simply some mechanism in his brain that refused to entertain the idea of the Jackal Man for even a second.

Shruff turned in a slow circle with the flashlight. "I've been trying to find him. While everybody else in Asheville tells stories, I've been doing something. It all came down to just one thing: where would such a creature hide—where would it live—for so long without being found?"

"In this tunnel?"

"Not just one tunnel, but a whole *system* of them, burrowed all through this clay under our feet. I don't think it always lived down there, but it was forced to go underground when man started taking over this land."

"That doesn't explain the nonsense about how it's been here for centuries. I mean, *nothing* is immortal."

"I don't have all the answers...but I want them."

Frank pointed to the bicycle. "What about those two?"

Shruff shook his head, his fingers rubbing against his neck as he spoke. "We don't have too many options here. We can't sound the alarm unless their parents confirm they're missing. Even so, with their track record, they'll just be treated as runaways."

"What do you mean, 'runaways?' Can't you get the police or somebody out here?" He waved his arms in frustrated circles like he was trying to take off. "Doesn't everybody believe in the Jackal Man? Isn't that the whole point?"

"We leave him alone, he leaves us alone. There's nobody in town that's gonna risk coming out here to look for two people that nobody is even crying over. Trust me, I've seen it happen. The Jackal Man gets what he wants and that's that."

"They would let a child die?"

"It's happened before. A case I was on about six years ago. Girl got lost in the woods. Nobody would even search for her until daylight and even then…"

"That's not insane, it's just…" Frank's brow furrowed, "stupid."

"I can't explain the psychology of this town to you in one easy bite, Mr. Stanford. The one rule they live by is, 'Don't fuck with him, and try to stop others from doing the same.'"

"Well, Jesus Christ, we have to do *something!*"

"I know!" Shruff shouted. "And it's always left to *me!* But even if we find the entrance to that tunnel again, are *you* willing to go down there?"

Frank wiped a hand across his forehead, smudging dirt and mud. "No."

"See? And you don't believe a word I've said, so imagine what it's like for someone that does."

Shruff set the bike back on its feet and began walking it back to his car. Frank joined him and lifted up the back tire to put it in the trunk.

"I'm going to talk to their parents tonight, if I can find them," the detective said. "You going to be around tomorrow? I'd like to talk to Willie."

"Sure. It's Sunday, but even if it wasn't, there's not much point in coming to work."

They climbed into the vehicle. Frank noticed the other man left the place with a hell of a lot more speed than he came to it, and the ugly woods seemed to be alive and watching.

34

Nelson Kredell—or Nails, as he'd been called since he was old enough to swipe his first pack of cigarettes—couldn't tell the difference between the darkness behind his eyelids and the one outside them. For a second, his mind insisted he was back in the storage shed his father had locked him in overnight once when he was six, to punish him for spilling a glass of grape juice on the carpet. The darkness had been so thick during that long night it became more than just the absence of light; it closed around him like dried rawhide, smothering him, a steel thread around his chest.

That darkness of the shed when he was six was very much like this one. Alive. Dangerous.

Hungry.

When he remembered the hands that had shoved him into the wall hard enough to knock him out, his breath came shorter. The cool, tough image he'd worked so hard to create was shed like old snakeskin.

But when he didn't faint and he didn't die, he gradually manhandled the fear into a manageable ball in a back corner of his brain and took stock of what his other senses could tell him.

He was still sopping wet, but wherever he was, the dirt floor under him was dry. It smelled worse than before; the heavy scent of packed bodies, like that of a zoo animal's cage, mixed with a wild musk and something far, far worse. He couldn't hear anything, and somehow that was worse than being in the shed, where the sound of the crickets was still audible, along with the passing of traffic. The lack of sound coupled with the darkness gave the impression of a coffin.

Nails flipped onto his knees. He would just have to find a way back. And after he got out of here, he was going to be *famous*. He would be on TV and in the paper and this would be some serious shit to spread around. Might even get him laid.

He crawled along the rough floor until his hand brushed against flesh.

It was an arm. He felt his way upward to the shoulder, then the head. A head with hair on only one side.

A relieved sigh exploded out of him. "Zerk, thank God! C'mon, get up, we gotta get outta here!" His voice no longer echoed, but fell flat in the dead air.

Zerk didn't answer or move. Nails patted his cheek and felt his head loll.

He waited, crouched in the dark, then leaned over to put his ear against his best friend's chest. His head landed in warm stickiness. He jerked away.

Nails raised a hand—he didn't need to see to know it shook—and moved to touch the damp patch on the other boy's stomach.

It landed on Zerk's chest and then went *into* it, entering a cavity where warm organs squished against his intruding hand.

Nails screamed and flung himself away.

He crawled in the opposite direction, away from Zerk, and got no further than a few feet when he heard the hiss.

It was low and quiet, but impossible to miss in the oppressive silence.

Two green ovals came into his field of vision on the left, the only thing to focus on in this sea of black. He froze.

They floated through the darkness, passing in front of him, disappearing on his right, and then reappearing on his left after a few seconds, coming in front of him again.

Circling.

The ovals (and it was a little bit late in the game to still be fooling himself; they were fucking *eyes*, and they belonged to the creature he'd been hearing about since he moved to Asheville but that he *never*, not for one *instant*, really believed in) continued around him in smaller circles until they stopped inches from his face. He could see every detail of those dazzling corneas.

Here kitty, kitty, he thought, and cracked a weary smile.

The eyes examined him, sized him up. He felt warm breath blowing across him and realized he was wrong; the darkness wasn't hungry, only what lurked in it.

Nails felt his bladder let go as claws closed around his throat, close to where his tattoo was etched on in a similar design.

RIVER MEADOWS

THE SITE SUFFERS A LOSS

35

The night was long on dreams for Shruff, hellish conjurations of Nails and Zerk in the dark, somewhere far from the light of day. He woke—two hours later than planned—with a feeling of intense helplessness. Nails's father had told him that he hoped the 'little fuck' was dead and slammed the door in his face. Zerk's parents were in Ireland, but the French-speaking maid communicated to him that they'd left word to just send the police report and any tickets their son incurred through the mail.

It was almost a certainty, he realized while showering, that both of those boys were dead. A sacrifice from Asheville, long overdue payment toward the debt accrued since the Lyles Corporation came to town. Their bodies would be found eventually, and he would have another SPECIES UNKNOWN report to file.

After a breakfast of old bagels, he called Frank. The man's wife answered on the third ring, and he introduced himself.

"How's your son today, Mrs. Stanford? Your husband said he was pretty shaken."

"He seems calmer but...I don't know. He couldn't sleep last night, and this morning he just seems dazed. Whatever he saw..."

She didn't finish, but she didn't have to, not with him. He was very familiar with this brand of morning-after. "Would you mind if I came by? Do you think he'll be able to talk to me?"

"I think so. Maybe you can make sense of this, because I have no idea what's going on."

"I'll see what I can do. I have to make one short stop, but I'll be there as soon as I can."

He arrived at the hospital to find that the great lion tamer had been moved from critical to intensive care after regaining consciousness.

Oakland was in a small room with impressionistic paintings of roses on the wall, occupied by one other male patient. He lay in a mechanical hospital bed adjusted so he could sit up. A bank of beeping monitors flanked him, and he had enough wires running into him to give power to half the city. An elderly woman sat in a chair by his side, leaning over his chest and talking to him quietly.

She caught sight of Shruff and stood up, her hip cracking audibly in the still hospital room, and crossed to him. She brushed past and laid a hand on his shoulder, whispering, "He's older than he thinks he is, Detective. Play nice with him."

"I'll try."

"Hurry up and get over there. You're the only person he's asked about since he woke up."

He nodded and waited till she swept out of the room before approaching the bed. Oakland's eyes were closed, his skin the dusty paleness of plaster. Shruff hesitated, caught between calling out and tapping him. Before he could do either, the man's eyes flew open and that cocky smile stretched his lips.

"So you finally decide to check up on me? You almost get me killed, then you just dump me in the ER doorway and go back to hunt your monster."

"It wasn't like that!" Shruff blurted. "You're the professional, how was I supposed to know you were gonna have a heart attack?"

The man in the other bed stirred across the room. "What? Who's here?"

"Oh, keep quiet! It's no one for you!" Oakland snapped. He looked at Shruff. "The last thing you want to do is get him riled up. I've heard so many war stories I'm starting to think I was there, too!"

"I heard that!" the other man called out.

"Good, then there's nothing wrong with your hearing. Now go back to your coma, we're having a private conversation over here!" Oakland kept a scowl pointed at the other bed until he was sure he had the last word. Shruff's teeth found a good-sized chunk of tongue to bite. He hadn't realized how relieved he was that the old man was okay until this moment. "Please Detective, have a seat. I detest when people hover."

Shruff sat down in the seat vacated by the elderly woman and asked, "How're you feeling?"

Oakland waved the question away. "I'll live, but my insurance rates won't. Anyway, that's not what I want to talk about and that's certainly not why you're here. I've done a lot of thinking while I was stuck in this bed. As you might have guessed, I'm a firm believer in the Jackal Man now."

Shruff felt his muscles go limp. "Thank God. I was afraid you'd have amnesia or something."

Oakland snickered. "No, quite the opposite. I remember every detail, and I've been trying to find some answers."

"Like what?"

"First, tell me: what's happened while I was out of the game?"

"Three boys were attacked last night at the site. Only one made it out; he's the foreman's son. The other two are still missing."

One of the monitors at Oakland's side increased its rate of beeps. "Oh God, that's horrible. Those poor boys. I was afraid of something like this. It must be getting desperate." He quieted for a moment, fumbling with his hospital sheets and the wires from his wrists. "You're right, Detective. This…this *creature*—I don't know what else to call it—is a menace, and it's up to us to stop it."

"You don't know how long I've been waiting to hear those words."

"Unfortunately, I can't do much more than help you understand what you're dealing with."

"Then help me, please. What did you see that I didn't? What the hell is this thing?"

"Quick and vicious, and more violent than any cat I've ever worked with." That monitor's beeping had increased yet again. Before Oakland could speak further, a nurse popped her head in and asked if everything was all right. After shooing her away, he said, "Let's start with that roar we heard as we were, um, 'ushered out.' Only four known big cats in the world can do that: lions, tigers, leopards, and jaguars. I've heard all of them, and though it sounded closest to the jaguar, there was more of a harsh quality to it, almost a bark. I agree with you that this must be the origin of its misnomer."

Shruff thought briefly of that ululation echoing across the

site. His breath tightened so hard his lungs might've been dipped in bronze.

"You all right? You suddenly look like maybe you ought to be lying here instead of me."

"No, I'm fine. Please go on. I need to hear this." The next breath wasn't coming. The image of that dark shape streaking toward them...of it clinging to the car as it looked in at them...

"Well, then you have its speed. When it crossed that field to get to us, it must've been clearing sixty miles an hour, maybe sixty-five. Cheetahs can get up to seventy."

"No, that's impossible," Shruff wheezed. He coughed once, short and rough, and his breathing jumpstarted. "I admit it was hauling, but it chased that boy last night on a bike and the boy got away. There's no way he could've outrun that thing if it's as fast as you say."

"Ah, but that only proves my point." Oakland held up one wrinkled finger. "Cheetah's are the fastest land animals on earth, but their longevity is surprisingly short lived. They can maintain top speed for only a few hundred yards. If their prey can outlast them in the wild for mere seconds... escape is simple. Plus, it had the jumping power of a puma on speed, the climbing agility of a leopard, and its eyes! They were brighter than any species of caracal I've ever seen."

"You're saying it's some kind of cat hybrid?"

"No, not at all! The idea that so many cats from such far corners of the globe could've gotten together to intermingle is preposterous. I'm merely showing you the similarities in attributes so that we can be certain that we *are* dealing with a cat, in whatever form it's evolved into. And let's not forget the 'Man' part of his name. That thing...it may have moved and sounded like a cat, but, God help me, it *looked* like a man. Its bone structure held it upright! And it obviously had more intelligence than your average housecat, but, well... where do you draw the line?"

"So do you believe it's a monster now? That it thinks like us?"

Oakland shrugged helplessly, the enthusiasm in the gesture making him look very much younger than he was. "If we let ourselves go down that route, we're just being paranoid about something that's miraculous enough with bringing the supernatural into it."

"You don't think there's anything supernatural about it? I mean, the Jackal Man has been spotted around here for centuries! I don't care if it's a cat or man or both, nothing that fits your theory could have lived so long!"

The beeping of Oakland's heart monitor was now so rapid it was almost one continuous drone under their conversation. He shook his head, frowning, lost in thought.

"So what do we do now?"

"Just like with any animal, when its habitat is being invaded, it starts to get reckless. That's why there's been so much drastic activity out there lately. I imagine it feels pretty cornered with civilization crowding in on all sides of it."

The nurse entered behind them. "I'm sorry, sir, you'll have to leave now. Mr. Oakland needs his rest."

"I'm a cop." Shruff flashed his badge. "Can I stay a few more minutes? This is police business."

"I don't care if you're God. Out, now." She waved him toward the door.

He looked at Oakland, who met his eyes around the nurse with what looked like panic. "Detective, you've got to find a way to seal off the area and keep people out of those woods until we figure out what to do next."

"If it were that easy, I'd've done it years ago."

"*Out*," the nurse insisted.

"If it's getting desperate, there are liable to be a lot more attacks, maybe even further into town!" the zookeeper shouted as the nurse pushed Shruff through the door. "Watch yourself! Big cats have a tendency to go for the skull and throat, as I'm sure you already know!"

"What the hell is wrong with you people?" the man in the other bed asked, initiating a fresh tirade from Oakland that Shruff couldn't make out on his way to the elevator.

His hand was on his throat, massaging the mass of wrecked tissue there.

36

Frank let Shruff into the house at close to one o'clock. "I can't seem to get rid of you."

"Trust me, you're not at the top of my list either. But for now, it looks like we need each other."

"Whatever you say, Mulder. You want lunch?"

"Thanks, but I haven't got the stomach for it. How's Willie?"

"Better than he was yesterday, but not as good as he was the day before." Frank realized the irony in the fact that he would give anything to have his son back in working order, even if it was just the one that liked multi-colored hair and eye shadow.

"Did you track down your boss yet?"

"I've been trying to reach him all morning. His own wife doesn't even know where he is." That was understatement. Lucy Bradford was worried to the point of nausea and had the police standing by for tomorrow morning if Frank didn't find him by then.

"There's no chance..."

"What?"

"That he might've gone out to the site by himself?"

Out of all the scenarios he'd come up with to explain Damon's disappearance, here was a new one. He kept returning to what the man had hinted, about Lyles having something to do with Gammon's disappearance. "I don't see any reason why he would."

"Do you know if he got out of town okay?"

"The last contact I had with him was when we left the Howler." Now Frank was thinking of brawlers like John Boyd and the gun salesmen, with their intense dislike of outsiders.

Shruff seemed to pick up on his thoughts. "I'll ask around, see if anybody that was there saw anything."

Before they could say more, Willie entered the room, shepherded by his mother. She sat him on the couch and told Frank, "Casey's upstairs. I didn't want her to hear this."

Willie perched on the edge of the couch, face drained of color. He hadn't bothered to spike his hair with the metric ton of gel that was usually required, and the orange stood out in puffs. His mother sat and put an arm around him while Frank stood across the room with his arms crossed.

"Hey, kid," Shruff said to the boy.

"Hi," Willie mumbled. "Here to say, 'I told you so?'"

"About?"

He glanced at Frank. "You know. Nails and Zerk. Your warning."

"Well...we all gotta be right some time."

"Let me know when it's my turn."

Shruff knelt in the floor and looked up at him. "Trust me, I know how hard this is on you."

Frank saw the kid's eyes slip from Shruff's face, down the side of his mangled neck. "Yeah...I kind of figure you do."

"Why don't you tell me the whole story? This is the last time anyone will make you repeat it."

The boy frowned and swallowed. "Nails and Zerk came to my window upstairs," he began miserably. He talked for the next fifteen minutes, including horrified pauses. "And then I just pedaled home as hard as I could, and when I looked back...it was gone."

Frank noticed Trisha sniffling beside Willie, though whether the tears were sympathy for those two punk idiots, their son, or something else altogether, he didn't know. He stared at Willie hard, waiting for some break in the terrified façade.

Why don't you face it Frankie: the boy ain't lying. He really believes *this.*

"Okay Willie, that's good, but I need to ask you something, and you won't get in trouble if you say yes. I just need to know that this isn't some hoax or trick, and that those two aren't going to suddenly pop up and make us all look like fools. So...were you doing any sort of drugs with them?"

"No, I've never done drugs in my whole life!" he shouted desperately, looking from mother to father.

"All right Willie, okay, I believe you. But were *they?* You won't be protecting them by lying."

"No goddamn it, all right? They didn't have any drugs! We weren't hallucinating or whatever you're trying to get me to admit!"

"All right, fair enough. What can you tell me about this tunnel?"

Willie continued to scowl as he said, "Nothing, really. It was dark and big and went pretty deep underground."

"Can you...describe the creature that chased you?"

The boy closed his eyes and began to shake. "It was him. The Jackal Man. He has green eyes just like they say."

Frank turned away with a smirk. "Gimme a fuckin break."

"Mr. Stanford, please, hold on," Shruff said without turning around.

"It's true!" Willie shouted over the detective. "He's real, why won't you believe me? Don't go back there Dad, don't go back to work! Let's just go home before he comes after me!"

"No one's coming after you, honey." Trisha put a hand on his shoulder, which he shook off as he rose from the couch.

"Yes he IS, so don't treat me like a kid! I've seen him, I've been inside his home, and he's gonna come for me! He killed Nails and he killed Zerk and their bodies are down there in the dark with him! I had…oh God, I had nightmares about them… that he was down there eating them…" He trailed off into blubbers, but the hysterical speech had been enough to put shivers down the room's collective spine. Trisha caught Frank's eye as she led their son back out like some kind of mental patient, and he couldn't interpret the look she gave him.

"Jesus, he might be in shock," Shruff said.

"No shit."

"So take him to the hospital."

"Here, in town?"

"God no, unless you want him to be a circus exhibit. Take him to Arlington."

"What are you gonna do?"

"There's nothing I can do, short of prospecting for Jackal Man burrows by myself. I'm back to square one, just like always. I have to admit though, I really thought something would happen this time, after your company moved to town."

"But we're just a footnote in the Jackal Man file, is that it?"

Shruff grunted. "I'd love to know what made you so cynical, Mr. Stanford." He turned and left the house without waiting for a reply.

~ ~ ~

Frank found Trisha standing over the kitchen sink. He watched her for several seconds, thinking of the night—Jesus, had it only been last week?—that he told her they were coming here, back in their own house where they might not be perfectly happy, but at least they weren't all on the verge of a nervous breakdown. Funny how much he missed that other life he'd complained so much about.

She sensed him and turned. Their eyes locked. Frank braced for a fight as she rushed across the kitchen and threw her arms around him. Her face pressed into his side until her nose felt like a dagger.

"What? What is it?"

"I've never been so scared in my life!" she said into his chest.

"Trish…babe…do you really think there's a monster out there in those woods?"

She lifted her head to look at him. "Why would he make something like this up?"

He took a deep breath before answering. "Okay, I admit, it doesn't seem like he's lying. But that doesn't mean I think it really happened that way."

"God Frank, the drug thing again?"

"Maybe it's not drugs," he conceded. "But the fact is, I would be more willing to believe he has some sort of late stage brain tumor giving him hallucinations than the fact that he saw a centuries-old cat monster chasing him down the street. It's utterly ridiculous, don't you see that?"

"Does it matter, Frank? I mean, does it *really* matter? *Willie* thinks it's real, and he's about to give himself a coronary at the age of fifteen."

"Then what do you wanna do?"

"Let's just go home. Coming here was a mistake. We haven't even been here a full week and we're falling apart at the seams. Whether this…this…whatever…is real or not, we have to get Willie away from it."

He held up his hands. "All right." As soon as he said it, a monstrous weight lifted off him. "If you wanna go home, we'll go home. I guess…there are plenty of other jobs I can take when we get back."

She hugged him again.

"Can I have some time to clear things up with Lyles?"

"Yes, of course. But you can't go back out there to work."

"There's no need. The dream is over, I think. River Meadows isn't gonna happen."

"It was a stupid idea anyway."

"*That*, I agree with."

He went upstairs to check on his children. Casey was in her room, playing quietly with dolls. He crept past to peek into Willie's room after pushing the door open a crack.

The boy had been asleep last time Trisha checked on him. In the late afternoon shadows, Frank had to peer hard to pierce the room's gloomy interior.

The bed was empty.

Frank shoved the door all the way open, his heart rate tripling. The window was closed, the room otherwise undisturbed.

He spun in a slow circle, panic leeching away his ability to think straight. At last he noticed light beneath the closet door. He turned the knob and yanked the door open to find Willie face up on the floor under a pile of his own clothes, arms beneath his head and staring at the ceiling.

"Wow," Frank said from the doorway. "You haven't

done this since you were eight."

The boy rolled his eyes to look at him. "Done what?"

"You used to go sleep in the closet when you got scared. Your mom and I would find you in a big pile of clothes every morning." The memory was as poignant and beautiful as a bouquet of flowers. "You know, most kids are scared of the closet."

"It always felt like a safe place. Still does."

Frank crawled into the small space on hands and knees and they sat for a moment in silence, him against one wall, Willie on the floor. It was a foot of carpeting that separated them, but it could've been a canyon. "Your mother and I have decided to go home. We're leaving."

"What about your job?"

"I don't care about my job. I just want you to be safe."

"You don't believe me anyway, so what does it matter?"

"Look Willie, this isn't about me not believing just you. I would say the same thing to anyone trying to tell me a story like that."

"But why? I don't get it."

Frank knocked the back of his head against the closet wall. This town had been trying to get the story out of him since he got here, so he might as well get it over with, especially if something good came of it. "When I was twelve, my father—your granddad—took me on a hunting trip with him and his friends."

"Really?" Willie sat up, pushing clothes off him, looking interested. "*You* went hunting?"

"God, I wanted to go so bad, I begged him for weeks. It was just me and a bunch of forty-year-old guys sitting around a campfire, shooting the shit, drinking beer. I felt like a man. And then, late that night, when they were good and drunk, they told me a story."

"About what?"

Frank hesitated, the word caught in his throat. For Christ's sake, he was actually still scared, after 30 years. His father's laughter floated through his head. "About...snipes."

Willie frowned. "What's a snipe?"

"It's a bird. Just a bird. But I didn't know that then. They'd decided to have some fun with me, and they told me this story about snipes half as tall as I was, with razor sharp claws and beaks that could tear your eyes out. Then they gave me an unloaded rifle and sent me off into the woods to hunt them."

"And?"

"And I cried like a baby and shit my pants. And then I came back and had a group of grown men laughing at me. All except my father, who just looked disgusted."

It was out now, a story he'd never told anyone, and there was no taking it back. He sat uncomfortably, waiting for his own son's response.

"Wait a minute, is that why we've never been camping?"

"Well..."

"And why you're scared of the woods?"

"I'm not exactly—"

"And why you won't go in the birdhouse at the zoo?"

"Hey, it smelled bad in there! But no, I'm only telling you this so...I don't know...maybe you'll understand why I have a hard time believing something like your story."

"Because...you don't wanna get laughed at?"

It sounded every bit as ridiculous as he feared when put like that. "Yeah. I guess so."

"But that's stupid," the boy argued. "I'm not messing with you. Why can't you just trust me?"

"Honestly? Because of all these changes you've gone

through lately. I don't know what's going through your head anymore, Willie. The fights, the orange hair, all the black clothes, that tongue ring—do you know what my father would've done if I'd come home with a tongue ring?"

"I don't *care!* So what if Grandpa was strict on you? He gave you a lifelong complex, so he probably wasn't a model parent!"

A laugh escaped Frank before he could stop it. "Okay, you got me there. But are you really comfortable looking like that? Is that you?"

"That has nothing to do with what happened. I just want you to believe me. That's all."

The boy watched him, studying every tic of his face. Frank tried to look past the hair and the clothes and just see his son. "All right, if you say you saw the Jackal Man in the woods, then you did. That's why, the sooner we get outta this town, the better."

"Thanks, Dad."

Frank crawled back out of the closet and stood up. "Come down when you feel like it."

He started to close the door, but Willie stopped him. "Dad?"

"Yeah?"

"You really shit your pants?"

He shut the door on his son's wicked grin.

37

Night again claimed River Meadows, and this time the summer evening's peace was broken by a rusted yellow Volkswagen trundling down the Dark Road, engine coughing and headlights off. It slowed and turned onto the dirt path to the construction site. The chain link surrounding the housing project began only yards from the road, and the driver barely had his back bumper off the pavement before encountering the barrier. Instead of stopping, the car turned again and drove parallel to the fence, running roughshod over grass and scrub weed until it reached the corner. It continued along the side to the back of the lot and parked directly behind Frank Stanford's trailer, neatly hiding the vehicle from the road.

With a squeal of hinges, the door swung open and Jaime Garcia—jittery previous employee of the Lyles Corporation under both Wesley Gammon and Frank Stanford—hopped out. He stayed low to the ground, leaving his car door open. The field was alive with crickets, masking the rustling of his feet. After clicking on a flashlight, he approached the fence on the backside of the lot with a small tool pouch.

His hands shook as he snipped a hole in the fence with a pair of wire-cutters. He was terrified, every muscle in his body quivering, nerves pumping out sweat by the gallon.

This would be the third time he'd robbed River Meadows. The nervous crewman's life had fallen apart when his wife was hospitalized nearly eight weeks ago with an unknown ailment that appeared almost overnight. The doctors spoke of surgery in the glib tones of those that didn't worry about how to make their yacht payment, let alone squeak by on next month's rent. Leaving him, in desperation, to commit acts he would've found deplorable under normal circumstances.

The first time, he took a few minor items from around the site to pawn and, though the money was swallowed up by the hospital in one gulp, he spent hours in self-imposed penance for it. The second time, he took something more substantial, and it brought enough to feed his children for a week, and pay enough medical bills to keep the doctors diagnosing.

When the fence went up and the guard dog was set loose, he searched for other ways to supplement his trickling income, but opportunities were few and far between. After the dog died, he convinced himself to move quickly for a last big score.

Of course, the dog's death was itself a concern. He'd seen the splashes of blood all over the site as he worked the past two days. The hard rainstorm last night had scoured most of it away, but the place still looked terrifying, with the solemn air of a cemetery. He wasn't from Asheville, but he had all the evidence he needed to believe in the Jackal Man. He looked back longingly at his car, but could think of nothing but his wife dying on their bed because they couldn't afford a permanent hospital room.

"*Chinga*," he exclaimed angrily under his breath. He went back to work, cutting at the thin metal links of the fence until there was a two foot gap at ground level. He slid the tool pouch to one side and knelt, casting a worried glance over his shoulder.

The crickets stopped as he crawled under the fence, but Jaime had too many other problems to notice.

Several prongs of the fence caught his shirt. There was a panicked moment where he thought he was stuck. He finally wriggled onto the other side with a ripped t-shirt and shallow gouges along his back brimming with blood, then reached for his tools.

Staying low, he made his way across the short patch of ground between his entry and the dynamite shed next to the foreman trailer. He wasn't going to waste time stealing tools again; the high-grade explosives he took last time had been purchased by a group of Arabic men in Dallas. He didn't know what they wanted it for, but he wasn't naïve enough to believe it was stump removal.

The shed was locked. Jaime used a pair of bolt cutters to break the flimsy chain, then opened the shed and shined the flashlight around the interior. The dynamite was still stacked inside, in their metal crates. Jaime didn't know how they worked, but he'd seen enough to make him handle them like newborn babies.

He pocketed the flashlight, stacked two crates on top of one another, and hoisted. There were about forty others in the interior of the shed. He meant to take every last one. Jaime walked as fast as he dared back to the hole in the fence. Each case was slid under, followed by Jaime, doing a backwards limbo. He retrieved them, but instead of heading for his car, he struck off in the opposite direction, heading toward the high marsh grass on the south side of the field.

His car would never be able to carry the entire load of heavy dynamite, and every extra trip he made out here only increased his chances of getting caught. He'd decided, on the way here, to move the stash to a location nearby, where he could pick it up at his leisure.

It was brilliant, but that didn't comfort him as he stepped into the thick waves of mushy grass and the curtain of high reeds closed after him. He couldn't even carry the flashlight because of his load. Jaime was forced to take one step at a time, making sure each foot was firmly planted in the muck before moving on. At this time of year, the sun had managed to dry up most of the marsh, but the rain the night before had left long patches of mud. Weighed down by the crates, Jaime struggled against the grass as it wrapped around his legs. In places it grew to his neck, and in others only the tip of his head bobbed above the surface like a submarine periscope. Somewhere on the other side was another clearing and then the woods would loom, a convenient spot to hide his treasure.

The grass to his right rustled. He paused, a thread of fear unspooling in his heart, until the wind repeated the noise.

Jaime got moving again, but went only another step before the grass in the same area swayed violently. Something low streaked in front of him. He gasped and jumped away, dropping one handle of the bottom crate. His knee came up to prevent a topple, and he balanced on one leg until he could find the grip again.

Just an animal. He closed his eyes, breathed deeply, and forced another step, the needs of his family outweighing his petty fears.

He whispered a Spanish prayer as the last short blades were crushed beneath his feet, then emerged on the far side of the marsh. The moon was full enough to show him the edge of the woods across the narrow strip of meadow.

Jaime ran across as fast as he could manage. It would require twenty trips to get all the dynamite moved, and, at this halting pace, the process would take all night. He dodged around trees until he was several yards into the dense forest, then pushed the crates into some low underbrush. No reason to think they would search this far if they thought it had been stolen, or so he hoped. He stood, rubbed his palms together, and tried to memorize the location.

Some of the branches that formed the canopy above him crashed together. A few shaken leaves drifted down.

There was a light *thud* as something hit the ground behind him.

Jaime turned, the hair on his neck hard enough to cut glass. His eyes wondered over trees dipped in black paint.

Nothing. No, wait. *There.* Wasn't that someone standing in the even deeper shadow of that oak tree? Jaime squinted. Yes, there was a bulge of shoulders and a head and...it looked like...it was wearing a strange hat with one side of the brim folded up...

He was hit from behind, knocked over and rolled three feet to crash into the base of a wide elm. Jaime flipped over, digging in his pocket for the flashlight, and turned it on.

Yellow light splashed onto a face he would've expected to see at the zoo. Eyes small, black slashes above a triangular nose, from which silvery whiskers sprouted. The nose twitched, nostrils flaring.

Sniffing in his direction.

Suddenly, Jaime thought of the blood on his back.

The black slits opened, and then he was staring into wildly luminous green eyes, like emeralds lit on fire. Its mouth peeled back in a hiss.

Jaime did the first thing that came to mind: he threw his flashlight and ran.

He made it back out of the woods, but the first glance back revealed the beast leaping over a bush and landing on all fours to give chase. It looked like a jungle cat back there, an escapee from "Wild Kingdom", and yet it didn't resemble anything that God ever intentionally created.

Jaime plunged back into the marsh grass and went sprawling over a root in the ground. The beast landed on his back. Furry appendages straddled his torn shirt. There was shrieking pain as his back was raked between the shoulders. A flood of warmth spread down his sides.

He pushed up, getting his hands and knees under him. For one moment, the Jackal Man was riding him like a cowboy on a mustang, and then the creature leaned forward and sank fangs into the tender area where his neck met his shoulder. Jaime bucked, thrashing violently, and his attacker's weight disappeared.

Adrenaline kicked in, giving him enough of a buzz to counter the blood loss. He stumbled into a patch of grass well above his head, hopelessly lost.

There was a roar behind him that echoed across the entire plain. Jaime found himself wrapped in tough blades of grass. He tore free, pulling them out by the root, then spun in a new direction, desperate for a way out. The Jackal Man was suddenly right in front of him, standing hunched on two legs, eyes ablaze.

Its arm shot out. Jaime looked down in time to see it rip into his stomach, plunging in up to a furry wrist. There was a curious sensation of pressure in his abdomen, followed by the unpleasant urge to vacate his bowels.

The hand yanked out, taking half his sternum and several ribs with it.

Jaime uttered a high, wordless whine and turned away.

Slippery organs oozed from the hole in him. He made feeble attempts to catch them as he fled. The Dark Road appeared out of nowhere. Headlights bore down on him and brakes squealed as Jaime toppled forward and landed on the pavement with a wet *thwak!* on top of his own viscera.

He heard feet running toward him, but Jaime was too far gone to care.

Back in the woods, misshapen hands lifted the boxes of dynamite he'd so carefully hidden.

38

Frank and Trisha went to bed after making sure Willie and Casey had gotten to sleep. Their son seemed a little calmer, and, for the first time since coming to Asheville, Frank felt like things were going to be okay. They lay together on top of the sheets in a cool breeze from the ceiling fan.

Her hand found his and squeezed. He rolled to look at her, and then they slid toward each other with no words, lips meeting, his hands under her sheer gown, and she began to moan in a curious ringing tone.

Then he realized it was his cell phone on the bedside stand.

"Let it go," she begged, moving to straddle him.

"Uh huh," he agreed. He reached for her (*snipes, Damon*), meaning to pull her close (*Lyles, Jackal Man, Willie*), and then it was gone, and he couldn't concentrate.

"Fuck." He reached for the phone.

"Not anymore," she growled, turning away from him.

"Hello?" Frank tried not to let his ragged breathing show.

"It's Shruff. We've got another problem."

"No, *you've* got a problem. I'm quitting and going home, just like you wanted. So there is absolutely nothing you can say that's gonna mean shit to me."

"We just had a body come in from River Meadows."

"Oh Jesus." He humbled his tone. "One of those kids?"

"No, this guy is Jaime Garcia. Hispanic. You recognize the name?"

Frank thought of the fidgety little man that always seemed to be watching him from the corner of his eyes. "Yeah, he's one of my employees."

"His car was found behind the site along with a hole he apparently cut in your fence. Do you have any idea why he would've done that?"

The tumblers clicked together hard and fast in Frank's head. "Jesus, he's the one that's been stealing from us!"

"They picked up his body half a mile down the road."

"I don't understand, what killed him?" He caught sight of Trisha, frozen on the other side of the bed, staring at him with round eyes.

There was sufficient silence at the opposite end of the line to let Frank know he wasn't going to be shitting himself with happiness over the answer. "He was...disemboweled. Torn apart. Like your dog. And before you say something wiseass, you should know that every reporter for a thousand miles is either calling the police station or holding vigil outside. They're gonna do an autopsy on Garcia's body, but it's all just for show. With the media swarming all over this, my chief can't just sweep it all away. They've been trying to get in touch with Mr. Lyles, but so far it's just been the run-around. I wanted you to be prepared in case you start getting calls."

"I don't care about that! What about Garcia? Did he steal anything?" Lyles would be arriving anytime, and, though Frank fully intended to go out with spectacular glory, he was still technically responsible for all the pricey equipment out there.

"There was nothing found with the body. Garcia's car is being towed in, but, like I told you before, the guys on the scene clear out of there pretty fast. And with my 'history,' my chief doesn't want me anywhere near this investigation, so I don't know how much more info I'll be able to get you." Shruff paused. "Listen Mr. Stanford, don't go out to the site anymore. I don't care whether you believe me or not, just stay away. This is getting out of control."

"Is that police talk or more friendly warnings?"

"Whatever it takes. With everyone's eyes on us, they'll be forced to issue a court order to shut the site down."

"Fine, Shruff! Shut it down, put your yellow police tape everywhere! I told you, I quit." He ended the call, hopped out of bed, and pulled on a pair of dirty jeans over his boxer shorts.

"Frank?" Trisha was up from the bed in a flash. "Where are you going? What happened?"

"There's been some kind of accident. I have to find out what's going on." He pulled on a shirt and sat on the edge of the bed to tie his boots.

"You said you weren't going back to the site!"

"And I'm not," he lied. Damned if he wasn't; he needed to know if Mr. Garcia's shopping spree had penetrated as far as a certain storage shed. "This is an emergency, Trish. I just have to check a few things out and I'll be right back."

She was still watching him through the open door of the bedroom as he sprinted into the living room, grabbing his truck keys from a dish on the television. He opened the front door and nearly stepped on a dark mass lying across the threshold. Frank squinted at it in the darkness until he remembered to turn on the porch light switch beside him.

A large dead rabbit, its body mashed and torn, a ragged hole in its neck leaking fresh blood.

Snipes, snipes! Not the voice of his father this time, but twelve-year old Frankie. Gooseflesh that felt the size of volleyballs broke out on his arms.

Frank kicked the mutilated corpse off the porch, into the bushes. Before he went to his truck, he took a quick detour into the garage.

Stress crushed every inch of him as he pulled out of the driveway and headed south through the maze of lit up streets. When his cell phone beeped at him for a low battery warning, he cracked the screen while trying to plug it into the cigarette lighter. He couldn't feel sorry for Jaime Garcia, no matter how hard he tried. The man was a thief, plain and simple. Probably had some sob story to tell, but Frank didn't get involved with his crews' personal lives. All he cared about right now was making sure that dynamite was where it should be.

He sped out of town, taking the curves of the Dark Road hazardously. Now that he was here, in these godawful woods, part of his determination died. His eyes roamed the trees, looking for anything out of place, and he hated himself for it. Within a few minutes, he could see the house frames and, sure enough, there were police barricades around the entrance to the site, but the interior was deserted.

The door to the shed hung open. He cursed as he stopped the truck just inside the gate and killed the engine, then started up the dirt lane toward the dynamite shack.

Before he got halfway there, a flat, resounding *crack!* rolled across the site.

Frank turned south, toward the dry marsh and the trees in the distance. He knew what that sound was, even if he hadn't heard it outside of the movies in years: the echo of a gunshot.

Someone had just discharged a weapon in the woods, close

to where Jaime Garcia was murdered earlier this very night.

And Frank suddenly thought it was very important to find out who.

He ran back to his truck, to the passenger side this time, and pulled the rifle from where he'd wedged it against the floorboard before leaving home. He hefted the weapon as he had in the store, expecting the wave of dizziness to hit him, and he wasn't disappointed. The weapon made him feel safe and sick at the same time.

The box of ammo was in his glovebox. There were twenty-five in the case. Twenty-five gleaming, pointed heads the width of a dime. He loaded one into the chamber, snapped the bolt closed again, and rammed it home. Suddenly the weapon felt like a live cobra in his hands. He put six more shells in his front jeans pocket.

Frank sprinted, back out of the gate and across the short stretch of field between the site and the marsh grass, bent at the waist, the rifle clutched in front of him with both hands. With his extra weight, he started wheezing after only a minute and slowed his pace until he could catch his breath.

He stayed low and crept forward into the marsh. A squishy layer of mud sucked at his work boots. For just a moment, he was back in those woods as a kid again, clutching a rifle as he hunted snipes. This was stupid, he saw that now. If anything he should pull out his phone and call Shruff or the Asheville PD to handle this, but it was the ghostly sound of his father's laughter that stopped him, and the disgusted look on the man's face when Frank had come back screaming and crying.

There would be no retreat this time. The rifle in his hands exuded that deadly feeling of power, calming his nerves. That was the real danger of a gun, he decided, to pump you up with a primitive species of confidence that made you feel invincible.

As he pushed further into the grass, he could hear the low crackle of burning wood. There was a burst of reddish light between the swaying blades ahead. He squatted behind a thick tuft of swamp weed, holding the rifle butt in one sweaty palm, and examined the scene.

The field on this side of the marsh was narrower than the one where River Meadows was being built, a thin strip no more than twenty yards across. It was bordered by the forest directly across from Frank and the Dark Road seventy or eighty yards down to his left, with random gatherings of trees and underbrush spread up and down its length. No more than fifteen feet from him was a dwindling campfire in a shallow pit bounded by a small circle of stones. This was nestled into a tightly packed stand of trees with thick bushes weaving among their bases that would've hidden the flames from anyone passing on the road.

The campsite was deserted. He could see a can of open food that looked like beans and beef, but the label was in a foreign language. Next to it was a knapsack, and an empty bedroll stretched out beside the sputtering fire. And resting on the bedroll was a distinctly familiar shape.

A hat. The kind with the brim folded up on one side, like an Aussie boomerang-tosser might wear.

"What are we lookin at?" a voice whispered, so close to his ear it might've been in his own skull.

39

Frank yelped in surprise and jumped away, propelling himself out of the marsh grass, and landed on hands and knees with the rifle's barrel still gripped in one fist. He spun onto his ass and continued to scoot away, past the fire.

The freaky, 'roided-out hunter strolled from the marsh as casually as if he were stepping out of a public restroom. He wore the same khaki shorts and blue shirt, and carried a rifle that put Frank's to shame: large and smooth black all over, with enough gadgets and enhancements sticking off of it to make it look like a prop from a sci-fi movie.

His name; what was his goddamned name?

"Deegan," the hunter reminded him with a grin.

Heart still thumping, Frank swung the rifle up from his position on the ground and pointed it at the man's chest, his right hand slipping up to caress the trigger.

"Hey now boyo, that's not nice." Deegan didn't seem the least perturbed about being on the business end of a weapon. In fact, his smile got even wider. "Didn't your father ever tell you not to point a gun at anything you didn't intend to kill?"

"Listen asshole, I *will* kill you if you don't freeze right there!" He could hear how shrill his voice sounded, but was powerless to stop it.

Deegan squinted in the dim light. "Stanford. I thought it was you. Saw you on TV, ya know. They definitely captured your bad side, Frankie."

The use of the nickname threw him off stride. "You're trespassing on private property!"

The hunter shrugged. That gun was still gripped loosely in his huge hands, but Frank was ready if it should start to swing his way. "You say 'poe-tayto,' I say 'poe-tawto.'"

It was a huge disadvantage sitting on his ass and aiming up at the guy, but shifting his weight would mean taking the rifle off his target. "I heard a gunshot. Was that you?"

Deegan nodded.

"What were you firing at?"

"Just squeezing off a few target rounds. The damn thing's been a tad busy the last couple hours, so I took the opportunity to build a fire and make myself some grub. Thought I was alone out here, but I gotta say, you did a great bit of stalkin! I smelled you when you got within thirty yards though. You should consider a less harsh cologne if you wanna be a hunter."

"What are you talking about, *what's* been busy?"

Deegan shook his head with that lop-sided grin still in place. "The Jackal Man, Frankie. I had him right where I wanted him, then some Mexican dude shows up and blows the whole thing. Course, he got paid back for it. With interest."

Frank swallowed. The man had just admitted to being here when Jaime Garcia was killed. And he could still be the person that butchered Caesar and left him on Frank's desk. In fact, the more he thought about it, every time a death occurred, here was this guy, right in the middle of it. He could very well have been the person chasing Willie and his friends in some kind of costume.

He could *be* the Jackal Man.

The thought of proving everyone in this horrid town wrong was so enticing, Frank chose to ignore the fact that his theory sounded like every *Scooby Doo* cartoon in existence.

"So you're aware there was a man killed out here to-night? Did you have anything to do with his death?"

"I'd have to be pretty stupid to still be here if I did, now wouldn't I?"

"Not stupid, just crazy."

"Oh Frankie, I'm not crazy." As if to demonstrate this, Deegan walked forward, in front of Frank and around the far side of the fire to his camp.

"*I said freeze!*" Frank bawled, scooting around to follow him with the gun.

The man lowered his own weapon to the ground, disarming himself before Frank even thought to ask. He hunkered down on the bedroll beside his hat and stretched out his legs. "Like your piece. Not much stopping power, but a good, solid weapon. You know how to use it?"

"I know how to pull the trigger."

"Good." Deegan let his gaze drift past Frank to the marsh. "You might need to. But for now, why don't you point that thing somewhere else and come have a seat?"

Frank decided that he *really* disliked the man, and it wasn't just from his aversion to hunting. He was just too cool, too calculating, too in control of the situation. That control had only slipped once, when he left the trailer a couple of days before and glared at Frank with absolute fury after his request was denied. "What's to stop me from taking you to the cops and letting them decide how innocent you are?"

Deegan looked at him, shook his head, the smile unfazed. "Because you're gonna have to kill me first. Gun me down in the coldest of blood. And both of us know ya ain't got the stones for that, Frankie. So either turn around and go back the way you came, or belly up to the bar."

Frank held the weapon on him a moment longer, contemplating those options, before letting the rifle barrel droop and then fall into his lap. His arms screamed from the released tension. He might not be able to take the hunter to the police, but, now that his hands were free, he could sure as hell bring the police to the hunter. Frank reached to the back of his jeans, meaning to grab his phone, and found the pocket empty.

The truck. He'd left the goddamn phone in his truck.

The hunter leaned back. "Have a seat," he repeated.

Frank reluctantly crawled closer to the fire and hunkered across from the other man. He laid the weapon on his legs.

"So what brought you out here, Frankie?"

"I told you, a man was killed on this land tonight. He was one of my employees."

"And you came all the way out here in the middle of the night to see if you could find his killer. Bravo."

"Actually I came out here to make sure the shit hadn't stolen anything. Did you really see him, or is that just more manure spilling from your mouth?"

"Oh, I saw him all right."

"And what was he doing?"

"He had these two big metal crates, carryin 'em out here to the woods. He stashed them in the bushes over there." He hooked a thumb over his shoulder at the expanse of woods behind him. "Couldn't tell what was in 'em though. Sealed up too tight for my nose."

"They were dynamite."

"Dynamite," Deegan whispered, with a raised eyebrow. "Interesting."

"Could you, by any chance, take me back to where you claim he put these crates?"

"I could, but they wouldn't be there. Jackal Man took 'em as soon as he was finished with your boy. I guess I shoulda taken a shot then, but I was still learnin his routines and such."

Frank snorted. "Spare me. You were the last person to see this man alive, minutes before he was gutted by an urban legend monster. Do you know how that would sound to a jury?"

"Am I not supposed to tell the truth?"

"The Jackal Man...is not truth."

Deegan paused, frowned, pursed his lips, blew air through them. "Do ya wanna know where I was this time last week, Frankie?"

"I don't care."

"Too bad, cause I'm gonna tell you anyway. I was in Canada followin up a Bigfoot sighting. The week before that I was in Mexico huntin vampires. The week before that I was in South America, lookin for the Mothman. How many you think I found?"

"None, because they don't exist."

Deegan's unnaturally blue eyes glittered in the remaining light from the campfire. "You got it in one. Now, I don't wanna lead you astray, I've been on plenty of other hunts where the creatures were as real as you or I, but they were never kills worthy of a trophy. I've seen some crazy shit—if you'll pardon the French—but nothing as dangerous as this thing."

Frank shook his head and looked away. How were you supposed to argue with someone like this? He glanced at his watch instead. It was near midnight. He needed to get away from this guy.

Deegan wasn't done yet. He pointed toward the woods behind him again. "You know what kind of trees those are?"

"Not a clue."

"You got cedar elms and Texas sumac. The woods in this area are full of 'em, but they grow in a pattern out here I bet nobody ever thought to check."

Best to keep the guy talking, but Frank's mind was still precoccupied with trying to figure a way out of this situation. "What pattern is that?"

"You see, they're tough, adaptable trees, so they grow well in places where other trees can't. Such as areas with poor drainage. Areas, let's say, where the soil was clay with nothin below to hold water. An area...where there might be a tunnel runnin right under the ground."

Frank looked up from the rifle and stared across the flames at the hunter.

"That's right, Frankie, you're gettin it. These trees trace the routes of the tunnels that he lives in. There's one branch right beside us here." He traced an invisible line in the trees that looked no different to Frank. "I haven't found the entrance points yet, but they must exist. Not only that, I heard about what happened to your kid. Saw some of it, actually. Thought that thing had 'im for a second, but he was quite a little trooper. You should be proud."

Anger flooded through Frank. He bounded to his feet, grabbing his rifle at the same time. "Goddamn it, quit calling me Frankie! I don't know what your game is here, but I'm leaving right now and calling the police!" He turned away from the hunter, determined to keep walking.

"You'll never make it."

The words froze him. Here it was, the overt threat he'd been waiting for. He brought the rifle up slowly, clutching it like a shield, and turned around. "I'm going home."

"And I'm not stoppin you. But we have company."

"Bullshit. If anything harms me between here and my truck, it'll be you."

"C'mon, I got an extra blanket for you. We're just two guys out in nature, roughin it, fightin a sleek killin machine." Deegan obviously took supreme pleasure in the sweat on Frank's brow.

He took another step away, keeping an eye on the hunter. Something in the marsh grass at his back moved. An entire section swayed as something streaked away. Frank jumped and swung toward the sound, feet tripping over themselves in his hurry to get back to the fire.

Deegan chuckled, pulling a blanket from his bag and spreading it on the opposite side of the fire. "Ya know, night isn't the safest time to go traipsing through a predator's territory. Especially for someone as bad with a firearm as you."

"You actually expect me to stay here?"

"Sure, take a load off. Sleep if you want. He ain't gonna attack yet. He's checkin us out, too. Probably never had anyone camp in his woods, and he's mighty pissed about it."

Frank looked back at the marsh. Whatever was in there had been big. He could walk around on the road, but that seemed no better an idea.

You're letting him get in your head!

He wasn't, he believed in the Jackal Man no more than when he arrived in Asheville, but there were devils you knew, and those you didn't.

Frank sat down on the blanket this time and laid the rifle aside, remembering to push the safety. "Don't suppose you have any cigarettes?"

"Nope. Clogs the lungs. You should quit."

"That's what my wife says."

"Smart lady." Deegan's chilly blue eyes drilled into him from the far side of the fire. "Why don't ya lie down, Frankie?"

"Why don't you fuck off?" Frank answered, but he found himself stretching out on the blanket, which was more comfortable than the couch at the rental house. Without the lights from town, he could see the stars for the first time.

"Now close your eyes."

Some part of Frank's mind screamed that this was absolute insanity, but closing his eyes suddenly sounded like heaven. Even though his nerves were still jangling, a wave of overwhelming tiredness swept over him. His eyelids fluttered. He let them slide closed.

When Frank came to, he was lying on his side, and no longer so comfortable. The fire had died, and he was in darkness. He started to turn on his back when he realized there was someone standing over him.

Frank yelped, rolling away from the lean figure. He heard a hiss as the form made a quick feint toward him. There was another flash of movement to his right. He spun on his hands and knees in circles, trying to figure out what was happening in the pale moonlight.

Gunfire boomed, and, before Frank could react, he was shoved roughly aside as something streaked past him. He caught a musty aroma, and felt fur against his skin.

A strong hand gripped his upper arm and hauled him to his feet. He could make out Deegan's face in the dark, holding his rifle upright while he helped Frank, but as soon as he was on his feet, the hunter returned to a firing position. He was looking past Frank, at the marsh.

"Goddamn it!" the hunter growled.

"What's going on?"

"I missed! I *never* miss! I knew he was comin, smelled him a mile off even though he circled upwind, and he *still* got away."

"I don't understand! What was that thing?" The fleeting impression Frank had received when it ran was that of a wild jungle cat.

But it stood upright.

A feeling of cool dread iced his veins.

Deegan set the rifle down and sniffed the air. Frank thought of him kneeling in front of the desk in the trailer, smelling the wood. "Why'd you let the fire go out?" he demanded.

Deegan cut him off by slashing his hand through the air. "You smell that?"

"What?"

The hunter produced a lighter from a hidden pocket of his pants and stepped into the circle of stones he'd used for a firepit, in about the same spot where the thing had stood over Frank. He squatted in the ashes and flicked the flame on. "Spoor."

Frank came forward and looked over his shoulder. In front of Deegan, nestled amid the charred fragments of wood, was a large pile of steaming feces.

"It's a challenge," Deegan said through clenched teeth. "He came and shit in our camp. He's intelligent...as intelligent as anything I've ever hunted." He glared at Frank in the pitiful illumination of his lighter. "You wanted proof, Frankie? Here it is. *The Jackal Man is real.*"

From behind them, in the marsh, came a roar, the kind of noise one expected to hear in the deepest, darkest places on the planet, where men had yet to tread.

And now it was fifty yards from them.

"We have to go!" Frank whispered. He was ready to believe now, oh yes, he was ready to believe in snipes or Bigfoot or vampires or anything else this man told him was gospel.

He was twelve again, in the woods, terrified and waiting for someone to drag him out.

"Just calm down. I told ya, this is the safest place until daybreak. He doesn't have any cover to sneak up on us."

"That didn't stop him last time!"

"I won't let that happen again. I underestimated him."

"I don't care! I'm not staying here!" Frank grabbed his rifle from where he'd left it by the extinguished fire. "I'll take the road and use my gun if it comes near me!"

"STOP!" Deegan grabbed him by the shoulder, and turned him until they faced one another. He looked down from his height advantage, eyes drilling into Frank all the way to his marrow, that blue sheen to his eyes all but glowing. "Lie down, Stanford," he commanded in a sharp, droning tone.

The words cut through Frank's frantic plans, threw a wet blanket on his consciousness. Those eyes...he couldn't look away. Weariness stole over him again, turned his muscles to water. He was actually going to sleep standing up. "No... but..."

"Go to sleep." There was no questioning the words. "And forget."

Frank collapsed to the blanket again and passed out.

40

It was behind him, but he didn't even know what 'it' was.

Frank ran through the woods, ripping through underbrush and crashing against trees. The forest was so black he could see nothing until he was inches away.

The creature behind him had no such problem.

What was it?

A *bird*, his mind insisted, *an imaginary bird*.

He looked back and saw nothing, but he could feel it coming, and it wasn't a bird and it certainly wasn't imaginary. He could only run, and delay the inevitable.

"Dad!" He recognized Willie's voice. The boy was lost somewhere in these same woods.

He changed direction, heading toward the sound, hoping that together they could escape the beast on his heels. He could sense the boy's location, but every time he got close, the cry would echo from a different part of the woods and he would head toward this new origin.

And the trees were getting thicker. Everywhere he turned, more branches thrust leaves at him, until he was practically suffocating.

Willie was ahead, standing helpless, and it was the old Willie, before the hair and the shirts and the makeup and the piercings, and then the creature came streaking out of the woods at him, a monster with the body of a cat but the head of a familiar hunter...

Frank jerked awake and sat up in broad daylight in the middle of the field. It was already scalding hot out, the sun baking his skin. He thought he might have a sunburn.

He didn't remember falling asleep. His head pounded. The previous night's events were a blur, solidifying one shaky image at a time until...

That *thing*.

Frank jumped again as though he'd been poked in the side and looked around the field. He was alone, no man or beast sneaking up on him. Even the hunter and all of his belongings were gone, the fire pit—and anything in it—covered over with dirt. The blanket under him and his rifle were the only other manufactured items out here.

He could recall only the impression of speed and power from that thing last night, the smell of something wild. Now, in the light, the fear was gone. The whole thing seemed like a hallucination.

How had he fallen asleep, not once but *twice?*

Maybe he'd been drugged. He couldn't recall eating or drinking anything Deegan offered, but it was the only idea he had. Anything to explain it all away, give him some wiggle room for denial.

Frank looked at his watch. It was almost nine a.m. Monday morning. He had, as far as Trisha knew, been missing for ten hours. Jesus, she was going to kill him, especially when he'd promised not to come near this place.

He was dirty, sweaty, and stubbly, but he got to his feet,

collected the rifle and blanket, and headed back to the site. The extra bullets were still in his pocket, and he rolled them between his fingers as he hiked out of the clearing beside the marsh grass and walked down the Dark Road.

The site was empty. No protestors or reporters or even crewmen. They might have come and gone already, but he thought it more likely they never showed up at all, the workers permanently spooked by the death of Jaime Garcia and the protestors confident they had done their job.

He was too tired to care. The albatross had been surgically removed from his neck.

Frank entered the lot, stopped at his truck to grab the cell, and proceeded into the trailer, where he plopped down in his leather chair and called Trish, breathing out a monumental sigh of resignation.

"Hello?" Her voice was frantic.

"It's me."

"God Frank, where the hell have you been? I called the police!" He had to hold the phone away from his ear for this outburst.

"I'm sorry, something really weird happened, but I'm okay, just call off the search party. I'll be home soon."

"That's not good enough, Frank! Where were you? Detective Shruff found your truck at the site last night when you *promised*—"

"I know," he cut her off. Had Shruff been here while he was snoozing away in the meadow? "I'll explain it all when I can. For now, just get packed. I want to be out of Asheville by sundown."

"Are you serious? Oh thank God!"

"I'll be home soon."

Frank pressed the button to end the call. It would be so

wonderful to tell Barry Lyles he quit. To see this damn town in his rearview. A smile played at the corners of his mouth.

"It's gonna be okay," he said aloud.

There was a sound above him like a boulder dropping on the tin roof of the trailer. His head jerked back. A large dimple in the ceiling bowed out toward him, just above his desk. There was a piercing screech, like a sharp object being dragged across the surface.

Something was on the fucking roof.

Frank reached for the rifle, keeping his eyes on the ceiling. Something moved up there, a quick, shuffling noise. He stayed still and tried to follow the sounds.

Images of last night raced on a continual loop in his head.

"Shoo!" he yelled, feeling ridiculous. The noises moved to a new position. He held the rifle upright and took aim, contemplated firing through the roof. He was on the verge of panic.

A new sound brought his finger off the trigger. A car horn blasted from somewhere out on the site. A second later, a voice shouted, *"Frank! Frank, are you here?"*

There was silence as both he and the thing on the roof considered this turn of events, then he heard it skitter to the edge and leap off. He saw its body for only a second as it passed in front of the broken window, but he caught a lot more detail in the sun. Taut muscles on a sleek back covered in dusty gold fur.

"Frank?" the person outside shouted.

He went to the window and peeked out. Whatever it was (*you know damn well what it was, Frankie*), the creature was gone. At the other end of the yard, by the gate, was Damon, standing by the open door of Frank's truck and leaning in to honk the horn. As Frank watched, he stumbled down the lane toward the trailer, looking disheveled and gazing goggle-eyed around the abandoned site. His shadow trailed out long behind him like a writhing snake.

Frank caught movement to his left. He turned in time to see a swishing tail vanish behind the closest house frame.

Moving in Damon's direction. The man was less than halfway across the lot.

"Damon, go back! Get in the truck!" Frank shoved open the door of the trailer hard enough to break the top hinge. The other man's head snapped up. He met Frank's eyes as he came to a halt.

Frank charged out onto the dirt, bellowing and waving his free hand. Damon looked confused, but the sight of the rifle got the point across. He about-faced and went for the truck.

Frank ran sideways, looking in the space between each of the houses. Where was the thing, goddamn it? He looked up to find that Damon had made it to the last house frame.

The creature leapt out behind him.

Frank skidded to a stop and screamed his friend's name.

Damon turned. Frank wasn't sure he even saw what was coming. The thing was a blur, switching from two legs to four, spine elongating with each bound. It leapt on Damon, bearing him to the ground. Frank watched as it raised paws—*hands*—and slashed at the man's chest, then leaned forward to bite into his throat.

"Get off him, you fuck!" Frank raised the rifle one handed and fired. In his unbalanced position, the recoil nearly tore the weapon out of his hand. It wrenched his arm, spun him halfway around.

The bullet kicked up dirt so far to the right of his target it was laughable, but it got the thing's attention. The creature turned and hissed over its prey, then slashed at the air as though to ward him off.

And Frank got a good look at the Jackal Man for the first time. In broad daylight. No more ignorance to hide behind, no more excuses.

It was at least part cat—mountain lion, cheetah, leopard, *something*—but it was shaped like a man, a hideous aberration, like something from Dr. Moreau's island. It was hunched when upright, body adapted more to a four-legged stance, and the effort put obvious strain on its back. It might have been a huge cheetah, if not for the hooked claws growing from its twisted hands.

And a glimmer of intelligence in its flashing green eyes.

Frank jammed a hand into his pocket for more bullets. His finger caught on the fabric of his jeans. Shells spilled across the ground. He managed to keep two, and chambered one with a shaking hand.

The Jackal Man leapt off Damon and darted between the two closest houses on the right. Frank continued forward, keeping the rifle trained on the space where it disappeared. He looked down at his boss.

Damon was dead.

His eyes were wide open but glazed behind his smashed spectacles. Mouth frozen in a snarl of pain and surprise. A ragged tear on the side of his throat bubbled blood onto the dirt where it pooled and made obscene mud.

Another of those awful growls echoed in the empty houses. Frank had no time to mourn if he wanted to stay alive.

This time, the snipes were *real*.

Maybe they always had been.

He walked slowly toward his trailer, taking one careful step at a time. Panicked flight would only get him killed; staying calm would be the only way to see the thing if it came for him. There was no further sign of its position, but he could feel hateful eyes crawling over him. He sidestepped rapidly, keeping the entire south side of the complex in sight.

A clatter came from one of the houses behind him. He spun and saw a quick form dash into hiding behind a house wall. How could it possibly have gotten past him? Sly, pit-a-patting footsteps to his left, and again, nothing there. Noises drifted from all directions, and Frank spun in a circle with the rifle held aloft across his chest.

And then the Jackal Man was coming at him.

Frank had no idea where it came from; the lot was empty one second, and then the creature was speeding toward him down the middle of the lane. It plowed into him head-on, hitting him in the stomach and bowling him over. Packed dirt walloped the air from his lungs. Gravity tried to steal the gun, but he kept a hand around the stock. Frank looked down, expecting to see a gaping hole in his torso. Still gasping for air, he raised the rifle with both hands.

The creature stood defiant and unafraid, then feinted toward him. Frank jerked, almost pulling the trigger, but kept the weapon from firing. The Jackal Man jumped behind the cover a nearby bulldozer instead.

He realized, beyond a doubt, that it was playing with him. Trying to get him to use his ammo. He was being toyed with by a creature that, until fifteen minutes ago, he had been positive was no more real than the Easter Bunny.

Frank heaved himself up, sweat soaking his entire upper body. He could see now he had no chance in the open. It was just too fast, like a ghost. He needed something at his back.

In front of him was the yawning garage of one of the houses. A partial ceiling blocked out most of the sunlight, giving it the appearance of a cave. Frank stepped inside and leaned against the sheet rock wall. Survival was kicking in.

Suddenly hunting no longer seemed like some forgotten skill from his father that gave him the heebie-jeebies. His breath caught at the back of his throat and he held it hostage there as he listened for movement.

A second passed. Two. Four.

The sheet rock several inches to the left of his cheek erupted outward in a shower of powdery debris. A clawed fist punched through, the spindly fingers uncurling to sink into his shoulder.

Frank screamed. His shirt shredded as he pulled away, those needles taking a hunk of flesh. He fired his next-to-last bullet as the furry hand withdrew. A perfect circle blossomed on the sheet rock to mark the bullet's path.

He fumbled for the last shell as the Jackal Man stepped around the corner.

Frank backed away and ran into something against the far wall that clattered. A ladder stretched up into the garage rafters. Burning sunlight slanted through; the roof had only the barest frame up, but it was still high ground.

The Jackal Man's nose twitched madly, taking in the scent of his bleeding shoulder, or maybe just his fear. It took a deliberate step forward.

Frank climbed the ladder, carrying the rifle awkwardly under his arm. When he was more than halfway, he chanced a look back. The creature was gone.

He finished climbing and emerged on a frying pan. Most of the second floor was just support beams, and the area over the garage had baked in the sun all morning. Frank fell to his knees, felt them burn against the wood through his jeans, and found his last bullet. He thumbed the pointed cylinder into the chamber. Rammed the bolt home.

There was an angry shriek from below. Frank crept to

the edge. The Jackal Man was behind the house now, framed between two wall supports, looking up at him. It crouched low, then sprang up in a vertical leap. Those hands wrapped around a beam on the second floor. Like a deformed acrobat, it swung up in an arc and let go, undulating in the air, caught another board one-handed, and then touched down feather-light on the garage.

Frank gawked. This is what house cats would be—as agile as a chimp on methamphetamines—given a million extra years of unhindered evolution.

He backpedaled from its advance, but there was precious little space to maneuver in up here.

The Jackal Man's hand flashed out. Claws raked the inside of Frank's arm. The rifle dropped from his spasming fingers as white-hot pain shot through them. He clutched the limb to his chest.

It moved fast, latching onto Frank's shoulders, driving him toward the edge of the roof.

He would've flown right off the second story, but a beam slammed into the small of his back, halting their progress. The Jackal Man hissed in his face, muzzle wrinkled back to reveal rows of wicked incisors. Frank smelled fetid breath before he grabbed the monster's shoulders in return, like a wrestler. Adrenaline surged. He gritted his teeth and shoved back, but the thing just moved in closer to snap at him.

The creature's claws tore into the meat of his shoulders. The beam crushed his spine. He thought the damn thing would snap him in half if blood loss didn't kill him first.

Something brushed against his leg. Through bleary eyes, he saw a striped tail twitching on the ground between its paw-like feet. He lifted his boot—almost costing him his balance—and ground his heel down on the tip.

The Jackal Man's roar was deafening. It let go of him, and Frank dug his fingers into that mat of shining fur and pulled.

He had just enough leverage to swing the creature around. His adversary fell from the scalding roof, twisted in midair, and landed on all fours in the dirt below.

Frank retrieved the rifle, took careful aim this time, and thought about his father.

He fired his last bullet.

Blood exploded from a wound deep in the creature's side. It yelped, then snarled up at him. He raised the rifle threateningly.

The Jackal Man streaked away from him, favoring its wounded side. When it reached the fence around the site, it climbed over in three swift motions and took off across the field. It made Frank think of a lion crossing the Serengeti as it paused at the marsh's edge to glare back at him.

Frank climbed down from the roof. He was limping as he reached the trailer, his shirt slowly changing from gray to red as blood crept down his shoulders. He went inside and picked up his cell phone.

41

The police arrived first, reinforcing the cordon around the site. Reporters from three states clogged the entrance within the hour, and the entire town of Asheville was right behind them. Damon's ravaged body was covered and taken away. A tissue paper thin preliminary statement involving a pack of rabid wolves was taken from Frank by a young officer named Walz while he was treated for minor cuts and bruises, deep puncture wounds on his shoulders, and one large slash on the inside of his forearm.

Then he was escorted into the trailer to wait. Wait for what, he didn't know. He ranged through emotions, from guilt to grief to rage to relief that it hadn't been him.

Then back to rage.

Shruff finally walked in through the broken door of the trailer.

"What are you doing here?" Frank asked.

"What else? Came to see if you were all right."

"No, I mean, I thought your chief didn't want you anywhere near this."

"Yeah, then he realized I might be the only one who could handle it." The detective stood quietly for a handful of seconds and then asked, "Rabid wolves?"

"I couldn't tell them what I saw. I just couldn't."

"And...what did you see?"

"It was him. The...you know." It wasn't so easy to say the words anymore. God, he probably sounded like Gerrardo and all those superstitious morons.

Then again, how could it be superstition if it was true?

"He really attacked you? In broad daylight? How close was he?" Shruff's questions almost tripped over one another in their haste to get out.

"Take a good look at this pincushion I used to a call a body and tell me what you think."

The detective's hand stole up to rub those scars on his throat, the motion so automatic Frank doubted he was aware of it. It made him think of Damon dead on the ground, of jagged teeth so blood-covered they would be stained pink. "I shot him. I just thought you'd want to know. He certainly ain't immortal. He was wounded when he ran off."

"Good." Shruff came back from whatever memory or daydream he'd slipped into and said, "I'm sorry about your boss. I tried to warn you both."

"You saved my life, Shruff. If I hadn't bought the gun, I'd be just as dead. But I don't wanna talk about it anymore. I wanna go home, get my family, and leave Asheville."

Shruff sighed. "I'm afraid it's not that easy anymore. You're a suspect in all this."

Frank jumped to his feet. Something in his shoulder pulled, and he felt fresh blood leaking down his back. "What the hell do you mean, I'm a suspect? They all know what did this! What, do I have to say the words? *Jackal Man*, all right? Your goddamn Jackal Man killed Damon and attacked me!"

Shruff held up his hands, still standing in the doorway. "Yes, they know, but everything has changed now, Stanford.

I tried to tell you that before. We have every eye in the state on us, and the media types out there are not listening to stories about monsters in the woods. There are bodies piling up here—your boss and Garcia—and the parents of one of your son's friends finally came home and declared him missing."

"Don't forget the horses," Frank added. "Oh, and the dog."

"Exactly. The press is already talking serial killer. And Asheville is willing to give them someone's head if it gets them the hell out of here."

"Wonderful." Frank laughed harshly. "If I'm not the scapegoat for one thing, I'm the scapegoat for another. Every redneck in this town can go on and on about the Jackal Man, but if I do it, I get blamed for murder!" He shook his head. "It doesn't matter though, there's no way they can pin this on me. Surely some kind of analysis will prove that."

"You're exactly right, any test of the wounds will come back as FAMILY *FELIDAE*, SPECIES UNKNOWN. Trust me, I know. But...there's something else." Shruff inspected the broken top hinge of the door before continuing. "Something I can't make sense of no matter how hard I try."

"So spit it out."

"Bradford...did you speak to him before...? Did he tell you where he'd been the last few days when you couldn't get in touch with him?"

"No, he just showed up here and started yelling for me. Why, what is it?"

Shruff finally moved out of the doorway, into the shadow of the trailer. "He had other injuries. Stuff the attack couldn't account for. They'll do an autopsy on him too, but...it's pretty obvious he had rope burns on his wrists and ankles."

"Rope burns?"

"He was tied up at some point very recently, Stanford. I think we can both agree the thing that killed him didn't do that. And unless his wife can confirm they were into S and M..."

"That's not funny," Frank said. "Not in the least."

"I'm sorry, you're right. But where's the man's car? How did he get out here? Something's wrong about all this, even by Asheville's standards."

"Maybe, but *I* didn't have anything to do with it!"

"Well, Jesus, what were you even doing out here last night? After I specifically told you to stay away!"

"I came to see if Garcia had taken anything. I didn't want to be charged for some piece of equipment by that shitheel Lyles."

"Your wife called me, I came out here, had a monster panic attack. Found your car, but you were gone. I figured you were already dead, I didn't know what to tell her! Where were you?"

Frank opened his mouth to give the answer...and was stunned to find the answer wasn't there. He frowned. "I...I was...I woke up in that field over on the other side of the marsh grass..."

"You *slept* out there? *Why?*"

Frank closed his eyes, bowed his head. His thoughts were muddled all of a sudden. What the hell *had* happened? He knew the memories were there just this morning, but now there was a big blank spot. He remembered driving out here...leaving the truck...and then something causing him to spin around...

"A gunshot," he muttered.

"What?"

"There was...someone else out here, I think. A—," he

had to fight to get the word out, his head full of molasses, "hunter."

"A hunter? Who was he?"

Frank tried to reach back into the mish-mash of his thoughts for a name, but it just wasn't there. He couldn't even remember what the guy looked like. Hadn't he seen him somewhere before?

"I don't know," he finally answered.

"Okay. Why don't you keep that one to yourself then? For Christ's sake, you start mumbling about mystery hunters and they *will* throw you in jail."

"You mean I'm not under arrest for being the River Meadows Slasher?"

"No, you're free to go. You just can't leave town."

"So, the same people that wanted me gone because they were scared I'd rile up the Jackal Man now want me to stay because I did? There's a joke in that somewhere, but damned if I see the punchline."

Shruff led him toward the door. "Just go home and wait for me to get in touch with you. They've opened up the fence in back of your trailer so you can get out without having to deal with the reporters. We're nearly done here, and then the circus will clear out. I'll try to talk some sense into the chief, I promise."

Frank looked back over his shredded shoulder as he stepped outside. "What about my rifle?"

"It's evidence now."

Frank shrugged, winced in pain, and then started for his truck.

42

There was no peace at home. Trisha demanded answers that he literally couldn't give. She was only upset for a few minutes that they wouldn't be leaving town, and then checked over his wounds herself. Both of their cells rang constantly, filling up with messages from every newspaper and television station for miles. They offered cash, check, charge, and everything short of a blowjob (and he deleted one from a female reporter who he could swear was going to say just that) to get the true story directly from him, some hinting at the connection with Asheville's "mythological" creature and others outright calling him the Asheville Wood Stalker, the more media-friendly version of the name he'd come up with. They hadn't found the house yet, but he figured it was only a matter of time before they traced it through the Lyles Corporation.

He tried to reach the man himself, but was only told he was out of the office and his urgent message would be put with the others coming in. He called Lucy Bradford, but the woman was too distraught to talk. Frank finally retired to the bedroom to recuperate.

After a few minutes, the door opened and Willie ventured into the room. The boy took in his bandaged body with haggard eyes.

"The Jackal Man killed Mr. Bradford, didn't he?"

Frank nodded. No sense keeping it from the boy. If he faced down that creature at night by himself and still retained his sanity, he was more than man enough to hear the truth now.

"Did you see it?"

He didn't know if the boy meant the beast or the murder, but it didn't matter. The answer was the same. "Yeah, I saw it."

"What is he, Dad?" The boy's voice cracked.

"Some kind of..." He came close to saying 'monster' but he still didn't think that was quite right. To him, a monster was supernatural, something beyond science, but there was nothing otherworldly about that thing. "Some kind of mutation. Just an animal."

Willie nodded slowly. "Do you think...he'll come here to get us?"

Frank was already shaking his head. "No, he lives in the woods. We're safe. And soon we'll be out of here, back home in Houston."

"But what about him? He's killing people! Aren't they gonna do something about it? Aren't they gonna stop him?"

The people of Asheville were more concerned with protecting the Jackal Man than they were with punishing him. He could finally see what Shruff was trying to explain all along, but it was a truth he couldn't give his son. "Don't worry about that. The Jackal Man will get what's coming to him, sooner or later."

Willie appeared to sense the uncertainty in the statement, but he let it go.

~ ~ ~

Frank slept the day away, trying to find a comfortable position amidst his injuries and escape the instant replay of Damon's death that kept playing behind his eyelids. The sun was just falling below the horizon as his cell went off on the dresser. He flopped over and snatched it up, ready to tear in to whomever was on the other end, be it reporter or Lyles.

"Hey Frankie, rise and shine!"

The nickname rocketed through his head. A flood of memories dumped over him like a gallon of cold water, and suddenly he could recall everything from the previous night.

"Deegan!" he blurted. Why couldn't he remember it earlier?

"The one and only. Now get up, we got work to do!"

"What work?"

"You don't think the Jackal Man's gonna hunt himself, do ya?"

Frank sat up. "Get one thing real clear, I'm not fucking going anywhere with you! You left me alone last night! That thing could've killed me! It *did* kill someone else, a friend of mine!"

Deegan's voice was solemn for the first time when he spoke again, but it was too easy to imagine a smile on his lips. "I know, I heard about that. All I can say is, I'm sorry. I thought everything was cool. The Jackal Man'd been gone for hours when I cleared out."

"Yeah, well that's twice you fucked up, and this time it cost someone his life!"

"I said I was sorry," Deegan repeated, "but *I* didn't kill 'im. The Jackal Man did. So let's put some of that anger to use and go hunt the thing down."

Frank's mind recoiled in horror at the idea. "Are you completely insane, or just deaf? I'm not going near that place again! I *hunted* him earlier today, and for putting just one bullet in him, all I got for my trouble is a buttload of scar tissue!"

"You shot 'im?" Deegan sounded impressed.

"Yeah, I did."

"He bleed?"

Frank recalled the wound in the thing's side, the crimson pouring out of it. A small thrill, fed by rage, seeped through him. "Yeah."

"Then he can die. Be even easier now that he's wounded. Get dressed and let's go."

Frank clenched the phone in frustration. "Why do you even want me to go? I'm no hunter, today was the first time I fired a rifle in nearly thirty years!"

"Look out your window."

"Huh?"

"Get your ass outta bed and look out the bedroom window."

Frank stood, bent the blinds aside, and peered out.

The bedroom looked down on the front yard and driveway. A shadowed figure with a familiar hat stood in the middle of the lawn looking up at him, a cell phone pressed to his ear.

"Oh my God," Frank whispered. "How'd you find me? How...how did you even get this number?"

"I'm not some dumbass reporter. I'm your goddamn guardian angel. Your mentor. The person that's gonna show you how to grow a pair. You wanna know why you have to come?" He raised his free arm above his head. A long bundle dangled from his hand, a limp and furry form.

"What is that?"

"A dead rabbit."

"Did you get that out of the bushes?"

"Oh, so there's more, huh? No, this one was laid out right here on your lawn. Fresh, too. Blood's still runnin. How long you been gettin Valentines from the Jackal Man, Frankie?"

The squirrel on their first day here. The rabbit last night. He felt dizzy. "Shit. You're telling me that thing's been here? At this house?"

"Yep, and sometime in the last twenty minutes, I'd say. He crapped in our camp last night, challenged us, and now he's marking this house for death. You better believe this is a warning."

"No, no it can't be..." Because if it was, he'd just lied to Willie, and his entire family was in danger as long as they stayed in Asheville. The abnormally bright lights of this town were no deterrent.

"You're part of this, whether you wanna be or not. He's not gonna stop until either us or him are dead, so we better make damn sure it's *him*. If you won't do it for yourself or your dead friend, then do it for that woman and those kids you got in there. Be a man for once in your miserable life."

God, that was so much like something his father would've said. Maybe something he *had* said, that night of the snipes, the last time he and his father had really done anything together, or been able to look each other in the eye. Frank felt so removed from reality, drifting further away with each word this man said. "I...I don't have a gun anymore, the police took it..."

"I got one for you. Just get dressed, come with me, and I'll handle the rest."

He let the blinds go. The more he thought about it, the more he realized he wanted that thing dead. What he said to Willie was true: he wanted the Jackal Man to get what was coming.

The question being, was Frank Stanford the person to give it to him?

Then again, if Trish and the kids were really in danger, what choice did he have? At least if he went with Deegan, he stood a chance. The bastard might be crazy, but he'd protected them last night.

"Look, just...stay out there, all right? Let me talk to my wife."

"You do that, Frankie. See if she'll let you come out and play."

43

He'd never really lied to Trisha before, and this made twice in as many days.

This time he told her Shruff had called his cell and asked him to come down to the station to go over his story. She balked, wanted to know why he had to go so late, demanded to come with him, and finally settled for checking over his wounds one more time before letting him go out. He would rather her believe he was having an affair than that he was stupid enough to go back out to the place where he'd almost died eight hours before. After soliciting a promise she and the kids would stay inside, he ventured out.

The front yard was empty. "Deegan!" he called.

"Let's go," the man said, as he brushed past Frank from behind.

"Would you stop doing that?"

"You're drivin."

That was a given. Deegan didn't even seem to have a car, but Frank put that at the bottom of a growing list of oddities. He lowered a knapsack and rifle case into the truck bed and, when Frank unlocked the vehicle, the man opened the passenger side still holding the dead rabbit.

"We're bringing that?"

"Return to sender, Frankie. Postage due."

"Can you at least throw it in the truck bed?"

"Nope. I want our scent on it."

"Oh. Just...don't get any blood on the seats, okay?"

They were outside River Meadows ten minutes later, in the deepening shadows of early dusk. There was no need to unlock the gate this time, because there was no gate to unlock. Most of the fence was torn down, either by the cops or the crowds, and sections of chain link were strewn and trampled everywhere. Frank pulled the truck into the site, past the spot where Damon was killed, and parked between two house frames complete enough to hide the vehicle from the street, just in case some reporters cruised by for a midnight blurb. He was shaking as he got out.

Deegan leaned over the truck bed, busying himself with the rifle case. He slung his knapsack over one shoulder, the heavily-modified weapon over the other, and then handed another, simpler model to Frank. "That's a thirty-aught. Step up from that pop gun you were usin before."

Frank hefted the weapon, expecting to feel that same sense of dizziness and revulsion, but this time there was nothing. After this morning, it actually felt kind of good. "Bullets?"

"Loaded and ready. Five shots. You need any more than that, you're already dead."

"That's comforting."

"I'm a realist, Frankie."

Deegan grabbed the dead rabbit out of the front seat and strode into the construction yard, heading back toward the gate. Frank—trying to look left, right and backward all at the same time—struggled to keep up with him. The only place he didn't want to look was the rooftop where he'd fought the thing.

Deegan glanced over when he came abreast. "You left handed?"

"No."

"Then for God's sake, hold your rifle the other way. It'll feel a lot more comfortable."

Frank did so, moving his opposite hand up the stock. The change was slight, but it did feel more natural.

"Was that true what you said earlier? You haven't fired a gun in thirty years?"

"Yeah, it's true."

"What's the story behind that one? You a libbie pacifist?"

"No," Frank said quickly. Willie was one thing, but he wasn't about to let this guy in on one of the darkest chapters of his life. "I'm just not much of a gun person."

Deegan chuckled. "Couldn't imagine. I've been around guns since I was old enough to hold one. My father taught me to hunt, and he was taught by his father, and so on and so on all the way back to when the first caveman Deegan realized it was fun to kill things even when you're not gonna eat 'em."

"Yeah, I'm sure it's a great hobby."

They were nearly to the gate, and Deegan halted. "A 'hobby?' Is *that* what you think I'm doin out here? That this is no different for me than collectin stamps or a nice, civil round of golf?"

"I didn't mean—"

"I don't care what you meant, you ignorant son of a bitch. Hunting is good for the soul. There's no rush, no high, no feeling on earth like takin another being's life. You can create all the babies you want with as many women as you can, but *ending* a life gets you so much closer to bein a god. It's all about lookin 'em in the eye while you do it, and knowin you've just made their last decision for 'em." He pressed an index finger into Frank's chest. "So if you ever call my life's work a 'hobby' again, I'm gonna put a bullet in each one of your kneecaps and let you see if it feels the same as buildin model airplanes."

Frank tightened his grip on the rifle's stock. He nodded. "Yeah. Okay."

Deegan glared at him for another few seconds beneath his hat brim, then broke into a smile. "Now...last one in the pool's a rotten egg!" He turned and broke into a trot, crossing over the two narrow lanes of the Dark Road and starting into the dense woods on the other side.

"Woah, hey, what are you doing?" Frank whisper-yelled from the opposite side of the street.

"I thought we'd already established that."

"Why are you going in *there*? Let's go back over to the meadow."

"He's too hesitant in the open. If he has some cover, it'll give him confidence, make him sneak closer before attack-in."

"And that's a good thing?"

"It is if you wanna end this thing as quickly as I think we both do."

"Yes, I want away from you and this gun and these woods as soon as possible, but believe me when I say, you don't wanna give that thing stuff to jump around on."

Deegan put his hands on his hips, the dead bunny dangling against his bare leg beneath the shorts. "If he's wounded like you say, I'll be able to smell him a mile off."

"Well...what makes you think he'll come if he's wounded?"

Deegan's smile was big enough to be seen even across the road in the dark, a searchlight with teeth. "I have a feelin he'll be along shortly." With that, he turned and pushed into the dense underbrush.

"Unless he's dead already," Frank grumbled, but he hurried after the man once more.

Under the canopy of trees, shadows lay in crisscrossing patterns everywhere, the moonlight flickering through the net of branches. His eyes adjusted all they were going to, but he still couldn't see more than a few feet ahead, barely to Deegan's massive silhouette in front of him. The sound of crickets was near deafening. Bushes and ground vines tangled in his feet, and he fought free with the rifle held in front of him. The trees crowded in all sides like in his dream, until every direction looked the same. He thought about what the hunter had said, that the foliage traced the route of the Jackal Man's lair, and wondered if they were following such a path now.

The hike went on until Frank was panting. He thought they were heading southeast, parallel to the Dark Road, toward the trickling creek bed that lay between Asheville and the Westwood Strip. Just when Frank's mind started to see imaginary snipes around every tree trunk, Deegan stopped next to a fallen log.

"We're here. Make yourself comfortable."

Two hours later, comfort was nearly impossible.

Just past the prone tree was a small clearing, and Deegan had laid the dead rabbit here, in a picture-perfect shaft of moonlight. He then came back, situated himself behind the log, rested his rifle on top of it, and remained motionless. At first, Frank tried to do the same, but as minutes dragged on, the painkillers he'd been given by the paramedics wore off, letting his muscles scream, followed by his injuries, until he was forced to sit back on the lumpy woods floor and try not to whimper. Deegan showed no such signs of unease, even as the clock wound around toward ten o'clock.

Frank checked his watch once again, pressing the button to light up its face in the gloom. He needed to get out of here before Trisha started trying to find him. He pulled out a cigarette and his lighter.

It was swiped from his mouth before he could touch the flame to it. "Hey!"

"Did you fail kindergarten or somethin?" Deegan demanded. "These things have a scent!"

"Sorry. I wasn't thinking."

"So try."

Frank sighed and leaned back against a tree. "This just seems kinda stupid. I can't imagine that thing I fought earlier—that angry, smart fucking creature—just wandering into a trap like a baby deer."

"Why don't you leave the hunting to me?"

Then why am I here? Frank thought, but didn't say it. "So have you really gone after things like this before?"

Deegan sighed, lowered his rifle from the log. "By the time I was twenty, I'd hunted just about everything this planet has to offer. When I was twenty-four, I was in Russia for a worldwide sharp shootin competition, when I hear this story."

A branch snapped in the woods behind Frank. He jerked around, bringing his rifle up.

"Don't worry. He's not here. Yet."

After his heart had resumed a somewhat normal pace, Frank asked, "What was the story about?"

"A monster, of course. Their word for it translated to 'Soul Taker,' somethin like that. Some creature they told bedtime stories about to the children, to make sure they don't go out after dark. In the city, everyone just said it was a tale to keep the children from freezin to death in the winter, but in one village up there…well, it was true."

The word 'bullshit' rose to Frank's lips before he realized how stupid it would be to say, considering their current undertaking. Urban legends—or in this case, *rural* legends— had taken on a whole new meaning for him.

Deegan grunted a laugh as though reading his thoughts. "Every night this thing was callin to the children, drawin 'em out so it could kill 'em without leavin a mark. They were gettin ready to abandon the town until I showed up. I staked out this village three nights before I saw it."

"What was it?"

"Damn wraith of some sort. Not a ghost exactly, had more substance than than, but for the first time, I found myself with a target my rifle wouldn't be any use against. That was my entrance into the world of the supernatural, the one most folks don't wanna see. Took hunting to a whole new level for me."

"So you get introduced to an amazing new world and the only way for you to express your feelings was to try and kill everything in it?"

This time Deegan's laughter rang out. "Spoken like a true libbie pacifist."

"So wait, what the hell happened with the ghost thing? How'd you kill it?"

"The same way you kill any prey. Find a weakness, and exploit it." He stood up and stretched with his huge weapon in one hand. "New game plan. I want you to take that rifle and set up on the other side of the clearing."

"What, by *myself*?"

"Yeah, I wanna catch 'im in a shooting gallery. And offset

yourself at an angle, so we don't end up pluggin each other."

"Wait, why? If he's not coming, how will us changing our positions do anything?"

"For God's sake, just do it. I wanna test something."

Frank stood up. His hands were slick with sudden sweat against the rifle barrel. He blundered forward, crashing through undergrowth, until he reached the edge of the clearing. The woods were still full of those buzzing crickets. Frank made his way around the rabbit and plowed into the woods on the far side, going deep enough in until he found a comfortable stump to sit down on where he could see the clearing. He couldn't even make out Deegan in the screen of shadows.

Frank sat for several long minutes before discomfort set in again. This was awful. The one thing he'd *not* expected to be while hunting a dangerous legend was bored. Maybe that snipe hunt had done more for him than he ever realized, by saving him from years of waiting in the woods.

He closed his eyes. Bad idea to let those memories sneak up on him. Now that he was alone, he was starting to get a little uneasy. What was he doing? He was no hunter, and if that thing got to Deegan first, he would just be dessert.

Unease was becoming panic. The woods were dead silent now. He lifted his face, trying to take in the stiff breeze moving through the trees...

Frank jerked his eyes open.

The breeze was blowing in his face. Against him...and then deeper into the woods.

Frank may not be a professional hunter, but he suddenly realized that Deegan's position change had maneuvered him directly downwind, past whatever scent the rabbit was broadcasting.

And then he heard the growl behind him.

44

Frank moved so fast he surprised himself. He pulled the rifle up against his shoulder, hands sliding into increasingly familiar positions, and swung around, coming up off the stump all in one smooth motion.

It was there, stalking through the shadows directly toward him, not even trying to hide this time. Its green eyes burned, giving him a target. He redirected the rifle, but the sight of the gun deterred it no more now than it had earlier.

Frank pulled the trigger before it could start leaping.

There was a brittle click.

At first he thought the weapon's safety was engaged, but part of him—*most* of him—knew that wasn't the case.

"*DEEGAN!*" he bellowed.

The Jackal Man moved in, claws flashing as it reached for his throat.

And then, with the uncanny timing of a choir of angels, the tinny music of his cell phone filled the dark woods.

The Jackal Man hissed and drew back like a vampire from a cross.

Frank swallowed the lump of acidic fear in his throat and pulled out his ringing phone. The tune got a little louder after it was out of his pocket, and the creature in front of him crouched and scrambled backward on all fours. Frank dropped the useless rifle and held the device up, driving it back.

"Yeah, it's my wife, asshole," he said. "I'm a little scared of her sometimes myself."

The Jackal Man darted forward, swiping out at him, then scuttled back. A few centuries of living out here alone in the woods meant this thing had probably never even seen a cell phone.

"Deegan, get the fuck OUT HERE!" he screamed.

The music cut off as the call went to voicemail, thereby ending his life and marriage simultaneously.

Frank threw the phone. He had time to see it strike the Jackal Man right along the top of the snout before he turned and ran.

The trees blurred by on both sides. He had no idea where he was going, toward the road or away from it, his only goal putting distance between himself and that thing. He could hear the beast somewhere behind him, the sound of padded feet treading dirt, and waited to feel those claws sink into him, but it didn't happen. Either its injury was slowing it down, or the trees were just too dense for it to run flat out. A sense of determination—to live, to *win*—filled him as he hurtled ground debris and dodged tree trunks.

And then, before he could slow, he burst out of a last tight clove of trees into the open. The land sloped sharply down in front of him toward that sluggish creek. His momentum carried him right over the lip of the bank, treading air momentarily until his foot struck loose dirt. Frank went down on his side, his wounds waking up with a squall, and rolled down the bank.

He came to rest on a flat shelf near the creek's edge, dizzy and wheezing. A low tide rushed by him on its course to destinations unknown.

There was a roar from above.

Frank looked up.

The Jackal Man descended with considerably more grace. The moonlight was brighter out here without the trees, and the creature's descent looked like ballet as it bounded down the slope. The bullet he'd put in it back at the construction site hadn't slowed it; in fact, from the short glimpses he caught of its torso, he couldn't even see the wound.

Frank jerked away, anticipating a killing blow. Instead, the Jackal Man landed next to him on all fours. The hideous face was thrust into his again, ears slicked against its flat skull, green eyes ringed in black fur, like a demented raccoon. Its lips pulled back from wicked fangs as it hissed at him. Flecks of spittle hit his forehead; that stinking breath washed over him. He couldn't look away, and part of him—even then, in the midst of panic—was screaming it wasn't right, that something was—

The crack of a rifle rolled down the embankment. The Jackal Man fell away from him, landing facedown at the shoreline. A dark spot high on its furry side spilled blood onto the riverbank. Frank scrambled up.

Deegan emerged from the tree line and came down practically skipping. "Straight through the heart!" he yelled gleefully. "Damn what a rush!"

"*Where were you, you goddamned piece of shit? He almost tore my throat out!*"

Deegan came to a stop and knelt over the body. "Trying to get a shot that wouldn't put a bullet through both of you."

Frank marched toward him, looking down at the hunter. *"You gave me an unloaded rifle!"*

Deegan seemed amused by his anger. "Maybe next time you'll check when someone gives you a weapon then. Now back off a sec, I wanna see him stop breathin."

Frank clinched a fist, weighing the odds of successfully striking the man, when there was motion between them. As fast as a striking cobra, the Jackal Man was on its feet. It raked claws across the hunter's chest and used the other hand to knock the rifle away into the water. Deegan made a gagging noise and fell back, slamming down on the muddy bank, shirt front torn to shreds.

The man was down, weak, ready for the kill.

And the Jackal Man ignored him, turning on Frank.

He splashed into the creek after the gun. The creature came at him on two legs, back hunched, holding the wound in its side and making a pitiful mewling sound.

Frank dropped to all fours in the sluggish water. Chips of moonlight reflected across its black surface. He moved deeper, hands frantically searching, and felt polished metal. Frank swung Deegan's larger and heavier weapon up and out of the water, hands clamoring for the proper positions and the oh-so-important trigger.

He aimed at the thing's head, no less than six feet away.

The Jackal Man hesitated. There was no fear in the eyes set into that dark fur, just an awful knowing, and a hurt frustration that was entirely too human.

Frank pulled the trigger.

The Jackal Man's face disintegrated.

45

"NOOOO!" Deegan bellowed.

It happened in a heartbeat. One second that face was snarling at him, the next it was a mangled pit. The short muzzle vanished, those awful eyes winked out. Bloody mist filled the air, and a single tooth sailed away. For another second, the Jackal Man pawed at the air, a questioning sound gurgling up from the hole in its head, and then its body fell backward to land half in and half out of the water.

The strength ran out of Frank's arms all at once. He let the rifle fall from his hands back into the water.

"No, goddamnit!" Deegan snarled, struggling to his feet. He pressed one hand to his chest. Dark blood seeped between his fingers. "He was *mine!* That was my kill!"

"Then you should've killed him," Frank croaked. He felt bile rising in his throat, nausea overcoming him. This didn't feel nearly as good as he'd imagined, especially with his own wounds reopening. He stepped up onto the muddy bank. "He's all yours anyway. I'm not gonna mount him over my fireplace."

"He's not mine if I didn't make the kill, dipshit! *How?* How the hell did *you* take him out?"

"What's your game here, Deegan? The unloaded rifle and

putting me downwind? Why the hell did you even want me to come if not to help you hunt the damn thing?"

Deegan looked away, down the creek, mumbling under his breath, and then splashed into the water to retrieve his rifle. The man was completely different now that he'd been deprived of his hunting high.

Frank went to stand over the corpse, wary for movement, circling in a step at a time. It had landed on its side, slightly curled into a fetal position. He could look at its short fur at leisure now, and the black claws on the end of each knobby finger. The pads on the underside that had made the print in the house back at the site, sectioned on the palm and digits. That echo of wrongness vibrated through him, vague and annoying. He was drawn to its face, but that was only a stew of blood, bone, and brain now.

He liked to think he was man enough to admit when he was wrong. The Jackal Man was real. He was staring at it.

He'd *killed* it.

Asheville was about to have its proof. This story would change history, and, most importantly, this corpse would clear his name and get him, Trish, and the kids out of this town.

Deegan was fiddling with his rifle, muttering about a busted scope and water damage.

"I'm leaving," Frank announced. "Help me get this thing up the bank."

The hunter gave him a black look as he slung his weapon over his shoulder.

Frank grabbed the shoulders of the corpse, his fingers sliding through rough fur, and Deegan reluctantly picked up the legs. The body was lean and surprisingly light, but still unwieldy. It smelled earthy and surprisingly clean, like rich potting soil. Together they manhandled it up the riverbank, getting themselves slathered in mud. They carted the body through the woods without a word, back to their trap. Frank found his phone, cracked but still working, while Deegan went about bandaging himself with first aid supplies out of his knapsack. The cell had three voicemails from Trisha that he didn't listen to. He could catch the live show when he got home.

Frank also retrieved the empty rifle. It felt small to him after using Deegan's. Maybe when he got back to civilization, he would buy a new one, a better one. Maybe he would take up hunting.

Teach Willie to shoot.

"What now?" he asked.

"You tell me," Deegan said sulkily.

"We need to get this thing into town, turn it over to the police."

"You're such a tool."

"Hey, you son of a bitch—!"

The sound of a car engine from the Dark Road cut the argument off. They could hear it idling somewhere on the other side of the woods.

"Sounds like someone at your site."

"Oh God, Trish." Frank took off toward the sound, with Deegan hot on his heels.

Several minutes later, they crouched in underbrush by the side of the road, watching two figures working in the trunk of a dark sedan parked in front of the site.

"More reporters," Deegan told him.

"No," Frank said, looking at the much shorter member of the duo. "Stay right here."

Frank pushed his way out of the bushes and emerged onto the Dark Road across from the vehicle. He still had the rifle, and didn't bother to hide it as he marched across toward them. When he got close enough to hear their conversation, he pulled out his phone.

"I don't think that's enough gas," the taller one said.

They both wore black, the shorter one with a ski mask. This one barked, "Just torch whatever the fuck you can and let's go!"

Frank didn't need a face to know who it was.

"You may be a creepy little pipsqueak," he said, snapping a picture of the two with the contents of the trunk, "but at least you do your own dirty work."

At the sound of his voice, both men jumped so hard the taller one banged his head on the open door of the trunk. Before they could react any further, Frank snatched the mask off the shorter one's head and took another snapshot of Barry Lyles the Third in all his dumbfounded glory.

"Jesus, Frank. What the hell are you—"

Frank cut the question off by swinging the rifle butt across the man's cheek. The construction magnate stumbled back against the taller guy, who stared at Frank in amazement. The expression on Lyles's face as he cupped his chin in his hands—outrage, shock and pain—was priceless.

"What the hell was it all for?" Frank demanded. "Why'd you buy the land when they told you not to? You have something to prove to Daddy? And why send me out here when you knew you were just gonna burn the place down anyway? Do you have any idea what my family and I have been through?"

"You can't hit me, you cretin, I'm going to—!"

Frank kicked the man square in the balls. He screeched and let go of the swelling bruise on his face to grab at his crotch.

"You open your mouth again except to answer my questions and I'm gonna use this rifle for what it was actually made for. Damon Bradford is dead because of you. Were you the one that tied him up? What'd you do, kidnap him to keep him from telling me something?"

"What the fuck are you talking about?" Lyles choked through tears. "Bradford's *dead?*"

"Did you kill Wesley Gammon?"

Lyles made an attempt to regain control of himself. "No! He disappeared after I told him he was fired! I'm going to sue you for every penny you don't have!"

Frank pulled the rifle up.

"*He's fuckin nuts!*" The tall guy screamed, running for the driver's side of the car.

"Consider this my resignation." Frank put the rifle barrel against his horrified boss's nose. "If you don't give yours to the Board by tomorrow morning, I'm going to the police with these pictures."

Lyles nodded, slid out from under the barrel, and ran for the passenger door. The car took off with a squeal.

Deegan was doubled over with laughter when he got back. "Oh Jesus, Frankie, I didn't know you had it in you."

"Let's just get outta here."

The body was gone.

"Are you sure this was where we left it?" Frank asked numbly, already knowing the answer.

"There's a blood trail here. I can still smell the corpse."

"Maybe something carried it away."

"That's bullshit and you know it. He ain't dead." Deegan had shifted back into hunting mode, those intense eyes blazing.

Frank looked around the dark woods. "I shot him this

morning, but he didn't have a mark on him when he came after me just now. If he walked away from a bullet to the face, then…maybe he *is* immortal."

"Everything's got a weakness," Deegan said softly.

Frank held up a hand. "I'm done with this. I'm not letting you put me on a plate with an apple in my mouth anymore." He moved to walk past Deegan and out of the woods.

The hunter's hand shot out to block his path.

"You're not goin anywhere. We're finishin this."

"The hell we are."

Deegan snarled, as animalistic in his own way as the Jackal Man. "You're so blind to what's goin on, you can't even begin to know."

"What the fuck does that mean?"

The hunter glared into his eyes. "Frankie…you're tired."

It was as if he'd taken a fast-acting muscle relaxer. A wave of dizziness passed over Frank. His muscled quivered with exertion.

"Lay down and go to sleep."

Frank brought the gun butt up, hitting Deegan in nearly the same place he'd hit Lyles, but he put all his force behind this one. There was a monstrous crack, and Deegan collapsed. As soon as the eye connection was broken, Frank's weariness was instantly sucked away.

"Who the hell are you?" Frank whispered. When the man didn't answer, he squatted quickly and went through his knapsack until he found a box of rifle ammunition. After a few seconds, he figured out how to load the weapon, then turned and fled through the woods, leaving the hunter unconscious on the ground.

If the Jackal Man wanted him, so be it.

THE JACKAL MAN

THE BEAST GETS ITS SAY

46

"I called you *THREE* times, Frank! Where were you? You didn't get that filthy answering questions in the police station! You can't keep doing this to me! I want some answers!"

It was past eleven when he arrived home, dirty, sore, and bloodstained. He'd barely touched the knob before Trisha yanked the door open and started screaming.

Frank brushed past her. If there was even a chance that thing was still alive, he had to act now. "Get dressed and get the kids up. I want all three of you in your car and on your way out of town in fifteen minutes."

"What? Frank, what's going on? Where did you get that gun?"

He looked down at the rifle he still clutched in his hands, then laid it against the couch. "I don't have time to explain, and you could probably live the rest of your life happy without hearing it. I just need to know you guys are safe back home."

"And leave you here?"

"For now. I'll be right behind you as soon as the police let me go. Or arrest me. Whatever. The important thing is that you and Willie and Casey leave Asheville."

She stared at him. "Tell me the truth. I want to know what you're hiding so I can understand what happened here!"

And he wanted to tell her. The last twenty-four hours had been so insane, he wanted to share it with her just to see if would sound as crazy coming out of his mouth. And maybe he would've done so, if a scream hadn't come from the back of the house.

Willie froze in the kitchen when his mother started yelling. He'd come down to get something to eat, sneaking around the dark house. Just knowing that his father had seen the Jackal Man too, that he wasn't alone, had brought his appetite back. His mother's voice had that angry tone that had been so common back home.

"Same shit, different day," he muttered. For the first time in a long while, the tongue ring got in the way of his speech. He reached up and removed the steel rod from his mouth, relieved the thing was finally gone. All it did was take away the feeling in his tongue, and he was done feeling numb.

He turned away from the fridge to head back upstairs, hand on the light switch, when a familiar tapping came from the back door on the far side of the kitchen, the one that led to the pecan orchard behind their house.

"Zerk?" he whispered. That soft tapping came again on the small pane of glass set into the top of the door. "Nails?"

He grinned in elation, so relieved they were okay that the ridiculousness of the fantasy didn't dawn on him until he was turning the knob and pulling it open.

And then a nightmare rushed into the kitchen on four legs.

"*DAAAAAAAAAD!*"
The terror in that voice sent ice chips through Frank's

blood stream. "Willie?" He plunged past Trisha, tearing through the living room and into the kitchen.

He halted on the threshold. Blinked to make sure this was real.

The Jackal Man stood hunched over Willie by the back door, face whole and horrifying once more. The boy was on his back against the slick tile, struggling under the beast's weight as it batted him around like a cat with a chew toy.

"NO!" Frank yelled.

The creature glanced up, its luminous eyes meeting Frank's, and there was no mistaking the look in them. This was revenge, pure and simple. It roared triumphantly, the sound as out of place in the bright kitchen as the beast itself.

"Oh Jesus, *what is that?*" Trisha screamed behind him.

The Jackal Man had only been playing with the boy, waiting for Frank to arrive, to make sure he witnessed this. Now it ran its thin, muscular arms under Willie, hoisted the boy over its shoulder, and bounded through the doorway into the night.

Frank charged after them, clomping onto the porch and leaping into the dirt yard in pursuit. Outside, the beast was a lumpy silhouette as it made a beeline for the grove of pecan trees, into the shadows they offered.

And once that happened...Willie would be gone.

He concentrated on running. Carrying the boy slowed the creature down. Frank actually found himself gaining ground in this second footrace of the night.

Captive and captor disappeared into the trees, and Frank plunged in a split second later.

"*Dad, help!*" Willie cried, just like in his dream, and reached out toward him. His other hand got a firm hold on a jutting branch. He held on, and the Jackal Man was yanked off stride.

Frank clamped onto Willie's forearm and pulled. The boy

slipped off the creature's shoulder. The Jackal Man turned and grabbed Willie's legs in their oversized jeans and pulled back.

"*Dad!*"

"Let go of my son, you bastard!"

It released the boy, who dropped half into Frank's arms and half onto the ground with a *whuff* of expelled air. Frank stumbled backward with him, trying to stay on his feet.

The Jackal Man came at them, reaching. Frank felt the rough pads against his throat.

A gunshot went off behind them. Wood exploded from the trunk of a tree to Frank's left. Both he and the creature turned.

Trisha was just a few feet away, outside the darkness of the pecan treetops, holding the rifle Frank had taken from Deegan. She fired again, the recoil causing her to fall back a step and cry out.

Two inches to the right and Frank's left lung would've had an extra breathing hole. As it was, the bullet slammed into the Jackal Man's outstretched arm.

It whimpered in pain as it brought the injured appendage to its chest. *Don't worry*, Frank thought, *you'll be healed up and ready to go again in an hour.* Then it turned and ran back into the thicket of pecan trees. They heard its roar several seconds later, echoing from far away.

Frank gasped and sank to his knees next to Willie.

"Are you okay?"

His son nodded with shocked eyes, then focused on him. He threw his arms around Frank. "Thank you Dad, thank you, thank you, thank you," he repeated.

"Was that it?" Trisha asked, crawling up next to them with the rifle. "The thing?"

"The Jackal Man," father and son said in unison, letting her into the embrace.

"Do you think I killed it?"

"I don't think it *can* be killed."

"But why, Frank? Why did it come here?"

"To hurt me," he said, breaking the circle. Willie clung to him. "I have royally pissed this thing off, and it tried to take Willie to get back at me. That's why you have to leave. Right now. All of you."

"No way!" Willie shouted. "I'm not going without you!"

"You have to."

He helped them both up and pushed them toward the house. Trisha carried the rifle as they hurried inside and then went upstairs to get Casey.

"Dad, I'm not going!" Willie declared again.

Frank grabbed his shoulder. "You have to take care of your mom and sister for me."

"They can go! They'll be safe! You didn't leave me and I'm not leaving you!"

"Yes, you *are!*" Frank growled. There was no time to do this properly, no time to bask in this earned love, and he hated the beast even more for it. He picked the boy up, something he hadn't done since he was eight, and carried him out the front door, his back screaming. He tossed Willie in the back seat and slammed the door as Trisha did the same on the other side with Casey.

His wife jumped behind the wheel and got the engine started. She rolled down the window, pushed her face out, and kissed him urgently.

"Go north through town and circle around. Stay away from River Meadows."

"Promise me you won't go back after that thing, Frank."

"I'm not setting foot out of this house. I'll call Shruff right now."

"*Daaaaad!*" Willie wailed as she rolled back up the window and flew down the driveway.

Frank stood long enough to see them disappear down the street and then ran back into the house.

"Mom, we can't just go!" Willie shouted again.

"It's just for a little while! He'll be safe, and as soon as this is over, he'll come home!" His mother was frantic, shaking badly. Casey bawled in the front seat as they flew down the tight residential streets of Asheville.

Willie could think of nothing else to say that would make her listen. The idea of staying was terrifying, but he couldn't just go. This felt like betrayal. There was pressure building in his chest and every minute they moved farther away from his father added to the desperation.

"Please Willie, just stop," she pleaded, slowing for a stop sign.

It was the only chance he would get. Willie pulled the door handle and leapt from the moving station wagon. He hit the concrete on his knees, tearing holes in the fabric of his jeans and the flesh beneath, then got to his feet and started running. From behind him, his mother screamed his name.

He lost her by running down several side streets, with the unfortunate side effect of becoming lost himself. When he couldn't run anymore, he stopped to catch his breath on the sidewalk under one of the blazing streetlamps.

The dark pressed in on him beyond the circle of illumination. His father had told him the town was safe, off limits to the Jackal Man, but that obviously wasn't true.

Willie ran another two blocks when a red Jeep roared out of nowhere and squealed to a stop in front of him. He had to throw himself back on the lawn of the house behind him to keep from being run over.

The driver was a muscular guy wearing a camouflage shirt and khaki shorts.

"You're Stanford's boy, right?" the man asked. He smiled, but it was far from friendly. A bruise engulfed the entire bottom of his chin, and there were bloodstains across his shirt.

Willie nodded.

"The name's Deegan. Want a ride?"

47

It took Frank fifteen minutes to get back inside, rebandage his seeping wounds, and grab a fresh shirt before a squeal of tires brought him back to the front door. He thought it must be the police; one of the neighbors had surely reported the rifle shots, probably crazy pecan lady.

But it was Trisha back in the driveway, running to him with Casey in her arms.

And no Willie.

A sinking feeling pulled him toward despair.

Never should've let them go...

"Where is he?"

"I don't know! He jumped out of the car!"

"Get inside," he said.

Once the door was secured again, Trisha said, "Call the police, Frank."

For once he didn't argue, didn't hesitate. He pulled out his phone, despair mixing with guilt and helplessness, and as he dialed the number, it began to ring in his hand. He answered even though he knew it could only be bad news.

"Hello?"

"Frankie," Deegan said. There was barely-contained anger beneath the surface of the words. "My jaw hurts like a bitch, ya know. That wasn't very nice. Ruthless—and I respect that—but not very nice. Fortunately, I have a new bundle of joy to ease my pain."

Frank heard the phone shift. Then his son's voice, achingly brief, "Dad, I—!"

Deegan came back instantly. "Hear that, Frankie?"

"*FUCK YOU!*" Frank thundered. "Don't you touch my boy! Let him go!"

"I intend to do just that, if you listen and do exactly what I say. We still have a lot to talk about, and work to finish. Get over to your trailer, and come unarmed. Don't even think about calling the pig patrol. Can you do that, or do I kill him right here and call it a day?"

"Why?" Frank asked miserably. "What do you want? What does torturing me and my family have to do with the Jackal Man?"

"More than you know. Now, are you comin?"

"I'm coming."

The phone beeped in his ear to terminate the call. Trisha asked numbly, "Who has him, Frank?"

"This guy. A hunter. His name's Deegan."

"None of this makes sense! What does he want?"

"For me to meet him at the site."

"No! Just call the police, right now!"

"You don't know this guy like I do. He's dangerous."

"Please, Frank, don't!"

He grabbed her, pulled her and Casey close, hugged them both. "Go into town, to the police station, and stay there." He couldn't say more, couldn't stay or he would never leave. Frank started for the door without looking back, but kept the phone out.

He had one more call to make before he met the hunter.

~ ~ ~

Deegan pushed the end button on his own phone, then turned his attention back to the struggling brat beside him. Little Frankie Junior was tied to the incomplete second floor of one of the River Meadows houses. He looked ready to be stretched on the rack, arms and legs splayed out and connected to four different wall supports.

"Lemme go!" The kid struggled to kick him, but the ropes were so taut it looked more like a muscle spasm.

"I said I would. *If* your father cooperates."

"What do you want from him?"

"Something very special. Something only he can give me."

"Dude, do you know how gay that sounds?"

Deegan laughed. "Like father, like son. If you really wanna know, I'm gonna feed him to the Jackal Man." The brat was still as this sank in, then renewed his struggling. "Relax kid. I'm sure that thing'll make a quicker job of it than I would, especially after all the trouble your dad caused me. Play your cards right and I might let you go."

The boy opened his mouth and let loose with a long string of obscenities. Deegan howled laughter at the sky.

"Kiss your mamma with that mouth?"

"You're gonna kiss your ass goodbye when my dad finds you."

"We'll see. Ol' Frankie's definitely got more spunk than I gave him credit for." Deegan looked at the boy, taking in his orange hair and ridiculous clothing. "What are you supposed to be anyway, with the clown getup?"

The boy's anger faded. "What? I'm...just me."

"Naw, that ain't you, kid. I can see it in your eyes. You

were meant for better things than the carnival freak show. Now be quiet. Your father's gonna be here soon. Wouldn't want him to find you quite yet."

"I'm gonna scream till my eyes bleed!"

"Go to sleep," Deegan commanded. The boy's eyes clamped shut, his head dropped against the wood, and he was out. That trick always worked better on children. It was something he'd picked up in Brazil, from a now extinct tribe in the rainforest.

An extinction he had caused, but, you know...semantics.

Deegan climbed down from the roof and headed toward the trailer to spring what he intended to be his next-to-last trap of the night.

48

Frank's truck swerved around the last bend in the road before the site came into view. He was hunched over the wheel, hands gripping the plastic, face dipped in granite. As instructed, he'd left the gun behind. He would play by the psycho's rules until he could get Willie to safety. That was all that mattered.

Pale light shone through the windows of the trailer. This time he drove right up to the busted door, not bothering to hide. He walked up the steps, hoping it would be the last time.

Deegan was at his desk, in his chair, boots propped on the scarred desktop the same way he'd been the first time they met. His rifle was across his lap. He'd changed into a new shirt, but was minus his hat. A camping lantern on the desk pulsed irregular light. The bruise across his face was mottled purple and black in its illumination. For the first time, Frank realized how much the hunter reminded him of his father.

"The man of the hour."

"I want my son, Deegan."

"Sit down and let's talk."

"Where is he? This is between you and me. At least, I guess it is. Let him go and we can talk all you want."

"Call him an insurance policy, so I have your full attention." He swung the rifle's business end around. Frank remembered how the weapon had turned the Jackal Man's face into pudding. "Sit down or I make it between him and me."

Frank went to the stool, pulled it in front of the blood-stained desk, and sat like an obedient student. "The Jackal Man's alive. You can hunt him and prove you're better than me. I'll do whatever you want. Just let Willie go."

"Don't tell me about bein *better*," Deegan snarled, swinging his boots off the desk. "I've devoted my life to hunting! And just because some clock-punchin stiff got lucky and blasted my prey doesn't change my destiny!"

Frank nodded. "Now I get it. I thought there was a reason for all this, but you're just insane."

"Oh, that hurts so much comin from *you*, Frankie!" Deegan picked the butt of the rifle up and laid it across the desk. Frank denied his instinct to leap for it. "A man with no purpose or vision, a man who wouldn't know greatness if it bit him on his hefty ass. Now...you say he was alive? You actually saw him?"

"He came to my house tonight, just like you said. Tried to kill my son."

Deegan sneered. "Might have to start a list for that particular honor."

Every last drop of blood in Frank's body rushed to his head. "You won't touch him. I promise you that."

"You just don't have any clue, do you? Your stupidity, your inability to see what's goin on around you at *any... given...moment*...it just sickens me. I've met mental patients that delude themselves less than you."

"Then say what you brought me here to say."

Deegan nodded and leaned back in the chair, putting him farther away from the rifle. "What did I tell you about hunting? Find a weakness and exploit it. Once I got to town, got a feel for the situation and saw what he did to your dog, I knew my best chance to get a crack at the Jackal Man was to get him stirred up, get him angry and attackin anything that moved out here. I just wasn't countin on the stubbornness of this town, and their willingness to ignore him. In any case, my plan was to pin a few deaths on him, have the cops traipsin through his territory. So I set my sights on someone already out here, someone a little higher profile than a lowly Mexican construction worker."

"Me."

"You got it, boyo. Did you really think I needed to ask your permission? I figured you for a rube like the rest of 'em, somebody I could romance with stories of the Jackal Man and get you out here alone, but you just wouldn't cooperate, just wouldn't believe. You know, it's jerks like you that kill Tinkerbell."

"What does it matter? You'd just goddamn shoot her if I didn't."

The smile dropped off the hunter's face. "When you wouldn't cooperate, I went a different route. First, I stirred up a bee's nest by killin those horses."

"That was *you?*"

"Sure was. I just wanted to cause some trouble, but I hadn't counted on that old coot havin more influence around here than the president. That protest was a nice side effect. There was more Jackal Man activity that night than ever before. Course, I didn't know that was gonna happen. By that point, I'd already taken steps to make sure the media's attention stayed out here by kidnapping your boss."

"Oh my God. Damon. What did you do to him?"

"Just kept him stashed until I could see if an actual body was gonna be necessary. I figured, rich guy like that, gone mis-

sin after everything else that's happened, FBI would be craw-
lin all over it. But you never even raised the alarm, Frankie!
I snatched him right after you left that bar in town, kept him
for two days, and you never bothered to say a thing!"

"That's not my fault! I-I didn't know where he was!"

"Tell that to him. Anyway, the rest of the story you know,
even if you don't understand it. I was trackin the beast, Garcia shows up and gets hisself killed, then you come along. I
thought I had him last night when we were camped, but I
missed. I left you out there hopin he would finish you off,
and, when I saw the damn thing was still creepin around this
mornin, I dropped your boss off to get rid of him, too. Told
him you were tied up in the trailer. Schmuck was comin to
save you."

Damon's death came back to him, hauntingly clear, and
Frank bit down on the grief. "So why haven't you killed me?
You've had every chance."

Deegan rolled his head back in exasperation. "And here
we go, once again you're missin the obvious. Have you really
not figured it out yet? The Jackal Man wants *you*."

"That supposed to be a surprise? You already said he
wants to kill us."

"Oh, I'm sure he'd love to get his claws on both of us, but
he had a special jones for you even before we went after him.
Last night, he finally shows up in my camp right after you do.
He went for *you* by the fire. He wanted you bad enough to
attack you in broad daylight. When we had him by the river,
he ignored me even when I was down, and went after you. He
came to *your* house, repeatedly, and left you warnings."

"I don't understand…"

"Think about it! He goes after anybody he sees as a threat,
and right now, who's the biggest threat? The guys tearin up his

land. And who's out there every day, givin the orders to the troops? He's just defendin his home, the same way you would if somebody dynamited their way into your living room."

"But...but that's not my fault! I didn't buy the land, I'm just—!"

"Followin orders?" Deegan chuckled. "Yeah, so were the soldiers at Auschwitz. The Jackal Man's smart, Frankie, but he doesn't understand concepts like corporations. You're the one in charge as far as he's concerned, and he's got your scent now. If you look at all this from above, the way God sees it, *you're* the bad guy, not him."

Frank digested this for a moment, then said gravely, "So he has every reason in the world to want me dead. So what do *you* want?"

"See, that's what I'm talkin about. You still haven't figured it out." He sneered. "You're the bait."

Frank lunged for the rifle on the desk. He was leaning across the wooden surface with outstretched hands before Deegan whipped out a revolver and shoved the barrel in his face. It was a six-cylinder, Dirty-Harry-job that looked scarily big.

"So predictable."

"Maybe, but I wouldn't be very good bait if I was dead."

Frank hit the desk itself this time, driving it into Deegan like a football linebacker. The hunter's gun hand flung to the side as the edge of the desk pounded into his broad sternum, pinning him against the wall. The lantern tipped off, shattering on the floor. The two of them struggled in darkness, grunting like animals.

Something hard smashed against Frank's head. He grabbed the man's wrist and held the revolver away from him while still keeping pressure on the desk. Frank was on top of the wooden surface now, practically in the hunter's lap.

A muscular arm wrapped around his neck, but loosened when Frank grabbed one of the fingers around the revolver's grip and twisted. The sound of bones snapping and Deegan's exclamation of pain were sweet music. The hunter squirmed out from between the chair and the desk, and Frank followed, still latched on to the man's gun arm.

They wrestled into a corner of the trailer, and the hunter attempted to kick him now that he was free. Frank waded into the blows, prying at his hand.

Finally, the revolver hung limp from Deegan's trigger finger, and Frank plucked it off. His own wrist was grabbed just as fast and bent backward until the weapon fell to the floor. A palm smashed into the underside of his chin, driving his teeth together, filling his mouth with blood. He fell back against the desk.

Through the haze that floated around his head, he heard Deegan say, "Let's do this the old-fashioned way."

This time it was a booted foot that shoved Frank violently into unconsciousness.

He was aware of the pain first.

Partly from the throbbing in his temple, but also because it felt like his blood was pushing the pathways of his head wide open, adding another lane to the freeway of his bloodstream. When Frank's eyes finally fluttered open, he understood.

The ground was a dark green field two feet above his head. He could see a blur of trees but couldn't pick out anything definite; the upside down viewpoint disoriented him to the point of queasiness. His arms were bound behind him at the wrists. He made an effort to raise his head. A heavy-duty rope was tied around his ankles and ran up into the branches of a large tree, dangling him like a side of beef in a butcher shop window.

The muscles in his neck quivered from the strain. He let his head drop. The sudden motion started his body swaying at the end of the rope.

"Help," he rasped. The words scraped over his throat. "Deegan? Anybody?"

"I'm here, you big baby," Deegan's voice came from his left. His boots clomped into Frank's vision. "Just tryin to figure what position would be best. I thought about climbin into the tree, but, like you said, that sucker can jump."

"Deegan, this is pointless, it won't work! He can't be killed, haven't we proved that by now?"

"When I get him down this time, I'm gonna cut the thing's head off. We'll see if he can come back from *that*."

"Please don't do this."

Deegan said nothing for a long second, then knelt so they were face-to-face. He had his rifle in his one good hand. "It didn't have to be like this, you know. It didn't have to be hard."

"So what, I was supposed to let you kill me?"

"I meant for *me*, Frankie. It didn't have to be hard for *me*."

"Please, you've got me, I'm all yours, I'll be your bait. Just let my son go. You promised you would."

"And I will, when this is over. As soon as you've done your part." With that, he reached out, tore open Frank's shirt, grabbed his shoulder, and pushed a thumb into the wound there.

Shrieking agony bloomed hot in his brain. He screamed.

"That's the spirit! Let it all out!" Deegan told him. He'd dug past the bandage, and now Frank could feel him wriggling the digit beneath the flesh. Blood flowed down his neck and dripped from the top of his head.

"*Stop!*" he begged. The pain was unbearable. He thrashed at the end of the rope, trying to think of Willie. "*Please, STOP!*"

Deegan pulled his thumb out—Frank could swear it made a pop-goes-the-weasel type noise—and sat back on his haunches. "He gets a whiff of that, he'll come runnin. If it's any consolation, I'll try to kill him before he tears you up too bad."

Frank blinked blood out of his eyes. He thought he was going to pass out, but he found the energy to raise his weary head once more.

"Deegan?"

"Yeah?"

"You can let me down now."

Deegan smirked. "Oh really? And why's that?"

"Cause otherwise Detective Shruff is gonna shoot you in the head."

49

The smile faded so slowly from the hunter's face it was almost impossible to see. He turned around until the barrel of the pistol in Shruff's hand was almost in his eye socket.

"You heard the man," the detective said through chattering teeth. "Drop the rifle and let him down."

"Thought I told you not to call the police, Frankie."

"Just do it!" Shruff shouted. He was shaking, the gun bouncing in his grip. "Drop the rifle!"

"He's got a pistol, too!"

Deegan still didn't move. "You can't kill me. You'll never find his son if you do."

"No, but I can shoot you in painful places until you talk. If you cooperate, you stand a chance of just walking away."

Deegan set the rifle down beside the base of the tree, then pulled the pistol out of his waistband and did the same with it, watching the detective. Shruff moved them away with his foot while Deegan untied the rope around the tree trunk that held Frank aloft.

"Took you long enough," Frank said. "The guy was bleeding me out a drop at a time."

"You said I had to come from downwind. You know how long it took me to figure out which way was downwind? I didn't even know where you were until I heard the screams."

"You two must've been separated at birth," Deegan muttered.

"Keep your mouth shut and let him down slow. I have to admit Stanford, I thought you were nuts talking about this hunter, but here the guy is."

Deegan braced himself to take Frank's weight, then lowered him an inch at a time, grunting each time his broken finger was jostled. Once he was on the ground, Shruff made the hunter untie his hands and step away. Frank got a head rush as he stood up. He could feel blood running down his chest on the inside of his shirt; the wound pulsed with each beat of his heart. Now he could see where they were, right on the edge of the woods on the far side of the meadow, close to where Deegan's camp had been.

"Thank you," he told the detective, as he wiped blood off his face with his shirttail.

"No problem. Do me a favor and grab his guns in case I faint."

"Oh, right!" Frank snatched up the revolver and jammed it in a pocket, then got the rifle and aimed it at the hunter. "Where is he, Deegan?"

The man remained silent.

"You might as well tell us," Shruff said. "You're not getting out of this, but my offer stands: give us the kid and we all go our separate ways. You wanna hunt the Jackal Man, I'm the last person that's gonna stop you."

"*Tell us, goddamnit!*" Frank shouted.

"Okay." Deegan pointed a finger past them.

Into the woods.

"He's in there. I left him tied to a tree."

"You asshole! If anything happened to him—!"

"Just show us where," Shruff said. "And you better pray he's alive."

Deegan shrugged and led the way into the trees at gun-point. Darkness closed in around them. Frank saw the gun in Shruff's hand jittering. "You gonna be okay?" he whispered.

Instead of answering, the detective asked Deegan, "How f-far is he?"

"Not too far." Deegan stopped, reached out, and touched one of the nearby trees, as if getting directions. When he started walking again, he said, "By the way, that's a real pretty scar you got there, Mr. Detective. Where does one come by somethin like that?"

"Shut up and keep walking."

"Bet you would love to get your hands on the thing that did that to you."

"I said shut up!"

"I just thought you might wanna know—"

"Deegan!" Frank shouted.

"We're at his front door right now."

There was a roar above and a crash of branches as the Jackal Man landed in their midst. The beast stood hunched in front of them, hissing.

Deegan never paused. He spun around it, wrenched the rifle from Frank's slack hands, and started producing bullets from somewhere like a magician, the broken finger on his trigger hand not slowing him a bit.

The Jackal Man leapt at him, and Deegan used the rifle to keep the creature at arm's length as they danced around one another. Frank watched helplessly and then looked over in time to see Shruff preparing to squeeze off a shot with his quavering pistol. He knocked the detective's arm away as the report barked through the woods.

"You can't risk hitting Deegan!" Frank shouted. "You kill him, we'll never find Willie!"

The sound of the shot broke the standoff. The Jackal Man turned, fixed Frank and Shruff with its lantern stare, and bolted into the woods with uncanny speed.

The three of them stood quietly for a moment before remembering they were enemies. Shruff and Deegan brought their weapons up at one another. Frank thought the detective started to yell, 'Freeze,' but Deegan, trained only in killing, afforded no such luxury.

The rifle boomed. Shruff stumbled back and went down.

Frank watched him fall, then turned back to Deegan. The hunter bared his teeth. "Your son will *die*," he spat, and turned to run in the direction the Jackal Man had gone.

Frank pulled the revolver from his waistband, but by the time he could've gotten off a shot, Deegan was gone, vanished into the darkness.

Time seemed to race by. Frank wanted to go after him, but first turned back to Shruff. The detective slumped in scraggly shrubs, blood soaking through a hole in the middle of his white shirt with alarming speed.

He struggled to get up.

"You can't move," Frank told him. "You're hurt bad."

Shruff grabbed Frank's arm and hauled him down. He could see the stark fear swimming in the detective's eyes beneath his sweat-covered brow. "*Don't leave me alone*," he pleaded.

"I have to." Frank tore off part of the man's shirt, balled it up, and pressed it against his stomach. The blood flow seemed to be slackening, which he took as an encouraging sign. Unless the man's heart was already stopping. "He's gonna kill Willie. I have to stop him. Hold this here and I'll be back as soon as I can."

Shruff bit his lip and nodded. He moved his hands over the rag and pressed, then fell back with his eyes closed. His breathing appeared regular, which was all Frank could ask for at the moment.

He stood with the revolver and started to run after Deegan, but made it only a few yards before his foot plummeted straight through the ground up to his knee.

Frank went down hard. Pain wracked his leg as his knee tried to bend the wrong direction. The gun flew from his hand.

The earth around him issued a creaking groan. It reminded him of the sound induced by Cracker's explosives just before the pit had opened up.

"Oh shit," Frank breathed, staying as still as possible. He suddenly felt like a skater on a thinly-frozen lake.

He shifted, trying to roll onto his side so he could pull his leg out of the hole.

That groan came again, and suddenly there was vibration beneath him. He saw cracks spreading outward through the dirt.

Then the ground under him was gone, and he was falling into even deeper darkness.

50

His legs absorbed most of the impact, but when they buckled, Frank was terrified they'd shattered. He collapsed backward, falling upon a bed of hard dirt and rubble. The back of his head came down on a sharp chunk of earth, and his vision fragmented like a kaleidoscope before he forced it back together.

Frank sat up with a groan. Tried to move his legs. They weren't broken, but they hurt like hell. He rubbed them until the worst of it faded and then looked at his new surroundings.

Far above was the jagged hole that had opened beneath him. Through it, he could see the canopy of the woods and a small snatch of the night sky. Very little light made it down here to him. He could make out rough-textured walls on either side, but ahead was only a darkness so thick it looked like oil.

He was in a tunnel.

Willie's story rushed back to him, followed by Deegan's claims. The hunter had goddamn been leading him and Shruff here the whole time, tracing the route of these underground corridors by way of the trees. Probably hoping the Jackal Man would give him a distraction for escape, and boy, had that paid off.

Now Frank was in the thing's *home*. And everything would be lost unless he could find a way out.

He stood gingerly on his aching legs. There wouldn't be any getting out the way he came in. Even if all four of his limbs weren't screaming, the hole was a good five yards above his head, and the walls were sheer. He called Shruff's name, but got no response. The man was unconscious or dead.

That left only forward, into the heart of that inky black. The idea of going blind into a maze where the Jackal Man could be lurking around every corner wasn't comforting, but the idea of Willie's death was *terrifying*.

Nothing to be scared of, he thought. *That thing is running around up there with Deegan, so don't make the same mistake Goldilocks did and still be here when it gets back.*

Frank stuck a hand out and plunged forward into the greedy darkness, moving as fast as he could hobble.

Deegan hadn't followed the beast too far into the woods. Number one rule of hunting: you never chased the quarry. A real hunter made the prey come to him.

Luckily for him, he knew exactly where the beast would go.

Or rather, to *whom* the beast would go.

He doubled back to where he'd left those other two wastes. He found the pig lying against a tree, unconscious but still breathing.

Deegan pressed the barrel of his rifle against the man's skull, preparing to send him to oblivion, then hesitated.

Things had gotten too messy in this town, and matters always got exponentially worse when you figured in the cops.

All of them would have to die before he left town, even the punk kid, but for now, he needed to get focused on what really mattered.

Like killing the Jackal Man, and making sure he stayed dead.

"Later for you, piggy." He turned toward the deeper woods, his nose twitching as he hunted for his bait's scent.

There was light ahead.

Frank thought he was imagining it, until he realized he could now see his hand trailing along the clay wall. He'd been having a panic attack of his own, the tunnel dead silent save for his breathing. A wild, earthy smell hung heavy in the air, the same way the creature's fur had smelled. The light ahead was too bright to be the moon. He followed it with needful intensity, passing by several junctions within the network of tunnels.

He came to a corner on his left, a gap in the wall that opened onto a chamber. The light, inconstant and shifting, came from within.

Frank peeked around the corner.

The room beyond was large, circular and domed, with several other tunnels leading into it. The rounded ceiling stretched up much higher than the distance Frank had fallen, which meant he'd been heading deeper underground all this time.

The light came from a firepit in the middle of this chamber, a neatly maintained blaze much larger than the one Deegan had created in the field the night before. The smoke from this fire curled lazily up to the ceiling, where it exited the chamber through a series of small holes. A screen like that, Frank realized, would break up the cloud so it dissipated easier in the air outside, and didn't leave a trail.

His construction-oriented mind saw the implication immediately.

This was higher-level thinking. It showed an understanding of not only fire and its properties, but building design and engineering.

This room was not the product of an animal. Hell, Frank knew plenty of human beings that couldn't've put together something like this.

If you look at all this from above, the way God sees it, you're *the bad guy...*

Deegan's words.

And now Frank was beginning to truly understand them.

The walls were decorated with sloping illustrations and skewed lines, some carved into the clay, some made with ash, some painted in dark maroon blood like the vandalism at the site, the combination reminding him of ancient cave paintings. They felt almost ceremonial.

Frank turned his attention away from the primitive artwork to the contents of the floor.

All around the fire—but a good enough distance from it so the flames didn't spread—bric-a-brac and garbage from the world above filled every corner of this room. It looked like a town dump. A small path led from each of the tunnel entrances to the cleared area around the fire, and Frank followed it, looking at everything the Jackal Man had collected over the long years in the flickering light of the fire. Old, faded couches, lamps with no shades, a broken table. Soda cans, beer bottles, ripped handbags, laceless sneakers, and other items were strewn and piled around the periphery of the room in some places up to his waist. Frank could imagine the cars that had thrown these things from their windows as they roared past, the trucks that had stopped to dump them by the side of the Dark Road.

A small, rusted, silver disc stuck out from under a physics textbook on the edge of a pile close to the path's edge. Frank knelt, his legs screaming, and picked it out with hands that were still stained with Shruff's blood. It was a compass, badly scarred, the tarnished needle still wobbling in an eternal attempt to point north.

There was an engraving inside the lid that he couldn't make out, and a year that he could.

1752.

Frank dropped it back into the pile. He might've used it to find a way out of here, but something about holding an object belonging to someone nearly three hundred years in their grave turned his stomach. He turned right, anxious to keep moving, and spotted something else of interest beside the arm of an old recliner.

These objects were more familiar, two large black metal boxes with a barcode on the side. Frank pulled one out onto the path around the fire, slid the lid off, and stared inside.

Cellophane wrapped blasting caps and white, circular mounds.

Dynamite. Jaime Garcia's stashed goods, no doubt.

He left the explosives out and continued around the circle, trying to figure out which of the other tunnel exits he wanted to take, letting his eyes wander over the torn suitcases, empty milk jugs, broken toys—

Frank yelped and jumped back from the garbage.

A face was staring back at him.

Here was a clear area in the piles, and four corpses were laid out side by side like bodies in the morgue. On the wall above their heads was a series of dramatic markings in blood.

He recognized the two on the left. The missing boys. Willie's friends. One of them without his throat, the other his stomach. Both holes had stopped bleeding long ago, but the wounds were still squirming with maggots. Their skin had turned pale and waxy. They'd both died with eyes open, one staring at the ceiling, but the other one, the one that wore the leather coat, seemed to follow Frank wherever he moved.

The third body was much older, not only in age but in the length of time since its demise. The decay was so advanced that bone showed through in several places. Frank wondered if the fire served to burn up the odors from these corpses.

He didn't recognize the man by face, but he didn't have to. The body wore the remains of a casual work shirt. On the right breast, a single word was stitched in gold thread, like all the others clothes that had been in the closet of their rental property.

Wesley.

Deegan was right. The Jackal Man had killed the previous foreman for his transgressions, and when Frank had replaced him, he became the target. He felt foolish for not seeing it sooner.

The fourth and last form was covered in an ancient cloth like a shroud. Frank didn't want to look, time was slipping by with the subtlety of a raging river, but now that he'd seen these bodies, it was his responsibility to bring news of their deaths back to the outside world. Unless he joined them before this hellish night was over.

His hand shook as he grasped the edge of the cover and lifted it.

Frank stared at what was underneath.

His mouth went dry.

He dropped the filthy cloth and scrambled away, this time almost falling into the fire. Realization rushed through him like a freight train, and suddenly he understood, understood it all, and if he felt foolish before, it was nothing compared to now. The need to get out of these tunnels became a blazing fire under his feet.

There was a shuffling step on the dirt floor behind him.

Frank froze.

A quiet hiss.

Too late.

He turned.

On the far side of the fire was the Jackal Man, hunched and low, half crouched with one leg splayed to the side. It watched Frank with those feline eyes glowing like radioactive coals.

He stared back at it, wanting to slap himself a good one for not seeing what was right in front of him the entire time. But then again, neither had the great hunter.

The Jackal Man took a step closer to him around the fire. Frank moved in the opposite direction. Right now, without a weapon, keeping the flames between them was the only option he had. The beast growled deep in its throat, tail twitching like a rattlesnake, hands flexing those long claws. As they circled the fire pit, Frank felt a chilled sweat break out under his arms.

It opened its muzzle wide, displaying monstrous teeth. Frank prepared himself for one of those awful roars.

But, as usual, the creature did the last thing he expected.

The goddamned thing *spoke*.

51

At first, it was a series of grunts, growls and snarls, too choppy and patterned to be anything but language. It was like listening to Chinese or Arabic; he may not understand the words, but it was identifiable as communication. Then it jutted its jaw uncomfortably, and strained out a single, identifiable syllable.

"*Hoommme*," it said, in a voice as guttural and scratchy as a lifelong smoker.

Frank stared, too amazed and horrified to react.

It dug a padded hand into the garbage pile closest to it. "*Hoommme*," it repeated, and when Frank still did nothing, it bounded around the fire, waving its arms in an exaggerated gesture unlike anything it had exhibited thus far. There was frustration in the movement, like a foreigner who can't communicate the nuances through a language barrier. "*HOOMMME!*" it howled desperately, in its gravelly voice. It stepped back on its awkward legs, meant for quadrapedal locomotion but evolving rapidly, the way man's spine had straightened over the long millennia. It went to each of the entrances on its side of this chamber and repeated the word, pointing down the tunnels with one finger, a gesture so human it was all the proof anyone would need that this was no mere animal.

Frank found that his terror had ebbed. "I understand," he said calmly. "This is your home."

The creature stopped, satisfied that it had gotten through. It pointed at Frank across the fire. "*Hurrrrt hoommme.*" The Jackal Man put its hands together, claw-tipped finger to finger, pebble-covered palm to palm, and made a strange static noise with its tongue as it expanded its hands.

Like a five-year-old doing a pantomime of an explosion.

Frank wanted to argue. Wanted to explain. The same way he would in a court of law, if held accountable for the Lyles Corporation's dealings. But Deegan was right. It would make no sense to this creature. Frank was the invader here, the villain, General Custer and Darth Vader all rolled into one.

"I know. I'm sorry."

The Jackal Man pointed one last time, toward the corpses behind Frank, or, more specifically, toward the shroud. This time, no words were needed.

"I'm so sorry," Frank repeated, feeling the ineptitude of those words. It was crazy, he'd been hunted by this monster, watched as it killed his friend and tried to take his son, but now that he knew the truth, he wanted to hide his head in shame.

He remembered history from school, stories about the more ruthless settlers doing whatever it took to get the Indians off their own land, giving them blankets infected with deadly diseases, pushing and needling them until they were cornered into nice, tiny reservations. This creature's kingdom had probably once stretched across the plains and woods of Texas, but now here it was, surrounded on all sides by civilization that was blowing holes into its last refuge.

The Jackal Man was no urban legend.

He was a cautionary tale.

Was it any wonder he was fighting back? They were lucky he hadn't slaughtered the entire town.

And from what Frank had seen under that cloth, he knew now that the beast probably could.

"I didn't know. I didn't understand. None of us did."

The Jackal Man gave a roar so loud it shook Frank's vision. It clawed at the air and hissed.

Apology not accepted. He waited for it to attack.

Then there was a shot behind him, deafening in the enclosed chamber. Something whizzed by his head. The Jackal Man's next roar was cut off as it stumbled back.

"Stay dead this time." Deegan emerged from the dark tunnel behind him. The hunter stepped into the light, rifle held ready.

"Stop!" Frank shouted.

Deegan fired again. The creature mewed like a kitten but remained on its feet. The hunter pulled the trigger a final time, and the Jackal Man swayed and fell forward onto the logs of the fire with a spray of sparks.

"Damn it!" Deegan rushed past Frank and pulled the body out by one arm. He stamped out the smoldering flesh as a heavy cloud of smoke drifted up to get sucked through the ceiling holes.

"Deegan, you son of a bitch! You don't know what you're doing!"

The hunter glanced up. "I think I have a pretty good idea."

"He was intelligent! He can speak!"

"So you think that makes him any less dangerous? Besides, he'll be back on his feet in no time, if I don't do somethin to stop it. *You're* not so lucky, I'm afraid." He swung the rifle up. "Back away. Let's get this over with."

"Where's my son?" Frank demanded.

"He never felt a thing."

Frank's stomach dropped. Something deep inside reached up and threatened to seal off his windpipe. "What? You... you didn't..."

"Too many loose ends. But you'll be joinin him shortly. And I'll have a nice new trophy that won't be comin back from the dead this time."

From the corner of his eye, Frank saw a shadow flit across the far side of the room.

He smiled.

"What?" Deegan asked. "What now, Frankie? I know your detective friend ain't behind me this time."

It was all Frank could do to keep from laughing. "Now you're the one who's a little slow on the uptake, Deegan. You still haven't figured it out yet?"

"Figured what out?"

"It's not one ancient, immortal creature," Frank said, thinking of the body under the tarp, the corpse of the Jackal Man that he'd shot in the head by the banks of the river.

The one whose face had nagged at him until he realized every time he'd encountered the creature, it had different markings.

"It's an entire race."

As if on cue, the ten Jackal *Men* that had stolen into the room behind Deegan filled the chamber with their growls, hisses, and roars. The hunter jumped and spun around, stepping away from the body to move closer to the fire in the middle of the room. Frank sensed movement behind him and turned to find even more coming from the other entrances, perching on the mounds of garbage all around them, sealing off every exit.

At least thirty of them filled this room now.

They clawed the air. They screeched at the sight of their dead brother and hissed at Frank and Deegan. Some of them circled warily, waiting for an opportunity to move in. Frank spotted one with its arm held close to its chest, surely the one that Trisha had shot, and another with a rudimentary bandage across its side—his friend from the site—both glaring at him.

Frank backed up and ran into Deegan.

"What do you think?" Frank asked over the din. He found he was at a loss for resolve. Willie. God, he'd failed the boy in so many ways. Even the thought of seeing Trisha again was overshadowed by the grief at having to look her in the eye and tell her their son was dead. "You better get to hunting."

"I don't even think I have enough bullets." Deegan sounded equally calm, but Frank glanced over his shoulder. There was a faraway look in the man's cold eyes.

And then, before Frank could understand what was happening, he dropped his rifle, lunged several feet away, and fell to his knees. He came up holding the box of dynamite from the site.

He stepped to the edge of the fire and held it aloft.

The Jackal Men froze in place. They made a collective sighing noise.

"Yeah, you know what this is, don't you?"

"Put it down, Deegan!"

The hunted never looked away from the creatures closing in on them. "Shut up, you pussy! I'm not bein taken out by my own prey!"

"They're never gonna let you outta here! They don't bargain!"

"Who's bargainin? We're all goin together. You, me, and them." The man looked like a trapped animal himself. He tilted the box toward the fire, the contents inside shifting. Frank didn't need Cracker to tell him that the dynamite in there would be sufficient to turn this place into a crater.

Killing them.

Killing these creatures.

Destroying their home.

And for a moment, that was all Frank could think about, the injustice that this species—this *race*—had suffered. Maybe he deserved everything that happened to him since coming to Asheville, but *they* didn't. They just wanted to be left alone.

If it was the last decent thing he did in his life, Frank intended to save them.

Even if they tore him to shreds afterward.

He bent and picked up Deegan's rifle for the second time. "Put it down."

Deegan lowered the box the tiniest bit, but still kept it hovering precariously over the fire. "Well, little Frankie Stanford thinks he's a hero now, huh?"

Frank tried to swallow the lump in his throat, but couldn't do it. "I just think they may be more human than you are."

Deegan didn't wisecrack. He reached into the crate and brought out one of the white caps, holding it in a trembling hand over the fire. "I'm not goin out like this. Not by them. I'd rather do it myself."

His fingers uncurled, dropping the mound of dynamite into the fire.

Frank jerked the trigger, sending a bullet high into Deegan's chest. The hunter flopped backward with the crate on the far side of the fire, throwing white dynamite caps across the room. Frank let go of the rifle and dove forward.

Without stopping to think, he thrust a hand into the fire.

The pain of the flames was instant and excruciating, worse than Deegan digging in his shoulder, but the fear that he was about to be blown to smithereens put it in perspective. He grabbed the smoking dynamite and flung it away, across the room. The Jackal Men scattered away from it. He fell back, clutching his burnt hand to his chest.

With a roar of his own, Deegan jumped to his feet. The man's ponytail had come undone, and a mane of hair flew around his deranged grimace. Blood poured down the front of his body.

The Jackal Men closed in. One of them leapt on Deegan's back. The hunter spun in circles with it clinging to his shoulders. Frank could hear screams, but they were muffled by the claws ripping at his face.

Deegan stumbled into the fire.

His clothes went up, shorts and camouflage shirt blackening almost instantly. His entire body was engulfed in flame. The creature on his back jumped away.

Deegan wailed in pain, oblivious to anything around him, as the Jackal Men moved away from the human pyre. He walked into the mountain of garbage, which drank up the flames. The items down here were dry and old, and eager to supply the fire with fuel. Deegan collapsed across one of the couches.

Frank got up. The Jackal Men worked to smother the spreading flames, but the fire was too fast. It engulfed the far side of the chamber in seconds. The creatures backed away toward Frank as smoke collected in the ceiling too fast to be dispersed.

Leaving the second crate of dynamite and all the caps Deegan had flung across the room to be swallowed up.

"Jesus, run!" he shouted at the beings around him. They turned their heads from side to side, staring at him. "*Go! It's gonna blow!*"

Amazingly, the throng parted, giving him a clear shot at one of the exits.

Frank ran. He jumped through the entrance of the chamber and into the pitch-black tunnel beyond, running with hands held in front of him. The Jackal Men moved with him, all around him, their eyes floating in the darkness.

It was impossible to tell how far he made it when the dynamite blew behind them.

The thunder of noise came first, a clap of pure concussive sound, followed by the shockwave of expanding air. Frank felt heat singe the hair on the back of his neck. Light flashed as if from a camera bulb, one right after the other as the dynamite caps blew in turn, leaving the ghostly afterimages of numerous Jackal Men on his eyes. In a frozen, white-hot second, he saw one of them cut in half by a piece of flying debris.

The entire place quaked. The earthen floor under his feet wobbled. He staggered drunkenly in the darkness.

A rain of dirt fell on him as the place shook itself apart, clogging his mouth and lungs. Everything was a jumble, shaking and vibrating, the tunnel walls closing in, and he couldn't even tell how fast or in what direction he was moving...

Larger chunks of earth made spattering noises as they struck. He took another step and a piece of clay twice as big as his head struck his back and drove him to the ground.

Within seconds, he was half buried in an inch of earth.

"Willie," he gasped, as his mouth filled up.

And then the rumbling increased to incredible levels, and the ceiling of the tunnel collapsed.

52

Willie Stanford awoke to find himself staring at the stars. When he remembered where he was, he screamed for his father.

He strained at the cords that bound him to the rooftop of the unfinished house. They were too tight for him to move.

That strange gut instinct he'd had on the day they left home came back to him. He didn't want to die. He didn't want to run away anymore. He just wanted to go home and outgrow the shituitary gland.

A vibration started in the wood beneath him, like sitting in one of those massage chairs at the mall. He thought he might be imagining it, until the movement became violent. The entire structure under him rattled and bucked. He could hear the sound of wood splintering from all over the construction site.

An earthquake?

Something vital in the house beneath him finally broke, and the incomplete upper floor tilted crazily. His body slid a few inches as gravity shifted, but he was held in place by the ropes. The floor came to rest at a slight angle.

After what seemed like several long minutes, it all ended. Silence returned to River Meadows. He was left on a surface that groaned with instability as he tried to figure out what to do next.

And then there were footsteps. He yelled his father's name again, but received no answer.

The hunter, he thought.

But this sounded like multiple people.

He heard other sounds from the edge of the roof, and lifted his head.

A figure appeared at the edge of the incomplete second floor, using the beams to climb up. A dark shape with green eyes.

Willie whimpered. "No, please. Anything but you."

And, as if nightmares could multiply, a *second* monster climbed up behind the first.

Another followed the first two...and another...and another. The creatures squatted around him in an uneven circle, noses sniffing the air.

Then they moved in, claws up and ready.

Willie closed his eyes and waited to be devoured.

There were rough, scratchy noises. The pressure at his wrists and ankles disappeared. When he dared to open his eyes again, he was alone.

The ropes had been cut away from the beams holding him. He climbed to his feet on the canted surface and waited for the creatures to come back and finish him off. The only sound now was crickets. Willie used one of the ropes to slide down from the roof and drop to the ground, then walked to the middle of River Meadows.

All of the houses were either twisted out of shape or collapsed completely from the earthquake. His father's trailer stuck halfway out of a huge pit in the ground. The light of the moon revealed other holes scattered across the entire site.

With a groan, the house he'd been tied to crashed into a heap. Willie didn't even flinch; he was too exhausted.

He started to walk away, but then turned back, pulled the tongue ring from his pocket, and tossed it into the wreckage. With that done, he trudged toward the front of the construction site.

As he passed the large tree that had once been beside the gate, someone lurched out and grabbed him.

"Detective Shruff?" The man was so pale he glowed in the dark. He had one fist balled against a bloody hole in his shirt.

"Hey W-Willie," the detective gasped. "What happened?"

"I don't know. Have you seen my dad?"

Shruff shook his head. "No. But we have to go right now, before the Jackal Man finds us."

Willie looked back at the junkyard that had been River Meadows. "I don't think we have to worry about them anymore."

"*Them?*" the man asked, as Willie slipped a hand around his waist and helped him toward his father's truck.

"That's right. There's nothing to be afraid of on the Dark Road anymore."

And that's the whole story, just exactly as I heard it, from at least two or three different people. You probably remember the news last year about the housing edition destroyed by the earthquake while they were hunting for that Australian serial killer. The guy that owned the whole thing—Giles or Lyles or something—he was brought up on fraud charges right after it happened. Had something to do with compromising pictures of him that turned up on the corporate website.

I think that was about the extent of the national media coverage, but you can still find local papers about how Asheville lobbied to have the whole place turned into a wildlife sanctuary. And you'll have to check the Weekly Digest for anything about the hero cop that saved the little kidnapped boy during all this. Buchanon claims he transferred to some precinct in California, never to be heard from again.

There's one other story that none of them managed to catch though. Not too long after Asheville got the ruling on the sanctuary, they all went out there to burn the remains of those houses to the ground. It was a somber bonfire, only attended by folks from town. Well...almost.

My friend John Boyd says there were two strangers that showed up. They didn't say anything, just stood away from the rest of them and watched those flames eat everything up once and for all. A clean-cut kid, pushing the wheelchair of a guy with a burned hand and most of his body in a cast. John Boyd claims it was the foreman, a fellow he'd had a run-in with not but a week before.

Then again, John Boyd always was full of shit.

Like this novel?

YOUR REVIEWS HELP!

In the modern world, customer reviews are essential for any product. The artists who create the work you enjoy need your help growing their audience. Please visit Goodreads or the website of the company that sold you this novel to leave a review, or even just a star rating. Posting about the book on social media is also appreciated.

About the Author

Russell C. Connor has been writing horror since the age of five, and is the author of two short story collections, four eNovellas, and ten novels. His most recent, *Good Neighbors*, won the silver medal for horror in the 2016 Independent Publisher Awards. He has been a member of the DFW Writers' Workshop since 2006, and served as president for two years. He lives in Fort Worth, Texas with his rabid dog, demented film collection, mistress of the dark, and demonspawn daughter.

His next novel—*The Halls of Moambati: Volume III of the Dark Filament Ephemeris*—will be available in 2021.

Made in the USA
Las Vegas, NV
21 November 2021

34877342R00249